PENGUIN BOOKS

THE PENGUIN BOOK OF
AMERICAN SHORT STORIES

The Penguin Book of

AMERICAN SHORT STORIES

*

EDITED BY
JAMES COCHRANE

PENGUIN BOOKS

PENGUIN BOOKS

Published by the Penguin Group
Penguin Books Ltd, 27 Wrights Lane, London W8 5TZ, England
Penguin Books USA Inc., 375 Hudson Street, New York, New York 10014, USA
Penguin Books Australia Ltd, Ringwood, Victoria, Australia
Penguin Books Canada Ltd, 10 Alcorn Avenue, Toronto, Ontario, Canada M4V 3B2
Penguin Books (NZ) Ltd, 182–190 Wairau Road, Auckland 10, New Zealand

Penguin Books Ltd, Registered Offices: Harmondsworth, Middlesex, England

First published in Penguin Books 1969
25 27 29 30 28 26 24

This selection copyright © Penguin Books Ltd, 1969
All rights reserved

Printed in England by Clays Ltd, St Ives plc

CONTENTS

CONTENTS

PREFACE

AMERICAN literature and the short story might be said to have come of age at about the same time, and this, along with something in the bustling and energetic American temperament, might go some way towards explaining why the two go together as well as they do. The Americans are at home here, as a fish is in water; it is a medium in which they move naturally, and, above all, unselfconsciously; no one, so far as one can tell, has seen it as his duty to write the 'Great American Short Story'. Nevertheless Melville and Henry James, and Hemingway and Scott Fitzgerald have written stories that take their place among the finest literature the world has known.

Above all, perhaps, the American short story has been an essentially democratic form, not troubling itself overmuch about the categories of High, Middle and Low, serious and light-weight, that bedevil other forms of creative writing. Quality or catchpenny, it has never, at least until recently, strayed far from the literary market-place. Whether, in the face of college Creative Writing courses, it will stay much longer in this state of innocence, remains to be seen.

No apology is therefore made for the very different kinds of mastery offered in this selection. The writers who rub shoulders here might have rubbed shoulders in the same magazine, without any raising of eyebrows. Ring Lardner the sports columnist becomes Ring Lardner the short-story writer without any sense of the rupturing of literary social barriers, and the anthology that includes Henry James but omits O. Henry simply isn't telling the whole truth.

Incompleteness is another matter. Considerations of space and of copyright make it impossible to include everyone who deserves to be included in an anthology purporting to represent the best of American short-story writing, let alone to give more than an inkling of the richness of the genre as a whole. Space has been found, however, for some writers who will be less familiar, to non-American readers at any rate, than others. If

7

this anthology induces such readers to explore further, it will have served a purpose beyond its immediate one of offering some of the diversity of pleasures that the American short story at its best provides.

ACKNOWLEDGEMENTS

FOR permission to reprint the stories specified we are indebted to Harold Ober Associates Inc. for Sherwood Anderson's 'Death in the Woods' (Copyright © The American Mercury Inc., 1926; copyright renewed by Eleanor Copenhaver Anderson, 1953); Hamish Hamilton Ltd for Truman Capote's 'Children on their Birthdays' from *Selected Writings of Truman Capote*; Alfred A. Knopf, Inc. for Willa Cather's 'Neighbor Rosicky' from *Obscure Destinies*; Chatto and Windus Ltd for William Faulkner's 'Delta Autumn' from *Go Down, Moses*; The Bodley Head for F. Scott Fitzgerald's 'The Rich Boy' from *The Diamond as Big as the Ritz and Other Stories*; Jonathan Cape Ltd for Ernest Hemingway's 'The Battler' from *In Our Time*; Chatto and Windus Ltd for Ring Lardner's 'Who Dealt?' from *The Best Short Stories of Ring Lardner*; Eyre and Spottiswoode for Bernard Malamud's 'The Jewbird' from *Idiots First*; Jonathan Cape Ltd for Katherine Anne Porter's 'Flowering Judas'; André Deutsch for John Updike's 'Wife-Wooing' from *Pigeon Feathers*.

Washington Irving

THE LEGEND OF SLEEPY HOLLOW

FOUND AMONG THE PAPERS OF THE LATE DIEDRICH KNICKERBOCKER

A pleasing land of drowsy head it was,
Of dreams that wave before the half-shut eye;
And of gay castles in the clouds that pass,
For ever flushing round a summer sky.

CASTLE OF INDOLENCE

IN the bosom of one of those spacious coves which indent the eastern shore of the Hudson, at that broad expansion of the river denominated by the ancient Dutch navigators the Tappan Zee, and where they always prudently shortened sail, and implored the protection of St Nicholas when they crossed, there lies a small market-town or rural port, which by some is called Greensburgh, but which is more generally and properly known by the name of Tarry Town. This name was given, we are told, in former days, by the good housewives of the adjacent country, from the inveterate propensity of their husbands to linger about the village tavern on market days. Be that as it may, I do not vouch for the fact, but merely advert to it, for the sake of being precise and authentic. Not far from this village, perhaps about two miles, there is a little valley, or rather lap of land, among high hills, which is one of the quietest places in the whole world. A small brook glides through it, with just murmur enough to lull one to repose; and the occasional whistle of a quail, or tapping of a woodpecker, is almost the only sound that ever breaks in upon the uniform tranquillity.

I recollect that, when a stripling, my first exploit in squirrel-shooting was in a grove of tall walnut-trees that shades one side of the valley. I had wandered into it at noon time, when all nature is peculiarly quiet, and was startled by the roar of my own gun, as it broke the Sabbath stillness around, and was prolonged and reverberated by the angry echoes. If ever I should wish for a retreat, whither I might steal from the world and its distractions, and dream quietly away the remnant of a troubled life, I know of none more promising than this little valley.

From the listless repose of the place, and the peculiar character of its inhabitants, who are descendants from the original Dutch settlers, this sequestered glen has long been known by the name of Sleepy Hollow, and its rustic lads are called the Sleepy Hollow Boys throughout all the neighboring country. A drowsy, dreamy influence seems to hang over the land, and to pervade the very atmosphere. Some say that the place was bewitched by a high German doctor, during the early days of the settlement; others, that an old Indian chief, the prophet or wizard of his tribe, held his pow-wows there before the country was discovered by Master Hendrick Hudson. Certain it is, the place still continues under the sway of some witching power, that holds a spell over the minds of the good people, causing them to walk in a continual reverie. They are given to all kinds of marvellous beliefs; are subject to trances and visions; and frequently see strange sights, and hear music and voices in the air. The whole neighborhood abounds with local tales, haunted spots, and twilight superstitions; stars shoot and meteors glare oftener across the valley than in any other part of the country, and the nightmare, with her whole nine fold, seems to make it the favorite scene of her gambols.

The dominant spirit, however, that haunts this enchanted region, and seems to be commander-in-chief of all the powers of the air, is the apparition of a figure on horseback without a head. It is said by some to be the ghost of a Hessian trooper, whose head had been carried away by a cannon-ball, in some nameless battle during the revolutionary war; and who is ever and anon seen by the country folk, hurrying along in the gloom of night, as if on the wings of the wind. His haunts are not confined to the valley, but extend at times to the adjacent roads, and especially to the vicinity of a church at no great distance. Indeed, certain of the most authentic historians of those parts, who have been careful in collecting and collating the floating facts concerning this spectre, allege that the body of the trooper having been buried in the churchyard, the ghost rides forth to the scene of battle in nightly quest of his head; and that the rushing speed with which he sometimes passes along the Hollow, like a midnight blast, is owing to his being belated, and in a hurry to get back to the church-yard before daybreak.

Such is the general purport of this legendary superstition, which has furnished materials for many a wild story in that region of shadows; and the spectre is known, at all the country firesides, by the name of the Headless Horseman of Sleepy Hollow.

It is remarkable that the visionary propensity I have mentioned is not confined to the native inhabitants of the valley, but is unconsciously imbibed by every one who resides there for a time. However wide awake they may have been before they entered that sleepy region, they are sure, in a little time, to inhale the witching influence of the air, and begin to grow imaginative — to dream dreams, and see apparitions.

I mention this peaceful spot with all possible laud; for it is in such little retired Dutch valleys, found here and there embosomed in the great State of New-York, that population, manners, and customs remain fixed; while the great torrent of migration and improvement, which is making such incessant changes in other parts of this restless country, sweeps by them unobserved. They are like those little nooks of still water which border a rapid stream; where we may see the straw and bubble riding quietly at anchor, or slowly revolving in their mimic harbor, undisturbed by the rush of the passing current. Though many years have elapsed since I trod the drowsy shades of Sleepy Hollow, yet I question whether I should not still find the same trees and the same families vegetating in its sheltered bosom.

In this by-place of nature, there abode, in a remote period of American history, that is to say, some thirty years since, a worthy wight of the name of Ichabod Crane; who sojourned, or, as he expressed it, 'tarried', in Sleepy Hollow, for the purpose of instructing the children of the vicinity. He was a native of

Connecticut; a State which supplies the Union with pioneers for the mind as well as for the forest, and sends forth yearly its legions of frontier woodsmen and country schoolmasters. The cognomen of Crane was not inapplicable to his person. He was tall, but exceedingly lank, with narrow shoulders, long arms and legs, hands that dangled a mile out of his sleeves, feet that might have served for shovels, and his whole frame most loosely hung together. His head was small, and flat at top, with huge ears, large green glassy eyes, and a long snipe nose, so that it looked like a weather-cock, perched upon his spindle neck, to tell which way the wind blew. To see him striding along the profile of a hill on a windy day, with his clothes bagging and fluttering about him, one might have mistaken him for the genius of famine descending upon the earth, or some scarecrow eloped from a cornfield.

His school-house was a low building of one large room, rudely constructed of logs; the windows partly glazed, and partly patched with leaves of old copy-books. It was most ingeniously secured at vacant hours, by a withe twisted in the handle of the door, and stakes set against the window shutters; so that, though a thief might get in with perfect ease, he would find some embarrassment in getting out; an idea most probably borrowed by the architect, Yost Van Houten, from the mystery of an eel-pot. The school-house stood in a rather lonely but pleasant situation, just at the foot of a woody hill, with a brook running close by, and a formidable birch tree growing at one end of it. From hence the low murmur of his pupils' voices, conning over their lessons, might be heard in a drowsy summer's day, like the hum of a bee-hive; interrupted now and then by the authoritative voice of the master, in the tone of menace or command; or, peradventure, by the appalling sound of the birch, as he urged some tardy loiterer along the flowery path of knowledge. Truth to say, he was a conscientious man, and ever bore in mind the golden maxim, 'Spare the rod and spoil the child.' – Ichabod Crane's scholars certainly were not spoiled.

I would not have it imagined, however, that he was one of those cruel potentates of the school, who joy in the smart of their subjects; on the contrary, he administered justice with discrimi-

nation rather than severity; taking the burthen off the backs of
the weak, and laying it on those of the strong. Your mere puny
stripling, that winced at the least flourish of the rod, was passed
by with indulgence; but the claims of justice were satisfied by
inflicting a double portion on some little, tough, wrong-headed,
broad-skirted Dutch urchin, who sulked and swelled and grew
dogged and sullen beneath the birch. All this he called 'doing his
duty by their parents'; and he never inflicted a chastisement
without following it by the assurance, so consolatory to the
smarting urchin, that 'he would remember it, and thank him
for it the longest day he had to live'.

When school hours were over, he was even the companion
and playmate of the larger boys; and on holiday afternoons
would convoy some of the smaller ones home, who happened to
have pretty sisters, or good housewives for mothers, noted for
the comforts of the cupboard. Indeed it behooved him to keep
on good terms with his pupils. The revenue arising from his
school was small, and would have been scarcely sufficient to
furnish him with daily bread, for he was a huge feeder, and
though lank, had the dilating powers of an anaconda; but to
help out his maintenance, he was, according to country custom
in those parts, boarded and lodged at the houses of the farmers,
whose children he instructed. With these he lived successively a
week at a time; thus going the rounds of the neighborhood,
with all his worldly effects tied up in a cotton handkerchief.

That all this might not be too onerous on the purses of his
rustic patrons, who are apt to consider the costs of schooling a
grievous burden, and schoolmasters as mere drones, he had
various ways of rendering himself both useful and agreeable. He
assisted the farmers occasionally in the lighter labors of their
farms; helped to make hay; mended the fences; took the horses
to water; drove the cows from pasture; and cut wood for the
winter fire. He laid aside, too, all the dominant dignity and
absolute sway with which he lorded it in his little empire, the
school, and became wonderfully gentle and ingratiating. He
found favor in the eyes of the mothers, by petting the children,
particularly the youngest; and like the lion bold, which whilom
so magnanimously the lamb did hold, he would sit with a child

on one knee, and rock a cradle with his foot for whole hours together.

In addition to his other vocations, he was the singing-master of the neighborhood, and picked up many bright shillings by instructing the young folks in psalmody. It was a matter of no little vanity to him, on Sundays, to take his station in front of the church gallery, with a band of chosen singers; where, in his own mind, he completely carried away the palm from the parson. Certain it is, his voice resounded far above all the rest of the congregation; and there are peculiar quavers still to be heard in that church, and which may even be heard half a mile off, quite to the opposite side of the mill-pond, on a still Sunday morning, which are said to be legitimately descended from the nose of Ichabod Crane. Thus, by divers little make-shifts in that ingenious way which is commonly denominated 'by hook and by crook', the worthy pedagogue got on tolerably enough, and was thought, by all who understood nothing of the labor of head-work, to have a wonderfully easy life of it.

The school-master is generally a man of some importance in the female circle of a rural neighborhood; being considered a kind of idle gentlemanlike personage, of vastly superior taste and accomplishments to the rough country swains, and, indeed, inferior in learning only to the parson. His appearance, therefore, is apt to occasion some little stir at the tea-table of a farm-house, and the addition of a supernumerary dish of cakes or sweetmeats, or, peradventure, the parade of a silver tea-pot. Our man of letters, therefore, was peculiarly happy in the smiles of all the country damsels. How he would figure among them in the church-yard, between services on Sundays! gathering grapes for them from the wild vines that over-run the surrounding trees; reciting for their amusement all the epitaphs on the tombstones; or sauntering, with a whole bevy of them, along the banks of the adjacent mill-pond; while the more bashful country bumpkins hung sheepishly back, envying his superior elegance and address.

From his half itinerant life, also, he was a kind of travelling gazette, carrying the whole budget of local gossip from house to house; so that his appearance was always greeted with satisfaction. He was, moreover, esteemed by the women as a man of great erudition, for he had read several books quite through, and was a perfect master of Cotton Mather's history of New-England Witchcraft, in which, by the way, he most firmly and potently believed.

He was, in fact, an odd mixture of small shrewdness and simple credulity. His appetite for the marvellous, and his powers of digesting it, were equally extraordinary; and both had been increased by his residence in this spellbound region. No tale was too gross or monstrous for his capacious swallow. It was often his delight, after his school was dismissed in the afternoon, to stretch himself on the rich bed of clover, bordering the little brook that whimpered by his school-house, and there con over old Mather's direful tales, until the gathering dusk of the evening made the printed page a mere mist before his eyes. Then, as he wended his way, by swamp and stream and awful woodland, to the farmhouse where he happened to be quartered, every sound of nature, at that witching hour, fluttered his excited imagination: the moan of the whip-poor-will from the hill-side; the boding cry of the tree-toad, that harbinger of storm; the dreary hooting of the screech-owl; or the sudden rustling in the thicket of birds frightened from their roost. The fire-flies, too, which sparkled most vividly in the darkest places, now and then startled him, as one of uncommon brightness would stream across his path; and if, by chance, a huge blockhead of a beetle came winging his blundering flight against him, the poor varlet was ready to give up the ghost, with the idea that he was struck with a witch's token. His only resource on such occasions, either to drown thought, or drive away evil spirits, was to sing psalm tunes; and the good people of Sleepy Hollow, as they sat by their doors of an evening, were often filled with awe, at hearing his nasal melody, 'in linked sweetness long drawn out', floating from the distant hill, or along the dusky road.

Another of his sources of fearful pleasure was, to pass long winter evenings with the old Dutch wives, as they sat spinning by the fire, with a row of apples roasting and spluttering along the hearth, and listen to their marvellous tales of ghosts and goblins, and haunted fields, and haunted brooks, and haunted bridges, and haunted houses, and particularly of the headless horseman, or galloping Hessian of the Hollow, as they sometimes called him. He would delight them equally by his anecdotes of witchcraft, and of the direful omens and portentous sights and sounds in the air, which prevailed in the earlier times of Connecticut; and would frighten them woefully with speculations upon comets and shooting stars; and with the alarming fact that the world did absolutely turn round, and that they were half the time topsy-turvy!

But if there was a pleasure in all this, while snugly cuddling in the chimney corner of a chamber that was all of a ruddy glow from the crackling wood fire, and where, of course, no spectre dared to show his face, it was dearly purchased by the terrors of his subsequent walk homewards. What fearful shapes and shadows beset his path amidst the dim and ghastly glare of a snowy night! – With what wistful look did he eye every trembling ray of light streaming across the waste fields from some distant window! How often was he appalled by some shrub covered with snow, which, like a sheeted spectre, beset his very path! How often did he shrink with curdling awe at the sound of his own steps on the frosty crust beneath his feet; and dread to look over his shoulder, lest he should behold some uncouth being tramping close behind him! And how often was he thrown into complete dismay by some rushing blast, howling among the trees, in the idea that it was the Galloping Hessian on one of his nightly scourings!

All these, however, were mere terrors of the night, phantoms of the mind that walk in darkness; and though he had seen many spectres in his time, and been more than once beset by Satan in divers shapes, in his lonely perambulations, yet daylight put an end to all these evils; and he would have passed a pleasant life of it, in despite of the devil and all his works, if his path had not been crossed by a being that causes more perplexity to mortal man than ghosts, goblins, and the whole race of witches put together, and that was – a woman.

Among the musical disciples who assembled, one evening in each week, to receive his instructions in psalmody, was Katrina Van Tassel, the daughter and only child of a substantial Dutch farmer. She was a blooming lass of fresh eighteen; plump as a partridge; ripe and melting and rosy cheeked as one of her father's peaches, and universally famed, not merely for her beauty, but her vast expectations. She was withal a little of a coquette, as might be perceived even in her dress, which was a mixture of ancient and modern fashions, as most suited to set off her charms. She wore the ornaments of pure yellow gold, which her great-great-grandmother had brought over from Saardam; the tempting stomacher of the olden time; and withal a provokingly short petticoat, to display the prettiest foot and ankle in the country round.

Ichabod Crane had a soft and foolish heart towards the sex; and it is not to be wondered at, that so tempting a morsel soon found favor in his eyes; more especially after he had visited her in her paternal mansion. Old Baltus Van Tassel was a perfect picture of a thriving, contented, liberal-hearted farmer. He seldom, it is true, sent either his eyes or his thoughts beyond the boundaries of his own farm; but within those every thing was snug, happy, and well-conditioned. He was satisfied with his wealth, but not proud of it; and piqued himself upon the hearty abundance, rather than the style in which he lived. His stronghold was situated on the banks of the Hudson, in one of those green, sheltered, fertile nooks, in which the Dutch farmers are so fond of nestling. A great elm-tree spread its broad branches over it; at the foot of which bubbled up a spring of the softest and sweetest water, in a little well, formed of a barrel; and then stole sparkling away through the grass, to a neighboring brook, that bubbled along among alders and dwarf willows. Hard by the farmhouse was a vast barn, that might have served for a church; every window and crevice of which seemed bursting forth with the treasures of the farm; the flail was busily resounding within it from morning to night; swallows and martins skimmed twittering about the eaves; and rows of pigeons, some with one eye turned up, as if watching the weather, some with their heads under their wings, or buried in their bosoms, and others swelling, and cooing, and bowing about their dames, were enjoying the sunshine on the roof. Sleek unwieldy porkers were grunting in the repose and abundance of their pens;

whence sallied forth, now and then, troops of sucking pigs, as if to snuff the air. A stately squadron of snowy geese were riding in an adjoining pond, convoying whole fleets of ducks; regiments of turkeys were gobbling through the farmyard, and guinea fowls fretting about it, like ill-tempered housewives, with their peevish discontented cry. Before the barn door strutted the gallant cock, that pattern of a husband, a warrior, and a fine gentleman, clapping his burnished wings, and crowing in the pride and gladness of his heart – sometimes tearing up the earth with his feet, and then generously calling his ever-hungry family of wives and children to enjoy the rich morsel which he had discovered.

The pedagogue's mouth watered, as he looked upon this sumptuous promise of luxurious winter fare. In his devouring mind's eye, he pictured to himself every roasting-pig running about with a pudding in his belly, and an apple in his mouth; the pigeons were snugly put to bed in a comfortable pie, and tucked in with a coverlet of crust; the geese were swimming in their own gravy; and the ducks pairing cosily in dishes, like snug married couples, with a decent competency of onion sauce. In the porkers he saw carved out the future sleek side of bacon, and juicy relishing ham; not a turkey but he beheld daintily trussed up, with its gizzard under its wing, and, peradventure, a necklace of savory sausages; and even bright chanticleer himself lay sprawling on his back, in a side-dish, with uplifted claws, as if craving that quarter which his chivalrous spirit disdained to ask while living.

As the enraptured Ichabod fancied all this and as he rolled his great green eyes over the fat meadow-lands, the rich fields of wheat, of rye, of buckwheat, and Indian corn, and the orchards burthened with ruddy fruit, which surrounded the warm tenement of Van Tassel, his heart yearned after the damsel who was to inherit these domains, and his imagination expanded with the idea, how they might be readily turned into cash, and the money invested in immense tracts of wild land, and shingle palaces in the wilderness. Nay, his busy fancy already realized his hopes, and presented to him the blooming Katrina, with a whole family of children, mounted on the top of a wagon loaded with household trumpery, with pots and kettles dangling beneath; and he beheld himself bestriding a pacing mare, with a colt at her heels, setting out for Kentucky, Tennessee, or the Lord knows where.

When he entered the house the conquest of his heart was complete. It was one of those spacious farmhouses, with high-ridged, but lowly-sloping roofs, built in the style handed down from the first Dutch settlers; the low projecting eaves forming a piazza along the front, capable of being closed up in bad weather. Under this were hung flails, harness, various utensils of husbandry, and nets for fishing in the neighboring river. Benches were built along the sides for summer use; and a great spinning-wheel at one end, and a churn at the other, showed the various uses to which this important porch might be devoted. From this piazza the wondering Ichabod entered the hall, which formed the centre of the mansion and the place of usual residence. Here, rows of resplendent pewter, ranged on a long dresser, dazzled his eyes. In one corner stood a huge bag of wool ready to be spun; in another a quantity of linsey-woolsey just from the loom; ears of Indian corn, and strings of dried apples and peaches, hung in gay festoons along the walls, mingled with the gaud of red peppers; and a door left ajar gave him a peep into the best parlor, where the claw-footed chairs, and dark mahogany tables, shone like mirrors; and irons, with their accompanying shovel and tongs, glistened from their covert of asparagus tops; mock-oranges and conch-shells decorated the mantelpiece; strings of various colored birds' eggs were suspended above it : a great ostrich egg was hung from the centre of the room, and a corner cupboard knowingly left open, displayed immense treasures of old silver and well-mended china.

From the moment Ichabod laid his eyes upon these regions of delight, the peace of his mind was at an end, and his only study was how to gain the affections of the peerless daughter of Van Tassel. In this enterprise, however, he had more real difficulties than generally fell to the lot of a knight-errant of yore, who seldom had any thing but giants, enchanters, fiery dragons, and such like easily-conquered adversaries, to contend with; and had to make his way merely through gates of iron and brass, and walls of adamant, to the castle keep, where the lady of his heart was confined; all which he achieved as easily as a man would carve his way to the centre of a Christmas pie; and then the lady gave him her hand as a matter of course. Ichabod, on the contrary, had to win his way to the heart of a country coquette, beset with a labyrinth of whims and caprices, which were for ever presenting new difficulties and impediments; and he had to encounter a host of fearful adversaries of real flesh and blood, the numerous rustic admirers, who beset every portal to her heart; keeping a watchful and angry eye upon each other, but ready to fly out in the common cause against any new competitor.

Among these the most formidable was a burly, roaring, roystering blade, of the name of Abraham, or, according to the Dutch abbreviation, Brom Van Brunt, the hero of the country round, which rang with his feats of strength and hardihood. He was broad-shouldered and double-jointed, with short curly black hair, and a bluff, but not unpleasant countenance, having a mingled air of fun and arrogance. From his Herculean frame and great powers of limb, he had received the nickname of Brom Bones, by which he was universally known. He was famed for great knowledge and skill in horsemanship, being as dexterous on horseback as a Tartar. He was foremost at all races and cock-fights; and, with the ascendancy which bodily strength acquires in rustic life, was the umpire in all disputes, setting his hat on one side, and giving his decisions with an air and tone admitting of no gainsay or appeal. He was always ready for either a fight or a frolic; but had more mischief than ill-will in his composition; and, with all his overbearing roughness, there was a strong dash of waggish good humor at bottom. He had three or four boon companions, who regarded him as their model, and at the head of whom he scoured the country, attending every scene of feud or merriment for miles round. In cold weather he was distinguished by a fur cap, surmounted with a flaunting fox's tail; and when the folks at a country gathering descried this well-known crest at a distance, whisking about among a squad of hard riders, they always stood by for a squall. Sometimes his crew would be heard dashing along past the farmhouses at midnight, with whoop and halloo, like a troop of

Don Cossacks; and the old dames, startled out of their sleep, would listen for a moment till the hurry-scurry had clattered by, and then exclaim, 'Ay, there goes Brom Bones and his gang!' The neighbors looked upon him with a mixture of awe, admiration, and good-will; and when any madcap prank, or rustic brawl, occurred in the vicinity, always shook their heads, and warranted Brom Bones was at the bottom of it.

This rantipole hero had for some time singled out the blooming Katrina for the object of his uncouth gallantries, and though his amorous toyings were something like the gentle caresses and endearments of a bear, yet it was whispered that she did not altogether discourage his hopes. Certain it is, his advances were signals for rival candidates to retire, who felt no inclination to cross a lion in his amours; insomuch, that when his horse was seen tied to Van Tassel's paling, on a Sunday night, a sure sign that his master was courting, or, as it is termed, 'sparking', within all other suitors passed by in despair, and carried the war into other quarters.

Such was the formidable rival with whom Ichabod Crane had to contend, and, considering all things, a stouter man than he would have shrunk from the competition, and a wiser man would have despaired. He had, however, a happy mixture of pliability and perseverance in his nature; he was in form and spirit like a supplejack – yielding, but tough; though he bent, he never broke; and though he bowed beneath the slightest pressure, yet, the moment it was away – jerk! he was erect, and carried his head as high as ever.

To have taken the field openly against his rival would have been madness; for he was not a man to be thwarted in his amours, any more than that stormy lover, Achilles. Ichabod, therefore, made his advances in a quiet and gently-insinuating manner. Under cover of his character of singing-master, he made frequent visits at the farmhouse; not that he had any thing to apprehend from the meddlesome interference of parents, which is so often a stumbling-block in the path of lovers. Balt Van Tassel was an easy indulgent soul; he loved his daughter better even than his pipe, and, like a reasonable man and an excellent father, let her have her way in every thing. His notable

little wife, too, had enough to do to attend to her housekeeping
and manage her poultry; for, as she sagely observed, ducks and
geese are foolish things, and must be looked after, but girls can
take care of themselves. Thus while the busy dame bustled
about the house, or plied her spinning-wheel at one end of the
piazza, honest Balt would sit smoking his evening pipe at the
other, watching the achievements of a little wooden warrior,
who, armed with a sword in each hand, was most valiantly
fighting the wind on the pinnacle of the barn. In the meantime,
Ichabod would carry on his suit with the daughter by the side of
the spring under the great elm, or sauntering along in the twilight, that hour so favorable to the lover's eloquence.

I profess not to know how women's hearts are wooed and
won. To me they have always been matters of riddle and admiration. Some seem to have but one vulnerable point, or door
of access; while others have a thousand avenues, and may be
captured in a thousand different ways. It is a great triumph of
skill to gain the former, but a still greater proof of generalship
to maintain possession of the latter, for the man must battle for
his fortress at every door and window. He who wins a thousand
common hearts is therefore entitled to some renown; but he who
keeps undisputed sway over the heart of a coquette, is indeed a
hero. Certain it is, this was not the case with the redoubtable
Brom Bones; and from the moment Ichabod Crane made his
advances, the interests of the former evidently declined; his
horse was no longer seen tied at the palings on Sunday nights,
and a deadly feud gradually arose between him and the pre-
ceptor of Sleepy Hollow.

Brom, who had a degree of rough chivalry in his nature,
would fain have carried matters to open warfare, and have
settled their pretensions to the lady, according to the mode of
those most concise and simple reasons, the knights-errant of
yore – by single combat; but Ichabod was too conscious of the
superior might of his adversary to enter the lists against him : he
had overheard a boast of Bones, that he would 'double the
school-master up, and lay him on a shelf of his own school-house';
and he was too wary to give him an opportunity. There was
something extremely provoking in this obstinately pacific

system; it left Brom no alternative but to draw upon the funds of rustic waggery in his disposition, and to play off boorish practical jokes upon his rival. Ichabod became the object of whimsical persecution to Bones, and his gang of rough riders. They harried his hitherto peaceful domains; smoked out his singing school, by stopping up the chimney; broke into the school-house at night, in spite of its formidable fastenings of withe and window stakes, and turned every thing topsy-turvy: so that the poor school-master began to think all the witches in the country held their meetings there. But what was still more annoying, Brom took all opportunities of turning him into ridicule in presence of his mistress, and had a scoundrel dog whom he taught to whine in the most ludicrous manner, and introduced as a rival of Ichabod's to instruct her in psalmody.

In this way matters went on for some time, without producing any material effect on the relative situation of the contending powers. On a fine autumnal afternoon, Ichabod, in pensive mood, sat enthroned on a lofty stool whence he usually watched all the concerns of his little literary realm. In his hand he swayed a ferule, that sceptre of despotic power; the birch of justice reposed on three nails, behind the throne, a constant terror to evil doers; while on the desk before him might be seen sundry contraband articles and prohibited weapons, detected upon the persons of idle urchins; such as half-munched apples, popguns, whirligigs, fly-cages, and whole legions of rampant little paper game-cocks. Apparently there had been some appalling act of justice recently inflicted, for his scholars were all busily intent upon their books, or slyly whispering behind them with one eye kept upon the master; and a kind of buzzing stillness reigned throughout the school-room. It was suddenly interrupted by the appearance of a Negro, in tow-cloth jacket and trowsers, a round-crowned fragment of a hat, like the cap of Mercury, and mounted on the back of a ragged, wild, half-broken colt, which he managed with a rope by way of halter. He came clattering up to the school door with an invitation to Ichabod to attend a merry-making or 'quilting frolic', to be held that evening at Mynheer Van Tassel's; and having delivered his message with that air of importance, and effort at fine language, which a

Negro is apt to display on petty embassies of the kind, he dashed over the brook, and was seen scampering away up the hollow, full of the importance and hurry of his mission.

All was now bustle and hubbub in the late quiet school-room. The scholars were hurried through their lessons, without stopping at trifles; those who were nimble skipped over half with impunity, and those who were tardy, had a smart application now and then in the rear, to quicken their speed, or help them over a tall word. Books were flung aside without being put away on the shelves, inkstands were overturned, benches thrown down, and the whole school was turned loose an hour before the usual time; bursting forth like a legion of young imps, yelping and racketing about the green, in joy at their early emancipation.

The gallant Ichabod now spent at least an extra half hour at his toilet, brushing and furbishing up his best, and indeed only suit of rusty black, and arranging his looks by a bit of broken looking-glass, that hung up in the school-house. That he might make his appearance before his mistress in the true style of a cavalier, he borrowed a horse from the farmer with whom he was domiciliated, a choleric old Dutchman, of the name of Hans Van Ripper, and thus gallantly mounted, issued forth, like a knight-errant in quest of adventures. But it is meet I should, in the true spirit of romantic story, give some account of the looks and equipments of my hero and his steed. The animal he bestrode was a broken-down plough-horse, that had outlived almost every thing but his viciousness. He was gaunt and shagged, with a ewe neck and a head like a hammer; his rusty mane and tail were tangled and knotted with burrs; one eye had lost its pupil, and was glaring and spectral; but the other had the gleam of a genuine devil in it. Still he must have had fire and mettle in his day, if we may judge from the name he bore of Gunpowder. He had, in fact, been a favorite steed of his master's, the choleric Van Ripper, who was a furious rider, and had infused, very probably, some of his own spirit into the animal; for, old and broken-down as he looked, there was more of the lurking devil in him than in any young filly in the country.

Ichabod was a suitable figure for such a steed. He rode with short stirrups, which brought his knees nearly up to the pommel of the saddle; his sharp elbows stuck out like grasshoppers'; he carried his whip perpendicularly in his hand, like a sceptre, and, as his horse jogged on, the motion of his arms was not unlike the flapping of a pair of wings. A small wool hat rested on the top of his nose, for so his scanty strip of forehead might be called; and the skirts of his black coat fluttered out almost to the horse's tail. Such was the appearance of Ichabod and his steed, as they shambled out of the gate of Hans Van Ripper, and it was altogether such an apparition as is seldom to be met with in broad daylight.

It was, as I have said, a fine autumnal day, the sky was clear and serene, and nature wore that rich and golden livery which we always associate with the idea of abundance. The forests had put on their sober brown and yellow, while some trees of the tenderer kind had been nipped by the frosts into brilliant dyes of orange, purple, and scarlet. Streaming files of wild ducks began to make their appearance high in the air; the bark of the squirrel might be heard from the groves of beech and hickory nuts, and the pensive whistle of the quail at intervals from the neighboring stubble-field.

The small birds were taking their farewell banquets. In the fulness of their revelry, they fluttered, chirping and frolicking, from bush to bush, and tree to tree, capricious from the very profusion and variety around them. There was the honest cock-robin, the favorite game of stripling sportsmen, with its loud querulous note; and the twittering blackbirds flying in sable clouds; and the golden-winged woodpecker, with his crimson crest, his broad black gorget, and splendid plumage; and the cedar bird, with its red-tipt wings and yellow-tipt tail, and its little monteiro cap of feathers; and the blue jay, that noisy cox-comb, in his gay light-blue coat and white under-clothes; scream-ing and chattering, nodding and bobbing and bowing, and pre-tending to be on good terms with every songster of the grove.

As Ichabod jogged slowly on his way, his eye, ever open to every symptom of culinary abundance, ranged with delight over the treasures of jolly autumn. On all sides he beheld vast store of apples; some hanging in oppressive opulence on the trees;

some gathered into baskets and barrels for the market; others heaped up in rich piles for the cider-press. Farther on he beheld great fields of Indian corn, with its golden ears peeping from their leafy coverts, and holding out the promise of cakes and hasty pudding; and the yellow pumpkins lying beneath them, turning up their fair round bellies to the sun, and giving ample prospects of the most luxurious of pies; and anon he passed the fragrant buckwheat fields, breathing the odor of the bee-hive, and as he beheld them, soft anticipation stole over his mind of dainty slapjacks, well buttered, and garnished with honey or treacle, by the delicate little dimpled hand of Katrina Van Tassel.

Thus feeding his mind with many sweet thoughts and 'sugar suppositions', he journeyed along the sides of a range of hills which look out upon some of the goodliest scenes of the mighty Hudson. The sun gradually wheeled his broad disk down into the west. The wide bosom of the Tappan Zee lay motionless and glassy, excepting that here and there a gentle undulation waved and prolonged the blue shadow of the distant mountain. A few amber clouds floated in the sky, without a breath of air to move them. The horizon was of a fine golden tint, changing gradually into a pure apple green, and from that into the deep blue of the mid-heaven. A slanting ray lingered on the woody crests of the precipices that overhung some parts of the river, giving greater depth to the dark-gray and purple of their rocky sides. A sloop was loitering in the distance, dropping slowly down with the tide, her sail hanging uselessly against the mast; and as the reflection of the sky gleamed along the still water, it seemed as if the vessel was suspended in the air.

It was toward evening that Ichabod arrived at the castle of the Heer Van Tassel, which he found thronged with the pride and flower of the adjacent country. Old farmers, a spare leathern-faced race, in homespun coats and breeches, blue stockings, huge shoes, and magnificent pewter buckles. Their brisk withered little dames, in close crimped caps, long-waisted short-gowns, homespun petticoats, with scissors and pincushions, and gay calico pockets hanging on the outside. Buxom lasses, almost as antiquated as their mothers, excepting where a straw hat, a fine ribbon or perhaps a white frock, gave symptoms of city innovation. The sons, in short square-skirted coats with rows of stupendous brass buttons, and their hair generally queued in the fashion of the times, especially if they could procure an eel-skin for the purpose, it being esteemed, throughout the country, as a potent nourisher and strengthener of the hair.

Brom Bones, however, was the hero of the scene, having come to the gathering on his favorite steed Daredevil, a creature, like himself, full of mettle and mischief, and which no one but himself could manage. He was, in fact, noted for preferring vicious animals, given to all kinds of tricks, which kept the rider in constant risk of his neck, for he held a tractable well-broken horse as unworthy of a lad of spirit.

Fain would I pause to dwell upon the world of charms that burst upon the enraptured gaze of my hero, as he entered the state parlor of Van Tassel's mansion. Not those of the bevy of buxom lasses, with their luxurious display of red and white: but the ample charms of a genuine Dutch country tea-table, in the sumptuous time of autumn. Such heaped-up platters of cakes of various and almost indescribable kinds, known only to experienced Dutch housewives! There was the doughty doughnut, the tenderer oly koek, and the crisp and crumbling cruller; sweet cakes and short cakes, ginger cakes and honey cakes, and the whole family of cakes. And then there were apple pies and peach pies and pumpkin pies; besides slices of ham and smoked beef; and moreover delectable dishes of preserved plums, and peaches, and pears, and quinces; not to mention broiled shad and roasted chickens; together with bowls of milk and cream, all mingled higgledy-piggledy, pretty much as I have enumerated them, with the motherly tea-pot sending up its clouds of vapor from the midst – Heaven bless the mark! I want breath and time to discuss this banquet as it deserves, and am too eager to get on with my story. Happily, Ichabod Crane was not in so great a hurry as his historian, but did ample justice to every dainty.

He was a kind and thankful creature, whose heart dilated in proportion as his skin was filled with good cheer; and whose spirits rose with eating as some men's do with drink. He could not help, too, rolling his large eyes round him as he ate, and chuckling with the possibility that he might one day be lord of all this scene of almost unimaginable luxury and splendor. Then, he thought, how soon he'd turn his back upon the old schoolhouse; snap his fingers in the face of Hans Van Ripper, and every other niggardly patron, and kick any itinerant pedagogue out of doors that should dare to call him comrade!

Old Baltus Van Tassel moved about among his guests with a face dilated with content and good humor, round and jolly as the harvest moon. His hospitable attentions were brief, but expressive, being confined to a shake of the hand, a slap on the shoulder, a loud laugh, and a pressing invitation to 'fall to, and help themselves'.

And now the sound of the music from the common room, or hall, summoned to the dance. The musician was an old gray-headed Negro, who had been the itinerant orchestra of the neighborhood for more than half a century. His instrument was as old and battered as himself. The greater part of the time he scraped on two or three strings, accompanying every movement of the bow with a motion of the head; bowing almost to the ground, and stamping with his foot whenever a fresh couple were to start.

Ichabod prided himself upon his dancing as much as upon his vocal powers. Not a limb, not a fibre about him was idle; and to have seen his loosely-hung frame in full motion, and clattering about the room, you would have thought Saint Vitus himself, that blessed patron of the dance, was figuring before you in person. He was the admiration of all the Negroes; who having gathered, of all ages and sizes, from the farm and the neighborhood, stood forming a pyramid of shining black faces at every door and window, gazing with delight at the scene, rolling their white eye-balls, and showing grinning rows of ivory from ear to ear. How could the flogger of urchins be otherwise than animated and joyous? The lady of his heart was his partner in the dance, and smiling graciously in reply to all his amorous oglings; while Brom Bones, sorely smitten with love and jealousy, sat brooding by himself in one corner.

When the dance was at an end, Ichabod was attracted to a

knot of the sager folks, who, with old Van Tassel, sat smoking at one end of the piazza, gossiping over former times, and drawing out long stories about the war.

This neighborhood, at the time of which I am speaking, was one of those highly-favored places which abound with chronicle and great men. The British and American line had run near it during the war; it had, therefore, been the scene of marauding, and infested with refugees, cow-boys, and all kinds of border chivalry. Just sufficient time had elapsed to enable each story-teller to dress up his tale with a little becoming fiction, and, in the indistinctness of his recollection, to make himself the hero of every exploit.

There was the story of Doffue Martling, a large blue-bearded Dutchman, who had nearly taken a British frigate with an old iron nine-pounder from a mud breastwork, only that his gun burst at the sixth discharge. And there was an old gentleman who shall be nameless, being too rich a mynheer to be lightly mentioned, who, in the battle of Whiteplains, being an excellent master of defence, parried a musket ball with a small sword, insomuch that he absolutely felt it whiz round the blade, and glance off at the hilt: in proof of which, he was ready at any time to show the sword, with the hilt a little bent. There were several more that had been equally great in the field, not one of whom but was persuaded that he had a considerable hand in bringing the war to a happy termination.

But all these were nothing to the tales of ghosts and apparitions that succeeded. The neighborhood is rich in legendary treasures of the kind. Local tales and superstitions thrive best in these sheltered long-settled retreats; but are trampled under foot by the shifting throng that forms the population of most of our country places. Besides, there is no encouragement for ghosts in most of our villages, for they have scarcely had time to finish their first nap, and turn themselves in their graves, before their surviving friends have travelled away from the neighborhood; so that when they turn out at night to walk their rounds, they have no acquaintance left to call upon. This is perhaps the reason why we so seldom hear of ghosts except in our long-established Dutch communities.

The immediate cause, however, of the prevalence of supernatural stories in these parts, was doubtless owing to the vicinity
of Sleepy Hollow. There was a contagion in the very air that
blew from that haunted region; it breathed forth an atmosphere
of dreams and fancies infecting all the land. Several of the
Sleepy Hollow people were present at Van Tassel's, and, as
usual, were doling out their wild and wonderful legends. Many
dismal tales were told about funeral trains, and mourning cries
and wailings heard and seen about the great tree where the unfortunate Major André was taken, and which stood in the
neighborhood. Some mention was made also of the woman in
white, that haunted the dark glen at Raven Rock, and was often
heard to shriek on winter nights before a storm, having perished
there in the snow. The chief part of the stories, however, turned
upon the favorite spectre of Sleepy Hollow, the headless horseman, who had been heard several times of late, patrolling the
country; and, it was said, tethered his horse nightly among the
graves in the church-yard.

The sequestered situation of this church seems always to have
made it a favorite haunt of troubled spirits. It stands on a knoll,
surrounded by locust-trees and lofty elms, from among which its
decent, whitewashed walls shine modestly forth, like Christian
purity beaming through the shades of retirement. A gentle slope
descends from it to a silver sheet of water, bordered by high
trees, between which, peeps may be caught at the blue hills of
the Hudson. To look upon its grass-grown yard, where the sun-
beams seem to sleep so quietly, one would think that there at
least the dead might rest in peace. On one side of the church
extends a wide woody dell, along which raves a large brook
among broken rocks and trunks of fallen trees. Over a deep
black part of the stream, not far from the church, was formerly
thrown a wooden bridge; the road that led to it, and the bridge
itself, were thickly shaded by overhanging trees, which cast a
gloom about it, even in the daytime; but occasioned a fearful
darkness at night. This was one of the favorite haunts of the
headless horseman; and the place where he was most frequently
encountered. The tale was told of old Brouwer, a most heretical
disbeliever in ghosts, how he met the horseman returning from

his foray into Sleepy Hollow, and was obliged to get up behind him; how they galloped over bush and brake, over hill and swamp, until they reached the bridge; when the horseman suddenly turned into a skeleton, threw old Brouwer into the brook, and sprang away over the tree-tops with a clap of thunder.

This story was immediately matched by a thrice marvellous adventure of Brom Bones, who made light of the galloping Hessian as an arrant jockey. He affirmed that, on returning one night from the neighboring village of Sing Sing, he had been overtaken by this midnight trooper; that he had offered to race with him for a bowl of punch, and should have won it too, for Daredevil beat the goblin horse all hollow, but, just as they came to the church-bridge, the Hessian bolted, and vanished in a flash of fire.

All these tales, told in that drowsy undertone with which men talk in the dark, the countenances of the listeners only now and then receiving a casual gleam from the glare of a pipe, sank deep in the mind of Ichabod. He repaid them in kind with large extracts from his invaluable author, Cotton Mather, and added many marvellous events that had taken place in his native State of Connecticut, and fearful sights which he had seen in his nightly walks about Sleepy Hollow.

The revel now gradually broke up. The old farmers gathered together their families in their wagons, and were heard for some time rattling along the hollow roads, and over the distant hills. Some of the damsels mounted on pillions behind their favorite swains, and their light-hearted laughter, mingling with the clatter of hoofs, echoed along the silent woodlands, sounding fainter and fainter until they gradually died away – and the late scene of noise and frolic was all silent and deserted. Ichabod only lingered behind, according to the custom of country lovers, to have a tête-à-tête with the heiress; fully convinced that he was now on the high road to success. What passed at this interview I will not pretend to say, for in fact I do not know. Something, however, I fear me, must have gone wrong, for he certainly sallied forth, after no very great interval, with an air quite desolate and chop-fallen. Oh these women! these women! Could that girl have been playing off any of her coquettish tricks? Was her encouragement of the poor pedagogue all a mere sham to secure her conquest of his rival? Heaven only knows, not I! Let it suffice to say, Ichabod stole forth with the air of one who had been sacking a hen-roost, rather than a fair lady's heart. Without looking to the right or left to notice the scene of rural wealth, on which he had so often gloated, he went straight to the stable, and with several hearty cuffs and kicks, roused his steed most uncourteously from the comfortable quarters in which he was soundly sleeping, dreaming of mountains of corn and oats, and whole valleys of timothy and clover.

It was the very witching time of night that Ichabod, heavy-hearted and crest-fallen, pursued his travel homewards, along the sides of the lofty hills which rise above Tarry Town, and which he had traversed so cheerily in the afternoon. The hour was as dismal as himself. Far below him, the Tappan Zee spread its dusky and indistinct waste of waters, with here and there the tall mast of a sloop, riding quietly at anchor under the land. In the dead hush of midnight, he could even hear the barking of the watch dog from the opposite shore of the Hudson; but it was so vague and faint as only to give an idea of his distance from this faithful companion of man. Now and then, too, the long-drawn crowing of a cock, accidentally awakened, would sound far, far off, from some farmhouse away among the hills – but it was like a dreaming sound in his ear. No signs of life occurred near him, but occasionally the melancholy chirp of a cricket, or perhaps the guttural twang of a bull-frog, from a neighbouring marsh, as if sleeping uncomfortably, and turning suddenly in his bed.

All the stories of ghosts and goblins that he had heard in the afternoon, now came crowding upon his recollection. The night grew darker and darker; the stars seemed to sink deeper in the sky, and driving clouds occasionally hid them from his sight. He had never felt so lonely and dismal. He was, moreover, approaching the very place where many of the scenes of the ghost stories had been laid. In the centre of the road stood an enormous tulip-tree, which towered like a giant above all the other trees of the neighborhood, and formed a kind of land-mark. Its limbs were gnarled, and fantastic, large enough to form trunks for ordinary trees, twisting down almost to the earth, and rising again into the air. It was connected with the tragical story of the unfortunate André, who had been taken prisoner hard by; and was universally known by the name of Major André's tree. The common people regarded it with a mixture of respect and superstition, partly out of sympathy for the fate of its ill-starred namesake, and partly from the tales of strange sights and doleful lamentations told concerning it.

As Ichabod approached this fearful tree, he began to whistle; he thought his whistle was answered – it was but a blast sweeping sharply through the dry branches. As he approached a little nearer, he thought he saw something white, hanging in the midst of the tree – he paused and ceased whistling; but on looking more narrowly, perceived that it was a place where the tree had been scathed by lightning, and the white wood laid bare. Suddenly he heard a groan – his teeth chattered and his knees smote against the saddle: it was but the rubbing of one huge bough upon another, as they were swayed about by the breeze. He passed the tree in safety, but new perils lay before him.

About two hundred yards from the tree a small brook crossed the road, and ran into a marshy and thickly-wooded glen, known by the name of Wiley's swamp. A few rough logs, laid side by side, served for a bridge over this stream. On that side of the road where the brook entered the wood, a group of oaks and chestnuts, matted thick with wild grapevines, threw a cavernous gloom over it. To pass this bridge was the severest trial. It was at this identical spot that the unfortunate André was captured, and under the covert of those chestnuts and vines were the sturdy yeomen concealed who surprised him. This has ever since been considered a haunted stream, and fearful are the feelings of the schoolboy who has to pass it alone after dark.

As he approached the stream, his heart began to thump; he summoned up, however, all his resolution, gave his horse half a score of kicks in the ribs, and attempted to dash briskly across the bridge; but instead of starting forward, the perverse old animal made a lateral movement, and ran broadside against the fence. Ichabod, whose fears increased with the delay, jerked the reins on the other side, and kicked lustily with the contrary foot: it was all in vain; his steed started, it is true, but it was only to plunge to the opposite side of the road into a thicket of brambles and alder bushes. The school-master now bestowed both whip and heel upon the starveling ribs of old Gunpowder, who dashed forward, snuffling and snorting, but came to a stand just by the bridge, with a suddenness that had nearly sent his rider sprawling over his head. Just at this moment a plashy tramp by the side of the bridge caught the sensitive ear of Ichabod. In the dark shadow of the grove, on the margin of the brook, he beheld something huge, misshapen, black and towering. It stirred not, but seemed gathered up in the gloom, like some gigantic monster ready to spring upon the traveller.

The hair of the affrighted pedagogue rose upon his head with terror. What was to be done? To turn and fly was now too late; and besides, what chance was there of escaping ghost or goblin, if such it was, which could ride upon the wings of the wind? Summoning up, therefore, a show of courage, he demanded in stammering accents – 'Who are you?' He received no reply. He repeated his demand in a still more agitated voice. Still there was no answer. Once more he cudgelled the sides of the inflexible Gunpowder, and, shutting his eyes, broke forth with involuntary fervor into a psalm tune. Just then the shadowy object of alarm put itself in motion, and, with a scramble and a bound, stood at once in the middle of the road. Though the night was dark and dismal, yet the form of the unknown might now in some degree be ascertained. He appeared to be a horseman of large dimensions, and mounted on a black horse of powerful frame. He made no offer of molestation or sociability, but kept aloof on one side of the road, jogging along on the blind side of old Gunpowder, who had now got over his fright and waywardness.

Ichabod, who had no relish for this strange midnight companion, and bethought himself of the adventure of Brom Bones with the Galloping Hessian, now quickened his steed, in hopes of leaving him behind. The stranger, however, quickened his horse to an equal pace. Ichabod pulled up, and fell into a walk, thinking to lag behind – the other did the same. His heart began to sink within him; he endeavoured to resume his psalm tune, but his parched tongue clove to the roof of his mouth, and he could not utter a stave. There was something in the moody and dogged silence of this pertinacious companion, that was mysterious and appalling. It was soon fearfully accounted for. On mounting a rising ground, which brought the figure of his fellow-traveller in relief against the sky, gigantic in height, and muffled in a cloak, Ichabod was horror-struck, on perceiving that he was headless! But his horror was still more increased, on observing that the head, which should have rested on his shoulders, was carried before him on the pommel of the saddle: his terror rose to desperation; he rained a shower of kicks and blows upon Gunpowder, hoping, by a sudden movement, to give his companion the slip – but the spectre started full jump with him. Away then they dashed, through thick and thin; stones flying, and sparks flashing at every bound. Ichabod's flimsy garments fluttering in the air, as he stretched his long lank body away over his horse's head, in the eagerness of his flight.

They had now reached the road which turns off to Sleepy Hollow; but Gunpowder, who seemed possessed with a demon, instead of keeping up it, made an opposite turn, and plunged headlong down hill to the left. This road leads through a sandy hollow, shaded by trees for about a quarter of a mile, where it crosses the bridge famous in goblin story, and just beyond swells the green knoll on which stands the whitewashed church.

As yet the panic of the steed had given his unskilful rider an apparent advantage in the chase; but just as he had got half way through the hollow, the girths of the saddle gave way, and he felt it slipping from under him. He seized it by the pommel, and endeavored to hold it firm, but in vain; and had just time to save himself by clasping old Gunpowder round the neck, when the saddle fell to the earth, and he heard it trampled under foot by his pursuer. For a moment the terror of Hans Van Ripper's wrath passed across his mind – for it was his Sunday saddle; but this was no time for petty fears; the goblin was hard on his haunches; and (unskilful rider that he was!) he had much ado to maintain his seat; sometimes slipping on one side, sometimes on another, and sometimes jolted on the high ridge of his horse's backbone, with a violence that he verily feared would cleave him asunder.

An opening in the trees now cheered him with the hopes that the church bridge was at hand. The wavering reflection of a silver-star in the bosom of the brook told him that he was not mistaken. He saw the walls of the church dimly glaring under the trees beyond. He recollected the place where Brom Bones's ghostly competitor had disappeared. 'If I can but reach that bridge,' thought Ichabod, 'I am safe.' Just then he heard the black steed panting and blowing close behind him; he even fancied that he felt his hot breath. Another convulsive kick in the ribs, and old Gunpowder sprang upon the bridge; he thundered over the resounding planks; he gained the opposite side; and now Ichabod cast a look behind to see if his pursuer should vanish, according to rule, in a flash of fire and brimstone. Just then he saw the goblin rising in his stirrups, and in the very act of hurling his head at him. Ichabod endeavored to dodge the horrible missile, but too late. It encountered his cranium with a tremendous crash – he was tumbled headlong into the dust, and Gunpowder, the black steed, and the goblin rider, passed by like a whirlwind.

The next morning the old horse was found without his saddle, and with the bridle under his feet, soberly cropping the grass at his master's gate. Ichabod did not make his appearance at breakfast – dinner-hour came, but no Ichabod. The boys assembled at the school-house, and strolled idly about the banks of the brook; but no schoolmaster. Hans Van Ripper now began to feel some uneasiness about the fate of poor Ichabod, and his saddle. An inquiry was set on foot, and after diligent investigation they came upon his traces. In one part of the road leading to the church was found the saddle trampled in the dirt; the tracks of horses' hoofs deeply dented in the road, and evidently at furious speed, were traced to the bridge, beyond which, on the bank of a broad part of the brook, where the water ran deep and black, was found the hat of the unfortunate Ichabod, and close beside it a shattered pumpkin.

The brook was searched, but the body of the school-master was not to be discovered. Hans Van Ripper, as executor of his estate, examined the bundle which contained all his worldly effects. They consisted of two shirts and a half; two stocks for the neck; a pair or two of worsted stockings; an old pair of corduroy small-clothes; a rusty razor; a book of psalm tunes, full of dogs' ears; and a broken pitch-pipe. As to the books and furniture of the school-house, they belonged to the community, excepting Cotton Mather's History of Witchcraft, a New England Almanac, and a book of dreams and fortune-telling; in which last was a sheet of foolscap much scribbled and blotted in several fruitless attempts to make a copy of verses in honor of the heiress of Van Tassel. These magic books and the poetic scrawl were forthwith consigned to the flames by Hans Van Ripper; who from that time forward determined to send his children no more to school; observing, that he never knew any good come of this same reading and writing. Whatever money the schoolmaster possessed, and he had received his quarter's pay but a day or two before, he must have had about his person at the time of his disappearance.

The mysterious event caused much speculation at the church on the following Sunday. Knots of gazers and gossips were collected in the church-yard, at the bridge, and at the spot where the hat and pumpkin had been found. The stories of Brouwer, of Bones, and a whole budget of others, were called to mind; and when they had diligently considered them all, and compared them with the symptoms of the present case, they shook their heads, and came to the conclusion that Ichabod had been carried off by the galloping Hessian. As he was a bachelor, and in nobody's debt, nobody troubled his head any more about him. The school was removed to a different quarter of the hollow, and another pedagogue reigned in his stead.

It is true, an old farmer, who had been down to New-York on a visit several years after, and from whom this account of the ghostly adventure was received, brought home the intelligence that Ichabod Crane was still alive; that he had left the neighborhood, partly through fear of the goblin and Hans Van Ripper, and partly in mortification at having been suddenly dismissed by the heiress; that he had changed his quarters to a distant part of the country; had kept school and studied law at the same time, had been admitted to the bar, turned politician, electioneered, written for the newspapers, and finally had been made a justice of the Ten Pound Court. Brom Bones too, who, shortly after his rival's disappearance, conducted the blooming Katrina in triumph to the altar, was observed to look exceedingly knowing whenever the story of Ichabod was related, and always burst into a hearty laugh at the mention of the pumpkin; which led some to suspect that he knew more about the matter than he chose to tell.

The old country wives, however, who are the best judges of these matters, maintain to this day that Ichabod was spirited away by supernatural means; and it is a favorite story often told about the neighborhood round the winter evening fire. The bridge became more than ever an object of superstitious awe, and that may be the reason why the road has been altered of late years, so as to approach the church by the border of the mill-pond. The school-house being deserted, soon fell to decay, and was reported to be haunted by the ghost of the unfortunate pedagogue; and the plough boy, loitering homeward of a still summer evening, has often fancied his voice at a distance, chanting a melancholy psalm tune among the tranquil solitudes of Sleepy Hollow.

POSTSCRIPT, FOUND IN THE HANDWRITING OF MR KNICKERBOCKER

The preceding Tale is given, almost in the precise words in which I heard it related at a Corporation meeting of the ancient city of Manhattoes, at which were present many of its sagest and most illustrious burghers. The narrator was a pleasant, shabby, gentlemanly old fellow, in pepper-and-salt clothes, with a sadly humorous face; and one whom I strongly suspected of being poor – he made such efforts to be entertaining. When his story was concluded, there was much laughter and approbation, particularly from two or three deputy aldermen, who had been asleep the greater part of the time. There was, however, one tall, dry-looking old gentleman, with beetling eyebrows, who maintained a grave and rather severe face throughout: now and then folding his arms, inclining his head, and looking down upon the floor, as if turning a doubt over in his mind. He was one of your wary men, who never laugh, but upon good grounds – when they have reason and the law on their side. When the mirth of the rest of the company had subsided, and silence was restored, he leaned one arm on the elbow of his chair, and sticking the other akimbo, demanded, with a slight, but exceedingly sage motion of the head, and contraction of the brow, what was the moral of the story, and what it went to prove?

The story-teller, who was just putting a glass of wine to his lips, as a refreshment after his toils, paused for a moment, looked at his inquirer with an air of infinite deference, and, lowering the glass slowly to the table, observed, that the story was intended most logically to prove:

'That there is no situation in life but has its advantages and pleasures – provided we will but take a joke as we find it.

'That, therefore, he that runs races with goblin troopers is likely to have rough riding of it.

'Ergo, for a country school-master to be refused the hand of a Dutch heiress, is a certain step to high preferment, in the state.'

The cautious old gentleman knit his brows tenfold closer after this explanation, being sorely puzzled by the ratiocination of the syllogism; while, methought, the one in pepper-and-salt eyed him with something of a triumphant leer. At length he observed, that all this was very well, but still he thought the story a little on the extravagant – there were one or two points on which he had his doubts.

'Faith, sir,' replied the story-teller, 'as to that matter, I don't believe one-half of it myself.'

D. K.

Nathaniel Hawthorne

YOUNG GOODMAN BROWN

YOUNG Goodman Brown came forth at sunset into the street at Salem village; but put his head back, after crossing the threshold, to exchange a parting kiss with his young wife. And Faith, as the wife was aptly named, thrust her own pretty head into the street, letting the wind play with the pink ribbons of her cap while she called to Goodman Brown.

'Dearest heart,' whispered she, softly and rather sadly, when her lips were close to his ear, 'prithee put off your journey until sunrise and sleep in your own bed tonight. A lone woman is troubled with such dreams and such thoughts that she's afeard of herself sometimes. Pray tarry with me this night, dear husband, of all nights in the year.'

'My love and my Faith,' replied young Goodman Brown, 'of all nights in the year, this one night must I tarry away from thee. My journey, as thou callest it, forth and back again, must needs be done 'twixt now and sunrise. What, my sweet, pretty wife, dost thou doubt me already, and we but three months married?'

'Then God bless you!' said Faith, with the pink ribbons; 'and may you find all well when you come back.'

'Amen!' cried Goodman Brown. 'Say thy prayers, dear Faith, and go to bed at dusk, and no harm will come to thee.'

So they parted; and the young man pursued his way until, being about to turn the corner by the meeting-house, he looked back and saw the head of Faith still peeping after him with a melancholy air, in spite of her pink ribbons.

'Poor little Faith!' thought he, for his heart smote him. 'What a wretch am I to leave her on such an errand! She talks of dreams, too. Methought as she spoke there was trouble in her face, as if a dream had warned her what work is to be done tonight. But no, no; 'twould kill her to think it. Well, she's a blessed angel on earth; and after this one night I'll cling to her skirts and follow her to heaven.'

With this excellent resolve for the future, Goodman Brown felt himself justified in making more haste on his present evil purpose. He had taken a dreary road, darkened by all the gloomiest trees of the forest, which barely stood aside to let the narrow path creep through, and closed immediately behind. It was all as lonely as could be; and there is this peculiarity in such a solitude, that the traveller knows not who may be concealed by the innumerable trunks and the thick boughs overhead; so that with lonely footsteps he may yet be passing through an unseen multitude.

'There may be a devilish Indian behind every tree,' said Goodman Brown to himself; and he glanced fearfully behind him as he added, 'What if the devil himself should be at my very elbow!'

His head being turned back, he passed a crook of the road, and, looking forward again, beheld the figure of a man, in grave and decent attire, seated at the foot of an old tree. He arose at Goodman Brown's approach and walked onward side by side with him.

'You are late, Goodman Brown,' said he. 'The clock of the Old South was striking as I came through Boston, and that is full fifteen minutes agone.'

'Faith kept me back a while,' replied the young man, with a tremor in his voice, caused by the sudden appearance of his companion, though not wholly unexpected.

It was now deep dusk in the forest, and deepest in that part of it where these two were journeying. As nearly as could be discerned, the second traveller was about fifty years old, apparently in the same rank of life as Goodman Brown, and bearing a considerable resemblance to him, though perhaps more in expression than features. Still they might have been taken for father and son. And yet, though the elder person was as simply clad as the younger, and as simple in manner too, he had an indescribable air of one who knew the world, and who would not have felt abashed at the governor's dinner table or in King William's court, were it possible that his affairs should call him thither. But the only thing about him that could be fixed upon as remarkable was his staff, which bore the likeness of a great black snake, so curiously wrought that it might almost be seen to twist and wriggle itself like a living serpent. This, of course, must have been an ocular deception, assisted by the uncertain light.

'Come, Goodman Brown,' cried his fellow-traveller, 'this is a dull pace for the beginning of a journey. Take my staff, if you are so soon weary.'

'Friend,' said the other, exchanging his slow pace for a full stop, 'having kept covenant by meeting thee here, it is my purpose now to return whence I came. I have scruples touching the matter thou wot'st of.'

'Sayest thou so?' replied he of the serpent, smiling apart. 'Let us walk on, nevertheless, reasoning as we go; and if I convince thee not thou shalt turn back. We are but a little way in the forest yet.'

'Too far! too far!' exclaimed the goodman, unconsciously resuming his walk. 'My father never went into the woods on such an errand, nor his father before him. We have been a race of honest men and good Christians since the days of the martyrs; and shall I be the first of the name of Brown that ever took this path and kept' —

'Such company, thou wouldst say,' observed the elder person, interpreting his pause. 'Well said, Goodman Brown! I have been as well acquainted with your family as with ever a one among the Puritans; and that's no trifle to say. I helped your grandfather, the constable, when he lashed the Quaker woman so smartly through the streets of Salem; and it was I that brought your father a pitch-pine knot, kindled at my own hearth, to set fire to an Indian village, in King Philip's war. They were my good friends, both; and many a pleasant walk have we had along this path, and returned merrily after midnight. I would fain be friends with you for their sake.'

'If it be as thou sayest,' replied Goodman Brown, 'I marvel they never spoke of these matters; or verily, I marvel not, seeing that the least rumor of the sort would have driven them from

New England. We are a people of prayer, and good works to boot, and abide no such wickedness.'

'Wickedness or not,' said the traveller with the twisted staff, 'I have a very general acquaintance here in New England. The deacons of many a church have drunk the communion wine with me; the selectmen of divers towns make me their chairman; and a majority of the Great and General Court are firm supporters of my interest. The governor and I, too — But these are state secrets.'

'Can this be so?' cried Goodman Brown, with a stare of amazement at his undisturbed companion. 'Howbeit, I have nothing to do with the governor and council; they have their own ways, and are no rule for a simple husbandman like me. But, were I to go on with thee, how should I meet the eye of that good old man, our minister, at Salem village? Oh, his voice would make me tremble both Sabbath day and lecture day.'

Thus far the elder traveller had listened with due gravity; but now burst into a fit of irrepressible mirth, shaking himself so violently that his snake-like staff actually seemed to wriggle in sympathy.

'Ha! ha! ha!' shouted he again and again; then composing himself, 'Well, go on Goodman Brown, go on; but, prithee, don't kill me with laughing.'

'Well, then, to end the matter at once,' said Goodman Brown, considerably nettled, 'there is my wife, Faith. It would break her dear little heart; and I'd rather break my own.'

'Nay, if that be the case,' answered the other, 'e'en go thy ways, Goodman Brown. I would not for twenty old women like the one hobbling before us that Faith should come to any harm.'

As he spoke he pointed his staff at a female figure on the path, in whom Goodman Brown recognized a very pious and exemplary dame, who had taught him his catechism in youth, and was still his moral and spiritual adviser, jointly with the minister and Deacon Gookin.

'A marvel, truly, that Goody Cloyse should be so far in the wilderness at nightfall,' said he. 'But with your leave, friend, I shall take a cut through the woods until we have left this Christian woman behind. Being a stranger to you, she might ask whom I was consorting with and whither I was going.'

'Be it so,' said his fellow-traveller. 'Betake you to the woods, and let me keep the path.'

Accordingly the young man turned aside, but took care to watch his companion, who advanced softly along the road until he had come within a staff's length of the old dame. She, meanwhile, was making the best of her way, with singular speed for so aged a woman, and mumbling some indistinct words – a prayer, doubtless – as she went. The traveller put forth his staff and touched her withered neck with what seemed the serpent's tail.

'The devil!' screamed the pious old lady.

'Then Goody Cloyse knows her old friend?' observed the traveller, confronting her and leaning on his writhing stick.

'Ah, forsooth, and is it your worship indeed?' cried the good dame. 'Yea, truly is it, and in the very image of my old gossip, Goodman Brown, the grandfather of the silly fellow that now is. But – would your worship believe it? – my broomstick hath strangely disappeared, stolen, as I suspect, by that unhanged witch, Goody Cory, and that, too, when I was all anointed with the juice of smallage, and cinquefoil, and wolf's bane' –

'Mingled with fine wheat and the fat of a new-born babe,' said the shape of old Goodman Brown.

'Ah, your worship knows the recipe,' cried the old lady, cackling aloud. 'So, as I was saying, being all ready for the meeting, and no horse to ride on, I made up my mind to foot it; for they tell me there is a nice young man to be taken into communion tonight. But now your good worship will lend me your arm, and we shall be there in a twinkling.'

'That can hardly be,' answered her friend. 'I may not spare you my arm, Goody Cloyse; but here is my staff, if you will.'

So saying, he threw it down at her feet, where, perhaps, it assumed life, being one of the rods which its owner had formerly lent to the Egyptian magi. Of this fact, however, Goodman Brown could not take cognizance. He had cast up his eyes in astonishment, and, looking down again, beheld neither Goody

Cloyse nor the serpentine staff, but his fellow-traveller alone, who waited for him as calmly as if nothing had happened.

'That old woman taught me my catechism,' said the young man; and there was a world of meaning in this simple comment.

They continued to walk onward, while the elder traveller exhorted his companion to make good speed and persevere in the path, discoursing so aptly that his arguments seemed rather to spring up in the bosom of his auditor than to be suggested by himself. As they went, he plucked a branch of maple to serve for a walking stick, and began to strip it of the twigs and little boughs, which were wet with evening dew. The moment his fingers touched them they became strangely withered and dried up as with a week's sunshine. Thus the pair proceeded, at a good free pace, until suddenly, in a gloomy hollow of the road, Goodman Brown sat himself down on the stump of a tree and refused to go any farther.

'Friend,' said he, stubbornly, 'my mind is made up. Not another step will I budge on this errand. What if a wretched old woman do choose to go to the devil when I thought she was going to heaven: is that any reason why I should quit my dear Faith and go after her?'

'You will think better of this by and by,' said his acquaintance, composedly. 'Sit here and rest yourself a while; and when you feel like moving again, there is my staff to help you along.'

Without more words, he threw his companion the maple stick, and was as speedily out of sight as if he had vanished into the deepening gloom. The young man sat a few moments by the roadside, applauding himself greatly, and thinking with how clear a conscience he should meet the minister in his morning walk, nor shrink from the eye of good old Deacon Gookin. And what calm sleep would be his that very night, which was to have been spent so wickedly, but so purely and sweetly now, in the arms of Faith! Amidst these pleasant and praiseworthy meditations, Goodman Brown heard the tramp of horses along the road, and deemed it advisable to conceal himself within the verge of the forest, conscious of the guilty purpose that had brought him thither, though now so happily turned from it.

On came the hoof tramps and the voices of the riders, two grave old voices, conversing soberly as they drew near. These mingled sounds appeared to pass along the road, within a few yards of the young man's hiding-place; but, owing doubtless to the depth of the gloom at that particular spot, neither the travellers nor their steeds were visible. Though their figures brushed the small boughs by the wayside, it would not be seen that they intercepted, even for a moment, the faint gleam from the strip of bright sky athwart which they must have passed. Goodman Brown alternately crouched and stood on tiptoe, pulling aside the branches and thrusting forth his head as far as he durst without discerning so much as a shadow. It vexed him the more, because he could have sworn, were such a thing possible, that he recognized the voices of the minister and Deacon Gookin, jogging along quietly, as they were wont to do, when bound to some ordination or ecclesiastical council. While yet within hearing, one of the riders stopped to pluck a switch.

'Of the two, reverend sir,' said the voice like the deacon's, 'I had rather miss an ordination dinner than tonight's meeting. They tell me that some of our community are to be here from Falmouth and beyond, and others from Connecticut and Rhode Island, besides several of the Indian pow-wows, who, after their fashion, know almost as much deviltry as the best of us. Moreover, there is a goodly young woman to be taken into communion.'

'Mighty well, Deacon Gookin!' replied the solemn old tones of the minister. 'Spur up, or we shall be late. Nothing can be done, you know, until I get on the ground.'

The hoofs clattered again; and the voices, talking so strangely in the empty air, passed on through the forest, where no church had ever been gathered or solitary Christian prayed. Whither, then, could could these holy men be journeying so deep into the heathen wilderness? Young Goodman Brown caught hold of a tree for support, being ready to sink down on the ground, faint and overburdened with the heavy sickness of his heart. He looked up to the sky, doubting whether there really was a heaven above him. Yet there was the blue arch, and the stars brightening in it.

'With heaven above and Faith below, I will yet stand firm against the devil!' cried Goodman Brown.

While he still gazed upward into the deep arch of the firmament and had lifted his hand to pray, a cloud, though no wind was stirring, hurried across the zenith and hid the brightening stars. The blue sky was still visible, except directly overhead, where this black mass of cloud was sweeping swiftly northward. Aloft in the air, as if from the depths of the cloud, came a confused and doubtful sound of voices. Once the listener fancied that he could distinguish the accents of towns-people of his own, men and women, both pious and ungodly, many of whom he had met at the communion table, and had seen others rioting at the tavern. The next moment, so indistinct were the sounds, he doubted whether he had heard aught but the murmur of the old forest, whispering without a wind. Then came a stronger swell of those familiar tones, heard daily in the sunshine at Salem village, but never until now from a cloud of night. There was one voice, of a young woman, uttering lamentations, yet with an uncertain sorrow, and entreating for some favor, which, perhaps, it would grieve her to obtain; and all the unseen multitude, both saints and sinners, seemed to encourage her onward.

'Faith!' shouted Goodman Brown, in a voice of agony and desperation; and the echoes of the forest mocked him, crying, 'Faith! Faith!' as if bewildered wretches were seeking her all through the wilderness.

The cry of grief, rage, and terror was yet piercing the night, when the uphappy husband held his breath for a response. There was a scream, drowned immediately in a louder murmur of voices, fading into far-off laughter, as the dark cloud swept away, leaving the clear and silent sky above Goodman Brown. But something fluttered lightly down through the air and caught on the branch of a tree. The young man seized it, and beheld a pink ribbon.

'My Faith is gone!' cried he, after one stupefied moment. 'There is no good on earth; and sin is but a name. Come, devil; for to thee is this world given.'

And, maddened with despair, so that he laughed loud and

long, did Goodman Brown grasp his staff and set forth again, at such a rate that he seemed to fly along the forest path rather than to walk or run. The road grew wilder and drearier and more faintly traced, and vanished at length, leaving him in the heart of the dark wilderness, still rushing onward with the instinct that guides mortal man to evil. The whole forest was peopled with frightful sounds – the creaking of the trees, the howling of wild beasts, and the yell of Indians; while sometimes the wind tolled like a distant church bell, and sometimes gave a broad roar around the traveller, as if all Nature were laughing him to scorn. But he was himself the chief horror of the scene, and shrank not from its other horrors.

'Ha! ha! ha!' roared Goodman Brown when the wind laughed at him. 'Let us hear which will laugh loudest. Think not to frighten me with your deviltry. Come witch, come wizard, come Indian pow-wow, come devil himself, and here comes Goodman Brown. You may as well fear him as he fears you.'

In truth, all through the haunted forest there could be nothing more frightful than the figure of Goodman Brown. On he flew among the black pines brandishing his staff with frenzied gestures, now giving vent to an inspiration of horrid blasphemy, and now shouting forth such laughter as set all the echoes of the forest laughing like demons around him. The fiend in his own shape is less hideous than when he rages in the breast of man. Thus sped the demoniac on his course, until, quivering among the trees, he saw a red light before him, as when the felled trunks and branches of a clearing have been set on fire, and throw up their lurid blaze against the sky, at the hour of midnight. He paused, in a lull of the tempest that had driven him onward, and heard the swell of what seemed a hymn, rolling solemnly from a distance with the weight of many voices. He knew the tune; it was a familiar one in the choir of the village meeting-house. The verse died heavily away, and was lengthened by a chorus, not of human voices, but of all the sounds of the benighted wilderness pealing in awful harmony together. Goodman Brown cried out, and his cry was lost to his own ear by its unison with the cry of the desert.

In the interval of silence he stole forward until the light

glared full upon his eyes. At one extremity of an open space, hemmed in by the dark wall of the forest, arose a rock, bearing some rude, natural resemblance either to an altar or a pulpit, and surrounded by four blazing pines, their tops aflame, their stems untouched, like candles at an evening meeting. The mass of foliage that had overgrown the summit of the rock was all on fire, blazing high into the night and fitfully illuminating the whole field. Each pendent twig and leafy festoon was in a blaze. As the red light arose and fell, a numerous congregation alternately shone forth, then disappeared in shadow, and again grew, as it were, out of the darkness, peopling the heart of the solitary woods at once.

'A grave and dark-clad company,' quoth Goodman Brown.

In truth they were such. Among them, quivering to and fro between gloom and splendor, appeared faces that would be seen next day at the council board of the province, and others which, Sabbath after Sabbath, looked devoutly heavenward, and benignantly over the crowded pews, from the holiest pulpits in the land. Some affirm that the lady of the governor was there. At least there were high dames well known to her, and wives of honoured husbands, and widows, a great multitude, and ancient maidens, all of excellent repute, and fair young girls, who trembled lest their mothers should espy them. Either the sudden gleams of light flashing over the obscure field bedazzled Goodman Brown, or he recognized a score of the church members of Salem village famous for their especial sanctity. Good old Deacon Gookin had arrived, and waited at the skirts of that venerable saint, his revered pastor. But, irreverently consorting with these grave, reputable, and pious people, these elders of the church, these chaste dames and dewy virgins, there were men of dissolute lives and women of spotted fame, wretches given over to all mean and filthy vice, and suspected even of horrid crimes. It was strange to see that the good shrank not from the wicked, nor were the sinners abashed by the saints. Scattered also among their pale-faced enemies were the Indian priests, or pow-wows, who had often scared their native forest with more hideous incantations than any known to English witchcraft.

'But where is Faith?' thought Goodman Brown; and, as hope came into his heart, he trembled.

Another verse of the hymn arose, a slow and mournful strain, such as the pious love, but joined to words which expressed all that our nature can conceive of sin, and darkly hinted at far more. Unfathomable to mere mortals is the lore of fiends. Verse after verse was sung; and still the chorus of the desert swelled between like the deepest tone of a mighty organ; and with the final peal of that dreadful anthem there came a sound, as if the roaring wind, the rushing streams, the howling beasts, and every other voice of the unconcerted wilderness were mingling and according with the voice of guilty man in homage to the prince of all. The four blazing pines threw up a loftier flame, and obscurely discovered shapes and visages of horror on the smoke wreaths above the impious assembly. At the same moment the fire on the rock shot redly forth and formed a glowing arch above its base, where now appeared a figure. With reverence be it spoken, the figure bore no slight similitude, both in garb and manner, to some grave divine of the New England churches.

'Bring forth the converts!' cried a voice that echoed through the field and rolled into the forest.

At the word, Goodman Brown stepped forth from the shadow of the trees and approached the congregation, with whom he felt a loathful brotherhood by the sympathy of all that was wicked in his heart. He could have well-nigh sworn that the shape of his own dead father beckoned him to advance, looking downward from a smoke wreath, while a woman, with dim features of despair, threw out her hand to warn him back. Was it his mother? But he had no power to retreat one step, nor to resist, even in thought, when the minister and good old Deacon Gookin seized his arms and led him to the blazing rock. Thither came also the slender form of a veiled female, led between Goody Cloyse, that pious teacher of the catechism, and Martha Carrier, who had received the devil's promise to be queen of hell. A rampant hag was she. And there stood the proselytes beneath the canopy of fire.

'Welcome, my children,' said the dark figure, 'to the communion of your race. Ye have found thus young your nature and your destiny. My children, look behind you!'

They turned; and flashing forth, as it were, in a sheet of flame, the fiend worshippers were seen; the smile of welcome gleamed darkly on every visage.

'There,' resumed the sable form, 'are all whom ye have reverenced from youth. Ye deemed them holier than yourselves, and shrank from your own sin, contrasting it with their lives of righteousness and prayerful aspirations heavenward. Yet here are they all in my worshipping assembly. This night it shall be granted you to know their secret deeds: how hoary-bearded elders of the church have whispered wanton words to the young maids of their households; how many a woman, eager for widows' weeds, has given her husband a drink at bedtime and let him sleep his last sleep in her bosom; how beardless youths have made haste to inherit their fathers' wealth; and how fair damsels – blush not, sweet ones – have dug little graves in the garden, and bidden me, the sole guest, to an infant's funeral. By the sympathy of your human hearts for sin ye shall scent out all the places – whether in church, bedchamber, street, field, or forest – where crime has been committed, and shall exult to behold the whole earth one stain of guilt, one mighty blood spot. Far more than this. It shall be yours to penetrate, in every bosom, the deep mystery of sin, the fountain of all wicked arts, and which inexhaustibly supplies more evil impulses than human power – than my power at its utmost – can make manifest in deeds. And now, my children, look upon each other.'

They did so; and, by the blaze of the hell-kindled torches, the wretched man beheld his Faith, and the wife her husband, trembling before that unhallowed altar.

'Lo, there ye stand, my children,' said the figure, in a deep and solemn tone, almost sad with its despairing awfulness, as if his once angelic nature could yet mourn for our miserable race. 'Depending upon one another's hearts, ye had still hoped that virtue were not all a dream. Now are ye undeceived. Evil is the nature of mankind. Evil must be your only happiness. Welcome again, my children, to the communion of your race.'

'Welcome,' repeated the fiend worshippers, in one cry of despair and trumph.

And there they stood, the only pair, as it seemed, who were yet hesitating on the verge of wickedness in this dark world. A basin was hollowed, naturally, in the rock. Did it contain water, reddened by the lurid light? or was it blood? or, perchance, a liquid flame? Herein did the shape of evil dip his hand and prepare to lay the mark of baptism upon their foreheads, that they might be partakers of the mystery of sin, more conscious of the secret guilt of others, both in deed and thought, than they could now be of their own. The husband cast one look at his pale wife, and Faith at him. What polluted wretches would the next glance show them to each other, shuddering alike at what they disclosed and what they saw!

'Faith! Faith!' cried the husband, 'look up to heaven, and resist the wicked one.'

Whether Faith obeyed he knew not. Hardly had he spoken when he found himself amid calm night and solitude, listening to a roar of the wind which died heavily away through the forest. He staggered against the rock, and felt it chill and damp; while a hanging twig, that had been all on fire, besprinkled his cheek with the coldest dew.

The next morning young Goodman Brown came slowly into the street of Salem village, staring around him like a bewildered man. The good old minister was taking a walk along the graveyard to get an appetite for breakfast and meditate his sermon, and bestowed a blessing, as he passed, on Goodman Brown. He shrank from the venerable saint as if to avoid an anathema. Old Deacon Gookin was at domestic worship, and the holy words of his prayer were heard through the open window. 'What God doth the wizard pray to?' quoth Goodman Brown. Goody Cloyse, that excellent old Christian, stood in the early sunshine at her own lattice, catechizing a little girl who had brought her a pint of morning's milk. Goodman Brown snatched away the child as from the grasp of the fiend himself. Turning the corner by the meeting-house, he spied the head of Faith, with the pink ribbons, gazing anxiously forth, and bursting into such joy at sight of him that she skipped along the street and almost kissed her husband before the whole village. But Goodman Brown looked sternly and sadly into her face, and passed on without a greeting.

Had Goodman Brown fallen asleep in the forest and only dreamed a wild dream of a witch-meeting?

Be it so if you will; but, alas! it was a dream of evil omen for young Goodman Brown. A stern, a sad, a darkly meditative, a distrustful, if not a desperate man did he become from the night of that fearful dream. On the Sabbath day, when the congregation were singing a holy psalm, he could not listen because an anthem of sin rushed loudly upon his ear and drowned all the blessed strain. When the minister spoke from the pulpit with power and fervid eloquence, and, with his hand on the open Bible, of the sacred truths of our religion, and of saint-like lives and triumphant deaths, and of future bliss or misery unutterable, then did Goodman Brown turn pale, dreading lest the roof should thunder down upon the grey blasphemer and his hearers. Often, awaking suddenly at midnight, he shrank from the bosom of Faith; and at morning or eventide, when the family knelt down at prayer, he scowled and muttered to himself and gazed sternly at his wife, and turned away. And when he had lived long, and was borne to his grave a hoary corpse, followed by Faith, an aged woman, and children and grandchildren, a goodly procession, besides neighbours not a few, they carved no hopeful verse upon his tombstone, for his dying hour was gloom.

Edgar Allan Poe

THE FALL OF THE HOUSE OF USHER

DURING the whole of a dull, dark, and soundless day in the autumn of the year, when the clouds hung oppressively low in the heavens, I had been passing alone, on horseback, through a singularly dreary tract of country; and at length found myself, as the shades of the evening drew on, within view of the melancholy House of Usher. I know not how it was – but, with the first glimpse of the building, a sense of insufferable gloom pervaded my spirit. I say insufferable; for the feeling was unrelieved by any of that half-pleasurable, because of poetic, sentiment with which the mind usually receives even the sternest natural images of the desolate or terrible. I looked upon the scene before me – upon the mere house, and the simple landscape features of the domain, upon the bleak walls, upon the vacant eye-like windows, upon a few rank sedges, and upon a few white trunks of decayed trees – with an utter depression of soul which I can compare to no earthly sensation more properly than to the after-dream of the reveller upon opium: the bitter lapse into everyday life, the hideous dropping off of the veil. There was an iciness, a sinking, a sickening of the heart, an unredeemed dreariness of thought which no goading of the imagination could torture into aught of the sublime. What was it – I paused to think – what was it that so unnerved me in the contemplation of the House of Usher? It was a mystery all insoluble; nor could I grapple with the shadowy fancies that crowded upon me as I pondered. I was forced to fall back upon the unsatisfactory conclusion, that while, beyond doubt, there *are* combinations of very simple natural objects which have the power of thus affecting us, still the analysis of this power lies among considerations beyond our depth. It was possible, I reflected, that a mere different arrangement of the particulars of the scene, of the details of the picture, would be sufficient to modify, or perhaps to annihilate, its capacity for sorrowful impression; and acting upon this idea, I reined my horse to the precipitous brink of a black and lurid tarn that lay in unruffled lustre by the dwelling, and gazed down – but with a shudder even more thrilling than before – upon the remodelled and inverted images of the grey sedge, and the ghastly tree-stems, and the vacant and eye-like windows.

Nevertheless, in this mansion of gloom I now proposed to myself a sojourn of some weeks. Its proprietor, Roderick Usher, had been one of my boon companions in boyhood; but many years had elapsed since our last meeting. A letter, however, had lately reached me in a distant part of the country – a letter from him – which in its wildly importunate nature had admitted of no other than a personal reply. The MS. gave evidence of nervous agitation. The writer spoke of acute bodily illness, of a mental disorder which oppressed him, and of an earnest desire to see me, as his best and indeed his only personal friend, with a view of attempting, by the cheerfulness of my society, some alleviation of his malady. It was the manner in which all this, and much more, was said – it was the apparent *heart* that went with his request – which allowed me no room for hesitation; and I accordingly obeyed forthwith what I still considered a very singular summons.

Although as boys we had been even intimate associates, yet I really knew little of my friend. His reserve had been always excessive and habitual. I was aware, however, that his very ancient family had been noted, time out of mind, for a peculiar sensibility of temperament, displaying itself, through long ages, in many works of exalted art, and manifested of late in repeated deeds of munificent yet unobtrusive charity, as well as in a passionate devotion to the intricacies, perhaps even more than to the orthodox and easily recognizable beauties, of musical science. I had learned, too, the very remarkable fact that the stem of the Usher race, all time-honored as it was, had put forth at no period any enduring branch; in other words, that the entire family lay in the direct line of descent, and had always, with very trifling and very temporary variation, so lain. It was this deficiency, I considered, while running over in thought the perfect keeping of the character of the premises with the accredited character of the people, and while speculating upon the possible influence which the one, in the long lapse of centuries, might have exercised upon the other – it was this deficiency, perhaps, of collateral issue, and the consequent undeviating transmission from sire to son of the patrimony with the name, which had, at length, so identified the two as to merge the original title of the estate in the quaint and equivocal appellation of the 'House of Usher' – an appellation which seemed to include, in the minds of the peasantry who used it, both the family and the family mansion.

I have said that the sole effect of my somewhat childish experiment, that of looking down within the tarn, had been to deepen the first singular impression. There can be no doubt that the consciousness of the rapid increase of my superstition – for why should I not so term it? – served mainly to accelerate the increase itself. Such, I have long known, is the paradoxical law of all sentiments having terror as a basis. And it might have been for this reason only, that, when I again uplifted my eyes to the house itself from its image in the pool, there grew in my mind a strange fancy – a fancy so ridiculous, indeed, that I but mention it to show the vivid force of the sensations which oppressed me. I had so worked upon my imagination as really to believe that about the whole mansion and domain there hung an atmosphere peculiar to themselves and their immediate vicinity: an atmosphere which had no affinity with the air of heaven, but which had reeked up from the decayed trees, and the gray wall, and the silent tarn: a pestilent and mystic vapor, dull, sluggish, faintly discernible, and leaden-hued.

Shaking off from my spirit what *must* have been a dream, I scanned more narrowly the real aspect of the building. Its principal feature seemed to be that of an excessive antiquity. The discoloration of ages had been great. Minute fungi overspread the whole exterior, hanging in a fine tangled web-work from the eaves. Yet all this was apart from any extraordinary dilapidation. No portion of the masonry had fallen; and there appeared to be a wild inconsistency between its still perfect adaptation of parts and the crumbling condition of the individual stones. In this there was much that reminded me of the specious totality of old woodwork which has rotted for long years in some neglected vault, with no disturbance from the breath of the external air. Beyond this indication of extensive decay, however, the fabric gave little token of instability. Perhaps the eye of a scrutinizing observer might have discovered a barely perceptible fissure, which, extending from the roof of the building in front, made its way down the wall in a zigzag direction, until it became lost in the sullen waters of the tarn.

Noticing these things, I rode over a short causeway to the house. A servant in waiting took my horse, and I entered the Gothic archway of the hall. A valet, of stealthy step, thence conducted me, in silence, through many dark and intricate passages in my progress to the studio of his master. Much that I encountered on the way contributed, I know not how, to heighten the vague sentiments of which I have already spoken. While the objects around me – while the carvings of the ceilings, the sombre tapestries of the walls, the ebon blackness of the floors, and the phantasmagoric armorial trophies which rattled as I strode, were but matters to which, or to such as which, I had been accustomed from my infancy – while I hesitated not to acknowledge how familiar was all this – I still wondered to find how unfamiliar were the fancies which ordinary images were stirring up. On one of the staircases, I met the physician of the family. His countenance, I thought, wore a mingled expression of low cunning and perplexity. He accosted me with trepidation and passed on. The valet now threw open a door and ushered me into the presence of his master.

The room in which I found myself was very large and lofty. The windows were long, narrow, and pointed, and at so vast a distance from the black oaken floor as to be altogether inaccessible from within. Feeble gleams of encrimsoned light made their way through the trellised panes, and served to render sufficiently distinct the more prominent objects around; the eye, however, struggled in vain to reach the remoter angles of the chamber, or the recesses of the vaulted and fretted ceiling. Dark draperies hung upon the walls. The general furniture was profuse, comfortless, antique, and tattered. Many books and musical instruments lay scattered about, but failed to give any vitality to the scene. I felt that I breathed an atmosphere of sorrow. An air of stern, deep, and irredeemable gloom hung over and pervaded all.

Upon my entrance, Usher arose from a sofa on which he had been lying at full length, and greeted me with a vivacious warmth which had much in it, I at first thought, of an overdone cordiality — of the constrained effort of the *ennuyé* man of the world. A glance, however, at his countenance convinced me of his perfect sincerity. We sat down; and for some moments, while he spoke not, I gazed upon him with a feeling half of pity, half of awe. Surely man had never before so terribly altered, in so brief a period, as had Roderick Usher! It was with difficulty that I could bring myself to admit the identity of the wan being before me with the companion of my early boyhood. Yet the character of his face had been at all times remarkable. A cadaverousness of complexion; an eye large, liquid, and luminous beyond comparison; lips somewhat thin and very pallid, but of a surpassingly beautiful curve; a nose of a delicate Hebrew model, but with a breadth of nostril unusual in similar formations; a finely moulded chin, speaking, in its want of prominence, of a want of moral energy; hair of a more than web-like softness and tenuity; these features, with an inordinate expansion above the regions of the temple, made up altogether a countenance not easily to be forgotten. And now in the mere exaggeration of the prevailing character of these features, and of the expression they were wont to convey, lay so much of change that I doubted to whom I spoke. The now ghastly pallor of the skin, and the now miraculous lustre of the eye, above all things startled and even awed me. The silken hair, too, had been suffered to grow all unheeded, and as, in its wild gossamer texture, it floated rather than fell about the face, I could not, even with effort, connect its arabesque expression with any idea of simple humanity.

In the manner of my friend I was at once struck with an incoherence, an inconsistency; and I soon found this to arise from a series of feeble and futile struggles to overcome an habitual trepidancy, an excess nervous agitation. For something of this nature I had indeed been prepared, no less by his letter than by reminiscences of certain boyish traits, and by conclusions deduced from his peculiar physical conformation and temperament. His action was alternately vivacious and sullen. His voice varied rapidly from a tremulous indecision (when the animal spirits seemed utterly in abeyance) to that species of energetic concision – that abrupt, weighty, unhurried, and hollow-sounding enunciation – that leaden, self-balanced, and perfectly modulated guttural utterance – which may be observed in the lost drunkard, or the irreclaimable eater of opium, during the periods of his most intense excitement.

It was thus that he spoke of the object of my visit, of his earnest desire to see me, and of the solace he expected me to afford him. He entered, at some length, into what he conceived to be the nature of his malady. It was, he said, a constitutional and a family evil, and one for which he despaired to find a remedy – a mere nervous affection, he immediately added, which would undoubtedly soon pass off. It displayed itself in a host of unnatural sensations. Some of these, as he detailed them, interested and bewildered me; although, perhaps, the terms and the general manner of the narration had their weight. He suffered much from a morbid acuteness of the senses; the most insipid food was alone endurable; he could wear only garments of certain texture; the odors of all flowers were oppressive; his eyes were tortured by even a faint light; and there were but peculiar sounds, and these from stringed instruments, which did not inspire him with horror.

To an anomalous species of terror I found him a bounden slave. 'I shall perish,' said he, 'I *must* perish in this deplorable folly. Thus, thus, and not otherwise, shall I be lost. I dread the events of the future, not in themselves, but in their results. I shudder at the thought of any, even the most trivial incident, which may operate upon this intolerable agitation of soul. I have indeed, no abhorrence of danger, except in its absolute effect – in terror. In this unnerved – in this pitiable condition, I feel that the period will sooner or later arrive when I must abandon life and reason together, in some struggle with the grim phantasm, F E A R.'

I learned moreover at intervals, and through broken and

equivocal hints, another singular feature of his mental condition. He was enchained by certain superstitious impressions in regard to the dwelling which he tenanted, and whence, for many years, he had never ventured forth – in regard to an influence whose supposititious force was conveyed in terms too shadowy here to be restated – an influence which some peculiarities in the mere form and substance of his family mansion, had, by dint of long sufference, he said, obtained over his spirit – an effect which the physique of the gray walls and turrets, and of the dim tarn into which they all looked down, had, at length, brought about upon the morale of his existence.

He admitted, however, although with hesitation, that much of the peculiar gloom which thus afflicted him could be traced to a more natural and far more palpable origin – to the severe and long-continued illness, indeed to the evidently approaching dissolution, of a tenderly beloved sister – his sole companion for long years, his last and only relative on earth. 'Her decease,' he said, with a bitterness which I can never forget, 'would leave him (him the hopeless and the frail) the last of the ancient race of the Ushers.' While he spoke the lady Madeline (for so was she called) passed slowly through a remote portion of the apartment, and, without having noticed my presence, disappeared. I regarded her with an utter astonishment not unmingled with dread, and yet I found it impossible to account for such feelings. A sensation of stupor oppressed me, as my eyes followed her retreating steps. When a door, at length, closed upon her, my glance sought instinctively and eagerly the countenance of the brother; but he had buried his face in his hands, and I could only perceive that a far more than ordinary wanness had overspread the emaciated fingers through which trickled many passionate tears.

The disease of the lady Madeline had long baffled the skill of her physicians. A settled apathy, a gradual wasting away of the person, and frequent although transient affections of a partially cataleptical character, were the unusual diagnosis. Hitherto she had steadily borne up against the pressure of her malady, and had not betaken herself finally to bed; but, on the closing in of the evening of my arrival at the house, she succumbed (as her brother told me at night with inexpressible agitation) to the prostrating power of the destroyer; and I learned that the glimpse I had obtained of her person would thus probably be the last I should obtain – that the lady, at least while living, would be seen by me no more.

For several days ensuing, her name was unmentioned by either Usher or myself; and during this period I was busied in earnest endeavors to alleviate the melancholy of my friend. We painted and read together; or I listened, as if in a dream, to the wild improvisations of his speaking guitar. And thus, as a closer and still closer intimacy admitted me more unreservedly into the recesses of his spirit, the more bitterly did I perceive the futility of all attempt at cheering a mind from which darkness, as if an inherent positive quality, poured forth upon all objects of the moral and physical universe, in one unceasing radiation of gloom.

I shall ever bear about me a memory of the many solemn hours I thus spent alone with the master of the House of Usher. Yet I should fail in any attempt to convey an idea of the exact character of the studies, or of the occupations, in which he involved me, or led me the way. An excited and highly distempered ideality threw a sulphureous luster over all. His long improvised dirges will ring forever in my ears. Among other things, I hold painfully in mind a certain singular perversion and amplification of the wild air of the last waltz of Von Weber. From the paintings over which his elaborate fancy brooded, and which grew, touch by touch, into vaguenesses at which I shuddered the more thrillingly because I shuddered knowing not why – from these paintings (vivid as their images now are before me) I would in vain endeavor to educe more than a small portion which should lie within the compass of merely written words. By the utter simplicity, by the nakedness of his designs, he arrested and overawed attention. If ever mortal painted an idea, that mortal was Roderick Usher. For me at least, in the circumstances then surrounding me, there arose, out of the pure abstractions which the hypochondriac contrived to throw upon his canvas, an intensity of intolerable awe, no shadow of which felt I ever yet in the contemplation of the certainly glowing yet too concrete reveries of Fuseli.

One of the phantasmagoric conceptions of my friend, partaking not so rigidly of the spirit of abstraction, may be shadowed forth, although feebly, in words. A small picture presented the interior of an immensely long and rectangular vault or tunnel, with low walls, smooth, white, and without interruption or device. Certain accessory points of the design served well to convey the idea that this excavation lay at an exceeding depth below the surface of the earth. No outlet was observed in any portion of its vast extent, and no torch or other artificial source of light was discernible; yet a flood of intense rays rolled throughout, and bathed the whole in a ghastly and inappropriate splendor.

I have just spoken of that morbid condition of the auditory nerve which rendered all music intolerable to the sufferer, with the exception of certain effects of stringed instruments. It was, perhaps, the narrow limits to which he thus confined himself upon the guitar, which gave birth, in great measure, to the fantastic character of his performances. But the fervid *facility* of his impromptus could not be so accounted for. They must have been, and were, in the notes, as well as in the words of his wild fantasias (for he not unfrequently accompanied himself with rhymed verbal improvisations), the result of that intense mental collectedness and concentration to which I have previously alluded as observable only in particular moments of the highest artificial excitement. The words of one of these rhapsodies I have easily remembered. I was, perhaps, the more forcibly impressed with it, as he gave it, because, in the under or mystic current of its meaning, I fancied that I perceived, and for the first time, a full consciousness, on the part of Usher, of the tottering of his lofty reason upon her throne. The verses, which were entitled 'The Haunted Palace', ran very nearly, if not accurately, thus:

I

In the greenest of our valleys
By good angels tenanted,
Once a fair and stately palace –
Radiant palace – reared its head.

In the monarch Thought's dominion,
   It stood there!
Never seraph spread a pinion
   Over fabric half so fair!

II

Banners yellow, glorious, golden,
   On its roof did float and flow,
(This – all this – was in the olden
   Time long ago)
And every gentle air that dallied,
   In that sweet day,
   Along the ramparts plumed and pallid,
   A wingèd odor went away.

III

Wanderers in that happy valley,
   Through two luminous windows, saw
Spirits moving musically
   To a lute's well-tunèd law,
Round about a throne where, sitting,
   Porphyrogene!
In state his glory well befitting,
   The ruler of the realm was seen.

IV

And all with pearl and ruby glowing
   Was the fair palace door,
Through which came flowing, flowing, flowing
   And sparkling evermore,
A troop of Echoes, whose sweet duty
   Was but to sing,
In voices of surpassing beauty,
   The wit and wisdom of their king.

V

But evil things, in robes of sorrow,
   Assailed the monarch's high estate.
(Ah, let us mourn! – for never morrow
   Shall dawn upon him, desolate!)

And round about his home the glory
   That blushed and bloomed
Is but a dim-remembered story
   Of the old time entombed.

VI

And travellers, now, within that valley,
   Through the red-litten windows see
Vast forms that move fantastically
   To a discordant melody;
While, like a ghastly rapid river,
   Through the pale door
A hideous throng rush out forever,
   And laugh – but smile no more.

I well remember that suggestions arising from this ballad led us into a train of thought, wherein there became manifest an opinion of Usher's which I mention not so much on account of its novelty (for other men have thought thus), as on account of the pertinacity with which he maintained it. This opinion, in its general form, was that of the sentience of all vegetable things. But in his disordered fancy the idea had assumed a more daring character, and trespassed, under certain conditions, upon the kingdom of inorganization. I lack words to express the full extent, or the earnest *abandon* of his persuasion. The belief, however, was connected (as I have previously hinted) with the gray stones of the home of his forefathers. The conditions of the sentience had been here, he imagined, fulfilled in the method of collocation of these stones – in the order of their arrangement, as well as in that of the many fungi which overspread them, and of the decayed trees which stood around – above all, in the long undisturbed endurance of this arrangement, and in its reduplication in the still waters of the tarn. Its evidence – the evidence of the sentience – was to be seen, he said (and I here started as he spoke), in the gradual yet certain condensation of an atmosphere of their own about the waters and the walls. The result was discoverable, he added, in that silent, yet importunate and terrible influence which for centuries had moulded the destinies of his family, and which made *him* what I now saw him

— what he was. Such opinions need no comment, and I will make none.

Our books — the books which, for years, had formed no small portion of the mental existence of the invalid — were, as might be supposed, in strict keeping with this character of phantasm. We pored together over such works as the *Ververt* and *Chartreuse* of Gresset; the *Belphegor* of Machiavelli; the *Heaven and Hell* of Swedenborg; the *Subterranean Voyage of Nicholas Klimm* by Holberg; the *Chiromancy* of Robert Flud, of Jean D'Indaginé, and of De la Chambre; the *Journey into the Blue Distance* of Tieck; and the *City of the Sun* of Campanella. One favorite volume was a small octavo edition of the *Directorium Inquisitorum* by the Dominican Eymeric de Gironne; and there were passages in Pomponius Mela, about the old African Satyrs and Ægipans, over which Usher would sit dreaming for hours. His chief delight, however, was found in the perusal of an exceedingly rare and curious book in quarto Gothic — the manual of a forgotten church — the *Vigilæ Mortuorum Secundum Chorum Ecclesiæ Maguntinæ.*

I could not help thinking of the wild ritual of this work, and of its probable influence upon the hypochondriac, when one evening, having informed me abruptly that the lady Madeline was no more, he stated his intention of preserving her corpse for a fortnight (previously to its final interment) in one of numerous vaults within the main walls of the building. The worldly reason, however, assigned for this singular proceeding, was one which I did not feel at liberty to dispute. The brother had been led to his resolution (so he told me) by consideration of the unusual character of the malady of the deceased, of certain obtrusive and eager inquiries on the part of her medical men, and of the remote and exposed situation of the burial-ground of the family. I will not deny that when I called to mind the sinister countenance of the person whom I met upon the staircase, on the day of my arrival at the house, I had no desire to oppose what I regarded as at best but a harmless, and by no means an unnatural precaution.

At the request of Usher, I personally aided him in the arrangements for the temporary entombment. The body having been encoffined, we two alone bore it to its rest. The vault in which we placed it (and which had been so long unopened that our torches, half smothered in its oppressive atmosphere, gave us little opportunity for investigation) was small, damp, and entirely without means of admission for light; lying, at great depth, immediately beneath that portion of the building in which was my own sleeping apartment. It had been used apparently, in remote feudal times, for the worst purposes of a donjon-keep, and in later days as a place of deposit for powder, or some other highly combustible substance, as a portion of its floor, and the whole interior of a long archway through which we reached it, were carefully sheathed with copper. The door, of massive iron, had been, also, similarly protected. Its immense weight caused an unusually sharp grating sound, as it moved upon its hinges.

Having deposited our mournful burden upon tressels within this region of horror, we partially turned aside the yet unscrewed lid of the coffin, and looked upon the face of the tenant. A striking similitude between the brother and sister now first arrested my attention; and Usher, divining, perhaps, my thoughts, murmured out some few words from which I learned that the deceased and himself had been twins, and that sympathies of a scarcely intelligible nature had always existed between them. Our glances, however, rested not long upon the dead – for we could not regard her unawed. The disease which had thus entombed the lady in the maturity of youth, had left, as usual in all maladies of a strictly cataleptical character, the mockery of a faint blush upon the bosom and the face, and that suspiciously lingering smile upon the lip which is so terrible in death. We replaced and screwed down the lid, and, having secured the door of iron, made our way, with toil, into the scarcely less gloomy apartments of the upper portion of the house.

And now, some days of bitter grief having elapsed, an observable change came over the features of the mental disorder of my friend. His ordinary manner had vanished. His ordinary occupations were neglected or forgotten. He roamed from chamber to chamber with hurried, unequal, and objectless step. The pallor of his countenance had assumed, if possible, a more ghastly hue – but the luminousness of his eye had utterly gone out. The once occasional huskiness of his tone was heard no more; and a tremulous quaver, as if of extreme terror, habitually characterized his utterance. There were times, indeed, when I thought his unceasingly agitated mind was laboring with some oppressive secret, to divulge which he struggled for the necessary courage. At times, again, I was obliged to resolve all into the mere inexplicable vagaries of madness, for I beheld him gazing upon vacancy for long hours, in an attitude of the profoundest attention, as if listening to some imaginary sound. It was no wonder that his condition terrified – that it infected me. I felt creeping upon me, by slow yet certain degrees, the wild influences of his own fantastic yet impressive superstitions.

It was, especially, upon retiring to bed late in the night of the seventh or eighth day after the placing of the lady Madeline within the donjon, that I experienced the full power of such feelings. Sleep came not near my couch, while the hours waned and waned away. I struggled to reason off the nervousness which had dominion over me. I endeavored to believe that much, if not all, of what I felt was due to the bewildering influence of the gloomy furniture of the room – of the dark and tattered draperies which, tortured into motion by the breath of a rising tempest, swayed fitfully to and fro upon the walls, and rustled uneasily about the decorations of the bed. But my efforts were fruitless. An irrepressible tremor gradually pervaded my frame; and at length there sat upon my very heart an incubus of utterly causeless alarm. Shaking this off with a gasp and a struggle, I uplifted myself upon the pillows, and, peering earnestly within the intense darkness of the chamber, hearkened – I know not why, except that an instinctive spirit prompted me – to certain low and indefinite sounds which came, through the pauses of the storm, at long intervals, I knew not whence. Overpowered by an intense sentiment of horror unaccountable yet unendurable, I threw on my clothes with haste (for I felt that I should sleep no more during the night) and endeavored to arouse myself from the pitiable condition into which I had fallen, by pacing rapidly to and fro through the apartment.

I had taken but few turns in this manner, when a light step on an adjoining staircase arrested my attention. I presently recognized it as that of Usher. In an instant afterward he rapped with a gentle touch at my door, and entered, bearing a lamp. His countenance was, as usual, cadaverously wan – but, moreover, there was a species of mad hilarity in his eyes – an evidently restrained hysteria in his whole demeanor. His air appalled me – but anything was preferable to the solitude which I had so long endured, and I even welcomed his presence as a relief.

'And you have not seen it?' he said abruptly, after having stared about him for some moments in silence – 'you have not then seen it? – but, stay! you shall.' Thus speaking, and having carefully shaded his lamp, he hurried to one of the casements, and threw it freely open to the storm.

The impetuous fury of the entering gust nearly lifted us from our feet. It was, indeed, a tempestuous yet sternly beautiful night, and one wildly singular in its terror and its beauty. A whirlwind had apparently collected its force in our vicinity; for there were frequent and violent alterations in the direction of the wind; and the exceeding density of the clouds (which hung so low as to press upon the turrets of the house) did not prevent our perceiving the life-like velocity with which they flew careering from all points against each other, without passing away into the distance. I say that even their exceeding density did not prevent our perceiving this; yet we had no glimpse of the moon or stars, nor was there any flashing forth of the lightning. But the under surfaces of the huge masses of agitated vapor, as well as all terrestrial objects immediately around us, were glowing in the unnatural light of a faintly luminous and distinctly visible gaseous exhalation which hung about and enshrouded the mansion.

'You must not – you shall not behold this!' said I, shudderingly, to Usher, as I led him with a gentle violence from the window to a seat. 'These appearances, which bewilder you, are merely electrical phenomena not uncommon – or it may be that they have their ghastly origin in the rank miasma of the tarn. Let us close this casement; the air is chilling and dangerous to your frame. Here is one of your favourite romances. I will read, and you shall listen – and so we will pass away this terrible night together.'

The antique volume which I had taken up was the *Mad Trist* of Sir Launcelot Canning; but I had called it a favorite of Usher's more in sad jest than in earnest; for, in truth, there is little in its uncouth and unimaginative prolixity which could have had interest for the lofty and spiritual ideality of my friend. It was, however, the only book immediately at hand; and I indulged a vague hope that the excitement which now agitated the hypochondriac might find relief (for the history of mental disorder is full of similar anomalies) even in the extremeness of the folly which I should read. Could I have judged, indeed, by the wild overstrained air of vivacity with which he hearkened, or apparently hearkened, to the words of the tale, I might well have congratulated myself upon the success of my design.

I had arrived at that well-known portion of the story where Ethelred, the hero of the *Trist*, having sought in vain for peaceable admission into the dwelling of the hermit, proceeds to make good an entrance by force. Here, it will be remembered, the words of the narrative run thus:

And Ethelred, who was by nature of a doughty heart, and who was now mighty withal, on account of the powerfulness of the wine which he had drunken, waited no longer to hold parley with the hermit, who, in sooth, was of an obstinate and maliceful turn, but, feeling the rain upon his shoulders, and fearing the rising of the tempest, uplifted his mace outright, and with blows made quickly room in the plankings of the door for his gauntleted hand; and now pulling therewith sturdily, he so cracked, and ripped, and tore all asunder, that the noise of the dry and hollow-sounding wood alarumed and reverberated throughout the forest.

At the termination of this sentence I started, and for a moment paused; for it appeared to me (although I at once concluded that my excited fancy had deceived me) – it appeared to me that from some very remote portion of the mansion there came, indistinctly, to my ears, what might have been, in its exact similarity of character, the echo (but a stifled and dull one certainly) of the very cracking and ripping round which Sir Launcelot had so particularly described. It was, beyond doubt, the coincidence alone which had arrested my attention; for, amid the rattling of the sashes of the casements, and the ordinary commingled noises of the still increasing storm, the sound, in itself, had nothing, surely, which should have interested or disturbed me. I continued the story:

But the good champion Ethelred, now entering within the door, was sore enraged and amazed to perceive no signal of the maliceful hermit; but, in the stead thereof, a dragon of a scaly and prodigious demeanor, and of a fiery tongue, which sate in guard before a palace of gold, with a floor of silver; and upon the wall there hung a shield of shining brass with his legend enwritten –

> *Who entereth herein, a conqueror hath bin,*
> *Who slayeth the dragon, the shield he shall win.*

And Ethelred uplifted his mace, and struck upon the head of the dragon, which fell before him, and gave up his pesty breath, with a shriek so horrid and harsh, and withal so piercing, that Ethelred had fain to close his ears with his hands against the dreadful noise of it, the like whereof was never before heard.

Here again I paused abruptly, and now with a feeling of wild amazement; for there could be no doubt whatever that, in this instance, I did actually hear (although from what direction it proceeded I found it impossible to say) a low and apparently distant, but harsh, protracted, and most unusual screaming or grating sound – the exact counterpart of what my fancy had already conjured up for the dragon's unnatural shriek as described by the romancer.

Oppressed, as I certainly was, upon the occurrence of this second and most extraordinary coincidence, by a thousand conflicting sensations, in which wonder and extreme terror were predominant, I still retained sufficient presence of mind to avoid exciting, by any observation, the sensitive nervousness of my companion. I was by no means certain that he had noticed the sounds in question; although, assuredly, a strange alteration had during the last few minutes taken place in his demeanor. From a position fronting my own, he had gradually brought round his chair, so as to sit with his face to the door of the chamber; and thus I could but partially perceive his features, although I saw that his lips trembled as if he were murmuring inaudibly. His head had dropped upon his breast – yet I knew that he was not asleep, from the wide and rigid opening of the eye as I caught a glance of it in profile. The motion of his body, too, was at variance with this idea – for he rocked from side to side with a gentle yet constant and uniform sway. Having rapidly taken notice of all this, I resumed the narrative of Sir Launcelot, which thus proceeded:

And now, the champion, having escaped from the terrible fury of the dragon, bethinking himself of the brazen shield, and of the breaking up of the enchantment which was upon it, removed the carcass from out of the way before him, and approached valorously over the silver pavement of the castle to where the shield was upon the wall; which in sooth tarried not for his full coming, but fell down at his feet upon the silver floor, with a mighty great and terrible ringing sound.

No sooner had these syllables passed my lips, than – as if a shield of brass had indeed at the moment, fallen heavily upon a floor of silver – I became aware of a distinct, hollow, metallic and clangorous yet apparently muffled reverberation. Completely unnerved, I leaped to my feet; but the measured rocking movement of Usher was undisturbed. I rushed to the chair in which he sat. His eyes were bent fixedly before him, and throughout his whole countenance there reigned a stony rigidity. But as I placed my hand upon his shoulder, there came a strong shudder over his whole person; a sickly smile quivered about his lips; and I saw that he spoke in a low, hurried, and gibbering murmur, as if unconscious of my presence. Bending closely over him, I at length drank in the hideous import of his words.

'Not hear it? – yes, I hear it, and *have* heard it. Long – long – long – many minutes, many hours, many days, have I heard it – yet I dared not – oh, pity me, miserable wretch that I am! – I dared not – I *dared* not speak! *We have put her living in the tomb!* Said I not that my senses were acute? I *now* tell you that I heard her first feeble movements in the hollow coffin. I heard them – many, many days ago – yet I dared not – *I dared not speak!* And now – tonight – Ethelred – ha! ha! – the breaking of the hermit's door, and the death-cry of the dragon, and the clangor of the shield! – say, rather, the rending of her coffin, and the grating of the iron hinges of her prison, and her struggles within the coppered archway of the vault! Oh, whither shall I fly? Will she not be here anon? Is she not hurrying to upbraid me for my haste? Have I not heard her footstep on the stair? Do I not distinguish that heavy and horrible beating of her heart? Madman!' – here he sprang furiously to his feet, and shrieked out his syllables, as if in the effort he were giving up his soul – *'Madman! I tell you that she now stands without the door!'*

As if in the superhuman energy of his utterance there had been found the potency of a spell, the huge antique panels to which the speaker pointed threw slowly back, upon the instant, their ponderous and ebony jaws. It was the work of the rushing gust – but then without those doors there *did* stand the lofty and enshrouded figure of the lady Madeline of Usher. There was blood upon her white robes, and the evidence of some bitter struggle upon every portion of her emaciated frame. For a moment she remained trembling and reeling to and fro upon the threshold – then, with a low moaning cry, fell heavily inward upon the person of her brother, and, in her violent and now final death agonies, bore him to the floor a corpse, and a victim to the terrors he had anticipated.

From that chamber, and from that mansion, I fled aghast. The storm was still abroad in all its wrath as I found myself crossing the old causeway. Suddenly there shot along the path a wild light, and I turned to see whence a gleam so unusual could have issued; for the vast house and its shadows were alone behind me. The radiance was that of the full, setting, and blood-red moon, which now shone vividly through that once barely discernible fissure, of which I have before spoken as extending from the roof of the building, in a zigzag direction, to the base. While I gazed, this fissure rapidly widened – there came a fierce breath of the whirlwind – the entire orb of the satellite burst at once upon my sight – my brain reeled as I saw the mighty walls rushing asunder – there was a long tumultuous shouting sound like the voice of a thousand waters – and the deep and dank tarn at my feet closed sullenly and silently over the fragments of the 'House of Usher'.

Herman Melville

BARTLEBY

I AM a rather elderly man. The nature of my avocations, for the last thirty years, has brought me into more than ordinary contact with what would seem an interesting and somewhat singular set of men, of whom, as yet, nothing, that I know of, has ever been written – I mean, the law-copyists, or scriveners. I have known very many of them, professionally and privately, and, if I pleased, could relate divers histories, at which good-natured gentlemen might smile, and sentimental souls might weep. But I waive the biographies of all other scriveners, for a few passages in the life of Bartleby, who was a scrivener, the strangest I ever saw, or heard of. While, of other law-copyists, I might write the complete life, of Bartleby nothing of that sort can be done. I believe that no materials exist, for a full and satisfactory biography of this man. It is an irreparable loss to literature. Bartleby was one of those beings of whom nothing is ascertainable, except from the original sources, and, in his case, those are very small. What my own astonished eyes saw of Bartleby, *that* is all I know of him, except, indeed, one vague report, which will appear in the sequel.

Ere introducing the scrivener, as he first appeared to me, it is fit I make some mention of myself, my *employés*, my business, my chambers, and general surroundings; because some such description is indispensable to an adequate understanding of the chief character about to be presented. Imprimis: I am a man who, from his youth upwards, has been filled with a profound conviction that the easiest way of life is the best. Hence, though I belong to a profession proverbially energetic and nervous, even to turbulence, at times, yet nothing of that sort have I ever suffered to invade my peace. I am one of those unambitious lawyers who never addresses a jury, or in any way draws down public applause; but, in the cool tranquillity of a snug retreat, do a snug business among rich men's bonds, and mortgages, and title-deeds. All who know me, consider me an eminently *safe* man. The late John Jacob Astor, a personage little given to poetic enthusiasm, had no hesitation in pronouncing my first grand point to be prudence; my next, method. I do not speak it in vanity, but simply record the fact, that I was not unemployed in my profession by the late John Jacob Astor; a name which, I admit, I love to repeat; for it hath rounded and orbicular sound to it, and rings like unto bullion. I will freely add, that I was not insensible to the late John Jacob Astor's good opinion.

Some time prior to the period at which this little history begins, my avocations had been largely increased. The good old office, now extinct in the State of New York, of a Master in Chancery, had been conferred upon me. It was not a very arduous office, but very pleasantly remunerative. I seldom lose my temper; much more seldom indulge in dangerous indignation at wrongs and outrages; but, I must be permitted to be rash here, and declare, that I consider the sudden and violent abrogation of the office of Master in Chancery, by the new Constitution, as a — premature act; inasmuch as I had counted upon a life-lease of the profits, whereas I only received those of a few short years. But this is by the way.

My chambers were up stairs, at No. — Wall Street. At one end, they looked upon the white wall of the interior of a spacious sky-light shaft, penetrating the building from top to bottom.

This view might have been considered rather tame than otherwise, deficient in what landscape painters call 'life'. But, if so, the view from the other end of my chambers offered, at least, a contrast, if nothing more. In that direction, my windows commanded an unobstructed view of a lofty brick wall, black by age and everlasting shade; which wall required no spy-glass to bring out its lurking beauties, but, for the benefit of all near-sighted spectators, was pushed up to within ten feet of my window panes. Owing to the great height of the surrounding buildings, and my chambers being on the second floor, the interval between this wall and mine not a little resembled a huge square cistern.

At the period just preceding the advent of Bartleby, I had two persons as copyists in my employment, and a promising lad as an office-boy. First, Turkey; second, Nippers; third, Ginger Nut. These may seem names, the like of which are not usually found in the Directory. In truth, they were nicknames, mutually conferred upon each other by my three clerks, and were deemed expressive of their respective persons or characters. Turkey was a short, pursy Englishman, of about my own age — that is, somewhere not far from sixty. In the morning, one might say, his face was of a fine florid hue, but after twelve o'clock, meridian — his dinner hour — it blazed like a grate full of Christmas coals; and continued blazing — but, as it were, with a gradual wane — till six o'clock, p.m., or thereabouts; after which, I saw no more of the proprietor of the face, which, gaining its meridian with the sun, seemed to set with it, to rise, culminate, and decline the following day, with the like regularity and undiminished glory. There are many singular coincidences I have known in the course of my life, not the least among which was the fact, that, exactly when Turkey displayed his fullest beams from his red and radiant countenance, just then, too, at that critical moment, began the daily period when I considered his business capacities as seriously disturbed for the remainder of the twenty-four hours. Not that he was absolutely idle, or averse to business, then; far from it. The difficulty was, he was apt to be altogether too energetic. There was a strange, inflamed, flurried, flighty recklessness of activity about him. He would be incautious in dipping his pen into his inkstand. All his blots upon my documents were dropped there after twelve o'clock, meridian. Indeed, not only would he be reckless, and sadly given to making blots in the afternoon, but, some days, he went further, and was rather noisy. At such times, too, his face flamed with augmented blazonry, as if cannel coal had been heaped on anthracite. He made an unpleasant racket with his chair; spilled his sand-box; in mending his pens, impatiently split them all to pieces, and threw them on the floor in a sudden passion; stood up, and leaned over his table, boxing his papers about in a most indecorous manner, very sad to behold in an elderly man like him. Nevertheless, as he was in many ways a most valuable person to me, and all the time before twelve o'clock, meridian, was the quickest, steadiest creature, too, accomplishing a great deal of work in a style not easily to be matched – for these reasons, I was willing to overlook his eccentricities, though, indeed, occasionally, I remonstrated with him. I did this very gently, however, because, though the civilest, nay, the blandest and most reverential of men in the morning, yet, in the afternoon, he was disposed, upon provocation, to be slightly rash with his tongue – in fact, insolent. Now, valuing his morning services as I did, and resolved not to lose them – yet, at the same time, made uncomfortable by his inflamed ways after twelve o'clock – and being a man of peace, unwilling by my admonitions to call forth unseemly retorts from him, I took upon me, one Saturday noon (he was always worse on Saturdays) to hint to him, very kindly, that perhaps, now that he was growing old, it might be well to abridge his labors; in short, he need not come to my chambers after twelve o'clock, but, dinner over, had best go home to his lodgings, and rest himself till tea-time. But no; he insisted upon his afternoon devotions. His countenance became intolerably fervid, as he oratorically assured me – gesticulating with a long ruler at the other end of the room – that if his services in the morning were useful, how indispensable, then, in the afternoon?

'With submission, sir,' said Turkey, on this occasion, 'I consider myself your right-hand man. In the morning I but marshal and deploy my columns; but in the afternoon I put myself at their head, and gallantly charge the foe, thus' – and he made a violent thrust with the ruler.

'But the blots, Turkey,' intimated I.

'True; but, with submission, sir, behold these hairs! I am getting old. Surely, sir, a blot or two of a warm afternoon is not to be severely urged against gray hairs. Old age – even if it blot the page – is honorable. With submission, sir, we *both* are getting old.'

This appeal to my fellow-feeling was hardly to be resisted. At all events, I saw that go he would not. So, I made up my mind to let him stay, resolving, nevertheless, to see to it that, during the afternoon, he had to do with my less important papers.

Nippers, the second on my list, was a whiskered, sallow, and,

upon the whole, rather piratical-looking young man, of about
five and twenty. I always deemed him the victim of two evil
powers — ambition and indigestion. The ambition was evinced
by a certain impatience of the duties of a mere copyist, an un-
warrantable usurpation of strictly professional affairs, such as
the original drawing up of legal documents. The indigestion
seemed betokened in an occasional nervous testiness and grinning irritability, causing the teeth to audibly grind together over
mistakes committed in copying; unnecessary maledictions,
hissed, rather than spoken, in the heat of business; and especially by a continual discontent with the height of the table
where he worked. Though of a very ingenious mechanical turn,
Nippers could never get this table to suit him. He put chips
under it, blocks of various sorts, bits of pasteboard, and at last
went so far as to attempt an exquisite adjustment, by final pieces
of folded blotting-paper. But no invention would answer. If, for
the sake of easing his back, he brought the table lid at a sharp
angle well up towards his chin, and wrote there like a man
using the steep roof of a Dutch house for his desk, then he declared that it stopped the circulation in his arms. If now he
lowered the table to his waistbands, and stooped over it in
writing, then there was a sore aching in his back. In short, the
truth of the matter was, Nippers knew not what he wanted. Or,
if he wanted anything, it was to be rid of a scrivener's table altogether. Among the manifestations of his diseased ambition
was a fondness he had for receiving visits from certain ambi-
guous-looking fellows in seedy coats, whom he called his clients.
Indeed, I was aware that not only was he, at times, considerable
of a ward-politician, but he occasionally did a little business at
the Justices' courts, and was not unknown on the steps of the
Tombs. I have good reason to believe, however, that one individual who called upon him at my chambers, and who, with a
grand air, he insisted was his client, was no other than a dun,
and the alleged title-deed, a bill. But, with all his failings, and
the annoyances he caused me, Nippers, like his compatriot
Turkey, was a very useful man to me; wrote a neat, swift hand;
and, when he chose, was not deficient in a gentlemanly sort of
deportment. Added to this, he always dressed in a gentlemanly

sort of way; and so, incidentally, reflected credit upon my chambers. Whereas, with respect to Turkey, I had much ado to keep him from being a reproach to me. His clothes were apt to look oily, and smell of eating-houses. He wore his pantaloons very loose and baggy in summer. His coats were execrable; his hat not to be handled. But while the hat was a thing of indifference to me, inasmuch as his natural civility and deference, as a dependent Englishman, always led him to doff it the moment he entered the room, yet his coat was another matter. Concerning his coats, I reasoned with him; but with no effect. The truth was, I suppose, that a man with so small an income could not afford to sport such a lustrous face and a lustrous coat at one and the same time. As Nippers once observed, Turkey's money went chiefly for red ink. One winter day, I presented Turkey with a highly respectable-looking coat of my own — a padded gray coat, of a most comfortable warmth, and which buttoned straight up from the knee to the neck. I thought Turkey would appreciate the favor, and abate his rashness and obstreperousness of afternoons. But no; I verily believe that buttoning himself up in so downy and blanket-like a coat had a pernicious effect upon him — upon the same principle that too much oats are bad for horses. In fact, precisely as a rash, restive horse is said to feel his oats, so Turkey felt his coat. It made him insolent. He was a man whom prosperity harmed.

Though, concerning the self-indulgent habits of Turkey, I had my own private surmises, yet, touching Nippers, I was well persuaded that, whatever might be his faults in other respects, he was, at least, a temperate young man. But, indeed, nature herself seemed to have been his vintner, and, at his birth, charged him so thoroughly with an irritable, brandy-like disposition, that all subsequent potations were needless. When I consider how, amid the stillness of my chambers, Nippers would sometimes impatiently rise from his seat, and stooping over his table, spread his arms wide apart, seize the whole desk, and move it, and jerk it, with a grim, grinding motion on the floor, as if the table were a perverse voluntary agent, intent on thwarting and vexing him, I plainly perceive that, for Nippers, brandy-and-water were altogether superfluous.

It was fortunate for me that, owing to its peculiar cause – indigestion – the irritability and consequent nervousness of Nippers were mainly observable in the morning, while in the afternoon he was comparatively mild. So that, Turkey's paroxysms only coming on about twelve o'clock, I never had to do with their eccentricities at one time. Their fits relieved each other, like guards. When Nippers's was on, Turkey's was off; and *vice versa*. This was a good natural arrangement, under the circumstances.

Ginger Nut, the third on my list, was a lad, some twelve years old. His father was a car-man, ambitious of seeing his son on the bench instead of a cart, before he died. So he sent him to my office, as student at law, errand-boy, cleaner and sweeper, at the rate of one dollar a week. He had a little desk to himself, but he did not use it much. Upon inspection, the drawer exhibited a great array of the shells of various sorts of nuts. Indeed, to this quick-witted youth, the whole noble science of the law was contained in a nutshell. Not the least among the employments of Ginger Nut, as well as one which he discharged with the most alacrity, was his duty as cake and apple purveyor for Turkey and Nippers. Copying law-papers being proverbially a dry, husky sort of business, my two scriveners were fain to moisten their mouths very often with Spitzenbergs, to be had at the numerous stalls nigh the Custom House and Post Office. Also, they sent Ginger Nut very frequently for that peculiar cake – small, flat, round, and very spicy – after which he had been named by them. Of a cold morning, when business was but dull, Turkey would gobble up scores of these cakes, as if they were mere wafers – indeed, they sell them at the rate of six or eight for a penny – the scrape of his pen blending with the crunching of the crisp particles in his mouth. Of all the fiery afternoon blunders and flurried rashnesses of Turkey, was his once moistening a ginger-cake between his lips, and clapping it on to a mortgage, for a seal. I came within an ace of dismissing him then. But he mollified me by making an oriental bow, and saying –

'With submission, sir, it was generous of me to find you in stationery on my own account.'

Now my original business — that of a conveyancer and title hunter, and drawer-up of recondite documents of all sorts — was considerably increased by receiving the master's office. There was now great work for scriveners. Not only must I push the clerks already with me, but I must have additional help.

In answer to my advertisement, a motionless young man one morning stood upon my office threshold, the door being open, for it was summer. I can see that figure now — pallidly neat, pitiably respectable, incurably forlorn! It was Bartleby.

After a few words touching his qualifications, I engaged him, glad to have among my corps of copyists a man of so singularly sedate an aspect, which I thought might operate beneficially upon the flighty temper of Turkey, and the fiery one of Nippers.

I should have stated before that ground glass folding-doors divided my premises into two parts, one of which was occupied by my scriveners, the other by myself. According to my humor, I threw open these doors, or closed them. I resolved to assign Bartleby a corner by the folding-doors, but on my side of them, so as to have this quiet man within easy call, in case any trifling thing was to be done. I placed his desk close up to a small side-window in that part of the room, a window which originally had afforded a lateral view of certain grimy back-yards and bricks, but which, owing to subsequent erections, commanded at present no view at all, though it gave some light. Within three feet of the panes was a wall, and the light came down from far above, between two lofty buildings, as from a very small opening in a dome. Still further to a satisfactory arrangement, I procured a high green folding screen, which might entirely isolate Bartleby from my sight, though not remove him from my voice. And thus, in a manner, privacy and society were conjoined.

At first, Bartleby did an extraordinary quantity of writing. As if long famishing for something to copy, he seemed to gorge himself on my documents. There was no pause for digestion. He ran a day and night line, copying by sun-light and by candle-light. I should have been quite delighted with his application, had he been cheerfully industrious. But he wrote on silently, palely, mechanically.

It is, of course, an indispensable part of a scrivener's business to verify the accuracy of his copy, word by word. Where there are two or more scriveners in an office, they assist each other in this examination, one reading from the copy, the other holding the original. It is a very dull, wearisome, and lethargic affair. I can readily imagine that, to some sanguine temperaments, it would be altogether intolerable. For example, I cannot credit that the mettlesome poet, Byron, would have contentedly sat down with Bartleby to examine a law document of, say five hundred pages, closely written in a crimpy hand.

Now and then, in the haste of business, it had been my habit to assist in comparing some brief document myself, calling Turkey or Nippers for this purpose. One object I had, in placing Bartleby so handy to me behind the screen, was, to avail myself of his services on such trivial occasions. It was on the third day, I think, of his being with me, and before any necessity had arisen for having his own writing examined, that, being much hurried to complete a small affair I had in hand, I abruptly called to Bartleby. In my haste and natural expectancy of instant compliance, I sat with my head bent over the original on my desk, and my right hand sideways, and somewhat nervously extended with the copy, so that, immediately upon emerging from his retreat, Bartleby might snatch it and proceed to business without the least delay.

In this very attitude did I sit when I called to him, rapidly stating what it was I wanted him to do – namely, to examine a small paper with me. Imagine my surprise, nay, my consternation, when, without moving from his privacy, Bartleby, in a singularly mild, firm voice, replied, 'I would prefer not to.'

I sat awhile in perfect silence, rallying my stunned faculties. Immediately it occurred to me that my ears had deceived me, or Bartleby had entirely misunderstood my meaning. I repeated my request in the clearest tone I could assume; but in quite as clear a one came the previous reply, 'I would prefer not to.'

'Prefer not to,' echoed I, rising in high excitement, and crossing the room with a stride. 'What do you mean? Are you moonstruck? I want you to help me compare this sheet here – take it,' and I thrust it towards him.

'I would prefer not to,' said he.

I looked at him steadfastly. His face was leanly composed; his gray eye dimly calm. Not a wrinkle of agitation rippled him. Had there been the least uneasiness, anger, impatience or impertinence in his manner; in other words, had there been any thing ordinarily human about him, doubtless I should have violently dismissed him from the premises. But as it was, I should have as soon thought of turning my pale plaster-of-paris bust of Cicero out of doors. I stood gazing at him awhile, as he went on with his own writing, and then reseated myself at my desk. This is very strange, thought I. What had one best do? But my business hurried me. I concluded to forget the matter for the present, reserving it for my future leisure. So calling Nippers from the other room, the paper was speedily examined.

A few days after this, Bartleby concluded four lengthy documents, being quadruplicates of a week's testimony taken before me in my High Court of Chancery. It became necessary to examine them. It was an important suit, and great accuracy was imperative. Having all things arranged, I called Turkey, Nippers, and Ginger Nut, from the next room, meaning to place the four copies in the hands of my four clerks, while I should read from the original. Accordingly, Turkey, Nippers, and Ginger Nut had taken their seats in a row, each with his document in his hand, when I called to Bartleby to join in this interesting group.

'Bartleby! quick, I am waiting.'

I heard a slow scrape of his chair legs on the uncarpeted floor, and soon he appeared standing at the entrance of his hermitage.

'What is wanted?' said he, mildly.

'The copies, the copies,' said I, hurriedly. 'We are going to examine them. There' – and I held towards him the fourth quadruplicate.

'I would prefer not to,' he said, and gently disappeared behind the screen.

For a few moments I was turned into a pillar of salt, standing at the head of my seated column of clerks. Recovering myself,

I advanced towards the screen, and demanded the reason for such extraordinary conduct.

'*Why* do you refuse?'

'I would prefer not to.'

With any other man I should have flown outright into a dreadful passion, scorned all further words, and thrust him ignominiously from my presence. But there was something about Bartleby that not only strangely disarmed me, but, in a wonderful manner, touched and disconcerted me. I began to reason with him.

'These are your own copies we are about to examine. It is labor saving to you, because one examination will answer for your four papers. It is common usage. Every copyist is bound to help examine his copy. Is it not so? Will you not speak? Answer!'

'I prefer not to,' he replied in a flute-like tone. It seemed to me that, while I had been addressing him, he carefully revolved every statement that I made; fully comprehended the meaning; could not gainsay the irresistible conclusion; but, at the same time, some paramount consideration prevailed with him to reply as he did.

'You are decided, then, not to comply with my request – a request made according to common usage and common sense?'

He briefly gave me to understand, that on that point my judgement was sound. Yes: his decision was irreversible.

It is not seldom the case that, when a man is browbeaten in some unprecedented and violently unreasonable way, he begins to stagger in his own plainest faith. He begins, as it were, vaguely to surmise that, wonderful as it may be, all the justice and all the reason is on the other side. Accordingly, if any disinterested persons are present, he turns to them for some reinforcement of his own faltering mind.

'Turkey,' said I, 'what do you think of this? Am I not right?'

'With submission, sir,' said Turkey, in his blandest tone, 'I think that you are.'

'Nippers,' said I, 'what do *you* think of it?'

'I think I should kick him out of the office.'

(The reader, of nice perceptions, will here perceive that, it being morning, Turkey's answer is couched in polite and tranquil terms, but Nippers replies in ill-tempered ones. Or, to repeat a previous sentence, Nippers's ugly mood was on duty, and Turkey's off.)

'Ginger Nut,' said I, willing to enlist the smallest suffrage in my behalf, 'what do *you* think of it?'

'I think, sir, he's a little *luny*,' replied Ginger Nut, with a grin.

'You hear what they say,' said I, turning towards the screen, 'come forth and do your duty.'

But he vouchsafed no reply. I pondered a moment in sore perplexity. But once more business hurried me. I determined again to postpone the consideration of this dilemma to my future leisure. With a little trouble we made out to examine the papers without Bartleby, though at every page or two Turkey deferentially dropped his opinion, that this proceeding was quite out of the common; while Nippers, twitching in his chair with a dyspeptic nervousness, ground out, between his set teeth, occasional hissing maledictions against the stubborn oaf behind the screen. And for his (Nippers's) part, this was the first and the last time he would do another man's business without pay.

Meanwhile Bartleby sat in his hermitage, oblivious to everything but his own peculiar business there.

Some days passed, the scrivener being employed upon another lengthy work. His late remarkable conduct led me to regard his ways narrowly. I observed that he never went to dinner; indeed, that he never went anywhere. As yet I had never, of my personal knowledge, known him to be outside of my office. He was a perpetual sentry in the corner. At about eleven o'clock though, in the morning, I noticed that Ginger Nut would advance toward the opening in Bartleby's screen, as if silently beckoned thither by a gesture invisible to me where I sat. The boy would then leave the office, jingling a few pence, and reappear with a handful of ginger-nuts, which he delivered in the hermitage, receiving two of the cakes for his trouble.

He lives, then, on ginger-nuts, thought I; never eats a dinner, properly speaking; he must be a vegetarian, then; but no; he never eats even vegetables, he eats nothing but ginger-nuts. My mind then ran on in reveries concerning the probable effects upon the human constitution of living entirely on ginger-nuts. Ginger-nuts are so called, because they contain ginger as one of their peculiar constituents, and the final flavoring one. Now, what was ginger? A hot, spicy thing. Was Bartleby hot and spicy? Not at all. Ginger, then, had no effect upon Bartleby. Probably he preferred it should have none.

Nothing so aggravates an earnest person as a passive resistance. If the individual so resisted be of a not inhumane temper, and the resisting one perfectly harmless in his passivity, then, in the better moods of the former, he will endeavor charitably to construe to his imagination what proves impossible to be solved by his judgement. Even so, for the most part, I regarded Bartleby and his ways. Poor fellow! thought I, he means no mischief; it is plain he intends no insolence; his aspect sufficiently evinces that his eccentricities are involuntary. He is useful to me. I can get along with him. If I turn him away, the chances are he will fall in with some less-indulgent employer, and then he will be rudely treated, and perhaps driven forth miserably to starve. Yes. Here I can cheaply purchase a delicious self-approval. To befriend Bartleby; to humor him in his strange willfulness, will cost me little or nothing, while I lay up in my soul what will eventually prove a sweet morsel for my conscience. But this mood was not invariable with me. The passiveness of Bartleby sometimes irritated me. I felt strangely goaded on to encounter him in new opposition – to elicit some angry spark from him answerable to my own. But, indeed, I might as well have essayed to strike fire with my knuckles against a bit of Windsor soap. But one afternoon the evil impulse in me mastered me, and the following little scene ensued:

'Bartleby,' said I, 'when those papers are all copied, I will compare them with you.'

'I would prefer not to.'

'How? Surely you do not mean to persist in that mulish vagary?'

No answer.

I threw open the folding-doors near by, and, turning upon Turkey and Nippers, exclaimed:

'Bartleby a second time says, he won't examine his papers. What do you think of it, Turkey?'

It was afternoon, be it remembered. Turkey sat glowing like a brass boiler; his bald head steaming; his hands reeling among his blotted papers.

'Think of it?' roared Turkey; 'I think I'll just step behind his screen, and black his eyes for him!'

So saying, Turkey rose to his feet and threw his arms into a pugilistic position. He was hurrying away to make good his promise, when I detained him, alarmed at the effect of incautiously rousing Turkey's combativeness after dinner.

'Sit down, Turkey,' said I, 'and hear what Nippers has to say. What do you think of it, Nippers? Would I not be justified in immediately dismissing Bartleby?'

'Excuse me, that is for you to decide, sir. I think his conduct quite unusual, and, indeed, unjust, as regards Turkey and myself. But it may only be a passing whim.'

'Ah,' exclaimed I, 'you have strangely changed your mind, then – you speak very gently of him now.'

'All beer,' cried Turkey; 'gentleness is effects of beer – Nippers and I dined together today. You see how gentle *I* am, sir. Shall I go and black his eyes?'

'You refer to Bartleby, I suppose. No, not today, Turkey,' I replied; 'pray, put up your fists.'

I closed the doors, and again advanced towards Bartleby. I felt additional incentives tempting me to my fate. I burned to be rebelled against again. I remembered that Bartleby never left the office.

'Bartleby,' said I, 'Ginger Nut is away; just step around to the Post Office, won't you? (it was but a three minutes' walk), and see if there is anything for me.'

'I would prefer not to.'

'You *will* not?'

'I *prefer* not.'

I staggered to my desk, and sat there in a deep study. My blind inveteracy returned. Was there any other thing in which I could procure myself to be ignominiously repulsed by this lean, penniless wight? – my hired clerk? What added thing is there, perfectly reasonable, that he will be sure to refuse to do?

'Bartleby l'

No answer.

'Bartleby,' in a louder tone.

No answer.

'Bartleby,' I roared.

Like a very ghost, agreeably to the laws of magical invocation, at the third summons, he appeared at the entrance of his hermitage.

'Go to the next room, and tell Nippers to come to me.'

'I prefer not to,' he respectfully and slowly said, and mildly disappeared.

'Very good, Bartleby,' said I, in a quiet sort of serenely-severe self-possessed tone, intimating the unalterable purpose of some terrible retribution very close at hand. At the moment I half intended something of the kind. But upon the whole, as it was drawing towards my dinner-hour, I thought it best to put on my hat and walk home for the day, suffering much from perplexity and distress of mind.

Shall I acknowledge it? The conclusion of this whole business was, that it soon became a fixed fact of my chambers, that a pale young scrivener, by the name of Bartleby, had a desk there; that he copied for me at the usual rate of four cents a folio (one hundred words); but he was permanently exempt from examining the work done by him, that duty being transferred to Turkey and Nippers, out of compliment, doubtless, to their superior acuteness; moreover, said Bartleby was never, on any account, to be dispatched on the most trivial errand of any sort; and that even if entreated to take upon him such a matter, it was generally understood that he would 'prefer not to' – in other words, that he would refuse point-blank.

As days passed on, I became considerably reconciled to Bartleby. His steadiness, his freedom from all dissipation, his incessant industry (except when he chose to throw himself into a standing revery behind his screen), his great stillness, his unalterableness of demeanor under all circumstances, made him a valuable acquisition. One prime thing was this – *he was always there* – first in the morning, continually through the day, and the last at night. I had a singular confidence in his honesty. I felt my most precious papers perfectly safe in his hands. Sometimes, to be sure, I could not, for the very soul of me, avoid falling into sudden spasmodic passions with him. For it was exceeding difficult to bear in mind all the time those strange peculiarities, privileges, and unheard of exemptions, forming the tacit stipulations on Bartleby's part under which he remained in my office. Now and then, in the eagerness of dispatching pressing business, I would inadvertently summon Bartleby, in a short, rapid tone, to put his finger, say, on the incipient tie of a bit of red tape with which I was about compressing some papers. Of course, from behind the screen the usual answer, 'I prefer not to', was sure to come; and then, how could a human creature, with the common infirmities of our nature, refrain from bitterly exclaiming upon such perverseness – such unreasonableness. However, every added repulse of this sort which I received only tended to lessen the probability of my repeating the inadvertence.

Here it must be said, that according to the custom of most legal gentlemen occupying chambers in densely-populated law buildings, there were several keys to my door. One was kept by a woman residing in the attic, which person weekly scrubbed and daily swept and dusted my apartments. Another was kept by Turkey for convenience sake. The third I sometimes carried in my own pocket. The fourth I knew not who had.

Now, one Sunday morning I happened to go to Trinity Church, to hear a celebrated preacher, and finding myself rather early on the ground I thought I would walk around to my chambers for a while. Luckily I had my key with me; but upon applying it to the lock, I found it resisted by something inserted from the inside. Quite surprised, I called out; when to my consternation a key was turned from within; and thrusting his lean visage at me, and holding the door ajar, the apparition of Bartleby appeared, in his shirt sleeves, and otherwise in a strangely tattered deshabille, saying quietly that he was sorry, but he was deeply engaged just then, and – preferred not admitting me at present. In a brief word or two, he moreover added, that perhaps

I had better walk around the block two or three times, and by
that time he would probably have concluded his affairs.

Now, the utterly unsurmised appearance of Bartleby, tenant-
ing my law-chambers of a Sunday morning, with his cadaverously gentlemanly *nonchalance*, yet withal firm and self-
possessed, had such a strange effect upon me, that incontinently
I slunk away from my own door, and did as desired. But not
without sundry twinges of impotent rebellion against the mild
effrontery of this unaccountable scrivener. Indeed, it was his
wonderful mildness chiefly, which not only disarmed me, but
unmanned me as it were. For I consider that one, for the time,
is a sort of unmanned when he tranquilly permits his hired
clerk to dictate to him, and order him away from his own premises. Furthermore, I was full of uneasiness as to what Bartleby
could possibly be doing in my office in his shirt sleeves, and in
an otherwise dismantled condition of a Sunday morning. Was
anything amiss going on? Nay, that was out of the question. It
was not to be thought of for a moment that Bartleby was an
immoral person. But what could he be doing there? – copying?
Nay again, whatever might be his eccentricities, Bartleby was an
eminently decorous person. He would be the last man to sit
down to his desk in any state approaching to nudity. Besides, it
was Sunday; and there was something about Bartleby that for-
bade the supposition that he would by any secular occupation
violate the proprieties of the day.

Nevertheless, my mind was not pacified; and full of a restless
curiosity, at last I returned to the door. Without hindrance I inserted my key, opened it, and entered. Bartleby was not to be
seen. I looked round anxiously, peeped behind his screen; but it
was very plain that he was gone. Upon more closely examining
the place, I surmised that for an indefinite period Bartleby must
have ate, dressed, and slept in my office, and that, too, without
plate, mirror, or bed. The cushioned seat of a ricketty old sofa
in one corner bore the faint impress of a lean, reclining form.
Rolled away under his desk, I found a blanket; under the empty
grate, a blacking box and brush; on a chair, a tin basin, with
soap and a ragged towel; in a newspaper a few crumbs of ginger-nuts and a morsel of cheese. Yes, thought I, it is evident

enough that Bartleby has been making his home here, keeping bachelor's hall all by himself. Immediately then the thought came sweeping across me, what miserable friendlessness and loneliness are here revealed! His poverty is great; but his solitude, how horrible! Think of it. Of a Sunday, Wall Street is deserted as Petra; and every night of every day it is an emptiness. This building, too, which of weekdays hums with industry and life, at nightfall echoes with sheer vacancy, and all through Sunday is forlorn. And here Bartleby makes his home; sole spectator of a solitude which he has seen all populous — a sort of innocent and transformed Marius brooding among the ruins of Carthage!

For the first time in my life a feeling of over-powering stinging melancholy seized me. Before, I had never experienced aught but a not unpleasing sadness. The bond of a common humanity now drew me irresistibly to gloom. A fraternal melancholy! For both I and Bartleby were sons of Adam. I remembered the bright silks and sparkling faces I had seen that day, in gala trim, swan-like sailing down the Mississippi of Broadway; and I contrasted them with the pallid copyist, and thought to myself, Ah, happiness courts the light, so we deem the world is gay; but misery hides aloof, so we deem that misery there is none. These sad fancyings — chimeras, doubtless, of a sick and silly brain — led on to other and more special thoughts, concerning the eccentricities of Bartleby. Presentiments of strange discoveries hovered round me. The scrivener's pale form appeared to me laid out, among uncaring strangers, in its shivering winding sheet.

Suddenly I was attracted by Bartleby's closed desk, the key in open sight left in the lock.

I mean no mischief, seek the gratification of no heartless curiosity, thought I; besides, the desk is mine, and its contents, too, so I will make bold to look within. Everything was methodically arranged, the papers smoothly placed. The pigeon holes were deep, and removing the files of documents, I groped into their recesses. Presently I felt something there, and dragged it out. It was an old bandanna handkerchief, heavy and knotted. I opened it, and saw it was a savings bank.

I now recalled all the quiet mysteries which I had noted in the man. I remembered that he never spoke but to answer; that, though at intervals he had considerable time to himself, yet I had never seen him reading – no, not even a newspaper; that for long periods he would stand looking out, at his pale window behind the screen, upon the dead brick wall; I was quite sure he never visited any refectory or eating house; while his pale face clearly indicated that he never drank beer like Turkey, or tea and coffee even, like other men; that he never went anywhere in particular that I could learn; never went out for a walk, unless, indeed, that was the case at present; that he had declined telling who he was, or whence he came, or whether he had any relatives in the world; that though so thin and pale, he never complained of ill health. And more than all, I remembered a certain unconscious air of pallid – how shall I call it? – of pallid haughtiness, say, or rather an austere reserve about him, which had positively awed me into my tame compliance with his eccentricities, when I had feared to ask him to do the slightest incidental thing for me, even though I might know, from his long-continued motionlessness, that behind his screen he must be standing in one of those dead-wall reveries of his.

Revolving all these things, and coupling them with the recently discovered fact, that he made my office his constant abiding place and home, and not forgetful of his morbid moodiness; revolving all these things, a prudential feeling began to steal over me. My first emotions had been those of pure melancholy and sincerest pity; but just in proportion as the forlornness of Bartleby grew and grew to my imagination, did that same melancholy merge into fear, that pity into repulsion. So true it is, and so terrible, too, that up to a certain point the thought or sight of misery enlists our best affections; but, in certain special cases, beyond that point it does not. They err who would assert that invariably this is owing to the inherent selfishness of the human heart. It rather proceeds from a certain hopelessness of remedying excessive and organic ill. To a sensitive being, pity is not seldom pain. And when at last it is perceived that such pity cannot lead to effectual succor, common sense bids the soul be rid of it. What I saw that morning persuaded me that the scrivener was the victim of innate and incurable disorder. I might give alms to his body; but his body did not pain him; it was his soul that suffered, and his soul I could not reach.

I did not accomplish the purpose of going to Trinity Church that morning. Somehow, the things I had seen disqualified me for the time from church-going. I walked homeward, thinking what I would do with Bartleby. Finally, I resolved upon this – I would put certain calm questions to him the next morning, touching his history, etc., and if he declined to answer them openly and unreservedly (and I supposed he would prefer not), then to give him a twenty dollar bill over and above whatever I might owe him, and tell him his services were no longer required; but that if in any other way I could assist him, I would be happy to do so, especially if he desired to return to his native place, wherever that might be, I would willingly help to defray the expenses. Moreover, if, after reaching home, he found himself at any time in want of aid, a letter from him would be sure of a reply.

The next morning came.

'Bartleby,' said I, gently calling to him behind his screen.

No reply.

'Bartleby,' said I, in a still gentler tone, 'come here; I am not going to ask you to do anything you would prefer not to do – I simply wish to speak to you.'

Upon this he noiselessly slid into view.

'Will you tell me, Bartleby, where you were born?'

'I would prefer not to.'

'Will you tell me *anything* about yourself?'

'I would prefer not to.'

'But what reasonable objection can you have to speak to me? I feel friendly towards you.'

He did not look at me while I spoke, but kept his glance fixed upon my bust of Cicero, which, as I then sat, was directly behind me, some six inches above my head.

'What is your answer, Bartleby,' said I, after waiting a considerable time for a reply, during which his countenance remained immovable, only there was the faintest conceivable tremor of the white attenuated mouth.

'At present I prefer to give no answer,' he said, and retired into his hermitage.

It was rather weak in me I confess, but his manner, on this occasion, nettled me. Not only did there seem to lurk in it a certain calm disdain, but his perverseness seemed ungrateful, considering the undeniable good usage and indulgence he had received from me.

Again I sat ruminating what I should do. Mortified as I was at his behavior, and resolved as I had been to dismiss him when I entered my office, nevertheless I strangely felt something superstitious knocking at my heart, and forbidding me to carry out my purpose, and denouncing me for a villain if I dared to breathe one bitter word against this forlornest of mankind. At last, familiarly drawing my chair behind his screen, I sat down and said: 'Bartleby, never mind, then, about revealing your history; but let me entreat you, as a friend, to comply as far as may be with the usages of this office. Say now, you will help to examine papers tomorrow or next day: in short, say now, that in a day or two you will begin to be a little reasonable – say so, Bartleby.'

'At present I would prefer not to be a little reasonable,' was his mildly cadaverous reply.

Just then the folding-doors opened, and Nippers approached. He seemed suffering from an unusually bad night's rest, induced by severer indigestion than common. He overheard those final words of Bartleby.

'*Prefer not*, eh?' gritted Nippers – 'I'd *prefer* him, if I were you, sir,' addressing me – 'I'd *prefer* him; I'd give him preferences, the stubborn mule! What is it, sir, pray, that he *prefers* not to do now?'

Bartleby moved not a limb.

'Mr Nippers,' said I, 'I'd prefer that you would withdraw for the present.'

Somehow, of late, I had got into the way of involuntarily using this word 'prefer' upon all sorts of not exactly suitable occasions. And I trembled to think that my contact with the scrivener had already and seriously affected me in a mental way. And what further and deeper aberration might it not yet produce? This apprehension had not been without efficacy in determining me to summary measures.

As Nippers, looking very sour and sulky, was departing, Turkey blandly and deferentially approached.

'With submission, sir,' said he, 'yesterday I was thinking about Bartleby here, and I think that if he would but prefer to take a quart of good ale every day, it would do much towards mending him, and enabling him to assist in examining his papers.'

'So you have got the word, too,' said I, slightly excited.

'With submission, what word, sir,' asked Turkey, respectfully crowding himself into the contracted space behind the screen, and by so doing, making me jostle the scrivener. 'What word, sir?'

'I would prefer to be left alone here,' said Bartleby, as if offended at being mobbed in his privacy.

'*That's* the word, Turkey,' said I – '*that's* it.'

'Oh, *prefer*? oh yes – queer word, I never use it myself. But, sir, as I was saying; if he would but prefer –'

'Turkey,' interrupted I, 'you will please withdraw.'

'Oh, certainly, sir, if you prefer that I should.'

As he opened the folding-door to retire, Nippers at his desk caught a glimpse of me, and asked whether I would prefer to have a certain paper copied on blue paper or white. He did not in the least roguishly accent the word prefer. It was plain that it involuntarily rolled from his tongue. I thought to myself, surely I must get rid of a demented man, who already has in some degree turned the tongues, if not the heads of myself and clerks. But I thought it prudent not to break the dismission at once.

The next day I noticed that Bartleby did nothing but stand at his window in his dead-wall revery. Upon asking him why he did not write, he said that he had decided upon doing no more writing.

'Why, how now? what next?' exclaimed I, 'do no more writing?'

'No more.'

'And what is the reason?'

'Do you not see the reason for yourself?' he indifferently replied.

I looked steadfastly at him, and perceived that his eyes looked dull and glazed. Instantly it occurred to me, that his un-exampled diligence in copying by his dim window for the first few weeks of his stay with me might have temporarily impaired his vision.

I was touched. I said something in condolence with him. I hinted that of course he did wisely in abstaining from writing for a while; and urged him to embrace that opportunity of taking wholesome exercise in the open air. This, however, he did not do. A few days after this, my other clerks being absent, and being in a great hurry to dispatch certain letters by the mail, I thought that, having nothing else earthly to do, Bartleby would surely be less inflexible than usual, and carry these letters to the post-office. But he blankly declined. So, much to my in-convenience, I went myself.

Still added days went by. Whether Bartleby's eyes improved or not, I could not say. To all appearance, I thought they did. But when I asked him if they did, he vouchsafed no answer. At all events, he would do no copying. At last, in reply to my urgings, he informed me that he had permanently given up copying.

'What!' exclaimed I; 'suppose your eyes should get entirely well – better than ever before – would you not copy then?'

'I have given up copying,' he answered, and slid aside.

He remained as ever, a fixture in my chamber. Nay – if that were possible – he became still more of a fixture than before. What was to be done? He would do nothing in the office; why should he stay there? In plain fact, he had now become a mill-stone to me, not only useless as a necklace, but afflictive to bear. Yet I was sorry for him. I speak less than truth when I say that, on his own account, he occasioned me uneasiness. If he would but have named a single relative or friend, I would instantly have written, and urged their taking the poor fellow away to some convenient retreat. But he seemed alone, absolutely alone in the universe. A bit of wreck in the mid Atlantic. At length, necessities connected with my business tyrannized over all other considerations. Decently as I could, I told Bartleby that in six days time he must unconditionally leave the office. I warned him to take measures, in the interval, for procuring some other abode. I offered to assist him in this endeavor, if he himself would but take the first step towards a removal. 'And when you finally quit me, Bartleby,' added I, 'I shall see that you go not away entirely unprovided. Six days from this hour, remember.'

At the expiration of that period, I peeped behind the screen, and lo! Bartleby was there.

I buttoned up my coat, balanced myself; advanced slowly towards him, touched his shoulder, and said, 'The time has come; you must quit this place; I am sorry for you; here is money; but you must go.'

'I would prefer not,' he replied, with his back still towards me.

'You *must*.'

He remained silent.

Now I had an unbounded confidence in this man's common honesty. He had frequently restored to me sixpences and shillings carelessly dropped upon the floor, for I am apt to be very reckless in such shirt-button affairs. The proceeding, then, which followed will not be deemed extraordinary.

'Bartleby,' said I, 'I owe you twelve dollars on account; here are thirty-two; the odd twenty are yours – Will you take it?' and I handed the bills towards him.

But he made no motion.

'I will leave them here, then,' putting them under a weight on the table. Then taking my hat and cane and going to the door, I tranquilly turned and added – 'After you have removed your things from these offices, Bartleby, you will of course lock the door – since every one is now gone for the day but you – and if you please, slip your key underneath the mat, so that I may have it in the morning. I shall not see you again; so good-bye to you. If, hereafter, in your new place of abode, I can be of any service to you, do not fail to advise me by letter. Good-bye, Bartleby, and fare you well.'

But he answered not a word; like the last column of some ruined temple, he remained standing mute and solitary in the middle of the otherwise deserted room.

As I walked home in a pensive mood, my vanity got the better of my pity. I could not but highly plume myself on my masterly management in getting rid of Bartleby. Masterly I call it, and such it must appear to any dispassionate thinker. The beauty of my procedure seemed to consist in its perfect quietness. There was no vulgar bullying, no bravado of any sort, no choleric hectoring, and striding to and fro across the apartment, jerking out vehement commands for Bartleby to bundle himself off with his beggarly traps. Nothing of the kind. Without loudly bidding Bartleby depart – as an inferior genius might have done – I *assumed* the ground that depart he must; and upon that assumption built all I had to say. The more I thought over my procedure, the more I was charmed with it. Nevertheless, next morning, upon awakening, I had my doubts – I had somehow slept off the fumes of vanity. One of the coolest and wisest hours a man has, is just after he awakes in the morning. My procedure seemed as sagacious as ever – but only in theory. How it would prove in practice – there was the rub. It was truly a beautiful thought to have assumed Bartleby's departure; but, after all, that assumption was simply my own, and none of Bartleby's. The great point was, not whether I had assumed that he would quit me, but whether he would prefer so to do. He was more a man of preferences than assumptions.

After breakfast, I walked down town, arguing the probabilities *pro* and *con*. One moment I thought it would prove a miserable failure, and Bartleby would be found all alive at my office as usual; the next moment it seemed certain that I should find his chair empty. And so I kept veering about. At the corner of Broadway and Canal Street, I saw quite an excited group of people standing in earnest conversation.

'I'll take odds he doesn't,' said a voice as I passed.

'Doesn't go? – done !' said I, 'put up your money.'

I was instinctively putting my hand in my pocket to produce my own, when I remembered that this was an election day. The words I had overheard bore no reference to Bartleby, but to the success or non-success of some candidate for the mayoralty. In my intent frame of mind, I had, as it were, imagined that all Broadway shared in my excitement, and were debating the same question with me. I passed on, very thankful that the uproar of the street screened my momentary absent-mindedness.

As I had intended, I was earlier than usual at my office door.

I stood listening for a moment. All was still. He must be gone. I tried the knob. The door was locked. Yes, my procedure had worked to a charm; he indeed must be vanished. Yet a certain melancholy mixed with this: I was almost sorry for my brilliant success. I was fumbling under the door mat for the key, which Bartleby was to have left there for me, when accidentally my knee knocked against a panel, producing a summoning sound, and in response a voice came to me from within – 'Not yet; I am occupied.'

It was Bartleby.

I was thunderstruck. For an instant I stood like the man who, pipe in mouth, was killed one cloudless afternoon long ago in Virginia, by summer lightning; at his own warm open window he was killed, and remained leaning out there upon the dreamy afternoon, till some one touched him, when he fell.

'Not gone!' I murmured at last. But again obeying that wondrous ascendancy which the inscrutable scrivener had over me, and from which ascendancy, for all my chafing, I could not completely escape, I slowly went down stairs and out into the street, and while walking round the block, considered what I should next do in this unheard-of perplexity. Turn the man out by an actual thrusting I could not; to drive him away by calling him hard names would not do; calling in the police was an unpleasant idea; and yet, permit him to enjoy his cadaverous triumph over me – this, too, I could not think of. What was to be done? or, if nothing could be done, was there anything further that I could *assume* in the matter? Yes, as before I had prospectively assumed that Bartleby would depart, so now I might retrospectively assume that departed he was. In the legitimate carrying out of this assumption, I might enter my office in a great hurry, and pretending not to see Bartleby at all, walk straight against him as if he were air. Such a proceeding would in a singular degree have the appearance of a home-thrust. It was hardly possible that Bartleby could withstand such an application of the doctrine of assumptions. But upon second thoughts the success of the plan seemed rather dubious. I resolved to argue the matter over with him again.

'Bartleby,' said I, entering the office, with a quietly severe expression, 'I am seriously displeased. I am pained, Bartleby. I had thought better of you. I had imagined you of such a gentlemanly organization, that in any delicate dilemma a slight hint would suffice – in short, an assumption. But it appears I am deceived. Why,' I added, unaffectedly starting, 'you have not even touched that money yet,' pointing to it, just where I had left it the evening previous.

He answered nothing.

'Will you, or will you not, quit me?' I now demanded in a sudden passion, advancing close to him.

'I would prefer *not* to quit you,' he replied, gently emphasizing the *not*.

'What earthly right have you to stay here? Do you pay any rent? Do you pay my taxes? Or is this property yours?'

He answered nothing.

'Are you ready to go on and write now? Are your eyes recovered? Could you copy a small paper for me this morning? or help examine a few lines? or step round to the post-office? In a word, will you do anything at all, to give a coloring to your refusal to depart the premises?'

He silently retired into his hermitage.

I was now in such a state of nervous resentment that I thought it but prudent to check myself at present from further demonstrations. Bartleby and I were alone. I remembered the tragedy of the unfortunate Adams and the still more unfortunate Colt in the solitary office of the latter; and how poor Colt, being dreadfully incensed by Adams, and imprudently permitting himself to get wildly excited, was at unawares hurried into his fatal act – an act which certainly no man could possibly deplore more than the actor himself. Often it had occurred to me in my ponderings upon the subject, that had that altercation taken place in the public street, or at a private residence, it would not have terminated as it did. It was the circumstance of being alone in a solitary office, up stairs, of a building entirely unhallowed by humanizing domestic associations – an uncarpeted office, doubtless, of a dusty, haggard sort of appearance – this must have been, which greatly helped to enhance the irritable desperation of the hapless Colt.

But when this old Adam of resentment rose in me and tempted me concerning Bartleby, I grappled him and threw him. How? Why, simply by recalling the divine injunction: 'A new commandment give I unto you, that ye love one another.' Yes, this it was that saved me. Aside from higher considerations, charity often operates as a vastly wise and prudent principle – a great safeguard to its possessor. Men have committed murder for jealousy's sake, and anger's sake, and hatred's sake, and selfishness' sake, and spiritual pride's sake; but no man, that ever I heard of, ever committed a diabolical murder for sweet charity's sake. Mere self-interest, then, if no better motive can be enlisted, should, especially with high-tempered men, prompt all beings to charity and philanthropy. At any rate, upon the occasion in question, I strove to drown my exasperated feelings towards the scrivener by benevolently construing his conduct. Poor fellow, poor fellow! thought I, he don't mean anything; and besides, he has seen hard times, and ought to be indulged.

I endeavored, also, immediately to occupy myself, and at the same time to comfort my despondency. I tried to fancy, that in the course of the morning, at such time as might prove agreeable to him, Bartleby, of his own free accord, would emerge from his hermitage and take up some decided line of march in the direction of the door. But no. Half past twelve o'clock came; Turkey began to glow in the face, overturn his inkstand, and became generally obstreperous; Nippers abated down into quietude and courtesy; Ginger Nut munched his noon apple; and Bartleby remained standing at his window in one of his profoundest dead-wall reveries. Will it be credited? Ought I to acknowledge it? That afternoon I left the office without saying one further word to him.

Some days now passed, during which, at leisure intervals, I looked a little into *Edwards on the Will*, and *Priestly on Necessity*. Under the circumstances, those books induced a salutary feeling. Gradually I slid into the persuasion that these troubles of mine, touching the scrivener, had been all predestinated from eternity, and Bartleby was billeted upon me for some mysterious purpose of an all-wise Providence, which it was not for a mere mortal like me to fathom. Yes, Bartleby, stay there behind your screen, thought I; I shall persecute you no more; you are harmless and noiseless as any of these old chairs; in short, I never feel so private as when I know you are here. At last I see it, I feel it; I penetrate to the predestinated purpose of my life. I am content. Others may have loftier parts to enact; but my mission in this world, Bartleby, is to furnish you with office-room for such period as you may see fit to remain.

I believe that this wise and blessed frame of mind would have continued with me, had it not been for the unsolicited and uncharitable remarks obtruded upon me by my professional friends who visited the rooms. But thus it often is, that the constant friction of liberal minds wears out at last the best resolves of the more generous. Though to be sure, when I reflected upon it, it was not strange that people entering my office should be struck by the peculiar aspect of the unaccountable Bartleby, and so be tempted to throw out some sinister observations concerning him. Sometimes an attorney, having business with me, and calling at my office, and finding no one but the scrivener there, would undertake to obtain some sort of precise information from him touching my whereabouts; but without heeding his idle talk, Bartleby would remain standing immovable in the middle of the room. So after contemplating him in that position for a time, the attorney would depart, no wiser than he came.

Also, when a reference was going on, and the room full of lawyers and witnesses, and business driving fast, some deeply occupied legal gentleman present, seeing Bartleby wholly unemployed, would request him to run round to his (the legal gentleman's) office and fetch some papers for him. Thereupon, Bartleby would tranquilly decline, and yet remain idle as before. Then the lawyer would give a great stare, and turn to me. And what could I say? At last I was made aware that all through the circle of my professional acquaintance, a whisper of wonder was running round, having reference to the strange creature I kept at my office. This worried me very much. And as the idea came upon me of his possibly turning out a long-lived man, and keep occupying my chambers, and denying my authority; and perplexing my visitors; and scandalizing my professional reputation; and casting a general gloom over the premises; keeping soul and body together to the last upon his savings (for doubtless he spent but half a dime a day), and in the end perhaps outlive me, and claim possession of my office by right of his perpetual occupancy: as all these dark anticipations crowded upon me more and more, and my friends continually intruded their relentless remarks upon the apparition in my room; a great change was wrought in me. I resolved to gather all my faculties together, and forever rid me of this intolerable incubus.

Ere revolving any complicated project, however, adapted to this end, I first simply suggested to Bartleby the propriety of his permanent departure. In a calm and serious tone, I commended the idea to his careful and mature consideration. But, having taken three days to meditate upon it, he apprised me, that his original determination remained the same; in short, that he still preferred to abide with me.

What shall I do? I now said to myself, buttoning up my coat to the last button. What shall I do? what ought I to do? what does conscience say I *should* do with this man, or, rather, ghost. Rid myself of him, I must; go, he shall. But how? You will not thrust him, the poor, pale, passive mortal – you will not thrust such a helpless creature out of your door? you will not dishonor yourself by such cruelty? No, I will not, I cannot do that. Rather would I let him live and die here, and then mason up his remains in the wall. What, then, will you do? For all your coaxing, he will not budge. Bribes he leaves under your own paperweight on your table; in short, it is quite plain that he prefers to cling to you.

Then something severe, something unusual must be done. What! surely you will not have him collared by a constable, and commit his innocent pallor to the common jail? And upon what ground could you procure such a thing to be done? – a vagrant, is he? What! he a vagrant, a wanderer, who refuses to budge? It is because he will *not* be a vagrant, then, that you seek to count him *as* a vagrant. That is too absurd. No visible means of support: there I have him. Wrong again: for indubitably he *does* support himself and that is the only unanswerable proof that any man can show of his possessing the means so to do. No more, then. Since he will not quit me, I must quit him. I will change my offices; I will move elsewhere, and give him fair notice, that if I find him on my new premises I will then proceed against him as a common trespasser.

Acting accordingly, next day I thus addressed him: 'I find these chambers too far from the City Hall; the air is unwholesome. In a word, I propose to remove my offices next week, and shall no longer require your services. I tell you this now, in order that you may seek another place.'

He made no reply, and nothing more was said.

On the appointed day I engaged carts and men, proceeded to my chambers, and, having but little furniture, everything was removed in a few hours. Throughout, the scrivener remained standing behind the screen, which I directed to be removed the last thing. It was withdrawn; and, being folded up like a huge folio, left him the motionless occupant of a naked room. I stood in the entry watching him a moment, while something from within me upbraided me.

I re-entered with my hand in my pocket — and — and my heart in my mouth.

'Good-bye, Bartleby; I am going — good-bye, and God some way bless you; and take that,' slipping something in his hand. But it dropped upon the floor, and then — strange to say — I tore myself from him whom I had so longed to be rid of.

Established in my new quarters, for a day or two I kept the door locked, and started at every footfall in the passages. When I returned to my rooms, after any little absence, I would pause at the threshold for an instant, and attentively listen, ere applying my key. But these fears were needless. Bartleby never came nigh me.

I thought all was going well, when a perturbed-looking stranger visited me, inquiring whether I was the person who had recently occupied rooms at No. — Wall Street.

Full of forebodings, I replied that I was.

'Then, sir,' said the stranger, who proved a lawyer, 'you are responsible for the man you left there. He refuses to do any copying; he refuses to do anything; he says he prefers not to; and he refuses to quit the premises.'

'I am very sorry, sir,' said I, with assumed tranquillity, but an inward tremor, 'but, really, the man you allude to is nothing to me – he is no relation or apprentice of mine, that you should hold me responsible for him.'

'In mercy's name, who is he?'

'I certainly cannot inform you. I know nothing about him. Formerly I employed him as a copyist; but he has done nothing for me now for some time past.'

'I shall settle him, then – good morning, sir.'

Several days passed, and I heard nothing more; and, though I often felt a charitable prompting to call at the place and see poor Bartleby, yet a certain squeamishness, of I know not what, withheld me.

All is over with him, by this time, thought I, at last, when, through another week, no further intelligence reached me. But, coming to my room the day after, I found several persons waiting at my door in a high state of nervous excitement.

'That's the man – here he comes,' cried the foremost one, whom I recognized as the lawyer who had previously called upon me alone.

'You must take him away, sir, at once,' cried a portly person among them, advancing upon me, and whom I knew to be the landlord of No. — Wall Street. 'These gentlemen, my tenants, cannot stand it any longer; Mr B—,' pointing to the lawyer, 'has turned him out of his room, and he now persists in haunting the building generally, sitting upon the banisters of the stairs by day, and sleeping in the entry by night. Everybody is concerned; clients are leaving the offices; some fears are entertained of a mob; something you must do, and that without delay.'

Aghast at this torrent, I fell back before it, and would fain have locked myself in my new quarters. In vain I persisted that Bartleby was nothing to me – no more than to any one else. In vain – I was the last person known to have anything to do with him, and they held me to the terrible account. Fearful, then, of being exposed in the papers (as one person present obscurely threatened), I considered the matter, and, at length, said, that if the lawyer would give me a confidential interview with the scrivener, in his (the lawyer's) own room, I would, that afternoon, strive my best to rid them of the nuisance they complained of.

Going up stairs to my old haunt, there was Bartleby silently sitting upon the banister at the landing.

'What are you doing here, Bartleby?' said I.

'Sitting upon the banister,' he mildly replied.

I motioned him into the lawyer's room, who then left us.

'Bartleby,' said I, 'are you aware that you are the cause of great tribulation to me, by persisting in occupying the entry after being dismissed from the office?'

No answer.

'Now one of two things must take place. Either you must do something, or something must be done to you. Now what sort of business would you like to engage in? Would you like to re-engage in copying for some one?'

'No; I would prefer not to make any change.'

'Would you like a clerkship in a dry-goods store?'

'There is too much confinement about that. No, I would not like a clerkship; but I am not particular.'

'Too much confinement,' I cried, 'why you keep yourself confined all the time!'

'I would prefer not to take a clerkship,' he rejoined, as if to settle that little item at once.

'How would a bar-tender's business suit you? There is no trying of the eye-sight in that.'

'I would not like it at all; though, as I said before, I am not particular.'

His unwonted wordiness inspirited me. I returned to the charge.

'Well, then, would you like to travel through the country collecting bills for the merchants? That would improve your health.'

'No, I would prefer to be doing something else.'

'How, then, would going as a companion to Europe, to entertain some young gentleman with your conversation — how would that suit you?'

'Not at all. It does not strike me that there is anything definite about that. I like to be stationary. But I am not particular.'

'Stationary you shall be, then,' I cried, now losing all patience, and, for the first time in all my exasperating connexion with him, fairly flying into a passion. 'If you do not go away from these premises before night, I shall feel bound – indeed, I *am* bound – to – to – to quit the premises myself!' I rather absurdly concluded, knowing not with what possible threat to try to frighten his immobility into compliance. Despairing of all further efforts, I was precipitately leaving him, when a final thought occurred to me – one which had not been wholly unindulged before.

'Bartleby,' said I, in the kindest tone I could assume under such exciting circumstances, 'will you go home with me now – not to my office, but my dwelling – and remain there till we can conclude upon some convenient arrangement for you at our leisure? Come, let us start now, right away.'

'No: at present I would prefer not to make any change at all.'

I answered nothing; but, effectually dodging every one by the suddenness and rapidity of my flight, rushed from the building, ran up Wall Street towards Broadway, and, jumping into the first omnibus, was soon removed from pursuit. As soon as tranquillity returned, I distinctly perceived that I had now done all that I possibly could, both in respect to the demands of the landlord and his tenants, and with regard to my own desire and sense of duty, to benefit Bartleby, and shield him from rude persecution. I now strove to be entirely care-free and quiescent; and my conscience justified me in the attempt; though, indeed it was not so successful as I could have wished. So fearful was I of being again hunted out by the incensed landlord and his exasperated tenants, that, surrendering my business to Nippers, for a few days, I drove about the upper part of the town and through the suburbs, in my rockaway; crossed over to Jersey City and Hoboken, and paid fugitive visits to Manhattanville and Astoria. In fact, I almost lived in my rockaway for the time.

When again I entered my office, lo, a note from the landlord lay upon the desk. I opened it with trembling hands. It informed me that the writer had sent to the police, and had Bartleby removed to the Tombs as a vagrant. Moreover, since I knew more about him than any one else, he wished me to appear at that place, and make a suitable statement of the facts. These tidings had a conflicting effect upon me. At first I was indignant; but, at last, almost approved. The landlord's energetic, summary disposition, had led him to adopt a procedure which I do not think I would have decided upon myself; and yet, as a last resort, under such peculiar circumstances, it seemed the only plan.

As I afterwards learned, the poor scrivener, when told that he must be conducted to the Tombs, offered not the slightest obstacle, but, in his pale, unmoving way, silently acquiesced.

Some of the compassionate and curious bystanders joined the party; and headed by one of the constables arm in arm with Bartleby, the silent procession filed its way through all the noise, and heat, and joy of the roaring thoroughfares at noon.

The same day I received the note, I went to the Tombs, or, to speak more properly, the Halls of Justice. Seeking the right officer, I stated the purpose of my call, and was informed that the individual I described was, indeed, within. I then assured the functionary that Bartleby was a perfectly honest man, and greatly to be compassionated, however unaccountably eccentric. I narrated all I knew, and closed by suggesting the idea of letting him remain in as indulgent confinement as possible, till something less harsh might be done – though, indeed, I hardly knew what. At all events, if nothing else could be decided upon, the alms-house must receive him. I then begged to have an interview.

Being under no disgraceful charge, and quite serene and harmless in all his ways, they had permitted him freely to wander about the prison, and, especially, in the inclosed grass-platted yards thereof. And so I found him there, standing all alone in the quietest of the yards, his face towards a high wall, while all around, from the narrow slits of the jail windows, I thought I saw peering out upon him the eyes of murderers and thieves.

'Bartleby!'

'I know you,' he said, without looking round – 'and I want nothing to say to you.'

'It was not I that brought you here, Bartleby,' said I, keenly pained at his implied suspicion. 'And to you, this should not be so vile a place. Nothing reproachful attaches to you by being here. And see, it is not so sad a place as one might think. Look, there is the sky, and here is the grass.'

'I know where I am,' he replied, but would say nothing more, and so I left him.

As I entered the corridor again, a broad meat-like man, in an apron, accosted me, and, jerking his thumb over his shoulder, said – 'Is that your friend?'

'Yes.'

'Does he want to starve? If he does, let him live on the prison fare, that's all.'

'Who are you?' asked I, not knowing what to make of such an unofficially speaking person in such a place.

'I am the grub-man. Such gentlemen as have friends here, hire me to provide them with something good to eat.'

'Is this so?' said I, turning to the turnkey.

He said it was.

'Well, then,' said I, slipping some silver into the grub-man's hands (for so they called him), 'I want you to give particular attention to my friend there; let him have the best dinner you can get. And you must be as polite to him as possible.'

'Introduce me, will you?' said the grub-man, looking at me with an expression which seemed to say he was all impatience for an opportunity to give a specimen of his breeding.

Thinking it would prove of benefit to the scrivener, I acquiesced; and, asking the grub-man his name, went up with him to Bartleby.

'Bartleby, this is a friend; you will find him very useful to you.'

'Your sarvant, sir, your sarvant,' said the grub-man, making a low salutation behind his apron. 'Hope you find it pleasant here, sir; nice grounds – cool apartments – hope you'll stay with us sometime – try to make it agreeable. What will you have for dinner today?'

'I prefer not to dine today,' said Bartleby, turning away. 'It would disagree with me; I am unused to dinners.' So saying, he slowly moved to the other side of the inclosure, and took up a position fronting the dead-wall.

'How's this?' said the grub-man, addressing me with a stare of astonishment. 'He's odd, ain't he?'

'I think he is a little deranged,' said I, sadly.

'Deranged? deranged is it? Well, now, upon my word, I thought that friend of yourn was a gentleman forger; they are always pale and genteel-like, them forgers. I can't help pity 'em – can't help it, sir. Did you know Monroe Edwards?' he added, touchingly, and paused. Then, laying his hand piteously on my shoulder, sighed, 'He died of consumption at Sing-Sing. So you weren't acquainted with Monroe?'

'No, I was never socially acquainted with any forgers. But I cannot stop longer. Look to my friend yonder. You will not lose by it. I will see you again.'

Some few days after this, I again obtained admission to the Tombs, and went through the corridors in quest of Bartleby; but without finding him.

'I saw him coming from his cell not long ago,' said a turnkey, 'may be he's gone to loiter in the yards.'

So I went in that direction.

'Are you looking for the silent man?' said another turnkey, passing me. 'Yonder he lies – sleeping in the yard there. 'Tis not twenty minutes since I saw him lie down.'

The yard was entirely quiet. It was not accessible to the common prisoners. The surrounding walls, of amazing thickness, kept off all sounds behind them. The Egyptian character of the masonry weighed upon me with its gloom. But a soft imprisoned turf grew under foot. The heart of the eternal pyramids, it seemed, wherein, by some strange magic, through the clefts, grass-seed, dropped by birds, had sprung.

Strangely huddled at the base of the wall, his knees drawn up, and lying on his side, his head touching the cold stones, I saw the wasted Bartleby. But nothing stirred. I paused; then went close up to him; stooped over, and saw that his dim eyes were open; otherwise he seemed profoundly sleeping. Something prompted me to touch him. I felt his hand, when a tingling shiver ran up my arm and down my spine to my feet.

The round face of the grub-man peered upon me now. 'His dinner is ready. Won't he dine today, either? Or does he live without dining?'

'Lives without dining,' said I, and closed the eyes.

'Eh! — He's asleep, ain't he?'

'With kings and counselors,' murmured I.

There would seem little need for proceeding further in this history. Imagination will readily supply the meagre recital of poor Bartleby's interment. But, ere parting with the reader, let me say, that if this little narrative has sufficiently interested him, to awaken curiosity as to who Bartleby was, and what manner of life he led prior to the present narrator's making his acquaintance, I can only reply, that in such curiosity I fully share, but am wholly unable to gratify it. Yet here I hardly know whether I should divulge one little item of rumor, which came to my ear a few months after the scrivener's decease. Upon what basis it rested, I could never ascertain; and hence, how true it is I cannot now tell. But, inasmuch as this vague report has not been without a certain suggestive interest to me, however sad, it may prove the same with some others; and so I will briefly mention it. The report was this: that Bartleby had been a subordinate clerk in the Dead Letter Office at Washington, from which he had been suddenly removed by a change in the administration. When I think over this rumor, hardly can I express the emotions which seize me. Dead letters! Does it not sound like dead men? Conceive a man by nature and misfortune prone to a pallid hopelessness, can any business seem more fitted to heighten it than that of continually handling these dead letters, and assorting them for the flames? For by the cart-load they are annually burned. Sometimes from out the folded paper the pale clerk takes a ring — the finger it was meant for, perhaps, moulders in the grave; a bank-note sent in swiftest charity — he whom it would relieve, nor eats nor hungers any more; pardon for those who died despairing; hope for those who died unhoping; good tidings for those who died stifled by unrelieved calamities. On errands of life, these letters speed to death.

Ah, Bartleby! Ah, humanity!

Mark Twain

THE MAN THAT
CORRUPTED HADLEYBURG

I

I T was many years ago. Hadleyburg was the most honest and upright town in all the region round about. It had kept that reputation unsmirched during three generations, and was prouder of it than of any other of its possessions. It was so proud of it, and so anxious to insure its perpetuation, that it began to teach the principles of honest dealing to its babies in the cradle, and made the like teachings the staple of their culture thenceforward through all the years devoted to their education. Also, throughout the formative years temptations were kept out of the way of the young people, so that their honesty could have every chance to harden and solidify, and become a part of their very bone. The neighboring towns were jealous of this honorable supremacy, and elected to sneer at Hadleyburg's pride in it and call it vanity; but all the same they were obliged to acknowledge that Hadleyburg was in reality an incorruptible town; and if pressed they would also acknowledge that the mere fact that a young man hailed from Hadleyburg was all the recommendation he needed when he went forth from his natal town to seek for responsible employment.

But at last, in the drift of time, Hadleyburg had the ill luck to offend a passing stranger – possibly without knowing it, certainly without caring, for Hadleyburg was sufficient unto itself, and cared not a rap for strangers or their opinions. Still, it would have been well to make an exception in this one's case, for he was a bitter man and revengeful. All through his wanderings during a whole year he kept his injury in mind, and gave all his leisure moments to trying to invent a compensating satisfaction for it. He contrived many plans, and all of them were good, but none of them was quite sweeping enough; the poorest of them would hurt a great many individuals, but what he wanted was a plan which would comprehend the entire town, and not let so much as one person escape unhurt. At last he had a fortunate idea, and when it fell into his brain it lit up his whole head with an evil joy. He began to form a plan at once, saying to himself, 'That is the thing to do – I will corrupt the town.'

Six months later he went to Hadleyburg, and arrived in a buggy at the house of the old cashier of the bank about ten at night. He got a sack out of the buggy, shouldered it, and staggered with it through the cottage yard, and knocked at the door. A woman's voice said 'Come in', and he entered, and set his sack behind the stove in the parlor, saying politely to the old lady who sat reading the *Missionary Herald* by the lamp:

'Pray keep your seat, madam, I will not disturb you. There – now it is pretty well concealed; one would hardly know it was there. Can I see your husband a moment, madam?'

No, he was gone to Brixton, and might not return before morning.

'Very well, madam, it is no matter. I merely wanted to leave that sack in his care, to be delivered to the rightful owner when he shall be found. I am a stranger; he does not know me; I am merely passing through the town tonight to discharge a matter which has been long in my mind. My errand is now completed, and I go pleased and a little proud, and you will never see me again. There is a paper attached to the sack which will explain everything. Good night, madam.'

The old lady was afraid of the mysterious big stranger, and was glad to see him go. But her curiosity was roused, and she went straight to the sack and brought away the paper. It began as follows:

TO BE PUBLISHED; or, the right man sought out by private inquiry – either will answer. This sack contains gold coin weighing a hundred and sixty pounds four ounces —

'Mercy on us, and the door not locked!'

Mrs Richards flew to it all in a tremble and locked it, then pulled down the window-shades and stood frightened, worried, and wondering if there was anything else she could do toward making herself and the money more safe. She listened awhile for burglars, then surrendered to curiosity and went back to the lamp and finished reading the paper:

I am a foreigner, and am presently going back to my own country, to remain there permanently. I am grateful to America for what I have received at her hands during my stay under her flag, and to one of her citizens – a citizen of Hadleyburg – I am especially grateful for a great kindness done me a year or two ago. Two great kindnesses, in fact. I will explain. I was a gambler. I say w a s. I was a ruined gambler. I arrived in this village at night, hungry and without a penny. I asked for help – in the dark, I was ashamed to beg in the light. I begged of the right man. He gave me twenty dollars – that is to say, he gave me life, as I considered it. He also gave me fortune, for out of that money I have made myself rich at the gaming-table. And finally, a remark which he made to me has remained with me to this day, and has at last conquered me, and in conquering has saved the remnant of my morals: I shall gamble no more. Now I have no idea who that man was, but I want him found, and I want him to have this money, to give away, throw away, or keep, as he pleases. It is merely my way of testifying my gratitude to him. If I could stay, I would find him myself, but no matter, he will be found. This is an honest town, an incorruptible town, and I know I can trust it without fear. This man can be identified by the remark which he made to me, I feel persuaded that he will remember it.

And now my plan is this: If you prefer to conduct the inquiry privately, do so. Tell the contents of this present writing to any one who is likely to be the right man. If he shall answer, 'I am the man, the remark I made was so-and-so,' apply the test – to wit: open the sack, and in it you will find a sealed envelope containing that remark. If the remark mentioned by the candidate tallies with it, give him the money, and ask no further questions, for he is certain the right man.

But if you shall prefer a public inquiry, then publish this present writing in the local paper – with these instructions added, to wit: Thirty days from now, let the candidate appear at the town-hall at eight in the evening (Friday), and hand his remark, in a sealed envelope, to the Rev. Mr Burgess (if he will be kind enough to act), and let Mr Burgess there and then destroy the seals on the sack, open it, and see if the remark is correct, if correct, let the money be delivered, with my sincere gratitude, to my benefactor thus identified.

Mrs Richards sat down, gently quivering with excitement, and was soon lost in thinking – after this pattern: 'What a strange thing it is! ... And what a fortune for that kind man who set his bread afloat upon the waters! ... If it had only been my husband that did it! – for we are so poor, so old and poor! ...' Then, with a sigh – 'But it was not my Edward; no, it was not he that gave a stranger twenty dollars. It is a pity too; I see it now. ...' Then, with a shudder – 'But it is *gambler's* money! the wages of sin; we couldn't take it; we couldn't touch it. I don't like to be near it; it seems a defilement.' She moved to a farther chair. ... 'I wish Edward would come, and take it to the bank; a burglar might come at any moment; it is dreadful to be here all alone with it.'

At eleven Mr Richards arrived, and while his wife was saying, 'I am *so* glad you've come!' he was saying, 'I'm so tired – tired clear out; it is dreadful to be poor, and have to make these dismal journeys at my time of life. Always at the grind, grind, grind, on a salary – another man's slave, and he sitting at home in his slippers, rich and comfortable.'

'I am so sorry for you, Edward, you know that; but be comforted; we have our livelihood; we have our good name –'

'Yes, Mary, and that is everything. Don't mind my talk – it's just a moment's irritation and doesn't mean anything. Kiss me – there, it's all gone now, and I am not complaining any more. What have you been getting? What's in the sack?'

Then his wife told him the great secret. It dazed him for a moment; then he said:

'It weighs a hundred and sixty pounds? Why, Mary, it's for-ty thou-sand dollars – think of it – a whole fortune! Not ten men in this village are worth that much. Give me the paper.'

He skimmed through it and said:

'Isn't it an adventure! Why, it's a romance; it's like the impossible things one reads about in books, and never sees in life.' He was well stirred up now; cheerful, even gleeful. He tapped his old wife on the cheek, and said, humorously, 'Why, we're rich, Mary, rich; all we've got to do is to bury the money and burn the papers. If the gambler ever comes to inquire, we'll merely look coldly upon him and say: "What is this nonsense you are talking? We have never heard of you and your sack of gold before"; and then he would look foolish, and —'

'And in the mean time, while you are running on with your jokes, the money is still here, and it is fast getting along toward burglar-time.'

'True. Very well, what shall we do — make the inquiry private? No, not that; it would spoil the romance. The public method is better. Think what a noise it will make! And it will make all the other towns jealous; for no stranger would trust such a thing to any town but Hadleyburg, and they know it. It's a great card for us. I must get to the printing-office now, or I shall be too late.'

'But stop — stop — don't leave me here alone with it, Edward!'

But he was gone. For only a little while, however. Not far from his own house he met the editor-proprietor of the paper, and gave him the document, and said, 'Here is a good thing for you, Cox — put it in.'

'It may be too late, Mr Richards, but I'll see.'

At home again he and his wife sat down to talk the charming mystery over; they were in no condition for sleep. The first question was, Who could the citizen have been who gave the stranger the twenty dollars? It seemed a simple one; both answered it in the same breath —

'Barclay Goodson.'

'Yes,' said Richards, 'he could have done it, and it would have been like him, but there's not another in the town.'

'Everybody will grant that, Edward — grant it privately, anyway. For six months, now, the village has been its own proper self once more — honest, narrow, self-righteous, and stingy.'

'It is what he always called it, to the day of his death — said it right out publicly, too.'

'Yes, and he was hated for it.'

'Oh, of course; but he didn't care. I reckon he was the best-hated man among us, except the Reverend Burgess.'

'Well, Burgess deserves it – he will never get another congregation here. Mean as the town is, it knows how to estimate *him*. Edward, doesn't it seem odd that the stranger should appoint Burgess to deliver the money?'

'Well, yes – it does. That is – that is –'

'Why so much that-*is*-ing? Would *you* select him?'

'Mary, maybe the stranger knows him better than this village does.'

'Much *that* would help Burgess!'

The husband seemed perplexed for an answer; the wife kept a steady eye upon him, and waited. Finally Richards said, with the hesitancy of one who is making a statement which is likely to encounter doubt,

'Mary, Burgess is not a bad man.'

His wife was certainly surprised.

'Nonsense!' she exclaimed.

'He is not a bad man. I know. The whole of his unpopularity had its foundation in that one thing – the thing that made so much noise.'

'That "one thing", indeed! As if that "one thing" wasn't enough, all by itself.'

'Plenty. Plenty. Only he wasn't guilty of it.'

'How you talk! Not guilty of it! Everybody knows he *was* guilty.'

'Mary, I give you my word – he was innocent.'

'I can't believe it, and I don't. How do you know?'

'It is a confession. I am ashamed, but I will make it. I was the only man who knew he was innocent. I could have saved him, and – and well, you know how the town was wrought up – I hadn't the pluck to do it. It would have turned everybody against me. I felt mean, ever so mean; but I didn't dare; I hadn't the manliness to face that.'

Mary looked troubled, and for a while was silent. Then she said, stammeringly:

'I – I don't think it would have done for you to – to – One mustn't – er – public opinion – one has to be so careful – so –' It was a difficult road, and she got mired; but after a little she got started again. 'It was a great pity, but – Why, we couldn't afford it, Edward – we couldn't indeed. Oh, I wouldn't have had you do it for anything!'

'It would have lost us the good-will of so many people, Mary; and then – and then –'

'What troubles me now is, what *he* thinks of us, Edward.'

'He? *He* doesn't suspect that I could have saved him.'

'Oh,' exclaimed the wife, in a tone of relief, 'I am glad of that. As long as he doesn't know that you could have saved him, he – he – well, that makes it a great deal better. Why, I might have known he didn't know, because he is always trying to be friendly with us, as little encouragement as we give him. More than once people have twitted me with it. There's the Wilsons, and the Wilcoxes, and the Harknesses, they take a mean pleasure in saying, *'Your friend* Burgess,' because they know it pesters me. I wish he wouldn't persist in liking us so; I can't think why he keeps it up.'

'I can explain it. It's another confession. When the thing was new and hot, and the town made a plan to ride him on a rail, my conscience hurt me so that I couldn't stand it, and I went privately and gave him notice, and he got out of the town and stayed out till it was safe to come back.'

'Edward! If the town had found it out –'

'*Don't!* It scares me yet, to think of it. I repented of it the minute it was done; and I was even afraid to tell you, lest your face might betray it to somebody. I didn't sleep any that night, for worrying. But after a few days I saw that no one was going to suspect me, and after that I got to feeling glad I did it. And I feel glad yet, Mary – glad through and through.'

'So do I, now, for it would have been a dreadful way to treat him. Yes, I'm glad; for really you did owe him that, you know. But, Edward, suppose it should come out yet, some day!'

'It won't.'

'Why?'

'Because everybody thinks it was Goodson.'

'Of course they would!'

'Certainly. And of course *he* didn't care. They persuaded poor old Sawlsberry to go and charge it on him, and he went blustering over there and did it. Goodson looked him over, like as if he was hunting for a place on him that he could despise the most, then he says, "So you are the Committee of Inquiry, are you?" Sawlsberry said that was about what he was. "Hm. Do they require particulars, or do you reckon a kind of a *general* answer will do?" "If they require particulars, I will come back, Mr Goodson; I will take the general answer first." "Very well, then, tell them to go to hell – I reckon that's general enough. And I'll give you some advice, Sawlsberry; when you come back for the particulars, fetch a basket to carry the relics of yourself home in." '

'Just like Goodson; it's got all the marks. He had only one vanity; he thought he could give advice better than any other person.'

'It settled the business, and saved us, Mary. The subject was dropped.'

'Bless you, I'm not doubting *that*.'

Then they took up the gold-sack mystery again, with strong interest. Soon the conversation began to suffer breaks – interruptions caused by absorbed thinkings. The breaks grew more and more frequent. At last Richards lost himself wholly in thought. He sat long, gazing vacantly at the floor, and by-and-by he began to punctuate his thoughts with little nervous movements of his hands that seemed to indicate vexation. Meantime his wife too had relapsed into a thoughtful silence, and her movements were beginning to show a troubled discomfort. Finally Richards got up and strode aimlessly about the room, ploughing his hands through his hair, much as a somnambulist might do who was having a bad dream. Then he seemed to arrive at a definite purpose; and without a word he put on his hat and passed quickly out of the house. His wife sat brooding, with a drawn face, and did not seem to be aware that she was alone. Now and then she murmured, 'Lead us not into t ... but – but – we are so poor, so poor ! ... Lead us not into ... Ah, who would be hurt by it? – and no one would ever know. ... Lead us. ...' The voice died out in mumblings. After a little she glanced up and muttered in a half-frightened, half-glad way –

'He is gone ! But, oh dear, he may be too late – too late. ... Maybe not – maybe there is still time.' She rose and stood thinking, nervously clasping and unclasping her hands. A slight shudder shook her frame, and she said, out of a dry throat, 'God forgive me – it's awful to think such things – but ... Lord, how we are made – how strangely we are made!'

She turned the light low, and slipped stealthily over and kneeled down by the sack and felt of its ridgy sides with her hands, and fondled them lovingly; and there was a gloating light in her poor old eyes. She fell into fits of absence; and came half out of them at times to mutter, 'If we had only waited! – oh, if we had only waited a little, and not been in such a hurry!'

Meantime Cox had gone home from his office and told his wife all about the strange thing that had happened, and they had talked it over eagerly, and guessed that the late Goodson was the only man in the town who could have helped a suffering stranger with so noble a sum as twenty dollars. Then there was a pause, and the two became thoughtful and silent. And by-and-by nervous and fidgety. At last the wife, said, as if to herself,

'Nobody knows this secret but the Richardses ... and us ... nobody.'

The husband came out of his thinkings with a slight start, and gazed wistfully at his wife, whose face was become very pale; then he hesitatingly rose, and glanced furtively at his hat, then at his wife – a sort of mute inquiry. Mrs Cox swallowed once or twice, with her hand at her throat, then in place of speech she nodded her head. In a moment she was alone, and mumbling to herself.

And now Richards and Cox were hurrying through the deserted streets from opposite directions. They met, panting, at the foot of the printing-office stairs; by the nightlights there they read each other's face. Cox whispered,

'Nobody knows about this but us?'

The whispered answer was,

'Not a soul – on honor, not a soul!'

'If it isn't too late to –'

The men were starting up-stairs; at this moment they were overtaken by a boy, and Cox asked,

'Is that you, Johnny?'

'Yes, sir.'

'You needn't ship the early mail – nor *any* mail; wait till I tell you.'

'It's already gone, sir.'

'*Gone?*' It had the sound of an unspeakable disappointment in it.

'Yes, sir. Time-table for Brixton and all the towns beyond changed today, sir – had to get the papers in twenty minutes earlier than common. I had to rush; if I had been two minutes later –'

The men turned and walked slowly away, not waiting to hear the rest. Neither of them spoke during ten minutes; then Cox said, in a vexed tone,

'What possessed you to be in such a hurry, *I* can't make out.'

The answer was humble enough:

'I see it now, but somehow I never thought, you know, until it was too late. But the next time –'

'Next time be hanged! It won't come in a thousand years.'

Then the friends separated without a good night, and dragged themselves home with the gait of mortally stricken men. At their homes their wives sprang up with an eager 'Well?' – then saw the answer with their eyes and sank down sorrowing, without waiting for it to come in words. In both houses a discussion followed of a heated sort – a new thing; there had been discussions before, but not heated ones, not ungentle ones. The discussions tonight were a sort of seeming plagiarisms of each other. Mrs Richards said,

'If you had only waited, Edward – if you had only stopped to think; but no, you must run straight to the printing-office and spread it all over the world.'

'It *said* publish it.'

'That is nothing; it also said do it privately, if you liked. There now – is that true, or not?'

'Why, yes – yes, it is true; but when I thought what a stir it would make, and what a compliment it was to Hadleyburg that a stranger should trust it so –'

'Oh, certainly, I know all that; but if you had only stopped to think, you would have seen that you *couldn't* find the right man, because he is in his grave, and hasn't left chick nor child nor relation behind him; and as long as the money went to somebody that awfully needed it, and nobody would be hurt by it, and – and –'

She broke down, crying. Her husband tried to think of some comforting thing to say, and presently came out with this:

'But after all, Mary, it must be for the best – it *must* be; we know that. And we must remember that it was so ordered –'

'Ordered! Oh, everything's *ordered*, when a person has to find some way out when he has been stupid. Just the same, it was *ordered* that the money should come to us in this special way, and it was you that must take it on yourself to go meddling with the designs of Providence – and who gave you the right? It was wicked, that is what it was – just blasphemous presumption, and no more becoming to a meek and humble professor of –'

'But, Mary, you know how we have been trained all our lives long, like the whole village, till it is absolutely second nature to us to stop not a single moment to think when there's an honest thing to be done –'

'Oh, I know it, I know it – it's been one everlasting training and training and training in honesty – honesty shielded, from the very cradle, against every possible temptation, and so it's *artificial* honesty, and weak as water when temptation comes, as we have seen this night. God knows I never had shade nor shadow of a doubt of my petrified and indestructible honesty until now – and now, under the very first big and real temptation, I – Edward, it is my belief that this town's honesty is as rotten as mine is; as rotten as yours is. It is a mean town, a hard, stingy town, and hasn't a virtue in the world but this honesty it is so celebrated for and so conceited about; and so help me, I do believe that if ever the day comes that its honesty falls under great temptation, its grand reputation will go to ruin like a house of cards. There, now, I've made confession, and I feel better; I am a humbug, and I've been one all my life, without knowing it. Let no man call me honest again – I will not have it.'

'I – well, Mary, I feel a good deal as you do; I certainly do. It

seems strange, too, so strange. I never could have believed it –
never.'

A long silence followed; both were sunk in thought. At last
the wife looked up and said,

'I know what you are thinking, Edward.'

Richards had the embarrassed look of a person who is caught.

'I am ashamed to to confess it, Mary, but –'

'It's no matter, Edward, I was thinking the same question
myself.'

'I hope so. State it.'

'You were thinking, if a body could only guess out *what the
remark was* that Goodson made to the stranger.'

'It's perfectly true. I feel guilty and ashamed. And you?'

'I'm past it. Let us make a pallet here; we've got to stand
watch till the bank vault opens in the morning and admits the
sack. ... Oh, dear, oh, dear – if we hadn't made the mistake!'

The pallet was made, and Mary said:

'The open sesame – what could it have been? I do wonder
what that remark could have been? But come; we will get to
bed now.'

'And sleep?'

'No; think.'

'Yes, think.'

By this time the Coxes too had completed their spat and their
reconciliation, and were turning in – to think, to think, and toss,
and fret, and worry over what the remark could possibly have
been which Goodson made to the stranded derelict: that golden
remark; that remark worthy forty thousand dollars, cash.

The reason that the village telegraph-office was open later
than usual that night was this: The foreman of Cox's paper
was the local representative of the Associated Press. One might
say its honorary representative, for it wasn't four times a year
that he could furnish thirty words that would be accepted. But
this time it was different. His despatch stating what he had
caught got an instant answer:

'*Send the whole thing – all the details – twelve hundred
words.*'

A colossal order! The foreman filled the bill; and he was the proudest man in the State. By breakfast-time the next morning the name of Hadleyburg the Incorruptible was on every lip in America, from Montreal to the Gulf, from the glaciers of Alaska to the orange-groves of Florida; and millions and millions of people were discussing the stranger and his money-sack, and wondering if the right man would be found, and hoping some more news about the matter would come soon – right away.

2

Hadleyburg village woke up world-celebrated – astonished – happy – vain. Vain beyond imagination. Its nineteen principal citizens and their wives went about shaking hands with each other, and beaming, and smiling, and congratulating, and saying *this* thing adds a new word to the dictionary – *Hadleyburg*, synonym for *incorruptible* – destined to live in dictionaries forever! And the minor and unimportant citizens and their wives went around acting in much the same way. Everybody ran to the bank to see the gold-sack; and before noon grieved and envious crowds began to flock in from Brixton and all neighboring towns; and that afternoon and next day reporters began to arrive from everywhere to verify the sack and its history and write the whole thing up anew, and make dashing free-hand pictures of the sack and of Richard's house, and the bank, and the Presbyterian church, and the Baptist church, and the public square, and the town-hall where the test would be applied and the money delivered; and damnable portraits of the Richardses, and Pinkerton the banker, and Cox, and the foreman, and Reverend Burgess, and the postmaster – and even of Jack Halliday, who was the loafing, good-natured, no-account, irreverent fisherman, hunter, boys' friend, stray-dogs' friend, typical 'Sam Lawson' of the town. The little mean, smirking, oily Pinkerton showed the sack to all comers, and rubbed his sleek palms together pleasantly, and enlarged upon the town's fine old reputation for honesty and upon this wonderful endorsement of it, and hoped and believed that the example would now spread far and wide over the American world, and be epoch-making in the matter of moral regeneration. And so on, and so on.

By the end of a week things had quieted down again; the wild intoxication of pride and joy had sobered to a soft, sweet, silent delight – a sort of deep, nameless, unutterable content. All faces bore a look of peaceful, holy happiness.

Then a change came. It was a gradual change: so gradual that its beginnings were hardly noticed; maybe were not noticed at all, except by Jack Halliday, who always noticed everything; and always made fun of it, too, no matter what it was. He began to throw out chaffing remarks about people not looking quite so happy as they did a day or two ago; and next he claimed that the new aspect was deepening to positive sadness; next, that it was taking on a sick look; and finally he said that everybody was become so moody, thoughtful, and absent-minded that he could rob the meanest man in town of a cent out of the bottom of his breeches pocket and not disturb his revery.

At this stage – or at about this stage – a saying like this was dropped at bedtime – with a sigh, usually – by the head of each of the nineteen principal households:

'Ah, what *could* have been the remark that Goodson made!'

And straightway – with a shudder – came this, from the man's wife:

'Oh, *don't*! What horrible thing are you mulling in your mind? Put it away from you, for God's sake!'

But that question was wrung from those men again the next night – and got the same retort. But weaker.

And the third night the men uttered the question yet again – with anguish, and absently. This time – and the following night – the wives fidgeted feebly, and tried to say something. But didn't.

And the night after that they found their tongues and responded – longingly.

'Oh, if we *could* only guess!'

Halliday's comments grew daily more and more sparkingly disagreeable and disparaging. He went diligently about, laughing at the town, individually and in mass. But his laugh was the only one left in the village: it fell upon a hollow and mournful vacancy and emptiness. Not even a smile was findable anywhere. Halliday carried a cigar-box around on a tripod, playing that it was a camera, and halted all passers and aimed the thing and said, 'Ready! – now look pleasant, please,' but not even this capital joke could surprise the dreary faces into any softening.

So three weeks passed – one week was left. It was Saturday evening – after supper. Instead of the aforetime Saturday-evening flutter and bustle and shopping and larking, the streets were empty and desolate. Richards and his old wife sat apart in their little parlor – miserable and thinking. This was become their evening habit now: the life-long habit which had preceded it, of reading, knitting, and contented chat, or receiving or paying neighborly calls, was dead and gone and forgotten, ages ago – two or three weeks ago; nobody talked now, nobody read, nobody visited – the whole village sat at home, sighing, worrying, silent. Trying to guess out that remark.

The postman left a letter. Richards glanced listlessly at the superscription and the post-mark – unfamiliar, both – and tossed the letter on the table and resumed his might-have-beens and his hopeless dull miseries where he had left them off. Two or three hours later his wife got wearily up and was going away to bed without a good night – custom now – but she stopped near the letter and eyed it awhile with a dead interest, then broke it open, and began to skim it over. Richards, sitting there with his chair tilted back against the wall and his chin between his knees, heard something fall. It was his wife. He sprang to her side, but she cried out:

'Leave me alone, I am too happy. Read the letter – read it!'

He did. He devoured it, his brain reeling. The letter was from a distant State, and it said:

I am a stranger to you, but no matter: I have something to tell. I have just arrived home from Mexico, and learned about that episode. Of course you do not know who made that remark, but I know, and I am the only person living who does know. It was GOODSON. I knew him well, many years ago. I passed through your village that very night, and was his guest till the midnight train came along. I overheard him make that remark to the stranger in the dark – it was in Hale Alley. He and I talked of it the rest of the way home, and while smoking in his house. He mentioned many of your villagers in the course of his talk – most of them in a very uncomplimentary way, but two or three favorably: among these latter yourself. I say 'favorably' – nothing stronger. I remember his saying he did not actually L I K E any person in the town – not one, but that you – I T H I N K he said you – am almost sure – had done him a very great service once, possibly without knowing the full value of it, and he wished he had a fortune, he would leave it to you when he died, and a curse apiece for the rest of the citizens. Now, then, if it was you that did him that service, you are his legitimate heir, and entitled to the sack of gold. I know that I can trust to your honor and honesty, for in a citizen of Hadleyburg these virtues are an unfailing inheritance, and so I am going to reveal to you the remark, well satisfied that if you are not the right man you will seek and find the right one and see that poor Goodson's debt of gratitude for the service referred to is paid. This is the remark: 'YOU ARE FAR FROM BEING A BAD MAN: GO, AND REFORM.'

'HOWARD L. STEPHENSON.'

'Oh, Edward, the money is ours, and I am so grateful, *oh*, so grateful – kiss me, dear, it's forever since we kissed – and we needed it so – the money – and now you are free of Pinkerton and his bank, and nobody's slave any more; it seems to me I could fly for joy.'

It was a happy half-hour that the couple spent there on the settee caressing each other; it was the old days come again– days that had begun with their courtship and lasted without a break till the stranger brought the deadly money. By-and-by the wife said:

'Oh, Edward, how lucky it was you did him that grand service, poor Goodson! I never liked him, but I love him now. And it was fine and beautiful of you never to mention it or brag about it.' Then, with a touch of reproach, 'But you ought to have told *me*, Edward, you ought to have told your wife, you know.'

'Well, I – er – well, Mary, you see –'

'Now stop hemming and hawing, and tell me about it, Edward. I always loved you, and now I'm proud of you. Everybody believes there was only one good generous soul in this village, and now it turns out that you – Edward, why don't you tell me?'

'Well – er – er – Why, Mary, I can't!'

'You *can't*? *Why* can't you?'

'You see, he – well, he – he made me promise I wouldn't.'

The wife looked him over, and said, very slowly,

'Made – you – promise? Edward, what do you tell me that for?'

'Mary, do you think I would lie?'

She was troubled and silent for a moment, then she laid her hand within his and said:

'No ... no. We have wandered far enough from our bearings – God spare us that! In all your life you have never uttered a lie. But now – now that the foundations of things seem to be crumbling from under us, we – we –' She lost her voice for a moment, then said, brokenly, 'Lead us not into temptation. ... I think you made the promise, Edward. Let it rest so. Let us keep away from that ground. Now – that is all gone by; let us be happy again; it is no time for clouds.'

Edward found it something of an effort to comply, for his mind kept wandering – trying to remember what the service was that he had done Goodson.

The couple lay awake the most of the night, Mary happy and busy, Edward busy, but not so happy. Mary was planning what she would do with the money. Edward was trying to recall that service. At first his conscience was sore on account of the lie he had told Mary – if it was a lie. After much reflection – suppose it *was* a lie? What then? Was it such a great matter? Aren't we always *acting* lies? Then why not *tell* them? Look at Mary – look what she had done. While he was hurrying off on his honest errand, what was she doing? Lamenting because the papers hadn't been destroyed and the money kept! Is theft better than lying?

That point lost its sting – the lie dropped into the background and left comfort behind it. The next point came to the front: *had* he rendered that service? Well, here was Goodson's own evidence as reported in Stephenson's letter; there could be no better evidence than that – it was even *proof* that he had rendered it. Of course. So that point was settled. ... No, not quite. He recalled with a wince that this unknown Mr Stephenson was

just a trifle unsure as to whether the performer of it was Richards
or some other – and, oh dear, he had put Richards on his honor !
He must himself decide whither that money must go – and
Mr Stephenson was not doubting that if he was the wrong man
he would go honorably and find the right one. Oh, it was odious
to put a man in such a situation – ah, why couldn't Stephenson
have left out that doubt ! What did he want to intrude that for?

Further reflection. How did it happen that *Richards's* name
remained in Stephenson's mind as indicating the right man, and
not some other man's name? That looked good. Yes, that looked
very good. In fact, it went on looking better and better, straight
along – until by-and-by it grew into positive *proof*. And then
Richards put the matter at once out of his mind, for he had a
private instinct that a proof once established is better left so.

He was feeling reasonably comfortable now, but there was
still one other detail that kept pushing itself on his notice: of
course he had done that service – that was settled; but what *was*
that service? He must recall it – he would not go to sleep till he
had recalled it; it would make his peace of mind perfect. And
so he thought and thought. He thought of a dozen things –
possible services, even probable services – but none of them
seemed adequate, none of them seemed large enough, none of
them seemed worth the money – worth the fortune Goodson
had wished he could leave in his will. And besides, he couldn't
remember having done them, anyway. Now, then – now, then
– what *kind* of a service would it be that would make a man so
inordinately grateful? Ah – the saving of his soul ! That must
be it. Yes, he could remember, now, how he once set himself
the task of converting Goodson, and labored at it as much as –
he was going to say three months; but upon closer examination
it shrunk to a month, then to a week, then to a day, then to
nothing. Yes, he remembered now, and with unwelcome vivid-
ness, that Goodson had told him to go to thunder and mind his
own business – *he* wasn't hankering to follow Hadleyburg to
heaven !

So that solution was a failure – he hadn't saved Goodson's
soul. Richards was discouraged. Then after a little came another
idea: had he saved Goodson's property? No, that wouldn't do

THE MAN THAT CORRUPTED HADLEYBURG

– he hadn't any. His life? That is it! Of course. Why, he might have thought of it before. This time he was on the right track, sure. His imagination-mill was hard at work in a minute, now.

Thereafter during a stretch of two exhausting hours he was busy saving Goodson's life. He saved it in all kinds of difficult and perilous ways. In every case he got it saved satisfactorily up to a certain point; then, just as he was beginning to get well persuaded that it had really happened, a troublesome detail would turn up which made the whole thing impossible. As in the matter of drowning, for instance. In that case he had swum out and tugged Goodson ashore in an unconscious state with a great crowd looking on and applauding, but when he had got it all thought out and was just beginning to remember all about it a whole swarm of disqualifying details arrived on the ground: the town would have known of it, it would glare like a limelight in his own memory instead of being an inconspicuous service which he had possibly rendered 'without knowing its full value'. And at this point he remembered that he couldn't swim, anyway.

Ah – *there* was a point which he had been overlooking from the start: it had to be a service which he had rendered 'possibly without knowing the full value of it'. Why, really, that ought to be an easy hunt – much easier than those others. And sure enough, by-and-by he found it. Goodson, years and years ago, came near marrying a very sweet and pretty girl, named Nancy Hewitt, but in some way or other the match had been broken off; the girl died, Goodson remained a bachelor, and by-and-by became a soured one and a frank despiser of the human species. Soon after the girl's death the village found out, or thought it had found out, that she carried a spoonful of negro blood in her veins. Richards worked at these details a good while, and in the end he thought he remembered things concerning them which must have gotten mislaid in his memory through long neglect. He seemed to dimly remember that it was *he* that found out about the negro blood; that it was he that told the village; that the village told Goodson where they got it; that he thus saved Goodson from marrying the tainted girl; that he had done him this great service 'without knowing the full value of it', in fact without knowing that he *was* doing it; but Goodson knew the value of it, and what a narrow escape he had had, and so went to his grave grateful to his benefactor and wishing he had a fortune to leave him. It was all clear and simple now, and the more he went over it the more luminous and certain it grew; and at last, when he nestled to sleep satisfied and happy, he remembered the whole thing just as if it had been yesterday. In fact, he dimly remembered Goodson's *telling* him his gratitude once. Meantime Mary had spent six thousand dollars on a new house for herself and a pair of slippers for her pastor, and then had fallen peacefully to rest.

That same Saturday evening the postman had delivered a letter to each of the other principal citizens – nineteen letters in all. No two of the envelopes were alike, and no two of the superscriptions were in the same hand, but the letters inside were just like each other in every detail but one. They were exact copies of the letter received by Richards – handwriting and all – and were all signed by Stephenson, but in place of Richards's name each receiver's own name appeared.

All night long eighteen principal citizens did what their caste-brother Richards was doing at the same time – they put in their energies trying to remember what notable service it was that they had unconsciously done Barclay Goodson. In no case was it a holiday job; still they succeeded.

And while they were at this work, which was difficult, their wives put in the night spending the money, which was easy. During that one night the nineteen wives spent an average of seven thousand dollars each out of the forty thousand in the sack – a hundred and thirty-three thousand altogether.

Next day there was a surprise for Jack Halliday. He noticed that the faces of the nineteen chief citizens and their wives bore that expression of peaceful and holy happiness again. He could not understand it, neither was he able to invent any remarks about it that could damage it or disturb it. And so it was his turn to be dissatisfied with life. His private guesses at the reasons for the happiness failed in all instances, upon examination. When he met Mrs Wilcox and noticed the placid ecstasy in her face, he said to himself, 'Her cat has had kittens' – and went and asked the cook; it was not so; the cook had detected the happiness, but did not know the cause. When Halliday found the duplicate ecstasy in the face of 'Shadbelly' Billson (village nickname), he was sure some neighbor of Billson's had broken his leg, but inquiry showed that this had not happened. The subdued ecstasy in Gregory Yates's face could mean but one thing – he was a mother-in-law short; it was another mistake. 'And Pinkerton – Pinkerton – he has collected ten cents that he thought he was going to lose.' And so on, and so on. In some cases the guesses had to remain in doubt, in the others, they proved distinct errors. In the end Halliday said to himself, 'Anyway, it foots up that there's nineteen Hadleyburg families temporarily in heaven: I don't know how it happened; I only know Providence is off duty today.'

An architect and builder from the next State had lately ventured to set up a small business in this unpromising village, and his sign had now been hanging out a week. Not a customer yet; he was a discouraged man, and sorry he had come. But his weather changed suddenly now. First one and then another chief citizen's wife said to him privately:

'Come to my house Monday week – but say nothing about it for the present. We think of building.'

He got eleven invitations that day. That night he wrote his daughter and broke off her match with her student. He said she could marry a mile higher than that.

Pinkerton the banker and two or three other well-to-do men planned country-seats – but waited. That kind don't count their chickens until they are hatched.

The Wilsons devised a grand new thing – a fancy-dress ball. They made no actual promises, but told all their acquaintance-ship in confidence that they were thinking the matter over and thought they should give it – 'and if we do, you will be invited, of course.' People were surprised, and said, one to another, 'Why, they are crazy, those poor Wilsons, they can't afford it.' Several among the nineteen said privately to their husbands, 'It is a good idea, we will keep still till their cheap thing is over, then *we* will give one that will make it sick.'

The days drifted along, and the bill of future squanderings
rose higher and higher, wilder and wilder, more and more
foolish and reckless. It began to look as if every member of the
nineteen would not only spend his whole forty thousand dollars
before receiving-day, but be actually in debt by the time he got
the money. In some cases light-headed people did not stop with
planning to spend, they really spent – on credit. They bought
land, mortgages, farms, speculative stocks, fine clothes, horses,
and various other things, paid down the bonus, and made themselves liable for the rest – at ten days. Presently the sober second
thought came, and Halliday noticed that a ghastly anxiety was
beginning to show up in a good many faces. Again he was
puzzled, and didn't know what to make of it. 'The Wilcox kittens aren't dead, for they weren't born; nobody's broken a leg;
there's no shrinkage in mother-in-laws; *nothing* has happened –
it is an insolvable mystery.'

There was another puzzled man, too – the Rev. Mr Burgess.
For days, wherever he went, people seemed to follow him or to
be watching out for him; and if he ever found himself in a retired spot, a member of the nineteen would be sure to appear,
thrust an envelope privately into his hand, whisper 'To be
opened at the town-hall Friday evening', then vanish away like
a guilty thing. He was expecting that there might be one
claimant for the sack – doubtful, however, Goodson being dead
– but it never occurred to him that all this crowd might be
claimants. When the great Friday came at last, he found that he
had nineteen envelopes.

3

The town-hall had never looked finer. The platform at the end
of it was backed by a showy draping of flags; at intervals along
the walls were festoons of flags; the gallery fronts were clothed
in flags; the supporting columns were swathed in flags; all this
was to impress the stranger, for he would be there in considerable force, and in a large degree he would be connected with the
press. The house was full. The 412 fixed seats were occupied;
also the 68 extra chairs which had been packed into the aisles;

the steps of the platform were occupied; some distinguished strangers were given seats on the platform; at the horseshoe of tables which fenced the front and sides of the platform sat a strong force of special correspondents who had come from everywhere. It was the best-dressed house the town had ever produced. There were some tolerably expensive toilets there, and in several cases the ladies who wore them had the look of being unfamiliar with that kind of clothes. At least the town thought they had that look, but the notion could have arisen from the town's knowledge of the fact that these ladies had never inhabited such clothes before.

The gold-sack stood on a little table at the front of the platform where all the house could see it. The bulk of the house gazed at it with a burning interest, a mouth-watering interest, a wistful and pathetic interest; a minority of nineteen couples gazed at it tenderly, lovingly, proprietarily, and the male half of this minority kept saying over to themselves the moving little impromptu speeches of thankfulness for the audience's applause and congratulations which they were presently going to get up and deliver. Every now and then one of these got a piece of paper out of his vest pocket and privately glanced at it to refresh his memory.

Of course there was a buzz of conversation going on – there always is; but at last when the Rev. Mr Burgess rose and laid his hand on the sack he could hear his microbes gnaw, the place was so still. He related the curious history of the sack, then went on to speak in warm terms of Hadleyburg's old and well-earned reputation for spotless honesty, and of the town's just pride in this reputation. He said that this reputation was a treasure of priceless value; that under Providence its value had now become inestimably enhanced, for the recent episode had spread this fame far and wide, and thus had focussed the eyes of the American world upon this village, and made its name for all time, as he hoped and believed, a synonym for commercial incorruptibility. [*Applause.*] 'And who is to be the guardian of this noble treasure – the community as a whole? No! The responsibility is individual, not communal. From this day forth each and every one of you is in his own person its special guardian, and individually responsible that no harm shall come to it. Do you – does each of you – accept this great trust? [*Tumultuous assent.*] Then all is well. Transmit it to your children and to your children's children. Today your purity is beyond reproach – see to it that it shall remain so. Today there is not a person in your community who could be beguiled to touch a penny not his own – see to it that you abide in this grace. ['*We will! we will!*'] This is not the place to make comparisons between ourselves and other communities – some of them ungracious toward us; they have their ways, we have ours; let us be content. [*Applause.*] I am done. Under my hand, my friend, rests a stranger's eloquent recognition of what we are: through him the world will always henceforth know what we are. We do not know who he is, but in your name I utter your gratitude, and ask you to raise your voices in indorsement.'

The house rose in a body and made the walls quake with the thunders of its thankfulness for the space of a long minute. Then it sat down, and Mr Burgess took an envelope out of his pocket. The house held its breath while he slit the envelope open and took from it a slip of paper. He read its contents – slowly and impressively – the audience listening with tranced attention to this magic document, each of whose words stood for an ingot of gold:

'"*The remark which I made to the distressed stranger was this: 'You are very far from being a bad man, go, and reform.'*"' Then he continued: 'We shall know in a moment now whether the remark here quoted corresponds with the one concealed in the sack; and if that shall prove to be so – and it undoubtedly will – this sack of gold belongs to a fellow-citizen who will henceforth stand before the nation as the symbol of the special virtue which has made our town famous throughout the land – Mr Billson!'

The house had gotten itself all ready to burst into a proper tornado of applause; but instead of doing it, it seemed stricken with a paralysis; there was a deep hush for a moment or two, then a wave of whispered murmurs swept the place – of about this tenor: '*Billson!* oh, come, this is *too* thin! twenty dollars to a stranger – or *anybody* – *Billson!* Tell it to the marines!' And now at this point the house caught its breath all of a sudden in a new access of astonishment, for it discovered that whereas in one part of the hall Deacon Billson was standing up with his head meekly bowed, in another part of it Lawyer Wilson was doing the same. There was a wondering silence now for a while. Everybody was puzzled, and nineteen couples were surprised and indignant.

Billson and Wilson turned and stared at each other. Billson asked, bitingly,

'Why do *you* rise, Mr Wilson?'

'Because I have a right to. Perhaps you will be good enough to explain to the house why *you* rise?'

'With great pleasure. Because I wrote that paper.'

'It is an impudent falsity! I wrote it myself.'

It was Burgess's turn to be paralysed. He stood looking vacantly at first one of the men and then the other, and did not seem to know what to do. The house was stupefied. Lawyer Wilson spoke up, now, and said,

'I ask the Chair to read the name signed to that paper.'

That brought the Chair to itself, and it read out the name,

' "John Wharton *Billson*." '

'There!' shouted Billson, 'what have you got to say for yourself, now? And what kind of apology are you going to make to me and to this insulted house for the imposture which you have attempted to play here?'

'No apologies are due, sir; and as for the rest of it, I publicly charge you with pilfering my note from Mr Burgess and substituting a copy of it signed with your own name. There is no other way by which you could have gotten hold of the test-remark; I alone, of living men, possessed the secret of its wording.'

There was likely to be a scandalous state of things if this went on; everybody noticed with distress that the short-hand scribes were scribbling like mad; many people were crying 'Chair, Chair! Order! order!' Burgess rapped with his gavel, and said:

'Let us not forget the proprieties due. There has evidently been a mistake somewhere, but surely that is all. If Mr Wilson gave me an envelope – and I remember now that he did – I still have it.'

He took one out of his pocket, opened it, glanced at it, looked surprised and worried, and stood silent a few moments. Then he waved his hand in a wandering and mechanical way, and made an effort or two to say something, then gave it up despondently. Several voices cried out:

'Read it! read it! What is it?'

So he began in a dazed and sleep-walker fashion:

' "The remark which I made to the unhappy stranger was this: 'You are far from being a bad man. [The house gazed at him, marvelling.] Go, and reform." '

[*Murmurs*: 'Amazing! What can this mean?'] This one,' said the Chair, 'is signed Thurlow G. Wilson.'

'There!' cried Wilson, 'I reckon that settles it! I knew perfectly well my note was purloined.'

'Purloined!' retorted Billson. 'I'll let you know that neither you nor any man of your kidney must venture to –'

The Chair, 'Order, gentlemen, order! Take your seats, both of you, please.'

They obeyed, shaking their heads and grumbling angrily. The house was profoundly puzzled; it did not know what to do with this curious emergency. Presently Thompson got up. Thompson was the hatter. He would have liked to be a Nineteener; but such was not for him; his stock of hats was not considerable enough for the position. He said:

'Mr Chairman, if I may be permitted to make a suggestion, can both of these gentlemen be right? I put it to you, sir, can both have happened to say the very same words to the stranger? It seems to me –'

The tanner got up and interrupted him. The tanner was a disgruntled man; he believed himself entitled to be a Nineteener, but he couldn't get recognition. It made him a little unpleasant in his ways and speech. Said he:

'Sho, *that's* not the point! *That* could happen – twice in a hundred years – but not the other thing. *Neither* of them gave the twenty dollars!' [*A ripple of applause.*]

Billson. 'I did!'

Wilson. 'I did!'

Then each accused the other of pilfering.

The Chair. 'Order! Sit down, if you please – both of you. Neither of the notes has been out of my possession at any moment.'

A Voice. 'Good – that settles *that*!'

The Tanner. 'Mr Chairman, one thing is now plain: one of these men has been eavesdropping under the other one's bed, and filching family secrets. If it is not unparliamentary to suggest it, I will remark that both are equal to it. [*The Chair.* 'Order! order!'] I withdraw the remark, sir, and will confine myself to suggesting that *if* one of them has overheard the other reveal the test-remark to his wife, we shall catch him now.'

A Voice. 'How?'

The Tanner. 'Easily. The two have not quoted the remark in exactly the same words. You would have noticed that, if there hadn't been a considerable stretch of time and an exciting quarrel inserted between the two readings.'

A Voice. 'Name the difference.'

The Tanner. 'The word *very* is in Billson's note, and not in the other.'

Many Voices. 'That's so – he's right!'

The Tanner. 'And so, if the Chair will examine the test-remark in the sack, we shall know which of these two frauds – [*The Chair.* 'Order!'] – which of these two adventurers – [*The Chair.* 'Order! order!'] – which of these two gentlemen – [*laughter and applause*] – is entitled to wear the belt as being the first dishonest blatherskite ever bred in this town – which he has dishonoured, and which will be a sultry place for him from now out!' [*Vigorous applause.*]

Many Voices. 'Open it! – open the sack!'

Mr Burgess made a slit in the sack, slid his hand in and brought out an envelope. In it were a couple of folded notes. He said:

'One of these is marked, 'Not to be examined until all written communications which have been addressed to the Chair – if any – shall have been read.' The other is marked *'The Test'*. Allow me. It is worded – to wit:

" 'I do not require that the first half of the remark which was made to me by my benefactor shall be quoted with exactness, for it was not striking, and could be forgotten; but its closing fifteen words are quite striking, and I think easily rememberable; unless *these* shall be accurately reproduced, let the applicant be regarded as an impostor. My benefactor began by saying he seldom gave advice to any one, but that it always bore the hallmark of high value when he did give it. Then he said this – and it has never faded from my memory: *'You are far from being a bad man –* ' " '

Fifty Voices. 'That settles it – the money's Wilson's! Wilson! Wilson! Speech! Speech!'

People jumped up and crowded around Wilson, wringing his hand and congratulating fervently – meantime the Chair was hammering with the gavel and shouting:

'Order, gentlemen! Order! Order! Let me finish reading, please.' When quiet was restored, the reading was resumed – as follows:

' " 'Go, and reform – or, mark my words – some day, for your sins, you will die and go to hell or Hadleyburg – TRY AND MAKE IT THE FORMER.' " '

A ghastly silence followed. First an angry cloud began to settle darkly upon the faces of the citizenship; after a pause the cloud began to rise, and a tickled expression tried to take its place; tried so hard that it was only kept under with great and painful difficulty; the reporters, the Brixtonites, and other strangers bent their heads down and shielded their faces with their hands, and managed to hold in by main strength and heroic courtesy. At this most inopportune time burst upon the stillness the roar of a solitary voice – Jack Halliday's:

'That's got the hall-mark on it!'

Then the house let go, strangers and all. Even Mr Burgess's gravity broke down presently, then the audience considered itself officially absolved from all restraint, and it made the most of its privilege. It was a good long laugh, and a tempestuously

THE MAN THAT CORRUPTED HADLEYBURG

whole-hearted one, but it ceased at last – long enough for Mr Burgess to try to resume, and for the people to get their eyes partially wiped; then it broke out again; and afterward yet again; then at last Burgess was able to get out these serious words:

'It is useless to try to disguise the fact – we find ourselves in the presence of a matter of grave import. It involves the honor of your town, it strikes at the town's good name. The difference of a single word between the test-remarks offered by Mr Wilson and Mr Billson was itself a serious thing, since it indicated that one or the other of these gentlemen had committed a theft –'

The two men were sitting limp, nerveless, crushed; but at these words both were electrified into movement, and started to get up –

'Sit down!' said the Chair, sharply, and they obeyed. 'That, as I have said, was a serious thing. And it was – but for only one of them. But the matter has become graver; for the honor of *both* is now in formidable peril. Shall I go even further, and say in inextricable peril? *Both* left out the crucial fifteen words.' He paused. During several moments he allowed the pervading still-ness to gather and deepen its impressive effects, then added: 'There would seem to be but one way whereby this could hap-pen. I ask these gentlemen – Was there *collusion*? – agree-ment?'

A low murmur sifted through the house; its import was, 'He's got them both.'

Billson was not used to emergencies; he sat in a helpless col-lapse. But Wilson was a lawyer. He struggled to his feet, pale and worried, and said:

'I ask the indulgence of the house while I explain this most painful matter. I am sorry to say what I am about to say, since it must inflict irreparable injury upon Mr Billson, whom I have always esteemed and respected until now, and in whose invul-nerability to temptation I entirely believed – as did you all. But for the preservation of my own honor I must speak – and with frankness. I confess with shame – and I now beseech your par-don for it – that I said to the ruined stranger all of the words contained in the test-remark, including the disparaging fifteen.

[*Sensation.*] When the late publication was made I recalled them, and I resolved to claim the sack of coin, for by every right I was entitled to it. Now I will ask you to consider this point, and weigh it well: that stranger's gratitude to me that night knew no bounds; he said himself that he could find no words for it that were adequate, and that if he should ever be able he would repay me a thousandfold. Now, then, I ask you this: could I expect – could I believe – could I even remotely imagine – that, feeling as he did, he would do so ungrateful a thing as to add those quite unnecessary fifteen words to his test? – set a trap for me? – expose me as a slanderer of my own town before my own people assembled in a public hall? It was preposterous; it was impossible. His test would contain only the kindly opening clause of my remark. Of that I had no shadow of doubt. You would have thought as I did. You would not have expected a base betrayal from one whom you had befriended and against whom you had committed no offence. And so, with perfect confidence, perfect trust, I wrote on a piece of paper the opening words – ending with 'Go, and reform', – and signed it. When I was about to put it in an envelope I was called into my back office, and without thinking I left the paper lying open on my desk.' He stopped, turned his head slowly toward Billson, waited a moment, then added: 'I ask you to note this: when I returned, a little later, Mr Billson was retiring by my street door.' [*Sensation.*]

In a moment Billson was on his feet and shouting:
'It's a lie! It's an infamous lie!'
The Chair. 'Be seated, sir! Mr Wilson has the floor.'

Billson's friends pulled him into his seat and quieted him, and Wilson went on:

'Those are the simple facts. My note was now lying in a different place on the table from where I had left it. I noticed that, but attached no importance to it, thinking a draught had blown it there. That Mr Billson would read a private paper was a thing which could not occur to me; he was an honorable man, and he would be above that. If you will allow me to say it, I think his extra word '*very*' stands explained; it is attributable to a defect of memory. I was the only man in the world who could furnish here any detail of the test-mark – by *honorable* means. I have finished.'

There is nothing in the world like a persuasive speech to fuddle the mental apparatus and upset the convictions and debauch the emotions of an audience not practised in the tricks and delusions of oratory. Wilson sat down victorious. The house submerged him in tides of approving applause; friends swarmed to him and shook him by the hand and congratulated him, and Billson was shouted down and not allowed to say a word. The Chair hammered and hammered with its gavel, and kept shouting,

'But let us proceed, gentlemen, let us proceed!'

At last there was a measurable degree of quiet, and the hatter said,

'But what is there to proceed with, sir, but to deliver the money?'

Voices. 'That's it! That's it! Come forward, Wilson!'

The Hatter. 'I move three cheers for Mr Wilson, Symbol of the special virtue which –'

The cheers burst forth before he could finish; and in the midst of them – and in the midst of the clamor of the gavel also – some enthusiasts mounted Wilson on a big friend's shoulder and were going to fetch him in triumph to the platform. The Chair's voice now rose above the noise –

'Order! To your places! You forget that there is still a document to be read.' When quiet had been restored he took up the document, and was going to read it, but laid it down again, saying, 'I forgot; this is not to be read until all written communications received by me have first been read.' He took an envelope out of his pocket, removed its enclosure, glanced at it – seemed astonished – held it out and gazed at it – stared at it.

Twenty or thirty voices cried out:

'What is it? Read it! read it!'

And he did – slowly, and wondering:

'"The remark which I made to the stranger – [*Voices.* 'Hello! how's this?'] – was this: 'You are far from being a bad man. [*Voices.* 'Great Scott!'] Go, and reform.' " [*Voice.* 'Oh, saw my leg off!'] Signed by Mr Pinkerton the banker.'

The pandemonium of delight which turned itself loose now was of a sort to make the judicious weep. Those whose withers were unwrung laughed till the tears ran down; the reporters, in throes of laughter, set down disordered pot-hooks which would never in the world be decipherable; and a sleeping dog jumped up, scared out of its wits, and barked itself crazy at the turmoil. All manner of cries were scattered through the din: 'We're getting rich – *two* Symbols of Incorruptibility! – without counting Billson!' '*Three!* – count Shadbelly in – we can't have too many!' 'All right – Billson's elected' 'Alas, poor Wilson—victim of *two* thieves!'

A powerful Voice. 'Silence! The Chair's fished up something more out of its pocket.'

Voices. 'Hurrah! Is it something fresh? Read it! read! read!'

The Chair [*reading*]. ' "The remark which I made," etc. "You are far from being a bad man. Go," etc. Signed, "Gregory Yates." '

Tornado of Voices. 'Four Symbols!' ' 'Rah for Yates!' 'Fish again!'

The house was in a roaring humor now, and ready to get all the fun out of the occasion that might be in it. Several Nineteeners, looking pale and distressed, got up and began to work their way towards the aisles, but a score of shouts went up:

'The doors, the doors – close the doors; no Incorruptible shall leave this place! Sit down, everybody!'

The mandate was obeyed.

'Fish again! Read! read!'

The Chair fished again, and once more the familiar words began to fall from its lips – ' "You are far from being a bad man –" '

'Name! name! What's his name?'

' "L. Ingoldsby Sargent." '

'Five elected! Pile up the Symbols! Go on, go on!'

' "You are far from being a bad –" '

'Name! Name!'

' "Nicholas Whitworth." '

'Hooray! hooray! it's a symbolical day!'

Somebody wailed in, and began to sing this rhyme (leaving

out 'it's') to the lovely 'Mikado' tune of 'When a man's afraid of a beautiful maid'; the audience joined in, with joy; then, just in time, somebody contributed another line –

'And don't you this forget –'

The house roared it out. A third line was at once furnished –

'Corruptibles far from Hadleyburg are –'

The house roared that one too. As the last note died, Jack Halliday's voice rose high and clear, freighted with a final line –

'But the Symbols are here, you bet !'

That was sung, with booming enthusiasm. Then the happy house started in at the beginning and sang the four lines through twice, with immense swing and dash, and finished up with a crashing three-times-three and a tiger for 'Hadleyburg the Incorruptible and all Symbols of it which we shall find worthy to receive the hall-mark tonight.'

Then the shoutings at the Chair began again, all over the place:

'Go on ! go on ! Read ! read some more ! Read all you've got !'

'That's it – go on ! We are winning eternal celebrity !'

A dozen men got up now and began to protest. They said that this farce was the work of some abandoned joker, and was an insult to the whole community. Without a doubt these signatures were all forgeries –

'Sit down ! sit down ! Shut up ! You are confessing. We'll find *your* names in the lot.'

'Mr Chairman, how many of those envelopes have you got?'

The Chair counted.

'Together with those that have been already examined, there are nineteen.'

A storm of derisive applause broke out.

'Perhaps they all contain the secret. I move that you open

them all and read every signature that is attached to a note of that sort – and read also the first eight words of the note.'

'Second the motion'

It was put and carried – uproariously. Then poor old Richards got up, and his wife rose and stood at his side. Her head was bent down, so that none might see that she was crying. Her husband gave her his arm, and so supporting her, he began to speak in a quavering voice:

'My friends, you have known us two – Mary and me – all our lives, and I think you have liked us and respected us –'

The Chair interrupted him.

'Allow me. It is quite true – that which you are saying, Mr Richards; this town *does* know you two; it *does* like you; it *does* respect you; more – it honors you and *loves* you –'

Halliday's voice rang out:

'That's the hall-marked truth, too! If the Chair is right, let the house speak up and say it. Rise! Now, then – hip! hip! hip! – all together!'

The house rose in mass, faced toward the old couple eagerly, filled the air with a snow-storm of waving handkerchiefs, and delivered the cheers with all its affectionate heart.

The Chair then continued:

'What I was going to say is this: We know your good heart, Mr Richards, but this is not a time for the exercise of charity toward offenders. [Shouts of 'Right! right!'] I see your generous purpose in your face, but I cannot allow you to plead for these men –'

'But I was going to –

'Please take your seat, Mr Richards. We must examine the rest of these notes – simple fairness to the men who have already been exposed requires this. As soon as that has been done – I give you my word for this – you shall be heard.'

Many Voices. 'Right! – the Chair is right – no interruption can be permitted at this stage! Go on! – the names! the names! – according to the terms of the motion!'

The old couple sat reluctantly down, and the husband whispered to the wife, 'It is pitifully hard to have to wait; the shame will be greater than ever when they find we were only going to plead for *ourselves*.'

Straightway the jollity broke loose again with the reading of the names.

'"You are far from being a bad man –" Signature, "Robert J. Titmarsh."

'"You are far from being a bad man –" Signature, "Eliphalet Weeks."

'"You are far from being a bad man –" Signature, "Oscar B. Wilder."

At this point the house lit upon the idea of taking the eight words out of the Chairman's hands. He was not unthankful for that. Thenceforward he held up each note in its turn, and waited. The house droned out the eight words in a massed and measured and musical deep volume of sound (with a daringly close resemblance to a well-known church chant) – '"You are f-a-r from being a b-a-a-a-d man."' Then the Chair said, 'Signature, "Archibald Wilcox."' And so on, and so on, name after name, and everybody had an increasingly and gloriously good time except the wretched Nineteen. Now and then, when a particularly shining name was called, the house made the Chair wait while it chanted the whole of the test-remark from the beginning to the closing words, 'And go to hell or Hadleyburg – try and make it the for-or-m-e-r l' and in these special cases they added a grand and agonized and imposing 'A-a-a-*men* l'

The list dwindled, dwindled, dwindled, poor old Richards keeping tally of the count, wincing when a name resembling his own was pronounced, and waiting in miserable suspense for the time to come when it would be his humiliating privilege to rise with Mary and finish his plea, which he was intending to word thus: '... for until now we have never done any wrong thing, but have gone our humble way unreproached. We are very poor, we are old, and have no chick nor child to help us; we were sorely tempted, and we fell. It was my purpose when I got up before to make confession and beg that my name might not be read out in this public place, for it seemed to us that we could not bear it; but I was prevented. It was just; it was our place to suffer with the rest. It has been hard for us. It is the first time we have ever heard our name fall from any one's lips – sullied. Be merciful – for the sake of the better days; make our shame as light to bear as in your charity you can.' At this point in his revery Mary nudged him, perceiving that his mind was absent. The house was chanting, 'You are f-a-r,' etc.

'Be ready,' Mary whispered. 'Your name comes now; he has read eighteen.'

The chant ended.

'Next! next! next!' came volleying from all over the house.

Burgess put his hand into his pocket. The old couple, trembling, began to rise. Burgess fumbled a moment, then said,

'I find I have read them all.'

Faint with joy and surprise, the couple sank into their seats, and Mary whispered,

'Oh, bless God, we are saved! – he has lost ours – I wouldn't give this for a hundred of those sacks!'

The house burst out with its 'Mikado' travesty, and sang it three times with ever-increasing enthusiasm, rising to its feet when it reached for the third time the closing line –

'But the Symbols are here, you bet!'

and finishing up with cheers and a tiger for 'Hadleyburg purity and our eighteen immortal representatives of it.'

Then Wingate, the saddler, got up and proposed cheers 'for the cleanest man in town, the one solitary important citizen in it who didn't try to steal that money – Edward Richards.'

They were given with great and moving heartiness; then somebody proposed that Richards be elected sole Guardian and Symbol of the now Sacred Hadleyburg Tradition, with power and right to stand up and look the whole sarcastic world in the face.

Passed, by acclamation; then they sang the 'Mikado' again, and ended it with,

'And there's one Symbol left, you bet!'

There was a pause; then –

A Voice. 'Now, then, who's to get the sack?'

The Tanner [*with bitter sarcasm*]. 'That's easy. The money has to be divided among the eighteen Incorruptibles. They gave the suffering stranger twenty dollars apiece – and that remark – each in his turn – it took twenty-two minutes for the procession to move past. Staked the stranger – total contribution, $360. All they want is just the loan back – and interest – forty thousand dollars altogether.'

Many Voices [*derisively*]. 'That's it! Divvy! divvy! Be kind to the poor – don't keep them waiting!'

The Chair. 'Order! I now offer the stranger's remaining document. It says: "If no claimant shall appear [*grand chorus of groans*], I desire that you open the sack and count out the money to the principal citizens of your town, they to take it in trust [*Cries of 'Oh! Oh! Oh!'*], and use it in such ways as to them shall seem best for the propagation and preservation of your community's noble reputation for incorruptible honesty [*more cries*] – a reputation to which their names and their efforts will add a new and far-reaching luster.' [*Enthusiastic outburst of sarcastic applause.*] That seems to be all. No – here is a postscript:

"'P.S. – CITIZENS OF HADLEYBURG: There *is* no test-remark – nobody made one. [*Great sensation.*] There wasn't any pauper stranger, nor any twenty-dollar contribution, nor any accompanying benediction and compliment – these are all inventions. [*General buzz and hum of astonishment and delight.*] Allow me to tell my story – it will take but a word or two. I passed through your town at a certain time, and received a deep offense which I had not earned. Any other man would have been content to kill one or two of you and call it square, but to me that would have been a trivial revenge, and inadequate; for the dead do not *suffer*. Besides, I could not kill you all – and, anyway, made as I am, even that would not have satisfied me. I wanted to damage every man in the place, and every woman – and not in their bodies or in their estate, but in their vanity – the place where feeble and foolish people are most vulnerable. So I disguised myself and came back and studied you. You were easy game. You had an old and lofty reputation for honesty, and naturally you were proud of it – it was your treasure of treasures, the very apple of your eye. As soon as I found out that you carefully and vigilantly kept yourselves and your children *out of temptation*, I knew how to proceed. Why, you simple creatures, the weakest of all weak things is a virtue which has not been tested in the fire. I laid a plan, and gathered a list of names. My project was to corrupt Hadleyburg the Incorruptible. My idea was to make liars and thieves of nearly half a hundred smirchless men and women who had never in their lives uttered a lie or stolen a penny. I was afraid of Goodson. He was neither born nor reared in Hadleyburg. I was afraid that if I started to operate my scheme by getting my letter laid before you, you would say to yourselves, 'Goodson is the only man among us who would give away twenty dollars to a poor devil' – and then you might not bite at my bait. But Heaven took Goodson; then I knew I was safe, and I set my trap and baited it. It may be that I shall not catch all the men to whom I mailed the pretended test secret, but I shall catch the most of them, if I know Hadleyburg nature. [*Voices.* 'Right – he got every last one of them.'] I believe they will even steal ostensible *gamble*-money, rather than miss, poor, tempted, and mistrained fellows. I am hoping to eternally and everlastingly squelch your vanity and give Hadleyburg a new renown – one that will *stick* – and spread far. If I have succeeded, open the sack and summon the Committee on Propagation and Preservation of the Hadleyburg Reputation." '

A Cyclone of Voices. 'Open it! Open it! The Eighteen to the front! Committee on Propagation of the Tradition! Forward – the Incorruptibles!'

The Chair ripped the sack wide, and gathered up a handful of bright, broad, yellow coins, shook them together, then examined them –

'Friends, they are only gilded disks of lead!'

There was a crashing outbreak of delight over this news, and when the noise had subsided, the tanner called out:

'By right of apparent seniority in this business, Mr Wilson is Chairman of the Committee on Propagation of the Tradition. I suggest that he step forward on behalf of his pals, and receive in trust the money.'

A Hundred Voices. 'Wilson! Wilson! Wilson! Speech! Speech!'

Wilson [*in a voice trembling with anger*]. 'You will allow me to say, and without apologies for my language, *damn* the money!'

A Voice. 'Oh, and him a Baptist!'

A Voice. 'Seventeen Symbols left! Step up, gentlemen, and assume your trust!'

There was a pause – no response.

The Saddler. 'Mr Chairman, we've got *one* clean man left, anyway, out of the late aristocracy; and he needs money, and deserves it. I move that you appoint Jack Halliday to get up there and auction off that sack of gilt twenty-dollar pieces, and give the result to the right man – the man whom Hadleyburg delights to honor – Edward Richards.'

This was received with great enthusiasm, the dog taking a hand again; the saddler started the bids at a dollar, the Brixton folk and Barnum's representative fought hard for it, the people cheered every jump that the bids made, the excitement climbed moment by moment higher and higher, the bidders got on their mettle and grew steadily more and more daring, more and more determined, the jumps went from a dollar up to five, then to ten, then to twenty, then fifty, then to a hundred, then –

At the beginning of the auction Richards whispered in distress to his wife: 'Oh, Mary, can we allow it? It – it – you see, it is an honor-reward, a testimonial to purity of character, and – and – can we allow it? Hadn't I better get up and – Oh, Mary, what ought we to do? – what do you think we –' [*Halliday's voice. 'Fifteen I'm bid! – fifteen for the sack! – twenty! – ah, thanks! – thirty – thanks again! Thirty, thirty, thirty! – do I hear forty! – forty it is! Keep the ball rolling, gentlemen, keep it rolling! – fifty! – thanks, noble Roman! – going at fifty, fifty, fifty! – seventy! – ninety! – splendid! – a hundred! – pile it up, pile it up! – hundred and twenty – forty – just in time! – hundred and fifty! –* TWO *hundred! – superb! Do I hear two h— thanks! – two hundred and fifty! –'*]

'It is another temptation, Edward – I'm all in a tremble – but, oh, we've escaped *one* temptation, and that ought to warn us, to – [*'Six did I hear? – thanks! – six fifty six f—* SEVEN *hundred!'*] And yet, Edward, when you think – nobody susp—

['*Eight hundred dollars! – hurrah! – make it nine! – Mr Par-
sons, did I hear you say – thanks! – nine! – this noble sack of
virgin lead going at only nine hundred dollars, gilding and all –
come! do I hear – a thousand! – gratefully yours! – did some
one say eleven? – a sack which is going to be the most celebrated
in the whole Uni—*'] Oh, Edward [*beginning to sob*], we are
so poor! – but – but – do as you think best – do as you think
best.'

Edward fell – that is, he sat still; sat with a conscience which
was not satisfied, but which was overpowered by circumstances.

Meantime a stranger, who looked like an amateur detective
gotten up as an impossible English earl, had been watching the
evening's proceedings with manifest interest, and with a contented expression in his face; and he had been privately com-
menting to himself. He was now soliloquizing somewhat like
this : 'None of the Eighteen are bidding; that is not satisfactory;
I must change that – the dramatic unities require it; they must
buy the sack they tried to steal; they must pay a heavy price,
too – some of them are rich. And another thing, when I make
a mistake in Hadleyburg nature the man that puts that error
upon me is entitled to a high honorarium, and some one must
pay it. This poor old Richards has brought my judgement to
shame; he is an honest man – I don't understand it, but I acknowledge it. Yes, he saw my deuces – *and* with a straight flush,
and by rights the pot is his. And it shall be a jackpot, too, if I
can manage it. He disappointed me, but let that pass.'

He was watching the bidding. At a thousand, the market
broke; the prices tumbled swiftly. He waited – and still
watched. One competitor dropped out; then another, and another. He put in a bid or two, now. When the bids had sunk to
ten dollars, he added a five; some one raised him a three; he
waited a moment, then flung in a fifty-dollar jump, and the sack
was his – at $1282. The house broke out in cheers – then
stopped; for he was on his feet, and had lifted his hand. He
began to speak.

'I desire to say a word, and ask a favor. I am a speculator in
rarities, and I have dealings with persons interested in numis-
matics all over the world. I can make a profit on this purchase,

just as it stands; but there is a way, if I can get your approval, whereby I can make every one of these leaden twenty-dollar pieces worth its face in gold, and perhaps more. Grant me that approval, and I will give part of my gains to your Mr Richards, whose invulnerable probity you have so justly and so cordially recognized tonight; his share shall be ten thousand dollars, and I will hand him the money tomorrow. [*Great applause from the house*. But the 'invulnerable probity' made the Richardses blush prettily; however, it went for modesty, and did no harm.] If you will pass my proposition by a good majority – I would like a two-thirds vote – I will regard that as the town's consent, and that is all I ask. Rarities are always helped by any device which will rouse curiosity and compel remark. Now if I may have your permission to stamp upon the faces of each of these ostensible coins the names of the eighteen gentlemen who –'

Nine-tenths of the audience were on their feet in a moment – dog and all – and the proposition was carried with a whirlwind of approving applause and laughter.

They sat down, and all the Symbols except 'Dr' Clay Harkness got up, violently protesting against the proposed outrage, and threatening to –

'I beg you not to threaten me,' said the stranger, calmly. 'I know my legal rights, and am not accustomed to being frightened at bluster.' [*Applause*.] He sat down. 'Dr' Harkness saw an opportunity here. He was one of the two very rich men of the place, and Pinkerton was the other. Harkness was proprietor of a mint; that is to say, a popular patent medicine. He was running for the Legislature on one ticket, and Pinkerton on the other. It was a close race and a hot one, and getting hotter every day. Both had strong appetites for money; each had bought a great tract of land, with a purpose; there was going to be a new railway, and each wanted to be in the Legislature and help locate the route to his own advantage; a single vote might make the decision, and with it two or three fortunes. The stake was large, and Harkness was a daring speculator. He was sitting close to the stranger. He leaned over while one or another of the other Symbols was entertaining the house with protests and appeals, and asked, in a whisper.

'What is your price for the sack?'

'Forty thousand dollars.'

'I'll give you twenty.'

'No.'

'Twenty-five.'

'No.'

'Say thirty.'

'The price is forty thousand dollars; not a penny less.'

'All right, I'll give it. I will come to the hotel at ten in the morning. I don't want it known; will see you privately.'

'Very good.' Then the stranger got up and said to the house:

'I find it late. The speeches of these gentlemen are not without merit, not without interest, not without grace; yet if I may be excused I will take my leave. I thank you for the great favor which you have shown me in granting my petition. I ask the Chair to keep the sack for me until tomorrow, and to hand these three five-hundred-dollar notes to Mr Richards.' They were passed up to the Chair. 'At nine I will call for the sack, and at eleven will deliver the rest of the ten thousand to Mr Richards in person, at his home. Good night.'

Then he slipped out, and left the audience making a vast noise, which was composed of a mixture of cheers, the 'Mikado' song, dog-disapproval, and the chant, 'You are f-a-r from being a b-a-a-d man – a-a-a-a-men!'

At home the Richardses had to endure congratulations and compliments until midnight. Then they were left to themselves. They looked a little sad, and they sat silent and thinking. Finally Mary sighed and said,

'Do you think we are to blame, Edward – *much* to blame?' and her eyes wandered to the accusing triplet of big bank-notes lying on the table, where the congratulators had been gloating over them and reverently fingering them. Edward did not answer at once; then he brought out a sigh and said, hesitatingly:

'We – we couldn't help it, Mary. It – well, it was ordered. *All* things are.'

Mary glanced up and looked at him steadily, but he didn't return the look. Presently she said:

'I thought congratulations and praises always tasted good. But – it seems to me, now – Edward?'

'Well?'

'Are you going to stay in the bank?'

'N-no.'

'Resign?'

'In the morning – by note.'

'It does seem best.'

Richards bowed his head in his hands and muttered:

'Before, I was not afraid to let oceans of people's money pour through my hands, but – Mary, I am so tired, so tired –'

'We will go to bed.'

At nine in the morning the stranger called for the sack and took it to the hotel in a cab. At ten Harkness had a talk with him privately. The stranger asked for and got five checks on a metropolitan bank – drawn to 'Bearer', – four for $1,500 each, and one for $34,000. He put one of the former in his pocket-book, and the remainder, representing $38,5000, he put in an envelope, and with these he added a note, which he wrote after Harkness was gone. At eleven he called at the Richards house and knocked. Mrs Richards peeped through the shutters, then went and received the envelope, and the stranger disappeared without a word. She came back flushed and a little unsteady on her legs, and gasped out:

'I am sure I recognized him! Last night it seemed to me that maybe I had seen him somewhere before.'

'He is the man that brought the sack here?'

'I am almost sure of it.'

'Then he is the ostensible Stephenson too, and sold every important citizen in this town with his bogus secret. Now if he has sent checks instead of money, we are sold too, after we thought we had escaped. I was beginning to feel fairly comfortable once more, after my night's rest, but the look of that envelope makes me sick. It isn't fat enough; $8,500 in even the largest banknotes makes more bulk than that.'

'Edward, why do you object to checks?'

'Checks signed by Stephenson! I am resigned to take the $8,500 if it could come in bank-notes – for it does seem that it was so ordered, Mary – but I have never had much courage, and I have not the pluck to try to market a check signed with that disastrous name. It would be a trap. That man tried to catch me; we escaped somehow or other; and now he is trying a new way. If it is checks –'

'Oh, Edward, it is *too* bad!' and she held up the checks and began to cry.

'Put them in the fire! quick! we mustn't be tempted. It is a trick to make the world laugh at *us*, along with the rest, and – Give them to *me*, since you can't do it!' He snatched them and tried to hold his grip till he could get to the stove; but he was human, he was a cashier, and he stopped a moment to make sure of the signature. Then he came near to fainting.

'Fan me, Mary, fan me! They are the same as gold!'

'Oh, how lovely, Edward! Why?'

'Signed by Harkness. What can the mystery of that be, Mary?'

'Edward, do you think –'

'Look here – look at this! Fifteen – fifteen – fifteen – thirty-four. Thirty-eight thousand five hundred! Mary, the sack isn't worth twelve dollars, and Harkness – apparently – has paid about par for it.'

'And does it all come to us, do you think – instead of the ten thousand?'

'Why, it looks like it. And the checks are made to "Bearer", too.'

'Is that good, Edward? What is it for?'

'A hint to collect them at some distant bank, I reckon. Perhaps Harkness doesn't want the matter known. What is that – a note?'

'Yes. It was with the checks.'

'It was the 'Stephenson' handwriting, but there was no signature. It said:

I am a disappointed man. Your honesty is beyond the reach of temptation. I had a different idea about it, but I wronged you in that, and I beg pardon, and do it sincerely. I honor you – and that is sincere, too. This town is not worthy to kiss the hem of your garment. Dear sir, I made a square bet with myself that there were nineteen debauchable men in your self-righteous community. I have lost. Take the whole pot, you are entitled to it.

Richards drew a deep sigh, and said:

'It seems written with fire – it burns so. Mary. – I am miserable again.'

'I, too. Ah, dear, I wish –'

'To think, Mary – he *believes* in me.'

'Oh, don't, Edward – I can't bear it.'

'If those beautiful words were deserved, Mary – and God knows I believed I deserved them once – I think I could give the forty thousand dollars for them. And I would put that paper away, as representing more than gold and jewels, and keep it always. But now – we could not live in the shadow of its accusing presence, Mary.'

He put it in the fire.

A messenger arrived and delivered an envelope. Richards took from it a note and read it; it was from Burgess.

You saved me, in a difficult time. I saved you last night. It was at cost of a lie, but I made the sacrifice freely, and out of a grateful heart. None in this village knows so well as I know how brave and good and noble you are. At bottom you cannot respect me, knowing as you do of that matter of which I am accused, and by the general voice condemned, but I beg that you will at least believe that I am a grateful man, it will help me to bear my burden.

[Signed] BURGESS.

'Saved, once more. And on such terms!' He put the note in the fire. 'I – I wish I were dead, Mary, I wish I were out of it all.'

'Oh, these are bitter, bitter days, Edward. The stabs, through their very generosity, are so deep – and they come so fast!'

Three days before the election each of two thousand voters suddenly found himself in possession of a prized memento – one of the renowned bogus double-eagles. Around one of its faces was stamped these words: 'THE REMARK I MADE TO THE POOR STRANGER WAS –' Around the other face was stamped these 'GO AND REFORM. [SIGNED] PINKERTON.' Thus the entire remaining refuse of the renowned joke was emptied upon a single head, and with calamitous effect.

It revived the recent vast laugh and concentrated it upon Pinkerton; and Harkness's election was a walk-over.

Within twenty-four hours after the Richardses had received their checks their consciences were quieting down, discouraged; the old couple were learning to reconcile themselves to the sin which they had committed. But they were to learn, now, that a sin takes on new and real terrors when there seems a chance that it is going to be found out. This gives it a fresh and most substantial and important aspect. At church the morning sermon was of the usual pattern; it was the same old things said in the same old way; they had heard them a thousand times and found them innocuous, next to meaningless, and easy to sleep under; but now it was different; the sermon seemed to bristle with accusations; it seemed aimed straight and especially at people who were concealing deadly sins. After church they got away from the mob of congratulators as soon as they could, and hurried homeward, chilled to the bone at they did not know what — vague, shadowy, indefinite fears. And by chance they caught a glimpse of Mr Burgess as he turned a corner. He paid no attention to their nod of recognition! He hadn't seen it but they did not know that. What could his conduct mean? It might mean — it might mean — oh, a dozen dreadful things. Was it possible that he knew that Richards could have cleared him of guilt in that bygone time, and had been silently waiting for a chance to even up accounts? At home, in their distress they got to imagining that their servant might have been in the next room listening when Richards revealed the secret to his wife that he knew of Burgess's innocence; next, Richards began to imagine that he had heard the swish of a gown in there at that time; next, he was sure he *had* heard it. They would call Sarah in, on a pretext, and watch her face: if she had been betraying them to Mr Burgess, it would show in her manner. They asked her some questions — questions which were so random and incoherent and seemingly purposeless that the girl felt sure that the old people's minds had been affected by their sudden good fortune; the sharp and watchful gaze which they bent upon her frightened her, and that completed the business. She blushed, she became nervous and confused, and to the old people these were plain signs of guilt – guilt of some fearful sort or other – without doubt she was a spy and a traitor. When they were alone again they began to piece many unrelated things together and get horrible results out of the combination. When things had got about to the worst, Richards was delivered of a sudden gasp, and his wife asked,

'Oh, what is it? – what is it?'

'The note – Burgess's note! Its language was sarcastic, I see it now.' He quoted: ' "At bottom you cannot respect me, *knowing*, as you do, of *that matter* of which I am accused" – oh, it is perfectly plain, now, God help me! He knows that I know! You see the ingenuity of the phrasing. It was a trap – and like a fool, I walked into it. And Mary –?'

'Oh, it is dreadful – I know what you are going to say – he didn't return your transcript of the pretended test-remark.'

'No – kept it to destroy us with. Mary, he has exposed us to some already. I know it – I know it well. I saw it in a dozen faces after church. Ah, he wouldn't answer our nod of recognition – *he* knew what he had been doing!'

In the night the doctor was called. The news went around in the morning that the old couple were rather seriously ill – prostrated by the exhausting excitement growing out of their great windfall, the congratulations, and the late hours, the doctor said. The town was sincerely distressed; for these old people were about all it had left to be proud of, now.

Two days later the news was worse. The old couple were delirious, and were doing strange things. By witness of the nurses, Richards had exhibited checks – for $8,500? No – for an amazing sum – $38,500! What could be the explanation of this gigantic piece of luck?

The following day the nurses had more news – and wonderful. They had concluded to hide the checks, lest harm come to them; but when they searched they were gone from under the patient's pillow – vanished away. The patient said:

'Let the pillow alone; what do you want?'

'We thought it best that the checks –'

'You will never see them again – they are destroyed. They came from Satan. I saw the hell-brand on them, and I knew they were sent to betray me to sin.' Then he fell to gabbling strange and dreadful things which were not clearly understandable, and which the doctor admonished them to keep to themselves.

Richards was right; the checks were never seen again.

A nurse must have talked in her sleep, for within two days the forbidden gabblings were the property of the town; and they were of a surprising sort. They seemed to indicate that Richards had been a claimant for the sack himself, and that Burgess had concealed that fact and then maliciously betrayed it.

Burgess was taxed with this and stoutly denied it. And he said it was not fair to attach weight to the chatter of a sick old man who was out of his mind. Still, suspicion was in the air, and there was much talk.

After a day or two it was reported that Mrs Richards's delirious deliveries were getting to be duplicates of her husband's. Suspicion flamed up into conviction, now, and the town's pride in the purity of its one undiscredited important citizen began to dim down and flicker toward extinction.

Six days passed, then came more news. The old couple were dying. Richards's mind cleared in his latest hour, and he sent for Burgess. Burgess said:

'Let the room be cleared. I think he wishes to say something in privacy.'

'No!' said Richards; 'I want witnesses. I want you all to hear my confession, so that I may die a man, and not a dog. I was clean – artificially – like the rest; and like the rest I fell when temptation came. I signed a lie, and claimed the miserable sack. Mr Burgess remembered that I had done him a service and in gratitude (and ignorance) he suppressed my claim and saved me. You know the thing that was charged against Burgess years ago. My testimony, and mine alone, could have cleared him, and I was a coward, and left him to suffer disgrace –'

'No – no – Mr Richards, you –'

'My servant betrayed my secret to him –'

'No one has betrayed anything to me –'

– 'and then he did a natural and justifiable thing, he repented of the saving kindness which he had done me, and he *exposed* me – as I deserved –'

'Never! — I make oath —'

'Out of my heart I forgive him.'

Burgess's impassioned protestations fell upon deaf ears; the dying man passed away without knowing that once more he had done poor Burgess a wrong. The old wife died that night.

The last of the sacred Nineteen had fallen a prey to the fiendish sack; the town was stripped of the last rag of its ancient glory. Its mourning was not showy, but it was deep.

By act of the Legislature — upon prayer and petition — Hadleyburg was allowed to change its name to (never mind what — I will not give it away), and leave one word out of the motto that for many generations had graced the town's official seal.

It is an honest town once more, and the man will have to rise early that catches it napping again.

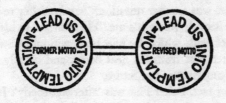

Francis Bret Harte

THE OUTCASTS OF POKER FLAT

As Mr John Oakhurst, gambler, stepped into the main street of
Poker Flat on the morning of the twenty-third of November
1850, he was conscious of a change in its moral atmosphere
since the preceding night. Two or three men, conversing earnestly together, ceased as he approached, and exchanged significant glances. There was a Sabbath lull in the air, which, in a
settlement unused to Sabbath influences, looked ominous.

Mr Oakhurst's calm, handsome face betrayed small concern
of these indications. Whether he was conscious of any predis-
posing cause, was another question. 'I reckon they're after somebody,' he reflected; 'likely it's me.' He returned to his pocket the
handkerchief with which he had been whipping away the red
dust of Poker Flat from his neat boots, and quietly discharged
his mind of any further conjecture.

In point of fact, Poker Flat was 'after somebody'. It had lately
suffered the loss of several thousand dollars, two valuable horses,
and a prominent citizen. It was experiencing a spasm of virtuous reaction, quite as lawless and ungovernable as any of the
acts that had provoked it. A secret committee had determined to
rid the town of all improper persons. This was done permanently in regard of two men who were then hanging from the
boughs of a sycamore in the gulch, and temporarily in the
banishment of certain other objectionable characters. I regret to
say that some of these were ladies. It is but due to the sex, however, to state that their impropriety was professional, and it was
only in such easily established standards of evil that Poker Flat
ventured to sit in judgement.

Mr Oakhurst was right in supposing that he was included in
this category. A few of the committee had urged hanging him as
a possible example, and a sure method of reimbursing themselves from his pockets of the sums he had won from them. 'It's

agin justice,' said Jim Wheeler, 'to let this yer young man from Roaring Camp – an entire stranger – carry away our money.' But a crude sentiment of equity residing in the breasts of those who had been fortunate enough to win from Mr Oakhurst overruled this narrower local prejudice.

Mr Oakhurst received his sentence with philosophic calmness, none the less coolly that he was aware of the hesitation of his judges. He was too much of a gambler not to accept Fate. With him life was at best an uncertain game, and he recognized the usual percentage in favor of the dealer.

A body of armed men accompanied the deported wickedness of Poker Flat to the outskirts of the settlement. Besides Mr Oakhurst, who was known to be a coolly desperate man, and for whose intimidation the armed escort was intended, the expatriated party consisted of a young woman familiarly known as 'The Duchess'; another, who had gained the infelicitous title of 'Mother Shipton'; and 'Uncle Billy,' a suspected sluice-robber and confirmed drunkard. The cavalcade provoked no comments from the spectators, nor was any word uttered by the escort. Only, when the gulch which marked the uttermost limit of Poker Flat was reached, the leader spoke briefly and to the point. The exiles were forbidden to return at the peril of their lives.

As the escort disappeared, their pent-up feelings found vent in a few hysterical tears from the Duchess, some bad language from Mother Shipton, and a Parthian volley of expletives from Uncle Billy. The philosophic Oakhurst alone remained still. He listened calmly to Mother Shipton's desire to cut somebody's heart out, to the repeated statements of the Duchess that she would die on the road, and to the alarming oaths that seemed to be bumped out of Uncle Billy as he rode forward. With the easy good humor characteristic of his class, he insisted upon exchanging his own riding-horse, Five Spot, for the sorry mule which the Duchess rode. But even this act did not draw the party into any closer sympathy. The young woman readjusted her somewhat draggled plumes with a feeble, faded coquetry; Mother Shipton eyed the possessor of Five Spot with malevolence, and Uncle Billy included the whole party in one sweeping anathema.

The road to Sandy Bar – a camp that, not having as yet experienced the regenerating influences of Poker Flat, consequently seemed to offer some invitation to the emigrants – lay over a steep mountain range. It was distant a day's severe journey. In that advanced season, the party soon passed out of the moist, temperate regions of the foothills into the dry, cold, bracing air of the Sierras. The trail was narrow and difficult. At noon the Duchess, rolling out of her saddle upon the ground, declared her intention of going no farther, and the party halted.

The spot was singularly wild and impressive. A wooded amphitheater, surrounded on three sides by precipitous cliffs of naked granite, sloped gently toward the crest of another precipice that overlooked the valley. It was undoubtedly the most suitable spot for a camp, had camping been advisable. But Mr Oakhurst knew that scarcely half the journey to Sandy Bar was accomplished, and the party were not equipped or provisioned for delay. This fact he pointed out to his companions curtly, with a philosophic commentary on the folly of 'throwing up their hand before the game was played out'. But they were furnished with liquor, which in this emergency stood them in place of food, fuel, rest, and prescience. In spite of his remonstrances, it was not long before they were more or less under its influence. Uncle Billy passed rapidly from a bellicose state into one of stupor, the Duchess became maudlin, and Mother Shipton snored. Mr Oakhurst alone remained erect, leaning against a rock, calmly surveying them.

Mr Oakhurst did not drink. It interfered with a profession which required coolness, impassiveness, and presence of mind, and, in his own language, he 'couldn't afford it'. As he gazed at his recumbent fellow-exiles, the loneliness begotten of his pariah-trade, his habits of life, his very vices, for the first time seriously oppressed him. He bestirred himself in dusting his black clothes, washing his hands and face, and other acts characteristic of his studiously neat habits, and for a moment forgot his annoyance. The thought of deserting his weaker and more pitiable companions never perhaps occurred to him. Yet he could not help feeling the want of that excitement which, singularly enough, was most conducive to the calm equanimity for which he was notorious. He looked at the gloomy walls that rose a thousand feet sheer above the circling pines around him; at the sky, ominously clouded; at the valley below, already deepening into shadow. And, doing so, suddenly he heard his own name called.

A horseman slowly ascended the trail. In the fresh, open face of the new-comer Mr Oakhurst recognized Tom Simson, otherwise known as 'The Innocent' of Sandy Bar. He had met him some months before over a 'little game', and had, with perfect equanimity, won the entire fortune – amounting to some forty dollars – of that guileless youth. After the game was finished, Mr Oakhurst drew the youthful speculator behind the door and thus addressed him: 'Tommy, you're a good little man, but you can't gamble worth a cent. Don't try it over again.' He then handed him his money back, pushed him gently from the room, and so made a devoted slave of Tom Simson.

There was a remembrance of this in his boyish and enthusiastic greeting of Mr Oakhurst. He had started, he said, to go to Poker Flat to seek his fortune. 'Alone?' No, not exactly alone; in fact – a giggle – he had run away with Piney Woods. Didn't Mr Oakhurst remember Piney? She that used to wait on the table at the Temperance House? They had been engaged a long time, but old Jake Woods had objected, and so they had run away, and were going to Poker Flat to be married, and here they were. And they were tired out, and how lucky it was they had found a place to camp and company. All this the Innocent delivered rapidly, while Piney – a stout, comely damsel of fifteen – emerged from behind the pine-tree, where she had been blushing unseen, and rode to the side of her lover.

Mr. Oakhurst seldom troubled himself with sentiment, still less with propriety; but he had a vague idea that the situation was not felicitous. He retained, however, his presence of mind sufficiently to kick Uncle Billy, who was about to say something, and Uncle Billy was sober enough to recognize in Mr Oakhurst's kick a superior power that would not bear trifling. He then endeavored to dissuade Tom Simson from delaying further, but in vain. He even pointed out the fact that there was no provision, nor means of making a camp. But, unluckily, the Innocent met this objection by assuring the party that he was provided with an extra mule loaded with provisions, and by the discovery of a rude attempt at a log-house near the trail. 'Piney can stay with Mrs Oakhurst,' said the Innocent, pointing to the Duchess, 'and I can shift for myself.'

Nothing but Mr Oakhurst's admonishing foot saved Uncle Billy from bursting into a roar of laughter. As it was, he felt compelled to retire up the canyon until he could recover his gravity. There he confided the joke to the tall pine-trees, with many slaps of his leg, contortions of his face, and the usual profanity. But when he returned to the party, he found them seated by a fire – for the air had grown strangely chill and the sky overcast – in apparently amicable conversation. Piney was actually talking in an impulsive, girlish fashion to the Duchess, who was listening with an interest and animation she had not shown for many days. The Innocent was holding forth, apparently with equal effect, to Mr Oakhurst and Mother Shipton, who was actually relaxing into amiability. 'Is this yer a d—d picnic?' said Uncle Billy, with inward scorn, as he surveyed the sylvan group, the glancing fire-light, and the tethered animals in the foreground. Suddenly an idea mingled with the alcoholic fumes that disturbed his brain. It was apparently of a jocular nature, for he felt impelled to slap his leg again and cram his fist into his mouth.

As the shadows crept slowly up the mountain, a slight breeze rocked the tops of the pine-trees, and moaned through their long and gloomy aisles. The ruined cabin, patched and covered with pine boughs, was set apart for the ladies. As the lovers parted, they unaffectedly exchanged a kiss, so honest and sincere that it might have been heard above the swaying pines. The frail Duchess and the malevolent Mother Shipton were probably too stunned to remark upon this last evidence of simplicity, and so turned without a word to the hut. The fire was replenished, the men lay down before the door, and in a few minutes were asleep.

Mr Oakhurst was a light sleeper. Toward morning he awoke benumbed and cold. As he stirred the dying fire, the wind, which was now blowing strongly, brought to his cheek that which caused the blood to leave it – snow!

THE OUTCASTS OF POKER FLAT

He started to his feet with the intention of awakening the sleepers, for there was no time to lose. But turning to where Uncle Billy had been lying, he found him gone. A suspicion leaped to his brain and a curse to his lips. He ran to the spot where the mules had been tethered; they were no longer there. The tracks were already rapidly disappearing in the snow.

The momentary excitement brought Mr Oakhurst back to the fire with his usual calm. He did not waken the sleepers. The Innocent slumbered peacefully, with a smile on his good humored, freckled face; the virgin Piney slept beside her frailer sisters as sweetly as though attended by celestial guardians, and Mr Oakhurst, drawing his blanket over his shoulders, stroked his mustachios and waited for the dawn. It came slowly in the whirling mist of snowflakes, that dazzled and confused the eye. What could be seen of the landscape appeared magically changed. He looked over the valley, and summed up the present and future in two words – 'Snowed in l'

A careful inventory of the provisions, which, fortunately for the party, had been stored within the hut, and so escaped the felonious fingers of Uncle Billy, disclosed the fact that with care and prudence they might last ten days longer. 'That is,' said Mr Oakhurst, *sotto voce* to the Innocent, 'if you're willing to board us. If you ain't – and perhaps you'd better not – you can wait till Uncle Billy gets back with provisions.' For some occult reason, Mr Oakhurst could not bring himself to disclose Uncle Billy's rascality, and so offered the hypothesis that he had wandered from the camp and had accidentally stampeded the animals. He dropped a warning to the Duchess and Mother Shipton, who of course knew the facts of their associate's defection. 'They'll find out the truth about us *all*, when they find out anything,' he added, significantly, 'and there's no good frightening them now.'

Tom Simson not only put all his worldly store at the disposal of Mr Oakhurst, but seemed to enjoy the prospect of their enforced seclusion. 'We'll have a good camp for a week, and then the snow'll melt, and we'll all go back together.' The cheerful gaiety of the young man and Mr Oakhurst's calm infected the others. The Innocent, with the aid of pine boughs, extemporized a thatch for the roofless cabin, and the Duchess directed Piney in the rearrangement of the interior with a taste and tact that opened the blue eyes of that provincial maiden to their fullest extent.

'I reckon now you're used to fine things at Poker Flat,' said Piney. The Duchess turned away sharply to conceal something that reddened her cheek through its professional tint, and Mother Shipton requested Piney not to 'chatter'. But when Mr Oakhurst returned from a weary search for the trail, he heard the sound of happy laughter echoed from the rocks. He stopped in some alarm, and his thoughts first naturally reverted to the whisky, which he had prudently *cached*. 'And yet it don't somehow sound like whisky,' said the gambler. It was not until he caught sight of the blazing fire through the still blinding storm, and the group around it, that he settled to the conviction that it was 'square fun'.

Whether Mr Oakhurst had *cached* his cards with the whisky as something debarred the free access of the community, I cannot say. It was certain that, in Mother Shipton's words, he 'didn't say cards once' during the evening. Haply the time was beguiled by an accordion, produced somewhat ostentatiously by Tom Simson, from his pack. Notwithstanding some difficulties attending the manipulation of this instrument, Piney Woods managed to pluck several reluctant melodies from its keys, to an accompaniment by the Innocent on a pair of bone castinets. But the crowning festivity of the evening was reached in a rude camp-meeting hymn, which the lovers, joining hands, sang with great earnestness and vociferation. I fear that a certain defiant tone and Covenanter's swing to its chorus, rather than any devotional quality, caused it speedily to infect the others who at last joined in the refrain:

> I'm proud to live in the service of the Lord,
> And I'm bound to die in His army.

The pines rocked, the storm eddied and whirled above the miserable group, and the flames of their altar leaped heavenward, as if in token of the vow.

At midnight the storm abated, the rolling clouds parted, and the stars glittered keenly above the sleeping camp. Mr Oakhurst, whose professional habits had enabled him to live on the smallest possible amount of sleep, in dividing the watch with Tom Simson, somehow managed to take upon himself the greater part of that duty. He excused himself to the Innocent, by saying that he had 'often been a week without sleep'. 'Doing what?' asked Tom. 'Poker !' replied Oakhurst, sententiously, 'when a man gets a streak of luck – nigger-luck – he don't get tired. The luck gives in first. Luck,' continued the gambler, reflectively, 'is a mighty queer thing. All you know about it for certain is that it's bound to change. And it's finding out when it's going to change that makes you. We've had a streak of bad luck since we left Poker Flat – you came along, and slap you get into it, too. If you can hold your cards right along you're all right. For,' added the gambler, with cheerful irrelevance,

> 'I'm proud to live in the service of the Lord,
> And I'm bound to die in His army.'

The third day came, and the sun, looking through the white-curtained valley, saw the outcasts divide their slowly decreasing store of provisions for the morning meal. It was one of the peculiarities of that mountain climate that its rays diffused a kindly warmth over the wintry landscape, as if in regretful commiseration of the past. But it revealed drift on drift of snow piled high around the hut; a hopeless, uncharted, trackless sea of white lying below the rocky shores to which the castaways still clung. Through the marvelously clear air, the smoke of the pastoral village of Poker Flat rose miles away. Mother Shipton saw it, and from a remote pinnacle of her rocky fastness, hurled in that direction a final malediction. It was her last vituperative attempt, and perhaps for that reason was invested with a certain degree of sublimity. It did her good, she privately informed the Duchess. 'Just to go out there and cuss, and see.' She then set herself to the task of amusing 'the child', as she and the Duchess were pleased to call Piney. Piney was no chicken, but it was a soothing and ingenious theory of the pair thus to account for the fact that she didn't swear and wasn't improper.

When night crept up again through the gorges, the reedy

notes of the accordion rose and fell in fitful spasms and long-drawn gasps by the flickering camp-fire. But music failed to fill entirely the aching void left by insufficient food, and a new diversion was proposed by Piney – story-telling. Neither Mr Oakhurst nor his female companions caring to relate their personal experiences, this plan would have failed, too, but for the Innocent. Some months before he had chanced upon a stray copy of Mr Pope's ingenious translation of the Iliad. He now proposed to narrate the principal incidents of that poem – having thoroughly mastered the argument and fairly forgotten the words – in the current vernacular of Sandy Bar. And so for the rest of that night the Homeric demi-gods again walked the earth. Trojan bully and wily Greek wrestled in the winds, and the great pines in the canyon seemed to bow to the wrath of the son of Peleus. Mr Oakhurst listened with quiet satisfaction. Most especially was he interested in the fate of 'Ash-heels', as the Innocent persisted in denominating the 'swift-footed Achilles'.

So with small food and much of Homer and the accordion, a week passed over the heads of the outcasts. The sun again forsook them, and again from leaden skies the snowflakes were sifted over the land. Day by day closer around them drew the snowy circle, until at last they looked from their prison over drifted walls of dazzling white, that towered twenty feet above their heads. It became more and more difficult to replenish their fires, even from the fallen trees beside them, now half-hidden in the drifts. And yet no one complained. The lovers turned from the dreary prospect and looked into each other's eyes, and were happy. Mr Oakhurst settled himself coolly to the losing game before him. The Duchess, more cheerful than she had been, assumed the care of Piney. Only Mother Shipton – once the strongest of the party – seemed to sicken and fade. At midnight on the tenth day she called Oakhurst to her side. 'I'm going,' she said, in a voice of querulous weakness, 'but don't say anything about it. Don't waken the kids. Take the bundle from under my head and open it.' Mr Oakhurst did so. It contained Mother Shipton's rations for the last week, untouched. 'Give 'em to the child,' she said, pointing to the sleeping Piney. 'You've starved yourself,' said the gambler. 'That's what they call it,' said the woman, querulously, as she lay down again, and, turning her face to the wall, passed quietly away.

The accordion and the bones were put aside that day, and Homer was forgotten. When the body of Mother Shipton had been committed to the snow, Mr Oakhurst took the Innocent aside, and showed him a pair of snowshoes, which he had fashioned from the old pack-saddle. 'There's one chance in a hundred to save her yet,' he said, pointing to Piney; 'but it's there,' he added, pointing toward Poker Flat. 'If you can reach there in two days she's safe.' 'And you?' asked Tom Simson. 'I'll stay here,' was the curt reply.

The lovers parted with a long embrace. 'You are not going, too?' said the Duchess, as she saw Mr Oakhurst apparently waiting to accompany him. 'As far as the canyon,' he replied. He turned suddenly, and kissed the Duchess, leaving her pallid face aflame, and her trembling limbs rigid with amazement.

Night came, but not Mr Oakhurst. It brought the storm again and the whirling snow. Then the Duchess, feeding the fire, found that some one had quietly piled beside the hut enough fuel to last a few days longer. The tears rose to her eyes, but she hid them from Piney.

The women slept but little. In the morning, looking into each other's faces, they read their fate. Neither spoke; but Piney, accepting the position of the stronger, drew near and placed her arm around the Duchess's waist. They kept this attitude for the rest of the day. That night the storm reached its greatest fury, and, rending asunder the protecting pines, invaded the very hut.

Toward morning they found themselves unable to feed the fire, which gradually died away. As the embers slowly blackened, the Duchess crept closer to Pincy, and broke the silence of many hours: 'Piney, can you pray?' 'No, dear,' said Piney, simply. The Duchess without knowing exactly why, felt relieved, and putting her head upon Piney's shoulder, spoke no more. And so reclining, the younger and purer pillowing the head of her soiled sister upon her virgin breast, they fell asleep.

The wind lulled as if it feared to waken them. Feathery drifts of snow, shaken from the long pine boughs, flew like white-winged birds, and settled about them as they slept. The moon through the rifted clouds looked down upon what had been the camp. But all human stain, all trace of earthly travail, was hidden beneath the spotless mantle mercifully flung from above.

They slept all that day and the next, nor did they waken when voices and footsteps broke the silence of the camp. And when pitying fingers brushed the snow from their wan faces, you could scarcely have told from the equal peace that dwelt upon them, which was she that had sinned. Even the Law of Poker Flat recognized this, and turned away, leaving them still locked in each other's arms.

But at the head of the gulch, on one of the largest pine trees, they found the deuce of clubs pinned to the bark with a bowie knife. It bore the following, written in pencil, in a firm hand:

†

BENEATH THIS TREE
LIES THE BODY
OF
JOHN OAKHURST,
WHO STRUCK A STREAK OF BAD LUCK
ON THE 23D OF NOVEMBER, 1850,
AND
HANDED IN HIS CHECKS
ON THE 7TH OF DECEMBER, 1850.

†

And pulseless and cold, with a Derringer by his side and a bullet in his heart, though still calm as in life, beneath the snow lay he who was at once the strongest and yet the weakest of the outcasts of Poker Flat.

Ambrose Bierce

ONE OF THE MISSING

JEROME SEARING, a private soldier of General Sherman's army, then confronting the enemy at and about Kenesaw Mountain, Georgia, turned his back upon a small group of officers, with whom he had been talking in low tones, stepped across a light line of earthworks, and disappeared in a forest. None of the men in line behind the works had said a word to him, nor had he so much as nodded to them in passing, but all who saw understood that this brave man had been intrusted with some perilous duty. Jerome Searing, though a private, did not serve in the ranks; he was detailed for service at division headquarters, being borne upon the rolls as an orderly. 'Orderly' is a word covering a multitude of duties. An orderly may be a messenger, a clerk, an officer's servant – anything. He may perform services for which no provision is made in orders and army regulations. Their nature may depend upon his aptitude, upon favour, upon accident. Private Searing, an incomparable marksman, young – it is surprising how young we all were in those days – hardy, intelligent, and insensible to fear, was a scout. The general commanding his division was not content to obey orders blindly without knowing what was in his front, even when his command was not on detached service, but formed a fraction of the line of the army; nor was he satisfied to receive his knowledge of his *vis-à-vis* through the customary channels; he wanted to know more than he was apprised of by the corps commander and the collisions of pickets and skirmishers. Hence Jerome Searing – with his extraordinary daring, his woodcraft, his sharp eyes and truthful tongue. On this occasion his instructions were simple: to get as near the enemy's lines as possible and learn all that he could.

In a few moments he had arrived at the picket line, the men on duty there lying in groups of from two to four behind little banks of earth scooped out of the slight depression in which they lay, their rifles protruding from the green boughs with which they had masked their small defences. The forest extended without a break toward the front, so solemn and silent that only by an effort of the imagination could it be conceived as populous with armed men, alert and vigilant – a forest formidable with possibilities of battle. Pausing a moment in one of the rifle pits to apprise the men of his intention, Searing crept stealthily forward on his hands and knees and was soon lost to view in a dense thicket of underbrush.

'That is the last of him,' said one of the men; 'I wish I had his rifle; those fellows will hurt some of us with it.'

Searing crept on, taking advantage of every accident of ground and growth to give himself better cover. His eyes penetrated everywhere, his ears took note of every sound. He stilled his breathing, and at the cracking of a twig beneath his knee stopped his progress and hugged the earth. It was slow work, but not tedious; the danger made it exciting, but by no physical signs was the excitement manifest. His pulse was as regular, his nerves were as steady, as if he were trying to trap a sparrow.

'It seems a long time,' he thought, 'but I cannot have come very far; I am still alive.'

He smiled at his own method of estimating distance, and crept forward. A moment later he suddenly flattened himself upon the earth and lay motionless, minute after minute. Through a narrow opening in the bushes he had caught sight of a small mound of yellow clay – one of the enemy's rifle pits. After some little time he cautiously raised his head, inch by inch, then his body upon his hands, spread out on each side of him, all the while intently regarding the hillock of clay. In another moment he was upon his feet, rifle in hand, striding rapidly forward with little attempt at concealment. He had rightly interpreted the signs, whatever they were; the enemy was gone.

To assure himself beyond a doubt before going back to report upon so important a matter, Searing pushed forward across the line of abandoned pits, running from cover to cover in the more open forest, his eyes vigilant to discover possible stragglers. He came to the edge of a plantation – one of those forlorn, deserted homesteads of the last years of the war, upgrown with brambles, ugly with broken fences, and desolate with vacant buildings having blank apertures in place of doors and windows. After a keen reconnoissance from the safe seclusion of a clump of young pines, Searing ran lightly across a field and through an orchard to a small structure which stood apart from the other farm buildings, on a slight elevation, which he thought would enable him to overlook a large scope of country in the direction that he supposed the enemy to have taken in withdrawing. This building, which had originally consisted of a single room, elevated upon four posts about ten feet high, was now little more than a roof; the floor had fallen away, the joists and planks loosely piled on the ground below or resting on end at various angles, not wholly torn from their fastenings above. The supporting posts were themselves no longer vertical. It looked as if the whole edifice would go down at the touch of a finger. Concealing himself in the débris of joists and flooring, Searing looked across the open ground between his point of view and a spur of Kenesaw Mountain, a half mile away. A road leading up and across this spur was crowded with troops – the rear guard of the retiring enemy, their gun barrels gleaming in the morning sunlight.

Searing had now learned all that he could hope to know. It was his duty to return to his own command with all possible speed and report his discovery. But the grey column of infantry toiling up the mountain road was singularly tempting. His rifle – an ordinary 'Springfield', but fitted with a globe sight and hair trigger – would easily send its ounce and a quarter of lead hissing into their midst. That would probably not affect the duration and result of the war, but it is the business of a soldier to kill. It is also his pleasure if he is a good soldier. Searing cocked his rifle and 'set' the trigger.

But it was decreed from the beginning of time that Private Searing was not to murder anybody that bright summer morning, nor was the Confederate retreat to be announced by him. For countless ages events had been so matching themselves together in that wondrous mosaic to some parts of which, dimly discernible, we give the name of history, that the acts which he had in will would have marred the harmony of the pattern.

Some twenty-five years previously the Power charged with the execution of the work according to the design had provided against that mischance by causing the birth of a certain male child in a little village at the foot of the Carpathian Mountains, had carefully reared it, supervised its education, directed its desires into a military channel, and in due time made it an officer of artillery. But the concurrence of an infinite number of favouring influences and their preponderance over an infinite number of opposing ones, this officer of artillery had been made to commit a breach of discipline and fly from his native country to avoid punishment. He had been directed to New Orleans (instead of New York), where a recruiting officer awaited him on the wharf. He was enlisted and promoted, and things were so ordered that he now commanded a Confederate battery some three miles along the line from where Jerome Searing, the Federal scout, stood cocking his rifle. Nothing had been neglected – at every step in the progress of both these men's lives, and in the lives of their ancestors and contemporaries, and of the lives of the contemporaries of their ancestors – the right thing had been done to bring about the desired result. Had anything in all this vast concatenation been overlooked, Private Searing might have fired on the retreating Confederates that morning, and would have perhaps have missed. As it fell out, a captain of artillery, having nothing better to do while awaiting his turn to pull out and be off, amused himself by sighting a field piece obliquely to his right at what he took to be some Federal officers on the crest of a hill, and discharged it. The shot flew high of its mark.

As Jerome Searing drew back the hammer of his rifle, and, with his eyes upon the distant Confederates, considered where he could plant his shot with the best hope of making a widow or an orphan or a childless mother – perhaps all three, for Private Searing, although he had repeatedly refused promotion, was not without a certain kind of ambition – he heard a rushing sound in the air, like that made by the wings of a great bird swooping down upon its prey. More quickly than he could apprehend the gradation, it increased to a hoarse and horrible roar, as the missile that made it sprang at him out of the sky, striking with a deafening impact one of the posts supporting the confusion of timbers above him, smashing it into matchwood, and bringing down the crazy edifice with a loud clatter, in clouds of blinding dust!

Lieutenant Adrian Searing, in command of the picket guard on that part of the line through which his brother Jerome had passed on his mission, sat with attentive ears in his breastwork behind the line. Not the faintest sound escaped him; the cry of a bird, the barking of a squirrel, the noise of the wind among the pines – all were anxiously noted by his overstrained sense. Suddenly, directly in front of his line, he heard a faint, confused rumble, like the clatter of a falling building translated by distance. At the same moment an officer approached him on foot from the rear and saluted.

'Lieutenant,' said the aide, 'the colonel directs you to move forward your line and feel the enemy if you find him. If not, continue the advance until directed to halt. There is reason to think that the enemy has retreated.'

The lieutenant nodded and said nothing; the other officer retired. In a moment the men, apprised of their duty by the non-commissioned officers in low tones, had deployed from their rifle pits and were moving forward in skirmishing order, with set teeth and beating hearts. The lieutenant mechanically looked at his watch. Six o'clock and eighteen minutes.

When Jerome Searing recovered consciousness, he did not at once understand what had occurred. It was, indeed, some time before he opened his eyes. For a while he believed that he had died and been buried, and he tried to recall some portions of the burial service. He thought that his wife was kneeling upon his grave, adding her weight to that of the earth upon his chest. The two of them, widow and earth, had crushed his coffin. Unless the children should persuade her to go home, he would not much longer be able to breathe. He felt a sense of wrong. 'I cannot speak to her,' he thought; 'the dead have no voice; and if I open my eyes I shall get them full of earth.'

He opened his eyes – a great expanse of blue sky, rising from a fringe of the tops of trees. In the foreground, shutting out some of the trees, a high, dun mound, angular in outline and crossed by an intricate, patternless system of straight lines; in the centre a bright ring of metal – the whole an immeasurable distance away – a distance so inconceivably great that it fatigued him, and he closed his eyes. The moment that he did so he was conscious of an insufferable light. A sound was in his ears like the low, rhythmic thunder of a distant sea breaking in successive waves upon the beach, and out of this noise, seeming a part of it, or possibly coming from beyond it, and intermingled with its ceaseless undertone, came the articulate words: 'Jerome Searing, you are caught like a rat in a trap – in a trap, trap, trap.'

Suddenly there fell a great silence, a black darkness, an infinite tranquillity, and Jerome Searing, perfectly conscious of his rathood, and well assured of the trap that he was in, remembered all, and nowise alarmed, again opened his eyes to reconnoitre, to note the strength of his enemy, to plan his defence.

He was caught in a reclining posture, his back firmly supported by a solid beam. Another lay across his breast, but he had been able to shrink a little way from it so that it no longer oppressed him, though it was immovable. A brace joining it at an angle had wedged him against a pile of boards on his left, fastening the arm on that side. His legs, slightly parted and straight along the ground, were covered upward to the knees with a mass of débris which towered above his narrow horizon. His head was as rigidly fixed as in a vice; he could move his eyes, his chin – no more. Only his right arm was partly free. 'You must help us out of this,' he said to it. But he could not get it from under the heavy timber athwart his chest, nor move it outward more than six inches at the elbow.

Searing was not seriously injured, nor did he suffer pain. A smart rap on the head from a flying fragment of the splintered post, incurred simultaneously with the frightfully sudden shock to the nervous system, had momentarily dazed him. His term of unconsciousness, including the period of recovery, during which he had had the strange fancies, had probably not exceeded a few seconds, for the dust of the wreck had not wholly cleared away as he began an intelligent survey of the situation.

With his partly free right hand he now tried to get hold of the beam which lay across, but not quite against, his breast. In no way could he do so. He was unable to depress the shoulder so as to push the elbow beyond that edge of the timber which was nearest his knees; failing in that, he could not raise the forearm and hand to grasp the beam. The brace that made an angle with it downward and backward prevented him from doing anything in that direction, and between it and his body the space was not half as wide as the length of his forearm. Obviously he could not get his hand under the beam nor over it; he could not, in fact, touch it at all. Having demonstrated his inability, he desisted, and began to think if he could reach any of the débris piled upon his legs.

In surveying the mass with a view to determining that point, his attention was arrested by what seemed to be a ring of shining metal immediately in front of his eyes. It appeared to him at first to surround some perfectly black substance, and it was somewhat more than a half inch in diameter. It suddenly occurred to his mind that the blackness was simply shadow, and that the ring was in fact the muzzle of his rifle protruding from the pile of débris. He was not long in satisfying himself that this was so – if it was a satisfaction. By closing either eye he could look a little way along the barrel – to the point where it was hidden by the rubbish that held it. He could see the one side, with the corresponding eye, at apparently the same angle as the other side with the other eye. Looking with the right eye, the weapon seemed to be directed at a point to the left of his head, and *vice versá*. He was unable to see the upper surface of the barrel, but could see the under surface of the stock at a slight angle. The piece was, in fact, aimed at the exact centre of his forehead.

In the perception of this circumstance, in the recollection that just previously to the mischance of which this uncomfortable situation was the result, he had cocked the gun and set the trigger so that a touch would discharge it, Private Searing was affected with a feeling of uneasiness. But that was as far as possible from fear; he was a brave man, somewhat familiar with the aspect of rifles from that point of view, and of cannon, too; and now he recalled, with something like amusement, an incident of his experience at the storming of Missionary Ridge, where, walking up to one of the enemy's embrasures from which he had seen a heavy gun throw charge after charge of grape among the assailants, he thought for a moment that the piece had been withdrawn; he could see nothing in the opening but a brazen circle. What that was he had understood just in time to step aside as it pitched another peck of iron down that swarming slope. To face firearms is one of the commonest incidents in a soldier's life – firearms, too, with malevolent eyes blazing behind them. That is what a soldier is for. Still, Private Searing did not altogether relish the situation, and turned away his eyes.

After groping, aimless, with his right hand for a time, he made an ineffectual attempt to release his left. Then he tried to disengage his head, the fixity of which was the more annoying from his ignorance of what held it. Next he tried to free his feet, but while exerting the powerful muscles of his legs for that purpose it occurred to him that a disturbance of the rubbish which held them might discharge the rifle; how it could have endured what had already befallen it he could not understand, although memory assisted him with various instances in point. One in particular he recalled, in which, in a moment of mental abstraction, he had clubbed his rifle and beaten out another gentleman's brains, observing afterward that the weapon which he had been diligently swinging by the muzzle was loaded, capped, and at full cock – knowledge of which circumstance would doubtless have cheered his antagonist to longer endurance. He had always smiled in recalling that blunder of his 'green and salad days' as a soldier, but now he did not smile. He turned his eyes again to the muzzle of the gun, and for a moment fancied that it had moved; it seemed somewhat nearer.

Again he looked away. The tops of the distant trees beyond the bounds of the plantation interested him; he had not before observed how light and feathery they seemed, nor how darkly blue the sky was, even among their branches, where they somewhat paled it with their green; above him it appeared almost black. 'It will be uncomfortably hot here,' he thought, 'as the day advances. I wonder which way I am looking.'

Judging by such shadows as he could see, he decided that his face was due north; he would at least not have the sun in his eyes, and north – well, that was toward his wife and children.

'Bah!' he exclaimed aloud, 'what have they to do with it?'

He closed his eyes. 'As I can't get out, I may as well go to sleep. The rebels are gone, and some of our fellows are sure to stray out here foraging. They'll find me.'

But he did not sleep. Gradually he became sensible of a pain in his forehead – a dull ache, hardly perceptible at first, but growing more and more uncomfortable. He opened his eyes and it was gone – closed them and it returned. 'The devil!' he said irrelevantly, and stared again at the sky. He heard the singing of birds, the strange metallic note of the meadow lark, suggesting the clash of vibrant blades. He fell into pleasant memories of his childhood, played again with his brother and sister, raced across the fields, shouting to alarm the sedentary larks, entered the sombre forest beyond, and with timid steps followed the faint path to Ghost Rock, standing at last with audible heart-throbs before the Dead Man's Cave and seeking to penetrate its awful mystery. For the first time he observed that the opening of the haunted cavern was encircled by a ring of metal. Then all else vanished, and left him gazing into the barrel of his rifle as before. But whereas before it had seemed nearer, it now seemed an inconceivable distance away, and all the more sinister for that. He cried out, and, startled by something in his own voice – the note of fear – lied to himself in denial: 'If I don't sing out I may stay here till I die.'

He now made no further attempt to evade the menacing stare of the gun barrel. If he turned away his eyes an instant it was to look for assistance (although he could not see the ground on either side the ruin), and he permitted them to return, obedient to the imperative fascination. If he closed them, it was from weariness, and instantly the poignant pain in his forehead – the prophecy and menace of the bullet – forced him to reopen them.

The tension of nerve and brain was too severe; nature came

to his relief with intervals of unconsciousness. Reviving from one of these, he became sensible of a sharp, smarting pain in his right hand, and when he worked his fingers together, or rubbed his palm with them, he could feel that they were wet and slippery. He could not see the hand, but he knew the sensation; it was running blood. In his delirium he had beaten it against the jagged fragments of the wreck, had clutched it full of splinters. He resolved that he would meet his fate more manly. He was a plain, common soldier, had no religion and not much philosophy; he could not die like a hero, with great and wise last words, even if there were someone to hear them, but he could die 'game', and he would. But if he could only know when to expect the shot!

Some rats which had probably inhabited the shed came sneaking and scampering about. One of them mounted the pile of débris that held the rifle; another followed, and another. Searing regarded them at first with indifference, then with friendly interest; then, as the thought flashed into his bewildered mind that they might touch the trigger of his rifle, he screamed at them to go away. 'It is no business of yours,' he cried.

The creatures left; they would return later, attack his face, gnaw away his nose, cut his throat – he knew that, but he hoped by that time to be dead.

Nothing could now unfix his gaze from the little ring of metal with its black interior. The pain in his forehead was fierce and constant. He felt it gradually penetrating the brain more and more deeply, until at last its progress was arrested by the wood at the back of his head. It grew momentarily more insufferable; he began wantonly beating his lacerated hand against the splinters again to counteract that horrible ache. It seemed to throb with a slow, regular, recurrence, each pulsation sharper than the preceding, and sometimes he cried out, thinking he felt the fatal bullet. No thoughts of home, of wife and children, of country, of glory. The whole record of memory was effaced. The world had passed away – not a vestige remained. Here, in this confusion of timbers and boards, is the sole universe. Here is immortality in time – each pain an everlasting life. The throbs tick off eternities.

Jerome Searing, the man of courage, the formidable enemy, the strong, resolute warrior, was as pale as a ghost. His jaw was fallen; his eyes protruded; he trembled in every fibre; a cold sweat bathed his entire body; he screamed with fear. He was not insane – he was terrified.

In groping about with his torn and bleeding hand he seized at last a strip of board, and, pulling, felt it give way. It lay parallel with his body, and by bending his elbow as much as the contracted space would permit, he could draw it a few inches at a time. Finally it was altogether loosened from the wreckage covering his legs; he could lift it clear of the ground its whole length. A great hope came into his mind: perhaps he could work it upward, that is to say backward, far enough to lift the end and push aside the rifle; or, if that were too tightly wedged, so hold the strip of board as to deflect the bullet. With this object he passed it backward inch by inch, hardly daring to breath, lest that act somehow defeat his intent, and more than ever unable to remove his eyes from the rifle, which might perhaps now hasten to improve its waning opportunity. Something at least had been gained; in the occupation of his mind in this attempt at self-defence he was less sensible of the pain in his head and had ceased to scream. But he was still dreadfully frightened, and his teeth rattled like castanets.

The strip of board ceased to move to the suasion of his hand. He tugged at it with all his strength, changed the direction of its length all he could, but it had met some extended obstruction behind him, and the end in front was still too far away to clear the pile of débris and reach the muzzle of the gun. It extended, indeed, nearly as far as the trigger-guard, which, uncovered by the rubbish, he could imperfectly see with his right eye. He tried to break the strip with his hand, but had no leverage. Perceiving his defeat, all his terror returned, augmented tenfold. The black aperture of the rifle appeared to threaten a sharper and more imminent death in punishment of his rebellion. The track of the bullet through his head ached with an intenser anguish. He began to tremble again.

Suddenly he became composed. His tremor subsided. He clinched his teeth and drew down his eyebrows. He had not exhausted his means of defence; a new design had shaped itself in his mind – another plan of battle. Raising the front end of the strip of board, he carefully pushed it forward through the wreckage at the side of the rifle until it pressed against the trigger guard. Then he moved the end slowly outward until he could feel that it had cleared it, then, closing his eyes, thrust it against the trigger with all his strength! There was no explosion; the rifle had been discharged as it dropped from his hand when the building fell. But Jerome Searing was dead.

A line of Federal skirmishes swept across the plantation toward the mountain. They passed on both sides of the wrecked building, observing nothing. At a short distance in their rear came their commander, Lieutenant Adrian Searing. He casts his eyes curiously upon the ruin and sees a dead body half buried in boards and timbers. It is so covered with dust that its clothing is Confederate grey. Its face is yellowish white; the cheeks are fallen in, the temples sunken, too, with sharp ridges about them, making the forehead forbiddingly narrow; the upper lip, slightly lifted, shows the white teeth, rigidly clinched. The hair is heavy with moisture, the face as wet as the dewy grass all about. From his point of view the officer does not observe the rifle; the man was apparently killed by the fall of the building.

'Dead a week,' said the officer curtly, moving on, mechanically pulling out his watch as if to verify his estimate of time. Six o'clock and forty minutes.

Henry James

THE REAL THING

I

W H E N the porter's wife, who used to answer the house-bell, announced 'A gentleman and a lady, sir,' I had, as I often had in those days – the wish being father to the thought – an immediate vision of sitters. Sitters my visitors in this case proved to be; but not in the sense I should have preferred. There was nothing at first however to indicate that they mightn't have come for a portrait. The gentleman, a man of fifty, very high and very straight, with a moustache slightly grizzled and a dark grey walking-coat admirably fitted, both of which I noted professionally – I don't mean as a barber or yet as a tailor – would have struck me as a celebrity if celebrities often were striking. It was a truth of which I had for some time been conscious that a figure with a good deal of frontage was, as one might say, almost never a public institution. A glance at the lady helped to remind me of this paradoxical law: she also looked too distinguished to be a 'personality'. Moreover one would scarcely come across two variations together.

Neither of the pair immediately spoke – they only prolonged the preliminary gaze suggesting that each wished to give the other a chance. They were visibly shy; they stood there letting me take them in – which, as I afterwards perceived, was the most practical thing they could have done. In this way their embarrassment served their cause. I had seen people painfully reluctant to mention that they desired anything so gross as to be represented on canvas; but the scruples of my new friends appeared almost insurmountable. Yet the gentleman might have said 'I should like a portrait of my wife,' and the lady might have said 'I should like a portrait of my husband.' Perhaps they weren't husband and wife – this naturally would make the matter more delicate. Perhaps they wished to be done together – in which case they ought to have brought a third person to break the news.

'We come from Mr Rivet,' the lady finally said with a dim smile that had the effect of a moist sponge passed over a 'sunk' piece of painting, as well as of a vague allusion to vanished beauty. She was as tall and straight, in her degree, as her companion, and with ten years less to carry. She looked as sad as a woman could look whose face was not charged with expression; that is her tinted oval mask showed waste as an exposed surface shows friction. The hand of time had played over her freely, but to an effect of elimination. She was slim and stiff, and so well-dressed, in dark blue cloth, with lappets and pockets and buttons, that it was clear she employed the same tailor as her husband. The couple had an indefinable air of prosperous thrift – they evidently got a good deal of luxury for their money. If I was to be one of their luxuries it would behoove me to consider my terms.

'Ah Claude Rivet recommended me?' I echoed; and I added that it was very kind of him, though I could reflect that, as he only painted landscape, this wasn't a sacrifice.

The lady looked very hard at the gentleman, and the gentleman looked round the room. Then staring at the floor a moment and stroking his moustache, he rested his pleasant eyes on me with the remark: 'He said you were the right one.'

'I try to be, when people want to sit.'

'Yes, we should like to,' said the lady anxiously.

'Do you mean together?'

My visitors exchanged a glance. 'If you could do anything with *me* I suppose it would be double,' the gentleman stammered.

'Oh yes, there's naturally a higher charge for two figures than for one.'

'We should like to make it pay,' the husband confessed.

'That's very good of you,' I returned, appreciating so unwonted a sympathy – for I supposed he meant pay the artist.

A sense of strangeness seemed to dawn on the lady. 'We mean for the illustrations – Mr Rivet said you might put one in.'

'Put in – an illustration?' I was equally confused.

'Sketch her off, you know,' said the gentleman, colouring.

It was only then that I understood the service Claude Rivet had rendered me; he had told them how I worked in black-and-white, for magazines, for storybooks, for sketches of contemporary life, and consequently had copious employment for models. These things were true, but it was not less true – I may confess it now; whether because the aspiration was to lead to everything or to nothing I leave the reader to guess – that I couldn't get the honours, to say nothing of the emoluments, of a great painter of portraits out of my head. My 'illustrations' were my pot-boilers; I looked to a different branch of art – far and away the most interesting it had always seemed to me – to perpetuate my fame. There was no shame in looking to it also to make my fortune; but that fortune was by so much further from being made from the moment my visitors wished to be 'done' for nothing. I was disappointed; for in the pictorial sense I had immediately *seen* them. I had seized their type – I had already settled what I would do with it. Something that wouldn't absolutely have pleased them, I afterwards reflected.

'Ah you're – you're – a?' I began as soon as I had mastered my surprise. I couldn't bring out the dingy word 'models': it seemed so little to fit the case.

'We haven't had much practice,' said the lady.

'We've got to *do* something, and we've thought that an artist in your line might perhaps make something of us,' her husband threw off. He further mentioned that they didn't know many artists and that they had gone first, on the off-chance – he painted views of course, but sometimes put in figures; perhaps I remembered – to Mr Rivet, whom they had met a few years before at a place in Norfolk where he was sketching.

'We used to sketch a little ourselves,' the lady hinted.

'It's very awkward, but we absolutely *must* do something,' her husband went on.

'Of course we're not so *very* young,' she admitted with a wan smile.

With the remark that I might as well know something more about them the husband had handed me a card extracted from a neat new pocket-book – their appurtenances were all of the freshest – and inscribed with the words 'Major Monarch'. Impressive as these words were they didn't carry my knowledge much further; but my visitor presently added: 'I've left the army and we've had the misfortune to lose our money. In fact our means are dreadfully small.'

'It's awfully trying – a regular strain,' said Mrs Monarch.

They evidently wished to be discreet – to take care not to swagger because they were gentlefolk. I felt them willing to recognize this as something of a drawback, at the same time that I guessed at an underlying sense – their consolation in adversity – that they *had* their points. They certainly had; but these advantages struck me as preponderantly social; such for instance as would help to make a drawing-room look well. However, a drawing-room was always, or ought to be, a picture.

In consequence of his wife's allusion to their age Major Monarch observed: 'Naturally it's more for the figure that we thought of going in. We can still hold ourselves up.' On the instant I saw that the figure was indeed their strong point. His 'naturally' didn't sound vain, but it lighted up the question. '*She* has the best one,' he continued, nodding at his wife with a pleasant after-dinner absence of circumlocution. I could only reply, as if we were in fact sitting over our wine, that this didn't prevent his own from being very good; which led him in turn to make answer: 'We thought that if you ever have to do people like us we might be something like it. *She* particularly – for a lady in a book, you know.'

I was so amused by them that, to get more of it, I did my best to take their point of view; and though it was an embarrassment to find myself appraising physically, as if they were animals on hire or useful blacks, a pair whom I should have expected to meet only in one of the relations in which criticism is tacit, I looked at Mrs Monarch judicially enough to be able to exclaim after a moment with conviction: 'Oh yes, a lady in a book!' She was singularly like a bad illustration.

'We'll stand up, if you like,' said the Major; and he raised himself before me with a really grand air.

I could take his measure at a glance – he was six feet two and a perfect gentleman. It would have paid any club in process of formation and in want of a stamp to engage him at a salary to stand in the principal window. What struck me at once was that in coming to me they had rather missed their vocation; they could surely have been turned to better account for advertising purposes. I couldn't of course see the thing in detail, but I could see them make somebody's fortune – I don't mean their own. There was something in them for a waistcoat-maker, an hotel-keeper or a soap-vendor. I could imagine. 'We always use it' pinned on their bosoms with the greatest effect; I had a vision of the brilliancy with which they would launch a table d'hôte.

Mrs Monarch sat still, not from pride but from shyness, and presently her husband said to her: 'Get up, my dear, and show how smart you are.' She obeyed, but she had no need to get up to show it. She walked to the end of the studio and then came back blushing, her fluttered eyes on the partner of her appeal. I was reminded of an incident I had accidentally had a glimpse of in Paris – being with a friend there, a dramatist about to produce a play, when an actress came to him to ask to be entrusted with a part. She went through her paces before him, walked up and down as Mrs Monarch was doing. Mrs Monarch did it quite as well, but I abstained from applauding. It was very odd to see such people apply for such poor pay. She looked as if she had ten thousand a year. Her husband had used the word that described her: she was in the London current jargon essentially and typically 'smart'. Her figure was, in the same order of ideas, conspicuously and irreproachably 'good'. For a woman of her age her waist was surprisingly small; her elbow moreover had the orthodox crook. She held her head at the conventional angle, but why did she come to *me*? She ought to have tried on jackets at a big shop. I feared my visitors were not only destitute but 'artistic' – which would be a great complication. When she sat down again I thanked her, observing that what a draughtsman most valued in his model was the faculty of keeping quiet.

'Oh *she* can keep quiet,' said Major Monarch. Then he added jocosely: 'I've always kept her quiet.'

'I'm not a nasty fidget, am I?' It was going to wring tears from me, I felt, the way she hid her head, ostrich-like, in the other broad bosom.

The owner of this expanse addressed his answer to me. 'Perhaps it isn't out of place to mention – because we ought to be quite business-like, oughtn't we? – that when I married her she was known as the Beautiful Statue.'

'Oh dear!' said Mrs Monarch ruefully.

'Of course I should want a certain amount of expression,' I rejoined.

'Of *course*!' – and I had never heard such unanimity.

'And then I suppose you know that you'll get awfully tired.'

'Oh we *never* get tired!' they eagerly cried.

'Have you had any kind of practice?'

They hesitated – they looked at each other. 'We've been photographed – *immensely*,' said Mrs Monarch.

'She means the fellows have asked us themselves,' added the Major.

'I see – because you're so good-looking.'

'I don't know what they thought, but they were always after us.'

'We always got our photographs for nothing,' smiled Mrs Monarch.

'We might have brought some, my dear,' her husband remarked.

'I'm not sure we have any left. We've given quantities away,' she explained to me.

'With our autographs and that sort of thing,' said the Major.

'Are they to be got in the shops?' I inquired as a harmless pleasantry.

'Oh yes, *hers* – they used to be.'

'Not now,' said Mrs Monarch with her eyes on the floor.

I could fancy the 'sort of thing' they put on the presentation
copies of their photograpns, and I was sure they wrote a beautiful hand. It was odd how quickly I was sure of everything that
concerned them. If they were now so poor as to have to earn
shillings and pence they could never have had much of a margin. Their good looks had been their capital, and they had good-
humouredly made the most of the career that this resource
marked out for them. It was in their faces, the blankness, the
deep intellectual repose of the twenty years of country-house
visiting that had given them pleasant intonations. I could see the
sunny drawing-rooms, sprinkled with periodicals she didn't
read, in which Mrs Monarch had continuously sat; I could see
the wet shrubberies in which she had walked, equipped to
admiration for either exercise. I could see the rich covers the
Major had helped to shoot and the wonderful garments in
which, late at night, he repaired to the smoking-room to talk
about them. I could imagine their leggings and waterproofs,
their knowing tweeds and rugs, their rolls of sticks and cases of
tackle and neat umbrellas; and I could evoke the exact appearance of their servants and the compact variety of their luggage
on the platforms of country stations.

They gave small tips, but they were liked; they didn't do
anything themselves, but they were welcome. They looked so
well everywhere; they gratified the general relish for stature,
complexion and 'form'. They knew it without fatuity or vulgarity, and they repected themselves in consequence. They
weren't superficial; they were thorough and kept themselves up
– it had been their line. People with such a taste for activity had
to have some line. I could feel how even in a dull house they
could have been counted on for the joy of life. At present something had happened – it didn't matter what, their little income
had grown less, it had grown least – and they had to do something for pocket-money. Their friends could like them, I made
out, without liking to support them. There was something
about them that represented credit – their clothes, their manners, their type; but if credit is a large empty pocket in which

an occasional chink reverberates, the chink at least must be audible. What they wanted of me was to help to make it so. Fortunately they had no children – I soon divined that. They would also perhaps wish our relations to be kept secret: this was why it was 'for the figure' – the reproduction of the face would betray them.

I liked them – I felt, quite as their friends must have done – they were so simple; and I had no objection to them if they would suit. But somehow with all their perfections I didn't easily believe in them. After all they were amateurs, and the ruling passion of my life was the detestation of the amateur. Combined with this was another perversity – an innate preference for the represented subject over the real one: the defect of the real one was so apt to be a lack of representation. I liked things that appeared; then one was sure. Whether they *were* or not was a subordinate and almost always a profitless question. There were other considerations, the first of which was that I already had two or three recruits in use, notably a young person with big feet, in alpaca, from Kilburn, who for a couple of years had come to me regularly for my illustrations and with whom I was still – perhaps ignobly – satisfied. I frankly explained to my visitors how the case stood, but they had taken more precautions than I supposed. They had reasoned out their opportunity, for Claude Rivet had told them of the projected *édition de luxe* of one of the writers of our day – the rarest of the novelists – who, long neglected by the multitudinous vulgar and dearly prized by the attentive (need I mention Philip Vincent?), had had the happy fortune of seeing, late in life, the dawn and then the full light of a higher criticism; an estimate in which on the part of the public there was something really of expiation. The edition preparing, planned by a publisher of taste, was practically an act of high reparation; the wood-cuts with which it was to be enriched were the homage of English art to one of the most independent representatives of English letters. Major and Mrs Monarch confessed to me they had hoped I might be able to work *them* into my branch of the enterprise. They knew I was to do the first of the books, *Rutland Ramsay*, but I had to make clear to them that my participation in the rest of the affair – this first book was to be a test – must depend on the satisfaction I should give. If this should be limited my employers would drop me with scarce common forms. It was therefore a crisis for me, and naturally I was making special preparations, looking about for new people, should they be necessary, and securing the best types. I admitted however that I should like to settle down to two or three good models who would do for everything.

'Should we have often to – a – put on special clothes?' Mrs Monarch timidly demanded.

'Dear yes – that's half the business.'

'And should we be expected to supply our own costumes?'

'Oh no; I've got a lot of things. A painter's models put on – or put off – anything he likes.'

'And you mean – a – the same?'

'The same?'

Mrs Monarch looked at her husband again.

'Oh she was just wondering,' he explained, 'if the costumes are in *general* use.' I had to confess that they were, and I mentioned further that some of them – I had a lot of genuine greasy last-century things – had served their time, a hundred years ago, on living world-stained men and women; on figures not perhaps so far removed, in that vanished world, from *their* type, the Monarchs', *quoi!* of a breeched and bewigged age. 'We'll put on anything that *fits*,' said the Major.

'Oh I arrange that – they fit in the pictures.'

'I'm afraid I should do better for the modern books. I'd come as you like,' said Mrs Monarch.

'She has got a lot of clothes at home: they might do for contemporary life,' her husband continued.

'Oh I can fancy scenes in which you'd be quite natural.' And indeed I could see the slipshod rearrangements of stale properties – the stories I tried to produce pictures for without the exasperation of reading them – whose sandy tracts the good lady might help to people. But I had to return to the fact that for this sort of work – the daily mechanical grind – I was already equipped: the people I was working with were fully adequate.

'We only thought we might be more like *some* characters,' said Mrs Monarch mildly, getting up.

Her husband also rose; he stood looking at me with a dim wistfulness that was touching in so fine a man. 'Wouldn't it be rather a pull sometimes to have – a – to have –?' He hung fire; he wanted me to help him by phrasing what he meant. But I couldn't – I didn't know. So he brought it out awkwardly: 'The *real* thing; a gentleman, you know, or a lady.' I was quite ready to give a general assent – I admitted that there was a great deal in that. This encouraged Major Monarch to say, following up his appeal with an unacted gulp: 'It's awfully hard – we've tried everything.' The gulp was communicative; it proved too much for his wife. Before I knew it Mrs Monarch had dropped again upon a divan and burst into tears. Her husband sat down beside her, holding one of her hands; whereupon she quickly dried her eyes with the other, while I felt embarrassed as she looked up at me. 'There isn't a confounded job I haven't applied for – waited for – prayed for. You can fancy we'd be pretty bad first. Secretaryships and that sort of thing? You might as well ask for a peerage. I'd be *anything* – I'm strong; a messenger or a coalheaver. I'd put on a gold-laced cap and open carriage-doors in front of the haberdasher's; I'd hang about a station to carry portmanteaux; I'd be a postman. But they won't *look* at you; there are thousands as good as yourself already on the ground. *Gentlemen*, poor beggars, who've drunk their wine, who've kept their hunters!'

I was as reassuring as I knew how to be, and my visitors were presently on their feet again while, for the experiment, we agreed on an hour. We were discussing it when the door opened and Miss Churm came in with a wet umbrella. Miss Churm had to take the omnibus to Maida Vale and then walk half a mile. She looked a trifle blowsy and slightly splashed. I scarcely ever saw her come in without thinking afresh how odd it was that, being so little in herself, she should yet be so much in others. She was a meagre little Miss Churm, but was such an ample heroine of romance. She was only a freckled cockney, but she could represent everything, from a fine lady to a shepherdess; she had the faculty as she might have had a fine voice or long hair. She couldn't spell and she loved beer, but she had two or three 'points', and practice, and a knack, and mother-wit, and a whimsical sensibility, and a love of the theatre, and seven sisters, and not an ounce of respect, especially for the *h*. The first thing my visitors saw was that her umbrella was wet, and in their spotless perfection they visibly winced at it. The rain had come on since their arrival.

'I'm all in a soak; there *was* a mess of people in the 'bus. I wish you lived near a styion,' said Miss Churm. I requested her to get ready as quickly as possible, and she passed into the room in which she always changed her dress. But before going out she asked me what she was to get into this time.

'It's the Russian princess, don't you know?' I answered; 'the one with the "golden eyes", in black velvet, for the long thing in the *Cheapside*.'

'Golden eyes? I *say*!' cried Miss Churm, while my companions watched her with intensity as she withdrew. She always arranged herself, when she was late, before I could turn round; and I kept my visitors a little on purpose, so that they might get an idea, from seeing her, what would be expected of themselves. I mentioned that she was quite my notion of an excellent model – she was really very clever.

'Do you think she looks like a Russian princess?' Major Monarch asked with lurking alarm.

'When I make her, yes.'

'Oh if you have to *make* her – !' he reasoned, not without point.

'That's the most you can ask. There are so many who are not makeable.'

'Well now, *here's* a lady' – and with a persuasive smile he passed his arm into his wife's – 'who's already made!'

'Oh I'm not a Russian princess,' Mrs Monarch protested a little coldly. I could see she had known some and didn't like them. There at once was a complication of a kind I never had to fear with Miss Churm.

This young lady came back in black velvet – the gown was rather rusty and very low on her lean shoulders – and with a Japanese fan in her red hands. I reminded her that in the scene I was doing she had to look over some one's head. 'I forget whose it is; but it doesn't matter. Just look over a head.'

'I'd rather look over a stove,' said Miss Churm; and she took her station near the fire. She fell into position, settled herself into a tall attitude, gave a certain backward inclination to her head and a certain forward droop to her fan, and looked, at least, to my prejudiced sense, distinguished and charming, foreign and dangerous. We left her looking so while I went downstairs with Major and Mrs Monarch.

'I believe I could come about as near it as that,' said Mrs Monarch.

'Oh you think she's shabby, but you must allow for the alchemy of art.'

However, they went off with an evident increase of comfort founded on their demonstrable advantage in being the real thing. I could fancy them shuddering over Miss Churm. She was very droll about them when I went back, for I told her what they wanted.

'Well, if *she* can sit I'll tyke to book-keeping,' said my model.

'She's very ladylike,' I replied as an innocent form of aggravation.

'So much the worse for *you*. That means she can't turn round.'

'She'll do for the fashionable novels.'

'Oh yes, she'll *do* for them!' my model humorously declared. 'Ain't they bad enough without her?' I had often sociably denounced them to Miss Churm.

3

It was for the elucidation of a mystery in one of these works that I first tried Mrs Monarch. Her husband came with her, to be useful if necessary – it was sufficiently clear that as a general thing he would prefer to come with her. At first I wondered if this were for 'propriety's' sake – if he were going to be jealous and meddling. The idea was too tiresome, and if it had been confirmed it would speedily have brought our acquaintance to a close. But I soon saw there was nothing in it and that if he accompanied Mrs Monarch it was – in addition to the chance of being wanted – simply because he had nothing else to do. When they were separate his occupation was gone and they never *had* been separate. I judged rightly that in their awkward situation their close union was their main comfort and that this union had no weak spot. It was a real marriage, an encouragement to the hesitating, a nut for pessimists to crack. Their address was humble – I remember afterwards thinking it had been the only thing about them that was really professional – and I could fancy the lamentable lodgings in which the Major would have been left alone. He could sit there more or less grimly with his wife – he couldn't sit there anyhow without her.

He had too much tact to try and make himself agreeable when he couldn't be useful; so when I was too absorbed in my work to talk he simply sat and waited. But I liked to hear him talk – it made my work, when not interrupting it, less mechanical, less special. To listen to him was to combine the excitement of going out with the economy of staying at home. There was only one hindrance – that I seemed not to know any of the people this brilliant couple had known. I think he wondered extremely, during the term of our intercourse, whom the deuce I *did* know. He hadn't a stray sixpence of an idea to fumble for, so we didn't spin it very fine; we confined ourselves to questions of leather and even of liquor – saddlers and breeches-makers and how to get excellent claret cheap – and matters like 'good trains' and the habits of small game. His lore on these last subjects was astonishing – he managed to interweave the station-master with the ornithologist. When he couldn't talk about greater things he could talk cheerfully about smaller, and since I couldn't accompany him into reminiscences of the fashionable world he could lower the conversation without a visible effort to my level.

So earnest a desire to please was touching in a man who could so easily have knocked one down. He looked after the fire and had an opinion on the draught of the stove without my asking him, and I could see that he thought many of my arrangements not half knowing. I remember telling him that if I were only rich I'd offer him a salary to come and teach me how to live. Sometimes he gave a random sigh of which the essence might have been: 'Give me even such a bare old barrack as *this*, and I'd do something with it!' When I wanted to use him he came alone; which was an illustration of the superior courage of women. His wife could bear her solitary second floor, and she was in general more discreet; showing by various small reserves that she was alive to the propriety of keeping our relations markedly professional – not letting them slide into sociability. She wished it to remain clear that she and the Major were employed, not cultivated, and if she approved of me as a superior, who could be kept in his place, she never thought me quite good enough for an equal.

She sat with great intensity, giving the whole of her mind to it, and was capable of remaining for an hour almost as motionless as before a photographer's lens. I could see she had been photographed often, but somehow the very habit that made her good for that purpose unfitted her for mine. At first I was extremely pleased with her ladylike air, and it was a satisfaction, on coming to follow her lines, to see how good they were and how far they could lead the pencil. But after a little skirmishing I began to find her too insurmountably stiff; do what I would with it my drawing looked like a photograph or a copy of a photograph. Her figure had no variety of expression – she herself had no sense of variety. You may say that this was my business and was only a question of placing her. Yet I placed her in every conceivable position and she managed to obliterate their differences. She was always a lady certainly, and into the bargain was always the same lady. She was the real thing, but always the same thing. There were moments when I rather writhed under the serenity of her confidence that she *was* the real thing. All her dealings with me and all her husband's were an implication that this was lucky for *me*. Meanwhile I found myself trying to invent types that approached her own, instead of making her own transform itself – in the clever way that was not impossible for instance to poor Miss Churm. Arrange as I would and take the precautions I would, she always came out, in my pictures, too tall – landing me in the dilemma of having represented a fascinating woman as seven feet high, which (out of respect perhaps to my own very much scantier inches) was far from my idea of such a personage.

The case was worse with the Major – nothing I could do would keep *him* down, so that he became useful only for the representation of brawny giants. I adored variety and range, I cherished human accidents, the illustrative note; I wanted to characterize closely, and the thing in the world I most hated was the danger of being ridden by a type. I had quarrelled with some of my friends about it; I had parted company with them for maintaining that one *had* to be, and that if the type was beautiful – witness Raphael and Leonardo – the servitude was only a gain. I was neither Leonardo nor Raphael – I might only be a presumptuous young modern searcher; but I held that everything was to be sacrificed sooner than character. When they claimed that the obsessional form could easily *be* character I retorted, perhaps superficially, 'Whose?' It couldn't be everybody's – it might end in being nobody's.

After I had drawn Mrs Monarch a dozen times I felt surer even than before that the value of such a model as Miss Churm resided precisely in the fact that she had no positive stamp, combined of course with the other fact that what she did have was a curious and inexplicable talent for imitation. Her usual appearance was like a curtain which she could draw up at request for a capital performance. This performance was simply suggestive; but it was a word to the wise – it was vivid and pretty. Sometimes even I thought it, though she was plain herself, too insipidly pretty; I made it a reproach to her that the figures drawn from her were monotonously (*bêtement*, as we used to say) graceful. Nothing made her more angry; it was so much her pride to feel she could sit for characters that had nothing in common with each other. She would accuse me at such moments of taking away her 'reputytion'.

It suffered a certain shrinkage, this queer quantity, from the repeated visits of my new friends. Miss Churm was greatly in demand, never in want of employment, so I had no scruple in putting her off occasionally, to try them more at my ease. It was certainly amusing at first to do the real thing – it was amusing to do Major Monarch's trousers. They *were* the real thing, even if he did come out colossal. It was amusing to do his wife's back hair – it was so mathematically neat – and the particular 'smart' tension of her tight stays. She lent herself especially to positions in which the face was somewhat averted or blurred; she abounded in ladylike back views and *profils perdus*. When she stood erect she took naturally one of the attitudes in which court-painters represent queens and princesses; so that I found myself wondering whether, to draw out this accomplishment, I couldn't get the editor of the *Cheapside* to publish a really royal romance, 'A Tale of Buckingham Palace'. Sometimes however the real thing and the make-believe came into contact; by which I mean that Miss Churm, keeping an appointment or coming to make one on days when I had much work in hand, encountered her invidious rivals. The encounter was not on their part, for they noticed her no more than if she had been the house-maid; not from intentional loftiness, but simply because as yet, professionally, they didn't know how to fraternize, as I could imagine they would have liked – or at least that the Major would. They couldn't talk about the omnibus – they always walked; and they didn't know what else to try – she wasn't interested in good trains or cheap claret. Besides, they must have felt – in the air – that she was amused at them, secretly derisive of their ever knowing how. She wasn't a person to conceal the limits of her faith if she had had a chance to show them. On the other hand Mrs Monarch didn't think her tidy; for why else did she take pains to say to me – it was going out of the way, for Mrs Monarch – that she didn't like dirty women?

One day when my young lady happened to be present with my other sitters – she even dropped in, when it was convenient, for a chat – I asked her to be so good as to lend a hand in getting tea, a service with which she was familiar and which was one of a class that, living as I did in a small way, with slender domestic resources, I often appealed to my models to render. They liked to lay hands on my property, to break the sitting, and sometimes the china – it made them feel Bohemian. The next time I saw Miss Churm after this incident she surprised me greatly by making a scene about it – she accused me of having wished to humiliate her. She hadn't resented the outrage at the time, but had seemed obliging and amused, enjoying the comedy of asking Mrs Monarch, who sat vague and silent, whether she would have cream and sugar, and putting an exaggerated simper into the question. She had tried intonations – as if she too wished to pass for the real thing – till I was afraid my other visitors would take offence.

Oh they were determined not to do this, and their touching patience was the measure of their great need. They would sit by the hour, uncomplaining, till I was ready to use them; they would come back on the chance of being wanted and would walk away cheerfully if it failed. I used to go to the door with them to see in what magnificent order they retreated. I tried to find other employment for them – I introduced them to several artists. But they didn't 'take', for reasons I could appreciate, and I became rather anxiously aware that after such disappointments they fell back upon me with a heavier weight. They did me the honour to think me most *their* form. They weren't romantic enough for the painters, and in those days there were few serious workers in black-and-white. Besides, they had an eye to the great job I had mentioned to them – they had secretly set their hearts on supplying the right essence for my pictorial vindication of our fine novelist. They knew that for this undertaking I should want no costume-effects, none of the frippery of past ages – that it was a case in which everything would be contemporary and satirical and presumably genteel. If I could work them into it their future would be assured, for the labour would of course be long and the occupation steady.

One day Mrs Monarch came without her husband – she explained his absence by his having had to go to the City. While she sat there in her usual relaxed majesty there came at the door a knock which I immediately recognized as the subdued appeal of a model out of work. It was followed by the entrance of a young man whom I at once saw to be a foreigner and who proved in fact an Italian acquainted with no English word but my name, which he uttered in a way that made it seem to include all others. I hadn't then visited his country, nor was I proficient in his tongue; but as he was not so meanly constituted – what Italian is? – as to depend only on that member for expression he conveyed to me, in familiar but graceful mimicry, that he was in search of exactly the employment in which the lady before me was engaged. I was not struck with him at first, and while I continued to draw I dropped few signs of interest or encouragement. He stood his ground however -- not importunately, but with a dumb dog-like fidelity in his eyes that amounted to innocent impudence, the manner of a devoted servant -- he might have been in the house for years -- unjustly suspected. Suddenly it struck me that this very attitude and expression made a picture; whereupon I told him to sit down and wait till I should be free. There was another picture in the way he obeyed me, and I observed as I worked that there were others still in the way he looked wonderingly, with his head thrown back, about the high studio. He might have been crossing himself in Saint Peter's. Before I finished I said to myself 'The fellow's a bankrupt orange-monger, but a treasure.'

When Mrs Monarch withdrew he passed across the room like a flash to open the door for her, standing there with the rapt pure gaze of the young Dante spellbound by the young Beatrice. As I never insisted, in such situations, on the blankness of the British domestic, I reflected that he had the making of a servant -- and I needed one, but couldn't pay him to be only that -- as well as of a model; in short I resolved to adopt my bright adventurer if he would agree to officiate in the double capacity. He jumped at my offer, and in the event my rashness -- for I had really known nothing about him -- wasn't brought home to me. He proved a sympathetic though a desultory ministrant, and had in a wonderful degree the *sentiment de la pose*. It was uncultivated, instinctive, a part of the happy instinct that had guided him to my door and helped him to spell out my name on the card nailed to it. He had had no other introduction to me than a guess, from the shape of my high north window, seen outside, that my place was a studio and that as a studio it would contain an artist. He had wandered to England in search of fortune, like other itinerants, and had embarked, with a partner and a small green hand-cart, on the sale of penny ices. The ices had melted away and the partner had dissolved in their train. My young man wore tight yellow trousers with reddish stripes and his name was Oronte. He was sallow but fair, and when I put him into some old clothes of my own he looked like an

Englishman. He was as good as Miss Churm, who could look, when requested, like an Italian.

4

I thought Mrs Monarch's face slightly convulsed when, on her coming back with her husband, she found Oronte installed. It was strange to have to recognize in a scrap of a lazzarone a competitor to her magnificent Major. It was she who scented danger first, for the Major was anecdotically unconscious. But Oronte gave us tea, with a hundred eager confusions – he had never been concerned in so queer a process – and I think she thought better of me for having at last an 'establishment'. They saw a couple of drawings that I had made of the establishment, and Mrs Monarch hinted that it never would have struck her he had sat for them. 'Now the drawings you make from *us*, they look exactly like us,' she reminded me, smiling in triumph; and I recognized that this was indeed just their defect. When I drew the Monarchs I couldn't anyhow get away from them – get into the character I wanted to represent; and I hadn't the least desire my model should be discoverable in my picture. Miss Churm never was, and Mrs Monarch thought I hid her, very properly, because she was vulgar; whereas if she was lost it was only as the dead who go to heaven are lost – in the gain of an angel the more.

By this time I had got a certain start with *Rutland Ramsay*, the first novel in the great projected series; that is I had produced a dozen drawings, several with the help of the Major and his wife, and I had sent them in for approval. My understanding with the publishers, as I have already hinted, had been that I was to be left to do my work, in this particular case, as I liked, with the whole book committed to me; but my connexion with the rest of the series was only contingent. There were moments when, frankly, it *was* a comfort to have the real thing under one's hand; for there were characters in *Rutland Ramsay* that were very much like it. There were people presumably as erect as the Major and women of as good a fashion as Mrs Monarch. There was a great deal of country-house life – treated, it is true, in a fine fanciful ironical generalized way – and there was a considerable implication of knickerbockers and kilts. There were certain things I had to settle at the outset; such things for instance as the exact appearance of the hero and the particular bloom and figure of the heroine. The author of course gave me a lead, but there was a margin for interpretation. I took the Monarchs into my confidence, I told them frankly what I was about, I mentioned my embarrassments and alternatives. 'Oh take *him* !' Mrs Monarch murmured sweetly, looking at her husband; and 'What could you want better than my wife?' the Major inquired with the comfortable candour that now prevailed between us.

I wasn't obliged to answer these remarks – I was only obliged to place my sitters. I wasn't easy in mind, and I postponed a little timidly perhaps the solving of my question. The book was a large canvas, the other figures were numerous, and I worked off at first some of the episodes in which the hero and the heroine were not concerned. When once I had set *them* up I should have to stick to them – I couldn't make my young man seven feet high in one place and five feet nine in another. I inclined on the whole to the latter measurement, though the Major more than once reminded me that *he* looked about as young as any one. It was indeed quite possible to arrange him, for the figure, so that it would have been difficult to detect his age. After the spontaneous Oronte had been with me a month, and after I had given him to understand several times over that his native exuberance would presently constitute an insurmountable barrier to our further intercourse, I waked to a sense of his heroic capacity. He was only five feet seven, but the remaining inches were latent. I tried him almost secretly at first, for I was really rather afraid of the judgement my other models would pass on such a choice. If they regarded Miss Churm as little better than a snare what would they think of the representation by a person so little the real thing as an Italian street-vendor of a protagonist formed by a public school?

If I went a little in fear of them it wasn't because they bullied me, because they had got an oppressive foothold, but because in their really pathetic decorum and mysteriously permanent newness they counted on me so intensely. I was therefore very glad when Jack Hawley came home: he was always of such good counsel. He painted badly himself, but there was no one like him for putting his finger on the place. He had been absent from England for a year; he had been somewhere – I don't remember where – to get a fresh eye. I was in a good deal of dread of any such organ, but we were old friends; he had been away for months and a sense of emptiness was creeping into my life. I hadn't dodged a missile for a year.

He came back with a fresh eye, but with the same old black velvet blouse, and the first evening he spent in my studio we smoked cigarettes till the small hours. He had done no work himself, he had only got the eye; so the field was clear for the production of my little things. He wanted to see what I had produced for the *Cheapside*, but he was disappointed in the exhibition. That at least seemed the meaning of two or three comprehensive groans which, as he lounged on my big divan, his leg folded under him, looking at my latest drawings, issued from his lips with the smoke of the cigarette.

'What's the matter with you?' I asked.

'What's the matter with *you*?'

'Nothing save that I'm mystified.'

'You are indeed. You're quite off the hinge. What's the meaning of this new fad?' And he tossed me, with visible irreverence, a drawing in which I happened to have depicted both my elegant models. I asked if he didn't think it good, and he replied that it struck him as execrable, given the sort of thing I had always represented myself to him as wishing to arrive at; but I let that pass – I was so anxious to see exactly what he meant. The two figures in the picture looked colossal, but I supposed this was *not* what he meant inasmuch as, for aught he knew to the contrary, I might have been trying for some such effect. I maintained that I was working exactly in the same way as when he last had done me the honour to tell me I might do something some day. 'Well, there's a screw loose somewhere,' he answered; 'wait a bit and I'll discover it.' I depended upon him to do so: where else was the fresh eye? But he produced at last nothing more luminous than 'I don't know – I don't like your types.'

This was lame for a critic who had never consented to discuss with me anything but the question of execution, the direction of strokes and the mystery of values.

'In the drawings you've been looking at I think my types are very handsome.'

'Oh they won't do!'

'I've been working with new models.'

'I see you have. *They* won't do.'

'Are you very sure of that?'

'Absolutely – they're stupid.'

'You mean *I* am – for I ought to get round that.'

'You *can't* – with such people. Who are they?'

I told him, so far as was necessary, and he concluded heartlessly: *'Ce sont des gens qu'il faut mettre à la porte.'*

'You've never seen them; they're awfully good' – I flew to their defence.

'Not seen them? Why all this recent work of yours drops to pieces with them. It's all I want to see of them.'

'No one else has said anything against it – the *Cheapside* people are pleased.'

'Every one else is an ass, and the *Cheapside* people the biggest asses of all. Come, don't pretend at this time of day to have pretty illusions about the public, especially about publishers and editors. It's not for *such* animals you work – it's for those who know, *coloro che sanno*; so keep straight for *me* if you can't keep straight for yourself. There was a certain sort of thing you used to try for – and a very good thing it was. But this twaddle isn't *in* it.' When I talked with Hawley later about *Rutland Ramsay* and its possible successors he declared that I must get back into my boat again or I should go to the bottom. His voice in short was the voice of warning.

I noted the warning, but I didn't turn my friends out of doors. They bored me a good deal; but the very fact that they bored me admonished me not to sacrifice them – if there was anything to be done with them – simply to irritation. As I look back at this phase they seem to me to have pervaded my life not a little. I have a vision of them as most of the time in my studio, seated against the wall on an old velvet bench to be out of the way, and resembling the while a pair of patient courtiers in a royal ante-chamber: I'm convinced that during the coldest weeks of the winter they held their ground because it saved them fire. Their newness was losing its gloss, and it was impossible not to feel them objects of charity. Whenever Miss Churm arrived they went away, and after I was fairly launched in *Rutland Ramsay* Miss Churm arrived pretty often. They managed to express to me tacitly that they supposed I wanted her for the low life of the book, and I let them suppose it, since they had attempted to study the work – it was lying about the studio – without discovering that it dealt only with the highest circles. They had dipped into the most brilliant of our novelists without deciphering many passages. I still took an hour from them, now and again, in spite of Jack Hawley's warning: it would be time enough to dismiss them, if dismissal should be necessary, when the rigour of the season was over. Hawley had made their acquaintance – he had met them at my fireside – and thought them a ridiculous pair. Learning that he was a painter they tried to approach him, to show him too that they were the real thing; but he looked at them, across the big room, as if they were miles away: they were a compendium of everything he most objected to in the social system of his country. Such people as that, all convention and patent-leather, with ejaculations that stopped conversation, had no business in a studio. A studio was a place to learn to see, and how could you see through a pair of feather-beds?

The main inconvenience I suffered at their hands was that at first I was shy of letting it break upon them that my artful little servant had begun to sit for me for *Rutland Ramsay*. They knew I had been odd enough – they were prepared by this time to allow oddity to artists – to pick a foreign vagabond out of the streets when I might have had a person with whiskers and credentials; but it was some time before they learned how high I rated his accomplishments. They found him in an attitude more than once, but they never doubted I was doing him as an organ-grinder. There were several things they never guessed, and one of them was that for a striking scene in the novel, in which a footman briefly figured, it occurred to me to make use of Major

Monarch as the menial. I kept putting this off, I didn't like to ask him to don the livery – besides the difficulty of finding a livery to fit him. At last, one day late in the winter, when I was at work on the despised Oronte, who caught one's idea on the wing, and was in the glow of feeling myself go very straight, they came in, the Major and his wife, with their society laugh about nothing (there was less and less to laugh at); came in like country-callers – they always reminded me of that – who have walked across the park after church and are presently persuaded to stay to luncheon. Luncheon was over, but they could stay to tea – I knew they wanted it. The fit was on me, however, and I couldn't let my ardour cool and my work wait, with the fading daylight, while my model prepared it. So I asked Mrs Monarch if she would mind laying it out – a request which for an instant brought all the blood to her face. Her eyes were on her husband's for a second, and some mute telegraphy passed between them. Their folly was over the next instant; his cheerful shrewdness put an end to it. So far from pitying their wounded pride, I must add, I was moved to give it as complete a lesson as I could. They bustled about together and got out the cups and saucers and made the kettle boil. I know they felt as if they were waiting on my servant, and when the tea was prepared I said: 'He'll have a cup, please – he's tired.' Mrs Monarch brought him one where he stood, and he took it from her as if he had been a gentleman at a party squeezing a crush-hat with an elbow.

Then it came over me that she had made a great effort for me – made it with a kind of nobleness – and that I owed her a compensation. Each time I saw her after this I wondered what the compensation could be. I couldn't go on doing the wrong thing to oblige them. Oh it *was* the wrong thing, the stamp of the work for which they sat – Hawley was not the only person to say it now. I sent in a large number of the drawings I had made for *Rutland Ramsay*, and I received a warning that was more to the point than Hawley's. The artistic adviser of the house for which I was working was of opinion that many of my illustrations were not what had been looked for. Most of these illustrations were the subjects in which the Monarchs had figured.

Without going into the question of what *had* been looked for, I had to face the fact that at this rate I shouldn't get the other books to do. I hurled myself in despair on Miss Churm – I put her through all her paces. I not only adopted Oronte publicly as my hero, but one morning when the Major looked in to see if I didn't require him to finish a *Cheapside* figure for which he had begun to sit the week before, I told him I had changed my mind – I'd do the drawing from my man. At this my visitor turned pale and stood looking at me. 'Is *he* your idea of an English gentleman?' he asked.

I was disappointed, I was nervous, I wanted to get on with my work; so I replied with irritation: 'Oh my dear Major – I can't be ruined for *you*!'

It was a horrid speech, but he stood another moment – after which, without a word, he quitted the studio. I drew a long breath, for I said to myself that I shouldn't see him again. I hadn't told him definitely that I was in danger of having my work rejected, but I was vexed at his not having felt the catastrophe in the air, read with me the moral of our fruitless collaboration, the lesson that in the deceptive atmosphere of art even the highest respectability may fail of being plastic.

I didn't owe my friends money, but I did see them again. They reappeared together three days later, and, given all the other facts, there was something tragic in that one. It was a clear proof they could find nothing else in life to do. They had threshed the matter out in a dismal conference – they had digested the bad news that they were not in for the series. If they weren't useful to me even for the *Cheapside* their function seemed difficult to determine, and I could only judge at first that they had come, forgivingly, decorously, to take a last leave. This made me rejoice in secret that I had little leisure for a scene; for I had placed both my other models in position together and I was pegging away at a drawing from which I hoped to derive glory. It had been suggested by the passage in which Rutland Ramsay, drawing up a chair to Artemisia's piano-stool, says extraordinary things to her while she ostensibly fingers out a difficult piece of music. I had done Miss Churm at the piano before – it was an attitude in which she knew how to

take on an absolutely poetic grace. I wished the two figures to
'compose' together with intensity, and my little Italian had
entered perfectly into my conception. The pair were vividly before me, the piano had been pulled out; it was a charming show
of blended youth and murmured love, which I had only to catch
and keep. My visitors stood and looked at it, and I was friendly
to them over my shoulder.

They made no response, but I was used to silent company and
went on with my work, only a little disconcerted – even though
exhilarated by the sense that *this* was at least the ideal thing –
at not having got rid of them after all. Presently I heard Mrs
Monarch's sweet voice beside or rather above me: 'I wish her
hair were a little better done.' I looked up and she was staring
with a strange fixedness at Miss Churm, whose back was turned
to her. 'Do you mind my just touching it?' she went on – a question which made me spring up for an instant as with the instinctive fear that she might do the young lady a harm. But she
quieted me with a glance I shall never forget – I confess I should
like to have been able to paint *that* – and went for a moment to
my model. She spoke to her softly, laying a hand on her shoulder and bending over her; and as the girl, understanding, gratefully assented, she disposed her rough curls, with a few quick
passes, in such a way as to make Miss Churm's head twice as
charming. It was one of the most heroic personal services I've
ever seen rendered. Then Mrs Monarch turned away with a low
sigh and, looking about her as if for something to do, stooped to
the floor with a noble humility and picked up a dirty rag that
had dropped out of my paint-box.

The Major meanwhile had also been looking for something to
do, and, wandering to the other end of the studio, saw before
him my breakfast-things neglected, unremoved. 'I say, can't I be
useful *here*?' he called out to me with an irrepressible quaver. I
assented with a laugh that I fear was awkward, and for the next
ten minutes, while I worked, I heard the light clatter of china
and the tinkle of spoons and glass. Mrs Monarch assisted her
husband – they washed up my crockery, they put it away. They
wandered off into my little scullery, and I afterwards found that
they had cleaned my knives and that my slender stock of plate

had an unprecedented surface. When it came over me, the latent eloquence of what they were doing, I confess that my drawing was blurred for a moment – the picture swam. They had accepted their failure, but they couldn't accept their fate. They had bowed their heads in bewilderment to the perverse and cruel law in virtue of which the real thing could be so much less precious than the unreal; but they didn't want to starve. If my servants were my models, then my models might be my servants. They would reverse the parts – the others would sit for the ladies and gentlemen and *they* would do the work. They would still be in the studio – it was an intense dumb appeal to me not to turn them out. 'Take us on,' they wanted to say – 'we'll do *anything*.'

My pencil dropped from my hand; my sitting was spoiled and I got rid of my sitters, who were also evidently rather mystified and awestruck. Then, alone with the Major and his wife, I had a most uncomfortable moment. He put their prayer into a single sentence: 'I say, you know – just let *us* do for you, can't you?' I couldn't – it was dreadful to see them emptying my slops; but I pretended I could, to oblige them, for about a week. Then I gave them a sum of money to go away, and I never saw them again. I obtained the remaining books, but my friend Hawley repeats that Major and Mrs Monarch did me a permanent harm, got me into false ways. If it be true I'm content to have paid the price – for the memory.

O. Henry

AN UNFINISHED STORY

WE no longer groan and heap ashes upon our heads when the flames of Tophet are mentioned. For, even the preachers have begun to tell us that God is radium, or ether or some scientific compound, and that the worst we wicked ones may expect is a chemical reaction. This is a pleasing hypothesis; but there lingers yet some of the old, goodly terror of orthodoxy.

There are but two subjects upon which one may discourse with a free imagination, and without the possibility of being controverted. You may talk of your dreams; and you may tell what you heard a parrot say. Both Morpheus and the bird are incompetent witnesses; and your listener dare not attack your recital. The baseless fabric of a vision, then, shall furnish my theme – chosen with apologies and regrets instead of the more limited field of pretty Polly's small talk.

I had a dream that was so far removed from the higher criticism that it had to do with the ancient, respectable, and lamented bar-of-judgement theory.

Gabriel had played his trump; and those of us who could not follow suit were arraigned for examination. I noticed at one side a gathering of professional bondsmen in solemn black and collars that buttoned behind; but it seemed there was some trouble about their real estate titles; and they did not appear to be getting any of us out.

A fly cop – an angel policeman – flew over to me and took me by the left wing. Near at hand was a group of very properous-looking spirits arraigned for judgement.

'Do you belong with that bunch?' the policeman asked.

'Who are they?' was my answer.

'Why,' said he, 'they are –'

But this irrelevant stuff is taking up space that the story hould occupy.

Dulcie worked in a department store. She sold Hamburg edging, or stuffed peppers, or automobiles, or other little trinkets such as they keep in department stores. Of what she earned, Dulcie received six dollars per week. The remainder was credited to her and debited to somebody else's account in the ledger kept by G— Oh, primal energy, you say, Reverend Doctor – Well then, in the Ledger of Primal Energy.

During her first year in the store, Dulcie was paid five dollars per week. It would be instructive to know how she lived on that amount. Don't care? Very well; probably you are interested in larger amounts. Six dollars is a larger amount. I will tell you how she lived on six dollars per week.

One afternoon at six, when Dulcie was sticking her hat-pin within an eighth of an inch of her *medulla oblongata*, she said to her chum, Sadie – the girl that waits on you with her left side:

'Say, Sade, I made a date for dinner this evening with Piggy.'

'You never did!' exclaimed Sadie admiringly. 'Well, ain't you the lucky one? Piggy's an awful swell; and he always takes a girl to swell places. He took Blanche up to the Hoffman House one evening, where they have swell music, and you see a lot of swells. You'll have a swell time, Dulcie.'

Dulcie hurried homeward. Her eyes were shining, and her cheeks showed the delicate pink of life's – real life's – approaching dawn. It was Friday; and she had fifty cents left of her last week's wages.

The streets were filled with the rush-hour floods of people. The electric lights of Broadway were glowing – calling moths from miles, from leagues, from hundreds of leagues out of darkness around to come in and attend the singeing school. Men in accurate clothes, with faces like those carved on cherry-stones by the old salts in sailors' homes, turned and stared at Dulcie as she sped, unheeding, past them. Manhattan, the night-blooming cereus, was beginning to unfold its dead-white, heavy-odoured petals.

Dulcie stopped in a store where goods were cheap and bought an imitation lace collar with her fifty cents. That money was to have been spent otherwise – fifteen cents for supper, ten cents for breakfast, ten cents for lunch. Another dime was to be added to her small store of savings; and five cents was to be squandered for liquorice drops – the kind that made your cheek look like the toothache, and last as long. The liquorice was an extravagance – almost a carouse – but what is life without pleasures?

Dulcie lived in a furnished room. There is this difference between a furnished room and a boarding-house. In a furnished room, other people do not know it when you go hungry.

Dulcie went up to her room – the third floor back in a West Side brownstone-front. She lit the gas. Scientists tell us that the diamond is the hardest substance known. Their mistake. Landladies know of a compound beside which the diamond is as putty. They pack it in the tips of gas-burners; and one may stand on a chair and dig at it in vain until one's fingers are pink and bruised. A hairpin will not remove it; therefore let us call it immovable.

So Dulcie lit the gas. In its one-fourth-candle-power glow we will observe the room.

Couch-bed, dresser, table, washstand, chair – of this much the landlady was guilty. The rest was Dulcie's. On the dresser were her treasures – a gilt china vase presented to her by Sadie, a calendar issued by a pickle works, a book on the divination of dreams, some rice powder in a glass dish, and a cluster of artificial cherries tied with a pink ribbon.

Against the wrinkly mirror stood pictures of General Kitchener, William Muldoon, the Duchess of Marlborough, and Benvenuto Cellini. Against one wall was a plaster of Paris plaque of an O'Callahan in a Roman helmet. Near it was a violent oleograph of a lemon-coloured child assaulting an inflammatory butterfly. This was Dulcie's final judgement in art; but it had never been upset. Her rest had never been disturbed by whispers of stolen copes; no critic had elevated his eyebrows at her infantile entomologist.

Piggy was to call for her at seven. While she swiftly makes ready, let us discreetly face the other way and gossip.

For the room, Dulcie paid two dollars per week. On weekdays her breakfast cost ten cents; she made coffee and cooked an

egg over the gaslight while she was dressing. On Sunday morn-
ings she feasted royally on veal chops and pineapple fritters at
'Billy's' restaurant, at a cost of twenty-five cents – and tipped
the waitress ten cents. New York presents so many temptations
for one to run into extravagance. She had her lunches in the
department-store restaurant at a cost of sixty cents for the week;
dinners were $1.05. The evening papers – show me a New
Yorker going without his daily paper ! – came to six cents; and
two Sunday papers – one for the personal column and the other
to read – were ten cents. The total amounts to $4.76. Now, one
has to buy clothes, and –

I give it up. I hear of wonderful bargain in fabrics, and of
miracles performed with needle and thread; but I am in doubt. I
hold my pen poised in vain when I would add to Dulcie's life
some of those joys that belong to woman by virtue of all the
unwritten, sacred, natural, inactive ordinances of the equity of
heaven. Twice she had been to Coney Island and had ridden the
hobby-horses. 'Tis a weary thing to count your pleasures by
summers instead of by hours.

Piggy needs but a word. When the girls named him, an
undeserving stigma was cast upon the noble family of swine.
The words-of-three-letters lesson in the old blue spelling book
begins with Piggy's biography. He was fat; he had the soul of a
rat, the habits of a bat, and the magnanimity of a cat. ... He
wore expensive clothes; and was a connoisseur in starvation. He
could look at a shop-girl and tell you to an hour how long it had
been since she had eaten anything more nourishing than marsh-
mallows and tea. He hung about the shopping districts, and
prowled around in department stores with his invitations to
dinner. Men who escort dogs upon the streets at the end of a
string look down upon him. He is a type; I can dwell upon him
no longer; my pen is not the kind intended for him; I am no
carpenter.

At ten minutes to seven Dulcie was ready. She looked at
herself in the wrinkly mirror. The reflection was satisfactory.
The dark blue dress, fitting without a wrinkle, the hat with its
jaunty black feather, the but-slightly-soiled gloves – all representing self-denial, even of food itself – were vastly becoming.

Dulcie forgot everything else for a moment except that she was beautiful, and that life was about to lift a corner of its mysterious veil for her to observe its wonders. No gentleman had ever asked her out before. Now she was going for a brief moment into the glitter and exalted show.

The girls said that Piggy was a 'spender'. There would be a grand dinner, and music, and splendidly dressed ladies to look at, and things to eat that strangely twisted the girls' jaws when they tried to tell about them. No doubt she would be asked out again.

There was a blue pongee suit in a window that she knew – by saving twenty cents a week instead of ten, in – let's see – Oh, it would run into years! But there was a second-hand store in Seventh Avenue where –

Somebody knocked at the door. Dulcie opened it. The land-lady stood there with a spurious smile, sniffing for cooking by stolen gas.

'A gentleman's downstairs to see you,' she said. 'Name is Mr Wiggins.'

By such epithet was Piggy known to unfortunate ones who had to take him seriously.

Dulcie turned to the dresser to get her handkerchief; then she stopped still, and bit her underlip hard. While looking in her mirror she had seen fairyland and herself, a princess, just awakening from a long slumber. She had forgotten one that was watching her with sad, beautiful, stern eyes – the only one there was to approve or condemn what she did. Straight and slender and tall, with a look of sorrowful reproach on his handsome, melancholy face, General Kitchener fixed his wonderful eyes on her out of his gilt photograph frame on the dresser.

Dulcie turned like an automatic doll to the landlady.

'Tell him I can't go,' she said dully. 'Tell him I'm sick, or something. Tell him I'm not going out.'

After the door was closed and locked, Dulcie fell upon her bed, crushing her black tip, and cried for ten minutes. General Kitchener was her only friend. He was Dulcie's ideal of a gallant knight. He looked as if he might have a secret sorrow, and his wonderful moustache was a dream, and she was a little afraid of that stern yet tender look in his eyes. She used to have little fancies that he would call at the house sometime, and ask for her, with his sword clanking against his high boots. Once, when a boy was rattling a piece of chain against a lamp-post, she had opened the window and looked out. But there was no use. She knew that General Kitchener was away over in Japan, leading his army against the savage Turks; and he would never step out of his gilt frame for her. Yet one look from him had vanquished Piggy that night. Yes, for that night.

When her cry was over Dulcie got up and took off her best dress, and put on her old blue kimono. She wanted no dinner. She sang two verses of 'Sammy'. Then she became intensely interested in a little red speck on the side of her nose. And after that was attended to, she drew up a chair to the rickety table, and told her fortune with an old deck of cards.

'The horrid, impudent thing!' she said aloud. 'And I never gave him a word or a look to make him think it!'

At nine o'clock Dulcie took a tin box of crackers and a little pot of raspberry jam out of her trunk, and had a feast. She offered General Kitchener some jam on a cracker; but he only looked at her as the sphinx would have looked at a butterfly – if there are butterflies in the desert.

'Don't eat it if you don't want to,' said Dulcie. 'And don't put on so many airs and scold so with your eyes. I wonder if you'd be so superior and snippy if you had to live on six dollars a week.'

It was not a good sign for Dulcie to be rude to General Kitchener. And then she turned Benvenuto Cellini face downward with a severe gesture. But that was not inexcusable; for she had always thought he was Henry VIII, and she did not approve of him.

At half past nine Dulcie took a last look at the pictures on the dresser, turned out the light, and skipped into bed. It's an awful thing to go to bed with a good night look at General Kitchener, William Muldoon, the Duchess of Marlborough, and Benvenuto Cellini.

This story really doesn't get anywhere at all. The rest of it comes later – sometime when Piggy asks Dulcie again to dine

with him, and she is feeling lonelier than usual, and General
Kitchener happens to be looking the other way; and then –

As I said before, I dreamed that I was standing near a crowd
of prosperous-looking angels, and a policeman took me by the
wing and asked if I belonged with them.

'Who are they?' I asked.

'Why,' said he, 'they are the men who hired working-girls,
and paid 'em five or six dollars a week to live on. Are you one
of the bunch?'

'Not on your immortality,' said I. 'I'm only the fellow that
set fire to an orphan asylum, and murdered a blind man for his
pennies.'

Stephen Crane

THE BRIDE COMES TO YELLOW SKY

I

T H E great Pullman was whirling onward with such dignity of
motion that a glance from the window seemed simply to prove
that the plains of Texas were pouring eastward. Vast flats of
green grass, dull-hued spaces of mesquit and cactus, little groups
of frame houses, woods of light and tender trees, all were sweeping into the east, sweeping over the horizon, a precipice.

A newly married pair had boarded this train at San Antonio.
The man's face was reddened from many days in the wind and
sun, and a direct result of his new black clothes was that his
brick-coloured hands were constantly performing in a most
conscious fashion. From time to time he looked down respectfully at his attire. He sat with a hand on each knee, like a man
waiting in a barber's shop. The glances he devoted to other
passengers were furtive and shy.

The bride was not pretty, nor was she very young. She wore
a dress of blue cashmere, with small reservations of velvet here
and there, and with steel buttons abounding. She continually
twisted her head to regard her puff-sleeves, very stiff, straight,
and high. They embarrassed her. It was quite apparent that she
had cooked, and that she expected to cook, dutifully. The
blushes caused by the careless scrutiny of some passengers as
she had entered the car were strange to see upon this plain,
under-class countenance, which was drawn in placid, almost
emotionless lines.

They were evidently very happy. 'Ever been in a parlour-car
before?' he asked, smiling with delight.

'No,' she answered; 'I never was. It's fine, ain't it?'

'Great. And then, after a while, we'll go forward to the diner, and get a big lay-out. Finest meal in the world. Charge, a dollar.'

'Oh, do they?' cried the bride. 'Charge a dollar? Why, that's too much – for us – ain't it, Jack?'

'Not this trip, anyhow,' he answered bravely. 'We're going to go the whole thing.'

Later, he explained to her about the train. 'You see it's a thousand miles from one end of Texas to the other, and this train runs right across it, and never stops but four times.'

He had the pride of an owner. He pointed out to her the dazzling fittings of the coach, and, in truth, her eyes opened wider as she contemplated the sea-green figured velvet, the shining brass, silver, and glass, the wood that gleamed as darkly brilliant as the surface of a pool of oil. At one end a bronze figure sturdily held a support for a separated chamber, and at convenient places on the ceiling were frescoes in olive and silver.

To the minds of the pair, their surroundings reflected the glory of their marriage that morning in San Antonio. This was the environment of their new estate, and the man's face, in particular, beamed with an elation that made him appear ridiculous to the Negro porter. This individual at times surveyed them from afar with an amused and superior grin. On other occasions he bullied them with skill in ways that did not make it exactly plain to them that they were being bullied. He subtly used all the manners of the most unconquerable kind of snobbery. He oppressed them, but of this oppression they had small knowledge, and they speedily forgot that unfrequently a number of travellers covered them with stares of derisive enjoyment. Historically there was supposed to be something infinitely humorous in their situation.

'We are due in Yellow Sky at 3.42,' he said, looking tenderly into her eyes.

'Oh, are we?' she said, as if she had not been aware of it.

To evince surprise at her husband's statement was part of her wifely amiability. She took from a pocket a little silver watch, and as she held it before her, and stared at it with a frown of attention, the new husband's face shone.

'I bought it in San Anton' from a friend of mine,' he told her gleefully.

'It's seventeen minutes past twelve,' she said, looking up at him with a kind of shy and clumsy coquetry.

A passenger, noting this play, grew excessively sardonic, and winked at himself in one of the numerous mirrors.

At last they went to the dining-car. Two rows of Negro waiters in dazzling white suits surveyed their entrance with the interest, and also the equanimity, of men who had been fore-warned. The pair fell to the lot of a waiter who happened to feel pleasure in steering them through their meal. He viewed them with the manner of a fatherly pilot, his countenance radiant with benevolence. The patronage entwined with the ordinary deference was not palpable to them. And yet as they returned to their coach they showed in their faces a sense of escape.

To the left, miles down a long purple slope, was a little ribbon of mist, where moved the keening Rio Grande. The train was approaching it at an angle, and the apex was Yellow Sky. Presently it was apparent that as the distance from Yellow Sky grew shorter, the husband became commensurately restless. His brick-red hands were more insistent in their prominence. Occasionally he was even rather absent-minded and far away when the bride leaned forward and addressed him.

As a matter of truth, Jack Potter was beginning to find the shadow of a deed weigh upon him like a leaden slab. He, the town-marshal of Yellow Sky, a man known, liked, and feared in his corner, a prominent person, had gone to San Antonio to meet a girl he believed he loved, and there, after the usual prayers, had actually induced her to marry him without con-sulting Yellow Sky for any part of the transaction. He was now bringing his bride before an innocent and unsuspecting com-munity.

Of course, people in Yellow Sky married as it pleased them in accordance with a general custom, but such was Potter's thought of his duty to his friends, or of their idea of his duty, or of an unspoken form which does not control men in these matters, that he felt he was heinous. He had committed an extraordinary crime. Face to face with this girl in San Antonio, and spurred by his sharp impulse, he had gone headlong over all the social hedges. At San Antonio he was like a man hidden in the dark. A knife to sever any friendly duty, any form, was easy to his hand in that remote city. But the hour of Yellow Sky, the hour of daylight, was approaching.

He knew full well that his marriage was an important thing to his town. It could only be exceeded by the burning of the new hotel. His friends would not forgive him. Frequently he had reflected upon the advisability of telling them by telegraph, but a new cowardice had been upon him. He feared to do it. And now the train was hurrying him toward a scene of amazement, glee, reproach. He glanced out of the window at the line of haze swinging slowly in toward the train.

Yellow Sky had a kind of brass band which played painfully to the delight of the populace. He laughed without heart as he thought of it. If the citizens could dream of his prospective arrival with his bride, they would parade the band at the station, and escort them, amid cheers and laughing congratulations, to his adobe home.

He resolved that he would use all the devices of speed and plainscraft in making the journey from the station to his house. Once within that safe citadel, he could issue some sort of a vocal bulletin, and then not go among the citizens until they had time to wear off a little of their enthusiasm.

The bride looked anxiously at him. 'What's worrying you, Jack?'

He laughed again. 'I'm not worrying, girl. I'm only thinking of Yellow Sky.'

She flushed in comprehension.

A sense of mutual guilt invaded their minds, and developed a finer tenderness. They looked at each other with eyes softly aglow. But Potter often laughed the same nervous laugh. The flush upon the bride's face seemed quite permanent.

The traitor to the feelings of Yellow Sky narrowly watched the speeding landscape.

'We're nearly there,' he said.

Presently the porter came and announced the proximity of

Potter's home. He held a brush in his hand, and, with all his airy superiority gone, he brushed Potter's new clothes, as the latter slowly turned this way and that way. Potter fumbled out a coin, and gave it to the porter as he had seen others do. It was a heavy and muscle-bound business, as that of a man shoeing his first horse.

The porter took their bag, and, as the train began to slow, they moved forward to the hooded platform of the car. Presently the two engines and their long string of coaches rushed into the station of Yellow Sky.

'They have to take water here,' said Potter, from a constricted throat, and in mournful cadence as one announcing death. Before the train stopped his eye had swept the length of the platform, and he was glad and astonished to see there was no one upon it but the station-agent, who, with a slightly hurried and anxious air, was walking toward the water-tanks. When the train had halted, the porter alighted first and placed in position a little temporary step.

'Come on, girl,' said Potter, hoarsely.

As he helped her down, they each laughed on a false note. He took the bag from the Negro, and bade his wife cling to his arm. As they slunk rapidly away, his hang-dog glance perceived that they were unloading the two trunks, and also that the station-agent, far ahead, near the baggage-car, had turned, and was running toward him, making gestures. He laughed, and groaned as he laughed, when he noted the first effect of his marital bliss upon Yellow Sky. He gripped his wife's arm firmly to his side, and they fled. Behind them the porter stood chuckling fatuously.

2

The California Express on the Southron Railway was due at Yellow Sky in twenty-one minutes. There were six men at the bar of the Weary Gentleman saloon. One was a drummer, who talked a great deal and rapidly; three were Texans, who did not care to talk at that time; and two were Mexican sheepherders, who did not talk as a general practice in the Weary

Gentleman saloon. The bar-keeper's dog lay on the board-walk that crossed in front of the door. His head was on his paws, and he glanced drowsily here and there with the constant vigilance of a dog that is kicked on occasion. Across the sandy street were some vivid green grass plots, so wonderful in appearance amid the sands that burned near them in a blazing sun, that they caused a doubt in the mind. They exactly resembled the grass-mats used to represent lawns on the stage. At the cooler end of the railway-station a man without a coat sat in a tilted chair and smoked his pipe. The fresh-cut bank of the Rio Grande circled near the town, and there could be seen beyond it a great plum-coloured plain of mesquit.

Save for the busy drummer and his companions in the saloon, Yellow Sky was dozing. The newcomer leaned grace-fully upon the bar, and recited many tales with the confidence of a bard who has come upon a new field.

'And at the moment that the old man fell downstairs, with the bureau in his arms, the old woman was coming up with two scuttles of coal, and, of course —'

The drummer's tale was interrupted by a young man who suddenly appeared in the open door. He cried —

'Scratchy Wilson's drunk, and has turned loose with both hands.'

The two Mexicans at once set down their glasses, and faded out of the rear entrance of the saloon.

The drummer, innocent and jocular, answered —

'All right, old man. S'pose he has. Come and have a drink, anyhow.'

But the information had made such an obvious cleft in every skull in the room, that the drummer was obliged to see its importance. All had become instantly morose.

'Say,' said he, mystified, 'what is this?'

His three companions made the introductory gesture of eloquent speech, but the young man at the door forestalled them.

'It means, my friend,' he answered, as he came into the saloon, 'that for the next two hours this town won't be a health resort.'

The bar-keeper went to the door, and locked and barred it. Reaching out of the window, he pulled in heavy wooden shutters and barred them. Immediately a solemn, chapel-like gloom was upon the place. The drummer was looking from one to another.

'But say,' he cried, 'what is this, anyhow? You don't mean there is going to be a gun-fight?'

'Don't know whether they'll be a fight or not,' answered one man grimly. 'But there'll be some shootin' – some good shootin'.'

The young man who had warned them waved his hand. 'Oh, there'll be a fight, fast enough, if any one wants it. Anybody can get a fight out there in the street. There's a fight just waiting.'

The drummer seemed to be swayed between the interest of a foreigner, and a perception of personal danger.

'What did you say his name was?' he asked.

'Scratchy Wilson,' they answered in chorus.

'And will he kill anybody? What are you going to do? Does this happen often? Does he rampage round like this once a week or so? Can he break in that door?'

'No, he can't break down that door,' replied the bar-keeper. 'He's tried it three times. But when he comes you'd better lay down on the floor, stranger. He's dead sure to shoot at it, and a bullet may come through.'

Thereafter the drummer kept a strict eye on the door. The time had not yet been called for him to hug the floor, but as a minor precaution he sidled near to the wall.

'Will he kill anybody?' he said again.

The men laughed low and scornfully at the question.

'He's out to shoot, and he's out for trouble. Don't see any good in experimentin' with him.'

'But what do you do in a case like this? What do you do?'

A man responded – 'Why, he and Jack Potter –'

But, in chorus, the other men interrupted – 'Jack Potter's in San Anton'.'

'Well, who is he? What's he got to do with it?'

'Oh, he's the town-marshal. He goes out and fights Scratchy when he gets on one of these tears.'

'Whow!' said the drummer, mopping his brow. 'Nice job he's got.'

The voices had toned away to mere whisperings. The drummer wished to ask further questions, which were born of an increasing anxiety and bewilderment, but when he attempted them, the men merely looked at him in irritation, and motioned him to remain silent. A tense waiting hush was upon them. In the deep shadows of the room their eyes shone as they listened for sounds from the street. One man made three gestures at the bar-keeper, and the latter, moving like a ghost, handed him a glass and a bottle. The man poured a full glass of whisky, and set down the bottle noiselessly. He gulped the whisky in a swallow, and turned again toward the door in immovable silence. The drummer saw that the bar-keeper, without a sound, had taken a Winchester from beneath the bar. Later, he saw this individual beckoning to him, so he tip-toed across the room.

'You better come with me back of the bar.'

'No thanks,' said the drummer, perspiring. 'I'd rather be where I can make a break for the back-door.'

Whereupon the man of bottles made a kindly but peremptory gesture. The drummer obeyed it, and finding himself seated on a box, with his head below the level of the bar, balm was laid upon his soul at sight of various zinc and copper fittings that bore a resemblance to plate armour. The bar-keeper took a seat comfortably upon an adjacent box.

'You see,' he whispered, 'this here Scratchy Wilson is a wonder with a gun – a perfect wonder – and when he goes on the war-trail, we hunt our holes – naturally. He's about the last one of the old gang that used to hang out along the river here. He's a terror when he's drunk. When he's sober he's all right – kind of simple – wouldn't hurt a fly – nicest fellow in town. But when he's drunk – whoo!'

There were periods of stillness.

'I wish Jack Potter was back from San Anton',' said the bar-keeper. 'He shot Wilson up once – in the leg – and he would sail in and pull out the kinks in this thing.'

Presently they heard from a distance the sound of a shot, followed by three wild yells. It instantly removed a bond from

the men in the darkened saloon. There was a shuffling of feet.
They looked at each other.

'Here he comes,' they said.

3

A man in a maroon-coloured flannel shirt, which had been
purchased for purposes of decoration, and made, principally,
by some Jewish women on the east side of New York, rounded
a corner and walked into the middle of the main street of Yellow Sky. In either hand the man held a long, heavy blue-black
revolver. Often he yelled, and these cries rang through a sem-
blance of a deserted village, shrilly flying over the roofs in a
volume that seemed to have no relation to the ordinary vocal
strength of a man. It was as if the surrounding stillness formed
the arch of a tomb over him. These cries of ferocious challenge
rang against walls of silence. And his boots had red tops with
gilded imprints, of the kind beloved in winter by little sledging
boys on the hillsides of New England.

The man's face flamed in a rage begot of whisky. His eyes,
rolling and yet keen for ambush, hunted the still door-ways and
windows. He walked with the creeping movement of the midnight cat. As it occurred to him, he roared menacing information. The long revolvers in his hands were as easy as straws;
they were moved with an electric swiftness. The little fingers of
each hand played sometimes in a musician's way. Plain from
the low collar of the shirt, the cords of his neck straightened and
sank as passion moved him. The only sounds were his terrible
invitations. The calm adobes preserved their demeanour at the
passing of this small thing in the middle of the street.

There was no offer of fight – no offer of fight. The man called
to the sky. There were no attractions. He bellowed and fumed
and swayed his revolver here and everywhere.

The dog of the bar-keeper of the Weary Gentleman saloon
had not appreciated the advance of events. He yet lay dozing in
front of his master's door. At sight of the dog, the man paused
and raised his revolver humorously. At sight of the man, the dog
sprang up and walked diagonally away, with a sullen head and

growling. The man yelled, and the dog broke into a gallop. As it was about to enter an alley, there was a loud noise, a whistling, and something spat the ground directly before it. The dog screamed, and, wheeling in terror, galloped headlong in a new direction. Again there was a noise, a whistling, and sand was kicked viciously before it. Fear-stricken, the dog turned and flurried like an animal in a pen. The man stood laughing, his weapons at his hips.

Ultimately the man was attracted by the closed door of the Weary Gentleman saloon. He went to it, and, hammering with a revolver, demanded drink.

The door remaining imperturbable, he picked a bit of paper from the walk, and nailed it to the framework with a knife. He then turned his back contemptuously upon this popular resort, and, walking to the opposite side of the street and spinning there on his heel quickly and lithely, fired at the bit of paper. He missed it by a half-inch. He swore at himself, and went away. Later, he comfortably fusiladed the windows of his most intimate friend. The man was playing with this town. It was a toy for him.

But still there was no offer of fight. The name of Jack Potter, his ancient antagonist, entered his mind, and he concluded that it would be a glad thing if he should go to Potter's house, and, by bombardment, induce him to come out and fight. He moved in the direction of his desire, chanting Apache scalp music.

When he arrived at it, Potter's house presented the same still, calm front as had the other adobes. Taking up a strategic position, the man howled a challenge. But this house regarded him as might a great stone god. It gave no sign. After a decent wait, the man howled further challenges, mingling with them wonderful epithets.

Presently there came the spectacle of a man churning himself into deepest rage over the immobility of a house. He fumed at it as the winter wind attacks a prairie cabin in the north. To the distance there should have gone the sound of a tumult like the fighting of two hundred Mexicans. As necessity bade him, he paused for breath or to reload his revolvers.

4

Potter and his bride walked sheepishly and with speed. Sometimes they laughed together shamefacedly and low.

'Next corner, dear,' he said finally.

They put forth the efforts of a pair walking bowed against a strong wind. Potter was about to raise a finger to point the first appearance of the new home, when, as they circled the corner, they came face to face with a man in a maroon-coloured shirt, who was feverishly pushing cartridges into a large revolver. Upon the instant the man dropped this revolver to the ground, and, like lightning, whipped another from its holster. The second weapon was aimed at the bridegroom's chest.

There was a silence. Potter's mouth seemed to be merely a grave for his tongue. He exhibited an instinct to at once loosen his arm from the woman's grip, and he dropped the bag to the sand. As for the bride, her face had gone as yellow as old cloth. She was a slave to hideous rites, gazing at the apparitional snake.

The two men faced each other at a distance of three paces. He of the revolver smiled with a new and quiet ferocity. 'Tried to sneak up on me!' he said. 'Tried to sneak up on me!' His eyes grew more baleful. As Potter made a slight movement, the man thrust his revolver venomously forward. 'No; don't you do it, Jack Potter. Don't you move a finger towards a gun just yet. Don't you move an eyelash. The time has come for me to settle with you, and I'm going to do it my own way, and loaf along with no interferin'. So if you don't want a gun bent on you, just mind what I tell you.'

Potter looked at his enemy. 'I ain't got a gun on me, Scratchy,' he said. 'Honest, I ain't.' He was stiffening and steadying, but yet somehow at the back of his mind a vision of the Pullman floated – the sea-green figured velvet, the shining brass, silver, and glass, the wood that gleamed as darkly brilliant as the surface of a pool of oil – all the glory of their marriage, the environment of the new estate.

'You know I fight when it comes to fighting, Scratchy Wilson, but I ain't got a gun on me. You'll have to do all the shootin' yourself.'

His enemy's face went livid. He stepped forward, and lashed his weapon to and fro before Potter's chest.

'Don't you tell me you ain't got no gun on you, you whelp. Don't tell me no lie like that. There ain't a man in Texas ever seen you without no gun. Don't take me for no kid.'

His eyes blazed with light and his throat worked like a pump.

'I ain't takin' you for no kid,' answered Potter. His heels had not moved an inch backward. 'I'm takin' you for a — fool. I tell you I ain't got a gun, and I ain't. If you're goin' to shoot me up, you'd better begin now. You'll never get a chance like this again.'

So much enforced reasoning had told on Wilson's rage. He was calmer.

'If you ain't got a gun, why ain't you got a gun?' he sneered. 'Been to Sunday School?'

'I ain't got a gun because I've just come from San Anton' with my wife. I'm married,' said Potter. 'And if I'd thought there was going to be any galoots like you prowling around when I brought my wife home, I'd had a gun, and don't you forget it.'

'Married!' said Scratchy, not at all comprehending.

'Yes, married! I'm married!' said Potter, distinctly.

'Married!' said Scratchy; seeming for the first time he saw the drooping drowning woman at the other man's side. 'No!' he said. He was like a creature allowed a glimpse of another world. He moved a pace backward, and his arm with the revolver dropped to his side. 'Is this — is this the lady?' he asked.

'Yes, this is the lady,' answered Potter.

There was another period of silence.

'Well,' said Wilson at last, slowly, 'I s'pose it's all off now?'

'It's all off if you say so, Scratchy. You know I didn't make the trouble.'

Potter lifted his valise.

'Well, I 'low it's off, Jack,' said Wilson. He was looking at the ground. 'Married!' He was not a student of chivalry; it was merely that in the presence of this foreign condition he was a simple child of the earlier plains. He picked up his starboard revolver, and placing both weapons in their holsters, he went away. His feet made funnel-shaped tracks in the heavy sand.

Willa Cather

NEIGHBOR ROSICKY

I

WHEN Doctor Burleigh told neighbour Rosicky he had a bad heart, Rosicky protested.

'So? No, I guess my heart was always pretty good. I got a little asthma, maybe. Just a awful short breath when I was pitchin' hay last summer, dat's all.'

'Well now, Rosicky, if you know more about it than I do, what did you come to me for? It's your heart that makes you short of breath, I tell you. You're sixty-five years old, and you've always worked hard, and your heart's tired. You've got to be careful from now on, and you can't do heavy work any more. You've got five boys at home to do it for you.'

The old farmer looked up at the Doctor with a gleam of amusement in his queer triangular-shaped eyes. His eyes were large and lively, but the lids were caught up in the middle in a curious way, so that they formed a triangle. He did not look like a sick man. His brown face was creased but not wrinkled, he had a ruddy colour in his smooth-shaven cheeks and in his lips, under his long brown moustache. His hair was thin and ragged around his ears, but very little grey. His forehead, naturally high and crossed by deep parallel lines, now ran all the way up to his pointed crown. Rosicky's face had the habit of looking interested – suggested a contented disposition and a reflective quality that was gay rather than grave. This gave him a certain detachment, the easy manner of an onlooker and observer.

'Well, I guess you ain't got no pills fur a bad heart, Doctor Ed. I guess the only thing is fur me to git me a new one.'

Doctor Burleigh swung round in his desk-chair and frowned

at the old farmer. 'I think if I were you I'd take a little care of the old one, Rosicky.'

Rosicky shrugged. 'Maybe I don't know how. I expect you mean fur me not to drink my coffee no more.'

'I wouldn't, in your place. But you'll do as you choose about that. I've never yet been able to separate a Bohemian from his coffee or his pipe. I've quit trying. But the sure thing is you've got to cut out farm work. You can feed the stock and do chores about the barn, but you can't do anything in the fields that makes you short of breath.'

'How about shelling corn?'

'Of course not!'

Rosicky considered with puckered brows.

'I can't make my heart go no longer'n it wants to, can I, Doctor Ed?'

'I think it's good for five or six years yet, maybe more, if you'll take the strain off it. Sit around the house and help Mary. If I had a good wife like yours, I'd want to stay around the house.'

His patient chuckled. 'It ain't no place fur a man. I don't like no old man hanging round the kitchen too much. An' my wife, she's a awful hard worker her own self.'

'That's it; you can help her a little. My Lord, Rosicky, you are one of the few men I know who has a family he can get some comfort out of; happy dispositions, never quarrel among themselves, and they treat you right. I want to see you live a few years and enjoy them.'

'Oh, they're good kids, all right,' Rosicky assented.

The Doctor wrote him a prescription and asked him how his oldest son, Rudolph, who had married in the spring, was getting on. Rudolph had struck out for himself, on rented land. 'And how's Polly? I was afraid Mary mightn't like an American daughter-in-law, but it seems to be working out all right.'

'Yes, she's a fine girl. Dat widder woman bring her daughters up very nice. Polly got lots of spunk, an' she got some style, too. Da's nice, for young folks to have some style.' Rosicky inclined his head gallantly. His voice and his twinkly smile were an affectionate compliment to his daughter-in-law.

'It looks like a storm, and you'd better be getting home before it comes. In town in the car?' Doctor Burleigh rose.

'No, I'm in de wagon. When you got five boys, you ain't got much chance to ride round in de Ford. I ain't much for cars, noway.'

'Well, it's a good road out to your place; but I don't want you bumping around in a wagon much. And never again on a hay-rake, remember!'

Rosicky placed the Doctor's fee delicately behind the desk-telephone, looking the other way, as if this were an absent-minded gesture. He put on his plush cap and his corduroy jacket with a sheepskin collar, and went out.

The Doctor picked up his stethoscope and frowned at it as if he were seriously annoyed with the instrument. He wished it had been telling tales about some other man's heart, some old man who didn't look the Doctor in the eye so knowingly, or hold out such a warm brown hand when he said good-bye. Doctor Burleigh had been a poor boy in the country before he went away to medical school; he had known Rosicky almost ever since he could remember, and he had a deep affection for Mrs Rosicky.

Only last winter he had had such a good breakfast at Rosicky's, and that when he needed it. He had been out all night on a long, hard confinement case at Tom Marshall's – a big rich farm where there was plenty of stock and plenty of feed and a great deal of expensive farm machinery of the newest model, and no comfort whatever. The woman had too many children and too much work, and she was no manager. When the baby was born at last, and handed over to the assisting neighbour woman, and the mother was properly attended to, Burleigh refused any breakfast in that slovenly house, and drove his buggy – the snow was too deep for a car – eight miles to Anton Rosicky's place. He didn't know another farmhouse where a man could get such a warm welcome, and such good strong coffee with rich cream. No wonder the old chap didn't want to give up his coffee!

He had driven in just when the boys had come back from the barn and were washing up for breakfast. The long table,

covered with a bright oilcloth, was set out with dishes waiting
for them, and the warm kitchen was full of the smell of coffee
and hot biscuit and sausage. Five big handsome boys, running
from twenty to twelve, all with what Burleigh called natural
good manners – they hadn't a bit of the painful self-conscious-
ness he himself had to struggle with when he was a lad. One
ran to put his horse away, another helped him off with his fur
coat and hung it up, and Josephine, the youngest child and the
only daughter, quickly set another place under her mother's
direction.

With Mary, to feed creatures was the natural expression of
affection – her chickens, the calves, her big hungry boys. It was
a rare pleasure to feed a young man whom she seldom saw and
of whom she was as proud as if he belonged to her. Some
country housekeepers would have stopped to spread a white
cloth over the oil-cloth, to change the thick cups and plates for
their best china, and the wooden-handled knives for plated ones.
But not Mary.

'You must take us as you find us, Doctor Ed. I'd be glad to
put out my good things for you if you was expected, but I'm
glad to get you any way at all.'

He knew she was glad – she threw back her head and spoke
out as if she were announcing him to the whole prairie. Rosicky
hadn't said anything at all; he merely smiled his twinkling
smile, put some more coal on the fire, and went into his own
room to pour the Doctor a little drink in a medicine glass. When
they were all seated, he watched his wife's face from his end of
the table and spoke to her in Czech. Then, with the instinct of
politeness which seldom failed him, he turned to the Doctor and
said slyly, 'I was just tellin' her not to ask you no questions
about Mrs Marshall till you eat some breakfast. My wife, she's
terrible fur to ask questions.'

The boys laughed, and so did Mary. She watched the Doctor
devour her biscuit and sausage, too much excited to eat anything
herself. She drank her coffee and sat taking in everything about
her visitor. She had known him when he was a poor country
boy, and was boastfully proud of his success, always saying:
'What do people go to Omaha for, to see a doctor, when we got

the best one in the State right here?' If Mary liked people at all, she felt physical pleasure in the sight of them, personal exultation in any good fortune that came to them. Burleigh didn't know many women like that, but he knew she was like that.

When his hunger was satisfied, he did, of course, have to tell them about Mrs Marshall, and he noticed what a friendly interest the boys took in the matter.

Rudolph, the oldest one (he was still living at home then), said: 'The last time I was over there, she was lifting them big heavy milk-cans, and I knew she oughtn't to be doing it.'

'Yes, Rudolph told me about that when he come home, and I said it wasn't right,' Mary put in warmly. 'It was all right for me to do them things up to the last, for I was terrible strong, but that woman's weakly. And do you think she'll be able to nurse it, Ed?' She sometimes forgot to give him the title she was so proud of. 'And to think of your being up all night and then not able to get a decent breakfast! I don't know what's the matter with such people.'

'Why, Mother,' said one of the boys, 'if Doctor Ed had got breakfast there, we wouldn't have him here. So you ought to be glad.'

'He knows I'm glad to have him, John, any time. But I'm sorry for that poor woman, how bad she'll feel the Doctor had to go away in the cold without his breakfast.'

'I wish I'd been in practice when these were getting born.' The doctor looked down the row of close-clipped heads. 'I missed some good breakfasts by not being.'

The boys began to laugh at their mother because she flushed so red, but she stood her ground and threw up her head. 'I don't care, you wouldn't have got away from this house without breakfast. No doctor ever did. I'd have had something ready fixed that Anton could warm up for you.'

The boys laughed harder than ever, and exclaimed at her: 'I'll bet you would!' 'She would, that!'

'Father, did you get breakfast for the doctor when we were born?'

'Yes, and he used to bring me my breakfast, too, mighty nice.

I was always awful hungry!' Mary admitted with a guilty laugh.

While the boys were getting the Doctor's horse, he went to the window to examine the house plants. 'What do you do to your geraniums to keep them blooming all winter, Mary? I never pass this house that from the road I don't see your windows full of flowers.'

She snapped off a dark red one, and a ruffled new green leaf, and put them in his buttonhole. 'There, that looks better. You look too solemn for a young man, Ed. Why don't you git married? I'm worried about you. Settin' at breakfast, I looked at you real hard, and I seen you've got some grey hairs already.'

'Oh, yes! They're coming. Maybe they'd come faster if I married.'

'Don't talk so. You'll ruin your health eating at the hotel. I could send your wife a nice loaf of nut bread, if you only had one. I don't like to see a young man getting grey. I'll tell you something, Ed; you make some strong black tea and keep it handy in a bowl, and every morning just brush it into your hair, an' it'll keep the grey from showin' much. That's the way I do!'

Sometimes the Doctor heard the gossipers in the drug-store wondering why Rosicky didn't get on faster. He was industrious, and so were his boys, but they were rather free and easy, weren't pushers, and they didn't always show good judgement. They were comfortable, they were out of debt, but they didn't get much ahead. Maybe, Doctor Burleigh reflected, people as generous and warm-hearted and affectionate as the Rosickys never got ahead much; maybe you couldn't enjoy your life and put it into the bank, too.

2

When Rosicky left Doctor Burleigh's office he went into the farm-implement store to light his pipe and put on his glasses and read over the list Mary had given him. Then he went into the general merchandise place next door and stood about until the pretty girl with the plucked eyebrows, who always waited on him, was free. Those eyebrows, two thin India-ink strokes, amused him, because he remembered how they used to be. Rosicky always prolonged his shopping by a little joking; the girl knew the old fellow admired her, and she liked to chaff with him.

'Seems to me about every other week you buy ticking, Mr Rosicky, and always the best quality,' she remarked as she measured off the heavy bolt with red stripes.

'You see, my wife is always makin' goose-fedder pillows, an' de thin stuff don't hold in dem little down-fedders.'

'You must have lots of pillows at your house.'

'Sure. She makes quilts of dem, too. We sleeps easy. Now she's makin' a fedder quilt for my son's wife. You know Polly, that married my Rudolph. How much my bill, Miss Pearl?'

'Eight eighty-five.'

'Chust make it nine, and put in some candy fur de women.'

'As usual. I never did see a man buy so much candy for his wife. First thing you know, she'll be getting too fat.'

'I'd like dat. I ain't much fur all dem slim women like what de style is now.'

'That's one for me, I suppose, Mr Bohunk!' Pearl sniffed and elevated her India-ink strokes.

When Rosicky went out to his wagon, it was beginning to snow – the first snow of the season, and he was glad to see it. He rattled out of town and along the highway through a wonderfully rich stretch of country, the finest farms in the county. He admired this High Prairie, as it was called, and always liked to drive through it. His own place lay in a rougher territory, where there was some clay in the soil and it was not so productive. When he bought his land, he hadn't the money to buy on High Prairie; so he told his boys, when they grumbled, that if their land hadn't some clay in it, they wouldn't own it at all. All the same, he enjoyed looking at these fine farms, as he enjoyed looking at a prize bull.

After he had gone eight miles, he came to the graveyard, which lay just at the edge of his own hay-land. There he stopped his horses and sat still on his wagon seat, looking about at the snowfall. Over yonder on the hill he could see his own house, crouching low, with the clump of orchard behind and the windmill before, and all down the gentle hill-slope the rows of pale gold cornstalks stood out against the white field. The snow was falling over the cornfield and the pasture and the hay-land, steadily, with very little wind — a nice dry snow. The graveyard had only a light wire fence about it and was all overgrown with long red grass. The fine snow, settling into this red grass and upon the few little evergreens and the headstones, looked very pretty.

It was a nice graveyard, Rosicky reflected, sort of snug and homelike, not cramped or mournful — a big sweep all round it. A man could lie down in the long grass and see the complete arch of the sky over him, hear the wagons go by; in summer the mowing-machine rattled right up to the wire fence. And it was so near home. Over there across the cornstalks his own roof and windmill looked so good to him that he promised himself to mind the Doctor and take care of himself. He was awful fond of his place, he admitted. He wasn't anxious to leave it. And it was a comfort to think that he would never have to go farther than the edge of his own hayfield. The snow, falling over his barnyard and the graveyard, seemed to draw things together like. And they were all old neighbors in the graveyard, most of them friends; there was nothing to feel awkward or embarrassed about. Embarrassment was the most disagreeable feeling Rosicky knew. He didn't often have it — only with certain people whom he didn't understand at all.

Well, it was a nice snowstorm; a fine sight to see the snow falling so quietly and graciously over so much open country. On his cap and shoulders, on the horses' backs and manes, light, delicate, mysterious it fell; and with it a dry cool fragrance was released into the air. It meant rest for vegetation and men and beasts, for the ground itself; a season of long nights for sleep, leisurely breakfasts, peace by the fire. This and much more went through Rosicky's mind, but he merely told himself that winter was coming, clucked to his horses, and drove on.

When he reached home, John, the youngest boy, ran out to put away his team for him, and he met Mary coming up from

the outside cellar with her apron full of carrots. They went into
the house together. On the table, covered with oilcloth figured
with clusters of blue grapes, a place was set, and he smelled hot
coffee-cake of some kind. Anton never lunched in town; he
thought that extravagant, and anyhow he didn't like the food.
So Mary always had something ready for him when he got
home.

After he was settled in his chair, stirring his coffee in a big
cup, Mary took out of the oven a pan of *kolache* stuffed with
apricots, examined them anxiously to see whether they had got
too dry, put them beside his plate, and then sat down opposite
him.

Rosicky asked her in Czech if she wasn't going to have any
coffee.

She replied in English, as being somehow the right language
for transacting business: 'Now what did Doctor Ed say, Anton?
You tell me just what.'

'He said I was to tell you some compliments, but I forgot
'em.' Rosicky's eyes twinkled.

'About you, I mean. What did he say about your asthma?'

'He says I ain't got no asthma.' Rosicky took one of the little
rolls in his broad brown fingers. The thickened nail of his right
thumb told the story of his past.

'Well, what is the matter? And don't try to put me off.'

'He don't say nothing much, only I'm a little older, and my
heart ain't so good like it used to be.'

Mary started and brushed her hair back from her temples
with both hands as if she were a little out of her mind. From
the way she glared, she might have been in a rage with him.

'He says there's something the matter with your heart? Doctor Ed says so?'

'Now don't yell at me like I was a hog in de garden, Mary.
You know I always did like to hear a woman talk soft. He
didn't say anything de matter wid my heart, only it ain't so
young like it used to be, an' he tell me not to pitch hay or run
de corn-sheller.'

Mary wanted to jump up, but she sat still. She admired the
way he never under any circumstances raised his voice or spoke

roughly. He was city-bred, and she was country-bred; she often said she wanted her boys to have their papa's nice ways.

'You never have no pain there, do you? It's your breathing and your stomach that's been wrong. I wouldn't believe nobody but Doctor Ed about it. I guess I'll go see him myself. Didn't he give you no advice?'

'Chust to take it easy like, an' stay round de house dis winter. I guess you got some carpenter work for me to do. I kin make some new shelves for you, and I want dis long time to build a closet in de boys' room and make dem two little fellers keep dere clo'es hung up.'

Rosicky drank his coffee from time to time, while he considered. His moustache was of the soft long variety and came down over his mouth like the teeth of a buggy-rake over a bundle of hay. Each time he put down his cup, he ran his blue handkerchief over his lips. When he took a drink of water, he managed very neatly with the back of his hand.

Mary sat watching him intently, trying to find any change in his face. It is hard to see anyone who has become like your own body to you. Yes, his hair had got thin, and his high forehead had deep lines running from left to right. But his neck, always clean shaved except in the busiest seasons, was not loose or baggy. It was burned a dark reddish brown, and there were deep creases in it, but it looked firm and full of blood. His cheeks had a good colour. On either side of his mouth there was a half-moon down the length of his cheek, not wrinkles, but two lines that had come there from his habitual expression. He was shorter and broader than when she married him; his back had grown broad and curved, a good deal like the shell of an old turtle, and his arms and legs were short.

He was fifteen years older than Mary, but she had hardly ever thought about it before. He was her man, and the kind of man she liked. She was rough, and he was gentle – city-bred, as she always said. They had been shipmates on a rough voyage and had stood by each other in trying times. Life had gone well with them because, at bottom, they had the same ideas about life. They agreed, without discussion, as to what was most important and what was secondary. They didn't often exchange opinions, even in Czech – it was as if they had thought the same thought together. A good deal had to be sacrificed and thrown overboard in a hard life like theirs, and they had never disagreed as to the things that could go. It had been a hard life, and a soft life, too. There wasn't anything brutal in the short, broad-backed man with the three-cornered eyes and the forehead that went on to the top of his skull. He was a city man, a gentle man, and though he had married a rough farm girl, he had never touched her without gentleness.

They had been at one accord not to hurry through life, not to be always skimping and saving. They saw their neighbours buy more land and feed more stock than they did, without discontent. Once when the creamery agent came to the Rosickys to persuade them to sell him their cream, he told them how much money the Fasslers, their nearest neighbours, had made on their cream last year.

'Yes,' said Mary, 'and look at them Fassler children! Pale, pinched little things, they look like skimmed milk. I'd rather put some colour into my children's faces than put money into the bank.'

The agent shrugged and turned to Anton.

'I guess we'll do like she says,' said Rosicky.

3

Mary very soon got into town to see Doctor Ed, and then she had a talk with her boys and set a guard over Rosicky. Even John, the youngest, had his father on his mind. If Rosicky went to throw hay down from the loft, one of the boys ran up the ladder and took the fork from him. He sometimes complained that though he was getting to be an old man, he wasn't an old woman yet.

That winter he stayed in the house in the afternoons and carpentered, or sat in the chair between the window full of plants and the wooden bench where the two pails of drinking-water stood. This spot was called 'Father's corner,' though it was not a corner at all. He had a shelf there, where he kept his Bohemian papers and his pipes and tobacco, and his shears and needles and thread and tailor's thimble. Having been a tailor in his youth, he couldn't bear to see a woman patching at his clothes, or at the boys'. He liked tailoring, and always patched all the overalls and jackets and work shirts. Occasionally he made over a pair of pants one of the older boys had outgrown, for the little fellow.

While he sewed, he let his mind run back over his life. He had a good deal to remember, really; life in three countries. The only part of his youth he didn't like to remember was the two years he had spent in London, in Cheapside, working for a German tailor who was wretchedly poor. Those days, when he was nearly always hungry, when his clothes were dropping off him for dirt, and the sound of a strange language kept him in continual bewilderment, had left a sore spot in his mind that wouldn't bear touching.

He was twenty when he landed at Castle Garden in New York, and he had a protector who got him work in a tailor shop in Vesey Street, down near the Washington Market. He looked upon that part of his life as very happy. He became a good workman, he was industrious, and his wages were increased from time to time. He minded his own business and envied nobody's good fortune. He went to night school and learned to read English. He often did overtime work and was well paid for it, but somehow he never saved anything. He couldn't refuse a loan to a friend, and he was self-indulgent. He liked a good dinner, and a little went for beer, a little for tobacco; a good deal went to the girls. He often stood through an opera on Saturday nights; he could get standing-room for a dollar. Those were the great days of opera in New York, and it gave a fellow something to think about for the rest of the week. Rosicky had a quick ear, and a childish love of all the stage splendour; the scenery, the costumes, the ballet. He usually went with a chum, and after the performance they had beer and maybe some oysters somewhere. It was a fine life; for the first five years or so it satisfied him completely. He was never hungry or cold or dirty, and everything amused him: a fire, a dog fight, a parade, a storm, a ferry ride. He thought New York the finest, richest, friendliest city in the world.

Moreover, he had what he called a happy home life. Very

near the tailor shop was a small furniture-factory, where an old Austrian, Loeffler, employed a few skilled men and made un- usual furniture, most of it to order, for the rich German house- wives up-town. The top floor of Loeffler's five-storey factory was a loft, where he kept his choice lumber and stored the odd pieces of furniture left on his hands. One of the young workmen he employed was a Czech, and he and Rosicky became fast friends. They persuaded Loeffler to let them have a sleeping-room in one corner of the loft. They bought good beds and bedding and had their pick of the furniture kept up there. The loft was low- pitched, but light and airy, full of windows, and good-smelling by reason of the fine lumber put up there to season. Old Loeffler used to go down to the docks and buy wood from South Ame- rica and the East from the sea captains. The young men were as foolish about their house as a bridal pair. Zichec, the young cabinet-maker, devised every sort of convenience, and Rosicky kept their clothes in order. At night and on Sundays, when the quiver of machinery underneath was still, it was the quietest place in the world, and on summer nights all the sea winds blew in. Zichec often practised on his flute in the evening. They were both fond of music and went to the opera together. Rosicky thought he wanted to live like that for ever.

But as the years passed, all alike, he began to get a little rest- less. When spring came round, he would begin to feel fretted, and he got to drinking. He was likely to drink too much of a Saturday night. On Sunday he was languid and heavy, getting over his spree. On Monday he plunged into work again. So he never had time to figure out what ailed him, though he knew something did. When the grass turned green in Park Place, and the lilac hedge at the back of Trinity churchyard put out its blossoms, he was tormented by a longing to run away. That was why he drank too much; to get a temporary illusion of freedom and wide horizons.

Rosicky, the old Rosicky, could remember as if it were yester- day the day when the young Rosicky found out what was the matter with him. It was on a Fourth of July afternoon, and he was sitting in Park Place in the sun. The lower part of New York was empty. Wall Street, Liberty Street, Broadway, all empty. So much stone and asphalt with nothing going on, so many empty windows. The emptiness was intense, like the stillness in a great factory when the machinery stops and the belts and bands cease running. It was too great a change, it took all the strength out of one. Those blank buildings, without the stream of life pouring through them, were like empty jails. It struck young Rosicky that this was the trouble with big cities; they built you in from the earth itself, cemented you away from any contact with the ground. You lived in an unnatural world, like the fish in an aquarium, who were probably much more comfortable than they ever were in the sea.

On that very day he began to think seriously about the articles he had read in the Bohemian papers, describing prosperous Czech farming communities in the West. He believed he would like to go out there as a farm hand; it was hardly possible that he could ever have land of his own. His people had always been workmen; his father and grandfather had worked in shops. His mother's parents had lived in the country, but they rented their farm and had a hard time to get along. Nobody in his family had ever owned any land – that belonged to a different station of life altogether. Anton's mother died when he was little, and he was sent into the country to her parents. He stayed with them until he was twelve, and formed those ties with the earth and the farm animals and growing things which are never made at all unless they are made early. After his grandfather died, he went back to live with his father and stepmother, but she was very hard on him, and his father helped him to get passage to London.

After that Fourth of July day in Park Place, the desire to return to the country never left him. To work on another man's farm would be all he asked; to see the sun rise and set and to plant things and watch them grow. He was a very simple man. He was like a tree that has not many roots, but one tap-root that goes down deep. He subscribed for a Bohemian paper printed in Chicago, then for one printed in Omaha. His mind got farther and farther west. He began to save a little money to buy his liberty. When he was thirty-five, there was a great meeting in New York of Bohemian athletic societies, and Rosicky left the

tailor shop and went home with the Omaha delegates to try his
fortune in another part of the world.

4

Perhaps the fact that his own youth was well over before he began to have a family was one reason why Rosicky was so fond
of his boys. He had almost a grandfather's indulgence for them.
He had never had to worry about any of them — except, just
now, a little about Rudolph.

On Saturday night the boys always piled into the Ford, took
little Josephine, and went to town to the moving-picture show.
One Saturday morning they were talking at the breakfast table
about starting early that evening, so that they would have an
hour or so to see the Christmas things in the stores before the
show began. Rosicky looked down the table.

'I hope you boys ain't disappointed, but I want you to let me
have de car tonight. Maybe some of you can go in with de neighbors.'

Their faces fell. They worked hard all week, and they were
still like children. A new jack-knife or a box of candy pleased
the older ones as much as the little fellow.

'If you and Mother are going to town,' Frank said, 'maybe
you could take a couple of us along with you, anyway.'

'No, I want to take de car down to Rudolph's, and let him
an' Polly go in to de show. She don't git into town enough,
an' I'm afraid she's gettin' lonesome, an' he can't afford no car
yet.'

That settled it. The boys were a good deal dashed. Their
father took another piece of apple-cake and went on: 'Maybe
next Saturday night de two little fellers can go along wid dem.'

'Oh, is Rudolph going to have the car every Saturday night?'

Rosicky did not reply at once; then he began to speak seriously: 'Listen, boys; Polly ain't lookin' so good. I don't like to see
nobody lookin' sad. It comes hard fur a town girl to be a farmer's wife. I don't want no trouble to start in Rudolph's family.
When it starts, it ain't so easy to stop. An American girl don't
git used to our ways all at once. I like to tell Polly she and

Rudolph can have the car every Saturday night till after New Year's, if it's all right with you boys.'

'Sure it's all right, Papa,' Mary cut in. 'And it's good you thought about that. Town girls is used to more than country girls. I lay awake nights, scared she'll make Rudolph discontented with the farm.'

The boys put as good a face on it as they could. They surely looked forward to their Saturday nights in town. That evening Rosicky drove the car the half-mile down to Rudolph's new, bare little house.

Polly was in a short-sleeved gingham dress, clearing away the supper dishes. She was a trim, slim little thing, with blue eyes and shingled yellow hair, and her eyebrows were reduced to a mere brush-stroke, like Miss Pearl's.

'Good evening, Mr Rosicky. Rudolph's at the barn, I guess.' She never called him father, or Mary mother. She was sensitive about having married a foreigner. She never in the world would have done it if Rudolph hadn't been such a handsome, persuasive fellow and such a gallant lover. He had graduated in her class in the high school in town, and their friendship began in the ninth grade.

Rosicky went in, though he wasn't exactly asked. 'My boys ain't goin' to town tonight, an' I brought de car over fur you two to go in to de picture show.'

Polly, carrying dishes to the sink, looked over her shoulder at him. 'Thank you. But I'm late with my work tonight, and pretty tired. Maybe Rudolph would like to go in with you.'

'Oh, I don't go to de shows! I'm too old-fashioned. You won't feel so tired after you ride in de air a ways. It's a nice clear night, an' it ain't cold. You go an' fix yourself up, Polly, an' I'll wash de dishes an' leave everything nice fur you.'

Polly blushed and tossed her bob. 'I couldn't let you do that, Mr Rosicky. I wouldn't think of it.'

Rosicky said nothing. He found a bib apron on a nail behind the kitchen door. He slipped it over his head and then took Polly by her two elbows and pushed her gently toward the door of her own room. 'I washed up de kitchen many times for my wife, when de babies was sick or somethin'. You go an' make yourself look nice. I like you to look prettier'n any of dem town girls when you go in. De young folks must have some fun, an' I'm goin' to look out fur you, Polly.'

That kind, reassuring grip on her elbows, the old man's funny bright eyes, made Polly want to drop her head on his shoulder for a second. She restrained herself, but she lingered in his grasp at the door of her room, murmuring tearfully: 'You always lived in the city when you were young, didn't you? Don't you ever get lonesome out here?'

As she turned round to him, her hand fell naturally into his, and he stood holding it and smiling into her face with his peculiar, knowing, indulgent smile without a shadow of reproach in it. 'Dem big cities is all right fur de rich, but dey is terrible hard fur de poor.'

'I don't know. Sometimes I think I'd like to take a chance. You lived in New York, didn't you?'

'An' London. Da's bigger still. I learned my trade dere. Here's Rudolph comin', you better hurry.'

'Will you tell me about London some time?'

'Maybe. Only I ain't no talker, Polly. Run an' dress yourself up.'

The bedroom door closed behind her, and Rudolph came in from the outside, looking anxious. He had seen the car and was sorry any of his family should come just then. Supper hadn't been a very pleasant occasion. Halting in the doorway, he saw his father in a kitchen apron, carrying dishes to the sink. He flushed crimson and something flashed in his eye. Rosicky held up a warning finger.

'I brought de car over fur you an' Polly to go to de picture show, an' I made her let me finish here so you won't be late. You go put on a clean shirt, quick !'

'But don't the boys want the car, Father?'

'Not tonight dey don't.' Rosicky fumbled under his apron and found his pants pocket. He took out a silver dollar and said in a hurried whisper: 'You go an' buy dat girl some ice cream an' candy tonight, like you was courtin'. She's awful good friends wid me.'

Rudolph was very short of cash, but he took the money as if

it hurt him. There had been a crop failure all over the county. He had more than once been sorry he'd married this year.

In a few minutes the young people came out, looking clean and a little stiff. Rosicky hurried them off, and then he took his own time with the dishes. He scoured the pots and pans and put away the milk and swept the kitchen. He put some coal in the stove and shut off the draughts, so the place would be warm for them when they got home late at night. Then he sat down and had a pipe and listened to the clock tick.

Generally speaking, marrying an American girl was certainly a risk. A Czech should marry a Czech. It was lucky that Polly was the daughter of a poor widow woman; Rudolph was proud, and if she had a prosperous family to throw up at him, they could never make it go. Polly was one of four sisters, and they all worked; one was book-keeper in the bank, one taught music, and Polly and her younger sister had been clerks, like Miss Pearl. All four of them were musical, had pretty voices, and sang in the Methodist choir, which the eldest sister directed.

Polly missed the sociability of a store position. She missed the choir, and the company of her sisters. She didn't dislike housework, but she disliked so much of it. Rosicky was a little anxious about this pair. He was afraid Polly would grow so discontented that Rudy would quit the farm and take a factory job in Omaha. He had worked for a winter up there, two years ago, to get money to marry on. He had done very well, and they would always take him back at the stockyards. But to Rosicky that meant the end of everything for his son. To be a landless man was to be a wage-earner, a slave, all your life; to have nothing, to be nothing.

Rosicky thought he would come over and do a little carpentering for Polly after the New Year. He guessed she needed jollying. Rudolph was a serious sort of chap, serious in love and serious about his work.

Rosicky shook out his pipe and walked home across the fields. Ahead of him the lamplight shone from his kitchen windows. Suppose he were still in a tailor shop on Vesey Street, with a bunch of pale, narrow-chested sons working on machines, all coming home tired and sullen to eat supper in a kitchen that was a parlor also; with another crowded, angry family quarrelling just across the dumb-waiter shaft, and squeaking pulleys at the windows where dirty washings hung on dirty lines above a court full of old brooms and mops and ash-cans. . . .

He stopped by the windmill to look up at the frosty winter stars and draw a long breath before he went inside. That kitchen with the shining windows was dear to him; but the sleeping fields and bright stars and the noble darkness were dearer still.

5

On the day before Christmas the weather set in very cold; no snow, but a bitter, biting wind that whistled and sang over the flat land and lashed one's face like fine wires. There was baking going on in the Rosicky kitchen all day, and Rosicky sat inside, making over a coat that Albert had outgrown into an overcoat for John. Mary had a big red geranium in bloom for Christmas, and a row of Jerusalem cherry trees, full of berries. It was the first year she had ever grown these; Doctor Ed brought her the seeds from Omaha when he went to some medical convention. They reminded Rosicky of plants he had seen in England; and all afternoon, as he stitched, he sat thinking about those two years in London, which his mind usually shrank from even after all this while.

He was a lad of eighteen when he dropped down into London, with no money and no connexions except the address of a cousin who was supposed to be working at a confectioner's. When he went to the pastry shop, however, he found that the cousin had gone to America. Anton tramped the streets for several days, sleeping in doorways and on the Embankment, until he was in utter despair. He knew no English, and the sound of the strange language all about him confused him. By chance he met a poor German tailor who had learned his trade in Vienna, and could speak a little Czech. This tailor, Lifschnitz, kept a repair shop in a Cheapside basement, underneath a cobbler. He didn't much need an apprentice, but he was sorry for the boy and took him in for no wages but his keep and what he could pick up. The pickings were supposed to be coppers given you when you took work home to a customer. But most of the customers called for their clothes themselves, and the coppers that came Anton's way were very few. He had, however, a place to sleep. The tailor's family lived upstairs in three rooms; a kitchen, a bedroom, where Lifschnitz and his wife and five children slept, and a living-room. Two corners of this living-room were curtained off for lodgers; in one Rosicky slept on an old horsehair sofa, with a feather quilt to wrap himself in. The other corner was rented to a wretched, dirty boy, who was studying the violin. He actually practised there. Rosicky was dirty, too. There was no way to be anything else. Mrs Lifschnitz got the water she cooked and washed with from a pump in a brick court, four flights down. There were bugs in the place, and multitudes of fleas, though the poor woman did the best she could. Rosicky knew she often went empty to give another potato or a spoonful of dripping to the two hungry, sad-eyed boys who lodged with her. He used to think he would never get out of there, never get a clean shirt to his back again. What would he do, he wondered, when his clothes actually dropped to pieces and the worn cloth wouldn't hold patches any longer?

It was still early when the old farmer put aside his sewing and his recollections. The sky had been a dark grey all day, with not a gleam of sun, and the light failed at four o'clock. He went to shave and change his shirt while the turkey was roasting. Rudolph and Polly were coming over for supper.

After supper they sat round in the kitchen, and the younger boys were saying how sorry they were it hadn't snowed. Everybody was sorry. They wanted a deep snow that would lie long and keep the wheat warm, and leave the ground soaked when it melted.

'Yes, sir!' Rudolph broke out fiercely; 'if we have another dry year like last year, there's going to be hard times in this country.'

Rosicky filled his pipe. 'You boys don't know what hard times is. You don't owe nobody, you got plenty to eat an' keep warm, an' plenty water to keep clean. When you got them, you can't have it very hard.'

Rudolph frowned, opened and shut his big right hand, and dropped it clenched upon his knee. 'I've got to have a good deal more than that, Father, or I'll quit this farming gamble. I can always make good wages railroading, or at the packing house, and be sure of my money.'

'Maybe so,' his father answered dryly.

Mary, who had just come in from the pantry and was wiping her hands on the roller towel, thought Rudy and his father were getting too serious. She brought her darning-basket and sat down in the middle of the group.

'I ain't much afraid of hard times, Rudy,' she said heartily. 'We've had a plenty, but we've always come through. Your father wouldn't never take nothing very hard, not even hard times. I got a mind to tell you a story on him. Maybe you boys can't hardly remember the year we had that terrible hot wind, that burned everything up on the Fourth of July? All the corn an' the gardens. An' that was in the days when we didn't have alfalfa yet – I guess it wasn't invented.

'Well, that very day your father was out cultivatin' corn, and I was here in the kitchen makin' plum preserves. We had bushels of plums that year. I noticed it was terrible hot, but it's always hot in the kitchen when you're preservin', an' I was too busy with my plums to mind. Anton come in from the field about three o'clock, an' I asked him what was the matter.

' "Nothin'," he says, "but it's pretty hot, an' I think I won't work no more today." He stood round for a few minutes, an' then he says: "Ain't you near through? I want you should git up a nice supper for us tonight. It's Fourth of July."

'I told him to git along, that I was right in the middle of preservin', but the plums would taste good on hot biscuit. "I'm goin' to have fried chicken, too," he says, and he went off an' killed a couple. You three oldest boys was little fellers, playin' round outside, real hot an' sweaty, an' your father took you to the horse tank down by the windmill an' took off your clothes an' put you in. Them two box-elder trees was little then, but they made shade over the tank. Then he took off all his own clothes, an' got in with you. While he was playin' in the water with you, the Methodist preacher drove into our place to say how all the neighbors was goin' to meet at the schoolhouse that night, to pray for rain. He drove right to the windmill, of course, and there was your father and you three with no clothes on. I was in the kitchen door, an' I had to laugh, for the preacher acted like he ain't never seen a naked man before. He surely was embarrassed, an' your father couldn't git to his clothes; they was all hangin' up on the windmill to let the sweat dry out of 'em. So he laid in the tank where he was, an' put one of you boys on top of him to cover him up a little, an' talked to the preacher.

'When you got through playin' in the water, he put clean clothes on you and a clean shirt on himself, an' by that time I'd begun to get supper. He says: "It's too hot in here to eat comfortable. Let's have a picnic in the orchard. We'll eat our supper behind the mulberry hedge, under them linden trees."

'So he carried our supper down, an' a bottle of my wild-grape wine, an' everything tasted good, I can tell you. The wind got cooler as the sun was goin' down, and it turned out pleasant, only I noticed how the leaves was curled up on the linden trees. That made me think, an' I asked your father if that hot wind all day hadn't been terrible hard on the gardens an' the corn.

' "Corn," he says, "there ain't no corn."

' "What you talkin' about?" I said. "Ain't we got forty acres?"

' "We ain't got an ear," he says, "nor nobody else ain't got none. All the corn in this country was cooked by three o'clock today, like you'd roasted it in an oven."

' "You mean you won't get no crop at all?" I asked him. I couldn't believe it, after he'd worked so hard.

' "No crop this year," he says. "That's why we're havin' a picnic. We might as well enjoy what we got."

'An' that's how your father behaved, when all the neighbours was so discouraged they couldn't look you in the face. An' we enjoyed ourselves that year, poor as we was, an' our neighbours wasn't a bit better off for bein' miserable. Some of 'em grieved till they got poor digestions and couldn't relish what they did have.'

The younger boys said they thought their father had the best of it. But Rudolph was thinking that, all the same, the neighbours had managed to get ahead more, in the fifteen years since that time. There must be something wrong about his father's way of doing things. He wished he knew what was going on in the back of Polly's mind. He knew she liked his father, but he knew, too, that she was afraid of something. When his mother sent over coffee-cake or prune tarts or a loaf of fresh bread, Polly seemed to regard them with a certain suspicion. When she observed to him that his brothers had nice manners, her tone implied that it was remarkable they should have. With his mother she was stiff and on her guard. Mary's hearty frankness and gusts of good humor irritated her. Polly was afraid of being unusual or conspicuous in any way, of being 'ordinary', as she said!

When Mary had finished her story, Rosicky laid aside his pipe.

'You boys like me to tell you about some of dem hard times I been through in London?' Warmly encouraged, he sat rubbing his forehead along the deep creases. It was bothersome to tell a long story in English (he nearly always talked to the boys in Czech), but he wanted Polly to hear this one.

'Well, you know about dat tailor shop I worked in in London? I had one Christmas dere I ain't never forgot. Times was awful bad before Christmas; de boss ain't got much work, an' have it awful hard to pay his rent. It ain't so much fun, bein' poor in a big city like London, I'll say! All de windows is full of good t'ings to eat, an' all de pushcarts in de streets is full, an' you smell 'em all de time, an' you ain't got no money – not a damn bit. I didn't mind de cold so much, though I didn't have no overcoat, chust a short jacket I'd outgrowed so it wouldn't meet on me, an' my hands was chapped raw. But I always had a good appetite, like you all know, an' de sight of dem pork pies in de windows was awful fur me!

'Day before Christmas was terrible foggy dat year, an' dat fog gits into your bones and makes you all damp like. Mrs Lifschnitz didn't give us nothin' but a little bread an' drippin' for supper, because she was savin' to try for to give us a good dinner on Christmas Day. After supper de boss say I can go an' enjoy myself, so I went into de streets to listen to de Christmas singers. Dey sing old songs an' make very nice music, an' I run round after dem a good ways, till I got awful hungry. I t'ink maybe if I go home, I can sleep till morning an' forgit my belly.

'I went into my corner real quiet, and roll up in my fedder quilt. But I ain't got my head down, till I smell somet'ing good. Seem like it git stronger an' stronger, an' I can't git to sleep noway. I can't understand dat smell. Dere was a gas light in a hall across de court, dat always shine in at my window a little. I got up an' look round. I got a little wooden box in my corner fur a stool, 'cause I ain't got no chair. I picks up dat box, and under it dere is a roast goose on a platter! I can't believe my eyes. I carry it to de window where de light comes in, an' touch it and smell it to find out, an' den I taste it to be sure. I say, I will eat chust one little bite of dat goose, so I can go to sleep, and to-morrow I won't eat none at all. But I tell you, boys, when I stop, one half of dat goose was gone!'

The narrator bowed his head, and the boys shouted. But little Josephine slipped behind his chair and kissed him on the neck beneath his ear.

'Poor little Papa, I don't want him to be hungry!'

'Da's long ago, child. I ain't never been hungry since I had your mudder to cook fur me.'

'Go on and tell us the rest, please,' said Polly.

'Well, when I come to realize what I done, of course, I felt terrible. I felt better in de stomach, but very bad in de heart. I set on my bed wid dat platter on my knees, an' it all come to me; how hard dat poor woman save to buy dat goose, and how she get some neighbour to cook it dat got more fire, an' how she put it in my corner to keep it away from dem hungry children. Dey was a old carpet hung up to shut my corner off, an' de children wasn't allowed to go in dere. An' I know she put it in my corner because she trust me more'n she did de violin boy. I can't stand it to face her after I spoil de Christmas. So I put on my shoes and go out into de city. I tell myself I better throw myself in de river; but I guess I ain't dat kind of a boy.

'It was after twelve o'clock, an' terrible cold, an' I start out to walk about London all night. I walk along de river awhile, but

255

dey was lots of drunks all along; men, and women too. I chust move along to keep away from de police. I git onto de Strand, an' den over to New Oxford Street, where dere was a big German restaurant on de ground floor, wid big windows all fixed up fine, an' I could see de people havin' parties inside. While I was lookin' in, two men and two ladies come out, laughin' and talkin' and feelin' happy about all dey been eatin' an' drinkin', and dey was speakin' Czech — not like de Austrians, but like de home folks talk it.

'I guess I went crazy, an' I done what I ain't never done before nor since. I went right up to dem gay people an' begun to beg dem: "Fellow-countrymen, for God's sake give me money enough to buy a goose!"

'Dey laugh, of course, but de ladies speak awful kind to me, an' dey take me back into de restaurant and give me hot coffee and cakes, an' make me tell all about how I happened to come to London, an' what I was doin' dere. Dey take my name and where I work down on paper, an' both of dem ladies give me ten shillings.

'De big market at Covent Garden ain't very far away, an' by dat time it was open. I go dere an' buy a big goose an' some pork pies, an' potatoes and onions, an' cakes an' oranges fur de children — all I could carry! When I git home, everybody is still asleep. I pile all I bought on de kitchen table, an' go in an' lay down on my bed, an' I ain't waken up till I hear dat woman scream when she come out into her kitchen. My goodness, but she was surprise! She laugh an' cry at de same time, an' hug me and waken all de children. She ain't stop fur no breakfast; she git de Christmas dinner ready dat morning, and we all sit down an' eat all we can hold. I ain't never seen dat violin boy have all he can hold before.

'Two three days after dat, de two men come to hunt me up, an' dey ask my boss, and he give me a good report an' tell dem I was a steady boy all right. One of dem Bohemians was very smart an' run a Bohemian newspaper in New York, an' de odder was a rich man, in de importing business, an' dey been travelling togedder. Dey told me how t'ings was easier in New York, an' offered to pay my passage when dey was goin' home soon on a boat. My boss say to me: "You go. You ain't got no chance here, an' I like to see you git ahead, fur you always been a good boy to my woman, and fur dat fine Christmas dinner you give us all." An' da's how I got to New York.'

That night when Rudolph and Polly, arm in arm, were running home across the fields with the bitter wind at their backs, his heart leaped for joy when she said she thought they might have his family come over for supper on New Year's Eve. 'Let's get up a nice supper, and not let your mother help at all; make her be company for once.'

'That would be lovely of you, Polly,' he said humbly. He was a very simple, modest boy, and he, too, felt vaguely that Polly and her sisters were more experienced and worldly than his people.

6

The winter turned out badly for farmers. It was bitterly cold, and after the first light snows before Christmas there was no snow at all – and no rain. March was as bitter as February. On those days when the wind fairly punished the country, Rosicky sat by his window. In the fall he and the boys had put in a big wheat planting, and now the seed had frozen in the ground. All that land would have to be ploughed up and planted over again, planted in corn. It had happened before, but he was younger then, and he never worried about what had to be. He was sure of himself and of Mary; he knew they could bear what they had to bear, that they would always pull through somehow. But he was not so sure about the young ones, and he felt troubled because Rudolph and Polly were having such a hard start.

Sitting beside his flowering window while the panes rattled and the wind blew in under the door, Rosicky gave himself to reflection as he had not done since those Sundays in the loft of the furniture-factory in New York, long ago. Then he was trying to find what he wanted in life for himself; now he was trying to find what he wanted for his boys, and why it was he so hungered to feel sure they would be here, working this very land, after he was gone.

They would have to work hard on the farm, and probably they would never do much more than make a living. But if he could think of them as staying here on the land, he wouldn't have to fear any great unkindness for them. Hardships, certainly; it was a hardship to have the wheat freeze in the ground when seed was so high; and to have to sell your stock because you had no feed. But there would be other years when everything came along right, and you caught up. And what you had was your own. You didn't have to choose between bosses and strikers, and go wrong either way. You didn't have to do with dishonest and cruel people. They were the only things in his experience he had found terrifying and horrible; the look in the eyes of a dishonest and crafty man, of a scheming and rapacious woman.

In the country, if you had a mean neighbour, you could keep off his land and make him keep off yours. But in the city, all the foulness and misery and brutality of your neighbours was part of your life. The worst things he had come upon in his journey through the world were human — depraved and poisonous specimens of man. To this day he could recall certain terrible faces in the London streets. There were mean people everywhere, to be sure, even in their own country town here. But they weren't tempered, hardened, sharpened, like the treacherous people in cities who live by grinding or cheating or poisoning their fellow-men. He had helped to bury two of his fellow-workmen in the tailoring trade, and he was distrustful of the organized industries that see one out of the world in big cities. Here, if you were sick, you had Doctor Ed to look after you; and if you died, fat Mr Haycock, the kindest man in the world, buried you.

It seemed to Rosicky that for good, honest boys like his, the worst they could do on the farm was better than the best they would be likely to do in the city. If he'd had a mean boy, now, one who was crooked and sharp and tried to put anything over on his brothers, then town would be the place for him. But he had no such boy. As for Rudolph, the discontented one, he would give the shirt off his back to anyone who touched his heart. What Rosicky really hoped for his boys was that they

could get through the world without ever knowing much about
the cruelty of human beings. 'Their mother and me ain't prepared them for that,' he sometimes said to himself.

These thoughts brought him back to a grateful consideration
of his own case. What an escape he had had, to be sure! He,
too, in his time, had had to take money for repair work from
the hand of a hungry child who let it go so wistfully; because it
was money due his boss. And now, in all these years, he had
never had to take a cent from anyone in bitter need – never had
to look at the face of a woman become like a wolf's from
struggle and famine. When he thought of these things, Rosicky
would put on his cap and jacket and slip down to the barn and
give his work-horses a little extra oats, letting them eat it out of
his hand in their slobbery fashion. It was his way of expressing
what he felt, and made him chuckle with pleasure.

The spring came warm, with blue skies – but dry, dry as a
bone. The boys began ploughing up the wheat-fields to plant
them over in corn. Rosicky would stand at the fence corner and
watch them, and the earth was so dry it blew up in clouds of
brown dust that hid the horses and the sulky plough and the
driver. It was a bad outlook.

The big alfalfa-field that lay between the home place and
Rudolph's came up green, but Rosicky was worried because during that open windy winter a great many Russian thistle plants
had blown in there and lodged. He kept asking the boys to rake
them out; he was afraid their seed would root and 'take the
alfalfa.' Rudolph said that was nonsense. The boys were working so hard planting corn, their father felt he couldn't insist
about the thistles, but he set great store by that big alfalfa field.
It was a feed you could depend on – and there was some deeper
reason, vague, but strong. The peculiar green of that clover
woke early memories in old Rosicky, went back to something in
his childhood in the old world. When he was a little boy, he had
played in fields of that strong blue-green color.

One morning, when Rudolph had gone to town in the car,
leaving a work-team idle in his barn, Rosicky went over to his
son's place, put the horses to the buggy-rake, and set about
quietly raking up those thistles. He behaved with guilty caution,

and rather enjoyed stealing a march on Doctor Ed, who was just then taking his first vacation in seven years of practice and was attending a clinic in Chicago. Rosicky got the thistles raked up, but did not stop to burn them. That would take some time, and his breath was pretty short, so he thought he had better get the horses back to the barn.

He got them into the barn and to their stalls, but the pain had come on so sharp in his chest that he didn't try to take the harness off. He started for the house, bending lower with every step. The cramp in his chest was shutting him up like a jack-knife. When he reached the windmill, he swayed and caught at the ladder. He saw Polly coming down the hill, running with the swiftness of a slim greyhound. In a flash she had her shoulder under his armpit.

'Lean on me, Father, hard! Don't be afraid. We can get to the house all right.'

Somehow they did, though Rosicky became blind with pain; he could keep on his legs, but he couldn't steer his course. The next thing he was conscious of was lying on Polly's bed, and Polly bending over him wringing out bath towels in hot water and putting them on his chest. She stopped only to throw coal into the stove, and she kept the tea-kettle and the black pot going. She put these hot applications on him for nearly an hour, she told him afterwards, and all that time he was drawn up stiff and blue, with the sweat pouring off him.

As the pain gradually loosed its grip, the stiffness went out of his jaws, the black circles round his eyes disappeared, and a little of his natural color came back. When his daughter-in-law buttoned his shirt over his chest at last, he sighed.

'Da's fine, de way I feel now, Polly. It was a awful bad spell, an' I was so sorry it all come on you like it did.'

Polly was flushed and excited. 'Is the pain really gone? Can I leave you long enough to telephone over to your place?'

Rosicky's eyelids fluttered. 'Don't telephone, Polly. It ain't no use to scare my wife. It's nice and quiet here, an' if I ain't too much trouble to you, just let me lay still till I feel like myself. I ain't got no pain now. It's nice here.'

Polly bent over him and wiped the moisture from his face.

'Oh, I'm so glad it's over!' she broke out impulsively. 'It just broke my heart to see you suffer so, Father.'

Rosicky motioned her to sit down on the chair where the tea-kettle had been, and looked up at her with that lively affectionate gleam in his eyes. 'You was awful good to me, I won't never forget dat. I hate it to be sick on you like dis. Down at de barn I say to myself, dat young girl ain't had much experience in sickness, I don't want to scare her, an' maybe she's got a baby comin' or somet'ing.'

Polly took his hand. He was looking at her so intently and affectionately and confidingly; his eyes seemed to caress her face, to regard it with pleasure. She frowned with her funny streaks of eyebrows, and then smiled back at him.

'I guess maybe there is something of that kind going to happen. But I haven't told anyone yet, not my mother or Rudolph. You'll be the first to know.'

His hand pressed hers. She noticed that it was warm again. The twinkle in his yellow-brown eyes seemed to come nearer.

'I like mighty well to see dat little child, Polly,' was all he said. Then he closed his eyes and lay half-smiling. But Polly sat still, thinking hard. She had a sudden feeling that nobody in the world, not her mother, not Rudolph, or anyone, really loved her as much as old Rosicky did. It perplexed her. She sat frowning and trying to puzzle it out. It was as if Rosicky had a special gift for loving people, something that was like an ear for music or an eye for color. It was quiet, unobtrusive; it was merely there. You saw it in his eyes — perhaps that was why they were merry. You felt it in his hands, too. After he dropped off to sleep, she sat holding his warm, broad, flexible brown hand. She had never seen another in the least like it. She wondered if it wasn't a kind of gypsy hand, it was so alive and quick and light in its communications — very strange in a farmer. Nearly all the farmers she knew had huge lumps of fists, like mauls, or they were knotty and bony and uncomfortable-looking, with stiff fingers. But Rosicky's was like quick-silver, flexible, muscular, about the colour of a pale cigar, with deep, deep creases across the palm. It wasn't nervous, it wasn't a stupid lump; it was a warm brown human hand, with some cleverness in it, a great deal of generosity, and something else which Polly could only call 'gypsy-like' – something nimble and lively and sure, in the way that animals are.

Polly remembered that hour long afterwards; it had been like an awakening to her. It seemed to her that she had never learned so much about life from anything as from old Rosicky's hand. It brought her to herself; it communicated some direct and untranslatable message.

When she heard Rudolph coming in the car, she ran out to meet him.

'Oh, Rudy, your father's been awful sick! He raked up those thistles he's been worrying about, and afterwards he could hardly get to the house. He suffered so I was afraid he was going to die.'

Rudolph jumped to the ground. 'Where is he now?'

'On the bed. He's asleep. I was terribly scared, because, you know, I'm so fond of your father.' She slipped her arm through his and they went into the house. That afternoon they took Rosicky home and put him to bed, though he protested that he was quite well again.

The next morning he got up and dressed and sat down to breakfast with his family. He told Mary that his coffee tasted better than usual to him, and he warned the boys not to bear any tales to Doctor Ed when he got home. After breakfast he sat down by his window to do some patching and asked Mary to thread several needles for him before she went to feed her chickens – her eyes were better than his, and her hands steadier. He lit his pipe and took up John's overalls. Mary had been watching him anxiously all morning, and as she went out of the door with her bucket of scraps, she saw that he was smiling. He was thinking, indeed, about Polly, and how he might never have known what a tender heart she had if he hadn't got sick over there. Girls nowadays didn't wear their heart on their sleeve. But now he knew Polly would make a fine woman after the foolishness wore off. Either a woman had that sweetness at her heart or she hadn't. You couldn't always tell by the look of them; but if they had that, everything came out right in the end.

After he had taken a few stitches, the cramp began in his chest, like yesterday. He put his pipe cautiously down on the window-sill and bent over to ease the pull. No use – he had better try to get to his bed if he could. He rose and groped his way across the familiar floor, which was rising and falling like the deck of a ship. At the door he fell. When Mary came in, she found him lying there, and the moment she touched him she knew that he was gone.

Doctor Ed was away when Rosicky died, and for the first few weeks after he got home he was hard driven. Every day he said to himself that he must get out to see that family that had lost their father. One soft, warm moonlight night in early summer he started for the farm. His mind was on other things, and not until his road ran by the graveyard did he realize that Rosicky wasn't over there on the hill where the red lamplight shone, but here, in the moonlight. He stopped his car, shut off the engine, and sat there for a while.

A sudden hush had fallen on his soul. Everything here seemed strangely moving and significant, though signifying what, he did not know. Close by the wire fence stood Rosicky's mowing-machine, where one of the boys had been cutting hay that afternoon; his own work-horses had been going up and down there. The new-cut hay perfumed all the night air. The moonlight silvered the long, billowy grass that grew over the graves and hid the fence; the few little evergreens stood out black in it, like shadows in a pool. The sky was very blue and soft, the stars rather faint because the moon was full.

For the first time it struck Doctor Ed that this was really a beautiful graveyard. He thought of city cemeteries; acres of shrubbery and heavy stone, so arranged and lonely and unlike anything in the living world. Cities of the dead, indeed; cities of the forgotten, of the 'put away'. But this was open and free, this little square of long grass which the wind for ever stirred. Nothing but the sky overhead, and the many-colored fields running on until they met that sky. The horses worked here in summer; the neighbors passed on their way to town; and over yonder, in the cornfield, Rosicky's own cattle would be eating fodder as winter came on. Nothing could be more undeathlike than this place; nothing could be more right for a man who had helped to do the work of great cities and had always longed for the open country and had got to it at last. Rosicky's life seemed to him complete and beautiful.

Jack London

TO BUILD A FIRE

D A Y had broken cold and gray, exceedingly cold and gray, when the man turned aside from the main Yukon trail and climbed the high earth-bank, where a dim and little-traveled trail led eastward through the fat spruce timberland. It was a steep bank, and he paused for breath at the top, excusing the act to himself by looking at his watch. It was nine o'clock. There was no sun nor hint of sun, though there was not a cloud in the sky. It was a clear day, and yet there seemed an intangible pall over the face of things, a subtle gloom that made the day dark, and that was due to the absence of sun. This did not worry the man. He was used to the lack of sun. It had been days since he had seen the sun, and he knew that a few more days must pass before that cheerful orb, due south, would just peep above the sky-line and dip immediately from view.

The man flung a look back along the way he had come. The Yukon lay a mile wide and hidden under three feet of ice. On top of this ice were as many feet of snow. It was all pure white, rolling in gentle undulations where the ice-jams of the freeze-up had formed. North and south, as far as his eye could see, it was unbroken white, save for a dark hair-line that curved and twisted from around the spruce-covered island to the south, and that curved and twisted away into the north, where it disappeared behind another spruce-covered island. This dark hair-line was the trail – the main trail – that led south five hundred miles to the Chilcoot Pass, Dyea, and salt water; and that led north seventy miles to Dawson, and still on to the north a thousand miles to Nulato, and finally to St Michael on Bering Sea, a thousand miles and half a thousand more.

But all this – the mysterious, far-reaching hair-line trail, the absence of sun from the sky, the tremendous cold, and the strangeness and weirdness of it all – made no impression on the man. It was not because he was long used to it. He was a new-comer in the land, a *chechaquo*, and this was his first winter. The trouble with him was that he was without imagination. He was quick and alert in the things of life, but only in the things, and not in the significances. Fifty degrees below zero meant eighty-odd degrees of frost. Such fact impressed him as being cold and uncomfortable, and that was all. It did not lead him to mediate upon his frailty as a creature of temperature, and upon man's frailty in general, able only to live within certain narrow limits of heat and cold; and from there on it did not lead him to the conjectural field of immortality and man's place in the universe. Fifty degrees below zero stood for a bite of frost that hurt and that must be guarded against by the use of mittens, ear-flaps, warm moccasins, and thick socks. Fifty degrees below zero was to him just precisely fifty degrees below zero. That there should be anything more to it than that was a thought that never entered his head.

As he turned to go on, he spat speculatively. There was a sharp, explosive crackle that startled him. He spat again. And again, in the air, before it could fall to the snow, the spittle crackled. He knew that at fifty below spittle crackled on the snow, but this spittle had crackled in the air. Undoubtedly it was colder than fifty below – how much colder he did not know. But the temperature did not matter. He was bound for the old claim on the left fork of Henderson Creek, where the boys were already. They had come over across the divide from the Indian Creek country, while he had come the roundabout way to take a look at the possibilities of getting out logs in the spring from the islands in the Yukon. He would be in to camp by six o'clock; a bit after dark, it was true, but the boys would be there, a fire would be going, and a hot supper would be ready. As for lunch, he pressed his hand against the protruding bundle under his jacket. It was also under his shirt, wrapped up in a handkerchief and lying against the naked skin. It was the only way to keep the biscuits from freezing. He smiled agreeably to himself as he thought of those biscuits, each cut open and sopped in bacon grease, and each enclosing a generous slice of fried bacon.

He plunged in among the big spruce trees. The trail was faint. A foot of snow had fallen since the last sled had passed over, and he was glad he was without a sled, traveling light. In fact, he carried nothing but the lunch wrapped in the handkerchief. He was surprised, however, at the cold. It certainly was cold, he concluded, as he rubbed his numb nose and cheek-bones with his mittened hand. He was a warm-whiskered man, but the hair on his face did not protect the high cheek-bones and the eager nose that thrust itself aggressively into the frosty air.

At the man's heels trotted a dog, a big native husky, the proper wolf-dog, gray-coated and without any visible or temperamental difference from its brother, the wild wolf. The animal was depressed by the tremendous cold. It knew that it was no time for traveling. Its instinct told it a truer tale than was told to the man by the man's judgement. In reality, it was not merely colder than fifty below zero; it was colder than sixty below, than seventy below. It was seventy-five below zero. Since the freezing point is thirty-two above zero, it meant that one hundred and seven degrees of frost obtained. The dog did not know anything about thermometers. Possibly in its brain there was no sharp consciousness of a condition of very cold such as was in the man's brain. But the brute had its instinct. It experienced a vague but menacing apprehension that subdued it and made it slink along at the man's heels, and that made it question eagerly every unwonted movement of the man as if expecting him to go into camp or to seek shelter somewhere and build a fire. The dog had learned fire, and it wanted fire, or else to burrow under the snow and cuddle its warmth away from the air.

The frozen moisture of its breathing had settled on its fur in a fine powder of frost, and especially were its jowls, muzzle, and eyelashes whitened by its crystalled breath. The man's red beard and mustache were likewise frosted, but more solidly, the deposit taking the form of ice and increasing with every warm, moist breath he exhaled. Also, the man was chewing tobacco, and the muzzle of ice held his lips so rigidly that he was unable to clear his chin when he expelled the juice. The result was that a crystal beard of the color and solidity of amber was increasing its length on his chin. If he fell down it would shatter itself, like glass, into brittle fragments. But he did not mind the appendage. It was the penalty all tobacco-chewers paid in that country, and he had been out before in two cold snaps. They had not been so cold as this, he knew, but by the spirit thermometer at Sixty Mile he knew they had been registered at fifty below and at fifty-five.

He held on through the level stretch of woods for several miles, crossed a wide flat of nigger-heads, and dropped down a bank to the frozen bed of a small stream. This was Henderson Creek, and he knew he was ten miles from the forks. He looked at his watch. It was ten o'clock. He was making four miles an hour, and he calculated that he would arrive at the forks at half-past twelve. He decided to celebrate that event by eating his lunch there.

The dog dropped in again at his heels, with a tail drooping discouragement, as the man swung along the creek-bed. The furrow of the old sled-trail was plainly visible, but a dozen inches of snow covered the marks of the last runners. In a month no man had come up or down that silent creek. The man held steadily on. He was not much given to thinking, and just then particularly he had nothing to think about save that he would eat lunch at the forks and that at six o'clock he would be in camp with the boys. There was nobody to talk to; and, had there been, speech would have been impossible because of the ice-muzzle on his mouth. So he continued monotonously to chew tobacco and to increase the length of his amber beard.

Once in a while the thought reiterated itself that it was very cold and that he had never experienced such cold. As he walked along he rubbed his cheek-bones and nose with the back of his mittened hand. He did this automatically, now and again changing hands. But rub as he would, the instant he stopped his cheek-bones went numb, and the following instant the end of his nose went numb. He was sure to frost his cheeks; he knew that, and experienced a pang of regret that he had not devised a nose-strap of the sort Bud wore in cold snaps. Such a strap passed across the cheeks, as well, and saved them. But it didn't matter much, after all. What were frosted cheeks? A bit painful, that was all; they were never serious.

Empty as the man's mind was of thoughts, he was keenly observant, and he noticed the changes in the creek, the curves and bends and timber-jams, and always he sharply noted where he placed his feet. Once, coming around a bend, he shied abruptly, like a startled horse, curved away from the place where he had been walking, and retreated several paces back along the trail. The creek he knew was frozen clear to the bottom – no creek could contain water in that artic winter – but he knew also that there were springs that bubbled out from the hillsides and ran along under the snow and on top the ice of the creek. He knew that the coldest snaps never froze these springs, and he knew likewise their danger. They were traps. They hid pools of water under the snow that might be three inches deep, or three feet. Sometimes a skin of ice half an inch thick covered them, and in turn was covered by the snow. Sometimes there were alternate layers of water and ice-skin, so that when one broke through he kept on breaking through for a while, sometimes wetting himself to the waist.

That was why he had shied in such panic. He had felt the give under his feet and heard the crackle of a snow-hidden ice-skin. And to get his feet wet in such a temperature meant trouble and danger. At the very least it meant delay, for he would be forced to stop and build a fire, and under its protection to bare his feet while he dried his socks and moccasins. He stood and studied the creek-bed and its banks, and decided that the flow of water came from the right. He reflected a while, rubbing his nose and cheeks, then skirted to the left, stepping gingerly and testing the footing for each step. Once clear of the danger, he took a fresh chew of tobacco and swung along at his four-mile gait.

In the course of the next two hours he came upon several similar traps. Usually the snow above the hidden pools had a sunken, candied appearance that advertised the danger. Once again, however, he had a close call; and once, suspecting danger, he compelled the dog to go on in front. The dog did not want to go. It hung back until the man shoved it forward, and then it went quickly across the white, unbroken surface. Suddenly it broke through, floundered to one side, and got away to firmer footing. It had wet its forefeet and legs, and almost immediately the water that clung to it turned to ice. It made quick efforts to lick the ice off its legs, then dropped down in the snow and began to bite out the ice that had formed between the toes. This was a matter of instinct. To permit the ice to remain would mean sore feet. It did not know this, it merely obeyed the mysterious prompting that arose from the deep crypts of its being. But the man knew, having achieved a judgement on the subject, and he removed the mitten from his right hand and helped tear out the ice-particles. He did not expose his fingers more than a minute, and was astonished at the swift numbness that smote them. It certainly was cold. He pulled on the mitten hastily, and beat the hand savagely across his chest.

At twelve o'clock the day was at its brightest. Yet the sun was too far south on its winter journey to clear the horizon. The bulge of the earth intervened between it and Henderson Creek, where the man walked under clear sky at noon and cast no shadow. At half past twelve, to the minute, he arrived at the forks of the creek. He was pleased at the speed he had made. If he kept it up, he would certainly be with the boys by six. He unbuttoned his jacket and shirt and drew forth his lunch. The action consumed no more than a quarter of a minute, yet in that brief moment the numbness laid hold of the exposed fingers. He did not put the mitten on, but, instead struck the fingers a dozen sharp smashes against his leg. Then he sat down on a snow-covered log to eat. The sting that followed upon the striking of his fingers against his leg ceased so quickly that he was startled. He had had no chance to take a bite of biscuit. He struck the fingers repeatedly and returned them to the mitten, baring the other hand for the purpose of eating. He tried to take a mouthful, but the ice-muzzle prevented. He had forgotten to build a fire and thaw out. He chuckled at his foolishness, and as he chuckled he noted the numbness creeping into the exposed fingers. Also, he noted that the stinging which had first come to his toes when he sat down was already passing away. He wondered whether the toes were warm or numb. He moved them inside the moccasins and decided that they were numb.

He pulled the mitten on hurriedly and stood up. He was a bit frightened. He stamped up and down until the stinging returned into the feet. It certainly was cold, was his thought. That man from Sulphur Creek had spoken the truth when telling how cold it sometimes got in the country. And he had laughed at him at the time! That showed one must not be too sure of things. There was no mistake about it, it *was* cold. He strode up and down, stamping his feet and threshing his arms, until reassured by the returning warmth. Then he got out matches and proceeded to make a fire. From the undergrowth, where high water of the previous spring had lodged a supply of seasoned twigs, he got his firewood. Working carefully from a small beginning, he soon had a roaring fire, over which he thawed the ice from his face and in the protection of which he ate his biscuits. For the moment the cold of space was outwitted. The dog took satisfaction in the fire, stretching out close enough for warmth and far enough away to escape being singed.

When the man had finished, he filled his pipe and took his comfortable time over a smoke. Then he pulled on his mittens, settled the earflaps of his cap firmly about his ears, and took the creek trail up the left fork. The dog was disappointed and yearned back toward the fire. This man did not know cold. Possibly all the generations of his ancestry had been ignorant of cold, of real cold, of cold one hundred and seven degrees below freezing point. But the dog knew; all its ancestry knew, and it had inherited the knowledge. And it knew that it was not good to walk abroad in such fearful cold. It was the time to lie snug in a hole in the snow and wait for a curtain of cloud to be drawn across the face of outer space whence this cold came. On the other hand, there was no keen intimacy between the dog and the man. The one was the toil-slave of the other, and the only caresses it had ever received were the caresses of the whiplash and of harsh and menacing throat-sounds that threatened the whiplash. So the dog made no effort to communicate its apprehension to the man. It was not concerned in the welfare of the man; it was for its own sake that it yearned back toward the fire. But the man whistled, and spoke to it with the sound of whiplashes, and the dog swung in at the man's heel and followed after.

The man took a chew of tobacco and proceeded to start a new amber beard. Also, his moist breath quickly powdered with white his mustache, eyebrows, and lashes. There did not seem to be so many springs on the left fork of the Henderson, and for half an hour the man saw no signs of any. And then it happened. At a place where there were no signs, where the soft, unbroken snow seemed to advertise solidity beneath, the man broke through. It was not deep. He wet himself halfway to the knees before he floundered out to the firm crust.

He was angry, and cursed his luck aloud. He had hoped to get into camp with the boys at six o'clock, and this would delay him an hour, for he would have to build a fire and dry out his foot-gear. This was imperative at that low temperature – he knew that much; and he turned aside to the bank, which he climbed. On top, tangled in the underbrush about the trunks of several small spruce trees, was a high-water deposit of dry firewood – sticks and twigs, principally, but also larger portions of seasoned branches and fine, dry, last-year's grasses. He threw down several large pieces on top of the snow. This served for a foundation and prevented the young flame from drowning itself in the snow it otherwise would melt. The flame he got by touching a match to a small shred of birch bark that he took from his pocket. This burned even more readily than paper. Placing it on the foundation, he fed the young flame with wisps of dry grass and with the tiniest dry twigs.

He worked slowly and carefully, keenly aware of his danger. Gradually, as the flame grew stronger, he increased the size of the twigs with which he fed it. He squatted in the snow, pulling the twigs out from their entanglement in the brush and feeding directly to the flame. He knew there must be no failure. When it is seventy-five below zero, a man must not fail in his first attempt to build a fire – that is, if his feet are wet. If his feet are dry, and he fails, he can run along the trail for half a mile and restore his circulation. But the circulation of wet and freezing feet cannot be restored by running when it is seventy-five below. No matter how fast he runs, the wet feet will freeze the harder.

All this the man knew. The old-timer on Sulphur Creek had

told him about it the previous fall, and now he was appreciating the advice. Already all sensation had gone out of his feet. To build the fire he had been forced to removed his mittens, and the fingers had quickly gone numb. His pace of four miles an hour had kept his heart pumping blood to the surface of his body and to all the extremities. But the instant he stopped, the action of the pump eased down. The cold of space smote the unprotected tip of the planet, and he, being on that unprotected tip, received the full force of the blow. The blood of his body recoiled before it. The blood was alive, like the dog, and like the dog it wanted to hide away and cover itself up from the fearful cold. So long as he walked four miles an hour, he pumped that blood, will-nilly, to the surface; but now, it ebbed away and sank down into the recesses of his body. The extremities were the first to feel its absence. His wet feet froze the faster, and his exposed fingers numbed the faster; though they had not yet begun to freeze. Nose and cheeks were already freezing, while the skin of all his body chilled as it lost its blood.

But he was safe. Toes and nose and cheeks would be only touched by the frost, for the fire was beginning to burn with strength. He was feeding it with twigs the size of his finger. In another minute he would be able to feed it with branches the size of his wrist, and then he could remove his wet foot-gear and, while it dried, he could keep his naked feet warm by the fire, rubbing them at first, of course, with snow. The fire was a success. He was safe. He remembered the advice of the old-timer on Sulphur Creek, and smiled. The old-timer had been very serious in laying down the law that no man must travel alone in the Klondike after fifty below. Well, here he was; he had had the accident; he was alone; and he had saved himself. Those old-timers were rather womanish, some of them, he thought. All a man had to do was to keep his head; and he was all right. Any man who was a man could travel alone. But it was surprising, the rapidity with which his cheeks and nose were freezing. And he had not thought his fingers could go lifeless in so short a time. Lifeless they were, for he could scarcely make them move together to grip a twig, and they seemed remote from his body and from him. When he touched a twig, he had to look and see whether or not he had hold of it. The wires were pretty well down between him and his finger-ends.

All of which counted for little. There was the fire, snapping and crackling and promising life with every dancing flame. He started to untie his moccasins. They were coated with ice; the thick German socks were like sheaths of iron halfway to the knees; and the moccasin strings were like rods of steel all twisted and knotted as by some conflagration. For a moment he tugged with his numb fingers, then, realizing the folly of it, he drew his sheath-knife.

But before he could cut the strings, it happened. It was his own fault or, rather, his mistake. He should not have built the fire under the spruce tree. He should have built it in the open. But it had been easier to pull the twigs from the brush and drop them directly on the fire. Now the tree under which he had done this carried a weight of snow on its boughs. No wind had blown for weeks, and each bough was fully freighted. Each time he had pulled a twig he had communicated a slight agitation to the tree – an imperceptible agitation, so far as he was concerned, but an agitation sufficient to bring about the disaster. High up in the tree one bough capsized its load of snow. This fell on the boughs beneath, capsizing them. This process continued, spreading out and involving the whole tree. It grew like an avalanche, and it descended without warning upon the man and the fire, and the fire was blotted out! Where it had burned was a mantle of fresh and disordered snow.

The man was shocked. It was as though he had just heard his own sentence of death. For a moment he sat and stared at the spot where the fire had been. Then he grew very calm. Perhaps the old-timer on Sulphur Creek was right. If he had only had a trail-mate he would have been in no danger now. The trail-mate could have built the fire. Well, it was up to him to build the fire over again, and this second time there must be no failure. Even if he succeeded, he would most likely lose some toes. His feet must be badly frozen by now, and there would be some time before the second fire was ready.

Such were his thoughts, but he did not sit and think them. He was busy all the time they were passing through his mind.

He made a new foundation for a fire, this time in the open, where no treacherous tree could blot it out. Next, he gathered dry grasses and tiny twigs from the high-water flotsam. He could not bring his fingers together to pull them out, but he was able to gather them by the handful. In this way he got many rotten twigs and bits of green moss that were undesirable, but it was the best he could do. He worked methodically, even collecting an armful of the larger branches to be used later when the fire gathered strength. And all the while the dog sat and watched him, a certain yearning wistfulness in its eyes, for it looked upon him as the fire-provider, and the fire was slow in coming.

When all was ready, the man reached in his pocket for a second piece of birch bark. He knew the bark was there, and, though he could not feel it with his fingers, he could hear its crisp rustling as he fumbled for it. Try as he would, he could not clutch hold of it. And all the time, in his consciousness, was the knowledge that each instant his feet were freezing. This thought tended to put him in a panic, but he fought against it and kept calm. He pulled on his mittens with his teeth, and threshed his arms back and forth, beating his hands with all his might against his sides. He did this sitting down, and he stood up to do it; and all the while the dog sat in the snow, its wolf-brush of a tail curled around warmly over its forefeet, its sharp wolf-ears pricked forward intently as it watched the man. And the man, as he beat and threshed with his arms and hands, felt a great surge of envy as he regarded the creature that was warm and secure in its natural covering.

After a time he was aware of the first far-away signals of sensation in his beaten fingers. The faint tingling grew stronger till it evolved into a stinging ache that was excruciating, but which the man hailed with satisfaction. He stripped the mitten from his right hand and fetched forth the birch bark. The exposed fingers were quickly going numb again. Next he brought out his bunch of sulphur matches. But the tremendous cold had already driven the life out of his fingers. In his effort to separate one match from the others, the whole bunch fell in the snow. He tried to pick it out of the snow, but failed. The dead fingers could neither touch nor clutch. He was very careful. He drove the thought of his freezing feet, and nose, and cheeks, out of his mind, devoting his whole soul to the matches. He watched, using the sense of vision in place of touch, and when he saw his fingers on each side the bunch, he closed them – that is, he willed to close them, for the wires were down, and the fingers did not obey. He pulled the mitten on the right hand, and beat it fiercely against his knee. Then, with both mittened hands he scooped the bunch of matches, along with much snow, into his lap. Yet he was no better off.

After some manipulation he managed to get the bunch between the heels of his mittened hands. In this fashion he carried it to his mouth. The ice crackled and snapped when by a violent effort he opened his mouth. He drew the lower jaw in, curled the upper lip out of the way, and scraped the bunch with his upper teeth in order to separate a match. He succeeded in getting one, which he dropped on his lap. He was no better off. He could not pick it up. Then he devised a way. He picked it up in his teeth and scratched it on his leg. Twenty times he scratched before he succeeded in lighting it. As it flamed he held it with his teeth to the birch bark. But the burning brimstone went up his nostrils and into his lungs, causing him to cough spasmodically. The match fell into the snow and went out.

The old-timer on Sulphur Creek was right, he thought in the moment of controlled despair that ensued: after fifty below, a man should travel with a partner. He beat his hands, but failed in exciting any sensation. Suddenly he bared both hands, removing the mittens with his teeth. He caught the whole bunch between the heels of his hands. His arm-muscles not being frozen enabled him to press the hand-heels tightly against the matches. Then he scratched the bunch along his leg. It flared into flame, seventy sulphur matches at once! There was no wind to blow them out. He kept his head to one side to escape the strangling fumes, and held the blazing bunch to the birch bark. As he so held it, he became aware of sensation in his hand. His flesh was burning. He could smell it. Deep down below the surface he could feel it. The sensation developed into pain that grew acute. And still he endured it, holding the flame of the

TO BUILD A FIRE

matches clumsily to the bark that would not light readily because his own burning hands were in the way, absorbing most
of the flame.

At last, when he could endure no more, he jerked his hands
apart. The blazing matches fell sizzling into the snow, but the
birch bark was alight. He began laying dry grasses and the
tiniest twigs on the flame. He could not pick and choose, for he
had to lift the fuel between the heels of his hands. Small pieces
of rotten wood and green moss clung to the twigs, and he bit
them off as well as he could with his teeth. He cherished the
flame carefully and awkwardly. It meant life, and it must not
perish. The withdrawal of blood from the surface of his body
now made him begin to shiver, and he grew more awkward. A
large piece of green moss fell squarely on the little fire. He tried
to poke it out with his fingers, but his shivering frame made him
poke too far, and he disrupted the nucleus of the little fire, the
burning grasses and tiny twigs separating and scattering. He
tried to poke them together again, but in spite of the tenseness
of the effort, his shivering got away with him, and the twigs
were hopelessly scattered. Each twig gushed a puff of smoke and
went out. The fire-provider had failed. As he looked apathetic-
ally about him, his eyes chanced on the dog, sitting across the
ruins of the fire from him, in the snow, making restless, hunching movements, slightly lifting one forefoot and then the other,
shifting its weight back and forth on them with wistful eagerness.

The sight of the dog put a wild idea into his head. He remembered the tale of the man, caught in a blizzard, who killed
a steer and crawled inside the carcass, and so was saved. He
would kill the dog and bury his hands in the warm body until
the numbness went out of them. Then he could build another
fire. He spoke to the dog, calling it to him; but in his voice was
a strange note of fear that frightened the animal, who had never
known the man to speak in such way before. Something was the
matter, and its suspicious nature sensed danger – it knew not
what danger, but somewhere, somehow, in its brain arose an
apprehension of the man. It flattened its ears down at the sound
of the man's voice, and its restless, hunching movements and

the liftings and shiftings of its forefeet became more pronounced; but it would not come to the man. He got on his hands
and knees and crawled toward the dog. This unusual posture
again excited suspicion, and the animal sidled mincingly away.

The man sat up in the snow for a moment and struggled for
calmness. Then he pulled on his mittens, by means of his teeth,
and got upon his feet. He glanced down at first in order to
assure himself that he was really standing up, for the absence
of sensation in his feet left him unrelated to the earth. His erect
position in itself started to drive the webs of suspicion from the
dog's mind; and when he spoke peremptorily, with the sound of
whiplashes in his voice, the dog rendered its customary allegi-
ance and came to him. As it came within reaching distance, the
man lost his control. His arms flashed out to the dog, and he
experienced genuine surprise when he discovered that his hands
could not clutch, that there was neither bend nor feeling in the
fingers. He had forgotten for the moment that they were frozen
and that they were freezing more and more. All this happened
quickly, and before the animal could get away, he encircled its
body with his arms. He sat down in the snow, and in this
fashion held the dog, while it snarled and whined and struggled.

But it was all he could do, hold its body encircled in his arms
and sit there. He realized that he could not kill the dog. There
was no way to do it. With his helpless hands he could neither
draw nor hold his sheath-knife nor throttle the animal. He released it, and it plunged wildly away, with tail between its legs,
and still snarling. It halted forty feet away and surveyed him
curiously, with ears sharply pricked forward. The man looked
down at his hands in order to locate them, and found them
hanging on the ends of his arms. It struck him as curious that
one should have to use his eyes in order to find out where his
hands were. He began threshing his arms back and forth, beating
the mittened hands against his sides. He did this for five
minutes, violently, and his heart pumped enough blood up to
the surface to put a stop to his shivering. But no sensation was
aroused in the hands. He had an impression that they hung like
weights on the ends of his arms, but when he tried to run the
impression down, he could not find it.

A certain fear of death, dull and oppressive, came to him. This fear quickly became poignant as he realized that it was no longer a mere matter of freezing his fingers and toes, or of losing his hands and feet, but that it was a matter of life and death with the chances against him. This threw him into a panic, and he turned and ran up the creek-bed along the old, dim trail. The dog joined in behind and kept up with him. He ran blindly, without intention, in fear such as he had never known in his life. Slowly, as he plowed and floundered through the snow, he began to see things again – the banks of the creeks, the old timber-jams, the leafless aspens, and the sky. The running made him feel better. He did not shiver. Maybe, if he ran on, his feet would thaw out; and, anyway, if he ran far enough, he would reach camp and the boys. Without doubt he would lose some fingers and toes and some of his face; but the boys would take care of him, and save the rest of him when he got there. And at the same time there was another thought in his mind that said he would never get to the camp and the boys; that it was too many miles away, that the freezing had too great a start on him, and that he would soon be stiff and dead. This thought he kept in the background and refused to consider. Sometimes it pushed itself forward and demanded to be heard, but he thrust it back and strove to think of other things.

It struck him as curious that he could run at all on feet so frozen that he could not feel them when they struck the earth and took the weight of his body. He seemed to himself to skim along the surface, and to have no connexion with the earth. Somewhere he had once seen a winged Mercury, and he wondered if Mercury felt as he felt when skimming over the earth.

His theory of running until he reached camp and the boys had one flaw in it: he lacked the endurance. Several times he stumbled, and finally he tottered, crumpled up, and fell. When he tried to rise, he failed. He must sit and rest, he decided, and next time he would merely walk and keep on going. As he sat and regained his breath, he noted that he was feeling quite warm and comfortable. He was not shivering, and it even seemed that a warm glow had come to his chest and trunk. And yet, when he touched his nose or cheeks, there was no sensation. Running would not thaw them out. Nor would it thaw out his hands and feet. Then the thought came to him that the frozen portions of his body must be extending. He tried to keep this thought down, to forget it, to think of something else; he was aware of the panicky feeling that it caused, and he was afraid of the panic. But the thought asserted itself, and persisted, until it produced a vision of his body totally frozen. This was too much, and he made another wild run along the trail. Once he slowed down to a walk, but the thought of the freezing extending itself made him run again.

And all the time the dog ran with him, at his heels. When he fell down a second time, it curled its tail over its forefeet and sat in front of him, facing him, curiously eager and intent. The warmth and security of the animal angered him, and he cursed it till it flattened down its ears appeasingly. This time the shivering came more quickly upon the man. He was losing in his battle with the frost. It was creeping into his body from all sides. The thought of it drove him on, but he ran no more than a hundred feet, when he staggered and pitched headlong. It was his last panic. When he had recovered his breath and control, he sat up and entertained in his mind the conception of meeting death with dignity. However, the conception did not come to him in such terms. His idea of it was that he had been making a fool of himself, running around like a chicken with its head cut off — such was the simile that occurred to him. Well, he was bound to freeze anyway, and he might as well take it decently. With this new-found peace of mind came the first glimmerings of drowsiness. A good idea, he thought, to sleep off to death. It was like taking an anaesthetic. Freezing was not so bad as people thought. There were lots worse ways to die.

He pictured the boys finding his body next day. Suddenly he found himself with them, coming along the trail and looking for himself. And, still with them, he came around a turn in the trail and found himself lying in the snow. He did not belong with himself any more, for even then he was out of himself, standing with the boys and looking at himself in the snow. It certainly was cold, was his thought. When he got back to the States he could tell the folks what real cold was. He drifted on from this to a vision of the old-timer on Sulphur Creek. He could see him quite clearly, warm and comfortable, and smoking a pipe.

'You were right, old hoss; you were right,' the man mumbled to the old-timer of Sulphur Creek.

Then the man drowsed off into what seemed to him the most comfortable and satisfying sleep he had ever known. The dog sat facing him and waiting. The brief day drew to a close in a long, slow twilight. There were no signs of a fire to be made, and, besides, never in the dog's experience had it known a man to sit like that in the snow and make no fire. As the twilight drew on, its eager yearning for the fire mastered it, and with a great lifting and shifting of forefeet, it whined softly, then flattened its ears down in anticipation of being chidden by the man. But the man remained silent. Later, the dog whined loudly. And still later it crept close to the man and caught the scent of death. This made the animal bristle and back away. A little longer it delayed, howling under the stars that leaped and danced and shone brightly in the cold sky. Then it turned and trotted up the trail in the direction of the camp it knew, where were the other food-providers and fire-providers.

Sherwood Anderson

DEATH IN THE WOODS

I

SHE was an old woman and lived on a farm near the town in which I lived. All country and small-town people have seen such old women, but no one knows much about them. Such an old woman comes into town driving an old worn-out horse or she comes afoot carrying a basket. She may own a few hens and have eggs to sell. She brings them in a basket and takes them to a grocer. There she trades them in. She gets some salt pork and some beans. Then she gets a pound or two of sugar and some flour.

Afterwards she goes to the butcher's and asks for some dog-meat. She may spend ten or fifteen cents, but when she does she asks for something. Formerly the butchers gave liver to any one who wanted to carry it away. In our family we were always having it. Once one of my brothers got a whole cow's liver at the slaughter-house near the fairgrounds in our town. We had it until we were sick of it. It never cost a cent. I have hated the thought of it ever since.

The old farm woman got some liver and a soup-bone. She never visited with any one, and as soon as she got what she wanted she lit out for home. It made quite a load for such an old lady. No one gave her a lift. People drive right down a road and never notice an old woman like that.

There was such an old woman who used to come into town past our house one summer and fall when I was a young boy and was sick with what was called inflammatory rheumatism. She went home later carrying a heavy pack on her back. Two or three large gaunt-looking dogs followed at her heels.

The old woman was nothing special. She was one of the nameless ones that hardly any one knows, but she got into my

282

thoughts. I have just suddenly now, after all these years, remembered her and what happened. It is a story. Her name was Grimes, and she lived with her husband and son in a small unpainted house on the bank of a small creek four miles from town.

The husband and son were a tough lot. Although the son was but twenty-one, he had already served a term in jail. It was whispered about that the woman's husband stole horses and ran them off to some other county. Now and then, when a horse turned up missing, the man had also disappeared. No one ever caught him. Once, when I was loafing at Tom Whitehead's livery-barn, the man came there and sat on the bench in front. Two or three other men were there, but no one spoke to him. He sat for a few minutes and then got up and went away. When he was leaving he turned around and stared at the men. There was a look of defiance in his eyes. 'Well, I have tried to be friendly. You don't want to talk to me. It has been so wherever I have gone in this town. If, some day, one of your fine horses turns up missing, well, then what?' He did not say anything actually. 'I'd like to bust one of you on the jaw,' was about what his eyes said. I remember how the look in his eyes made me shiver.

The old man belonged to a family that had had money once. His name was Jake Grimes. It all comes back clearly now. His father, John Grimes, had owned a sawmill when the country was new, and had made money. Then he got to drinking and running after women. When he died there wasn't much left.

Jake blew in the rest. Pretty soon there wasn't any more lumber to cut and his land was nearly all gone.

He got his wife off a German farmer, for whom he went to work one June day in the wheat harvest. She was a young thing then and scared to death. You see, the farmer was up to something with the girl – she was, I think, a bound girl and his wife had her suspicions. She took it out on the girl when the man wasn't around. Then, when the wife had to go off to town for supplies, the farmer got after her. She told young Jake that nothing really ever happened, but he didn't know whether to believe it or not.

SHERWOOD ANDERSON

He got her pretty easy himself, the first time he was out with her. He wouldn't have married her if the German farmer hadn't tried to tell him where to get off. He got her to go riding with him in his buggy one night when he was threshing on the place, and then he came for her the next Sunday night.

She managed to get out of the house without her employer's seeing, but when she was getting into the buggy he showed up. It was almost dark, and he just popped up suddenly at the horse's head. He grabbed the horse by the bridle and Jake got out his buggy-whip.

They had it out all right! The German was a tough one. Maybe he didn't care whether his wife knew or not. Jake hit him over the face and shoulders with the buggy-whip, but the horse got to acting up and he had to get out.

Then the two men went for it. The girl didn't see it. The horse started to run away and went nearly a mile down the road before the girl got him stopped. Then she managed to tie him to a tree beside the road. (I wonder how I know all this. It must have stuck in my mind from small-town tales when I was a boy.) Jake found her there after he got through with the German. She was huddled up in the buggy seat, crying, scared to death. She told Jake a lot of stuff, how the German had tried to get her, how he chased her once into the barn, how another time, when they happened to be alone in the house together, he tore her dress open clear down the front. The German, she said, might have got her that time if he hadn't heard his old woman drive in at the gate. She had been off to town for supplies. Well, she would be putting the horse in the barn. The German managed to sneak off to the fields without his wife seeing. He told the girl he would kill her if she told. What could she do? She told a lie about ripping her dress in the barn when she was feeding the stock. I remember now that she was a bound girl and did not know where her father and mother were. Maybe she did not have any father. You know what I mean.

Such bound children were often enough cruelly treated. They were children who had no parents, slaves really. There were very few orphan homes then. They were legally bound into some home. It was a matter of pure luck how it came out.

2

She married Jake and had a son and daughter, but the daughter
died.

Then she settled down to feed stock. That was her job. At the
German's place she had cooked the food for the German and his
wife. The wife was a strong woman with big hips and worked
most of the time in the fields with her husband. She fed them
and fed the cows in the barn, fed the pigs, the horses and the
chickens. Every moment of every day, as a young girl, was spent
feeding something.

Then she married Jake Grimes and he had to be fed. She was
a slight thing, and when she had been married for three or four
years, and after the two children were born, her slender shoulders became stooped.

Jake always had a lot of big dogs around the house, that stood
near the unused sawmill near the creek. He was always trading
horses when he wasn't stealing something and had a lot of poor
bony ones about. Also he kept three or four pigs and a cow.
They were all pastured in the few acres left of the Grimes place
and Jake did little enough work.

He went into debt for a threshing outfit and ran it for several
years, but it did not pay. People did not trust him. They were
afraid he would steal the grain at night. He had to go a long
way off to get work and it cost too much to get there. In the
winter he hunted and cut a little fire-wood, to be sold in some
near-by town. When the son grew up he was just like the father.
They got drunk together. If there wasn't anything to eat in the
house when they came home the old man gave his old woman a
cut over the head. She had a few chickens of her own and had
to kill one of them in a hurry. When they were all killed she
wouldn't have any eggs to sell when she went to town, and then
what would she do?

She had to scheme all her life about getting things fed, getting the pigs fed so they would grow fat and could be butchered
in the fall. When they were butchered her husband took most of
the meat off to town and sold it. If he did not do it first the boy

did. They fought sometimes and when they fought the old woman stood aside trembling.

She had got the habit of silence anyway – that was fixed. Sometimes, when she began to look old – she wasn't forty yet – and when the husband and son were both off, trading horses or drinking or hunting or stealing, she went around the house and the barnyard muttering to herself.

How was she going to get everything fed? – that was her problem. The dogs had to be fed. There wasn't enough hay in the barn for the horses and the cow. If she didn't feed the chickens how could they lay eggs? Without eggs to sell how could she get things in town, things she had to have to keep the life of the farm going? Thank heaven, she did not have to feed her husband – in a certain way. That hadn't lasted long after their marriage and after the babies came. Where he went on his long trips she did not know. Sometimes he was gone from home for weeks, and after the boy grew up they went off together.

They left everything at home for her to manage and she had no money. She knew no one. No one ever talked to her in town. When it was winter she had to gather sticks of wood for her fire, had to try to keep the stock fed with very little grain.

The stock in the barn cried to her hungrily, the dogs followed her about. In the winter the hens laid few enough eggs. They huddled in the corners of the barn and she kept watching them. If a hen lays an egg in the barn in the winter and you do not find it, it freezes and breaks.

One day in winter the old woman went off to town with a few eggs and the dogs followed her. She did not get started until nearly three o'clock and the snow was heavy. She hadn't been feeling very well for several days and so she went muttering along, scantily clad, her shoulders stooped. She had an old grain bag in which she carried her eggs, tucked away down in the bottom. There weren't many of them, but in winter the price of eggs is up. She would get a little meat in exchange for the eggs, some salt pork, a little sugar, and some coffee perhaps. It might be the butcher would give her a piece of liver.

When she had got to town and was trading in her eggs the

dogs lay by the door outside. She did pretty well, got the things she needed, more than she had hoped. Then she went to the butcher and he gave her some liver and some dog-meat.

It was the first time any one had spoken to her in a friendly way for a long time. The butcher was alone in his shop when she came in and was annoyed by the thought of such a sick-looking old woman out on such a day. It was bitter cold and the snow, that had let up during the afternoon, was falling again. The butcher said something about her husband and her son, swore at them, and the old woman stared at him, a look of mild surprise in her eyes as he talked. He said that if either the husband or the son were going to get any of the liver or the heavy bones with scraps of meat hanging to them that he had put into the grain bag, he'd see him starve first.

Starve, eh? Well, things had to be fed. Men had to be fed, and the horses that weren't any good but maybe could be traded off, and the poor thin cow that hadn't given any milk for three months.

Horses, cows, pigs, dogs, men.

3

The old woman had to get back before darkness came if she could. The dogs followed at her heels, sniffing at the heavy grain bag she had fastened on her back. When she got to the edge of town she stopped by a fence and tied the bag on her back with a piece of rope she had carried in her dress-pocket for just that purpose. That was an easier way to carry it. Her arms ached. It was hard when she had to crawl over fences and once she fell over and landed in the snow. The dogs went frisking about. She had to struggle to get to her feet again, but she made it. The point of climbing over the fences was that there was a short cut over a hill and through a woods. She might have gone around by the road, but it was a mile farther that way. She was afraid she couldn't make it. And then, besides, the stock had to be fed. There was a little hay left and a little corn. Perhaps her husband and son would bring some home when they came. They had driven off in the only buggy the Grimes family had, a rickety thing, a rickety horse hitched to the buggy, two other rickety horses led by halters. They were going to trade horses, get a little money if they could. They might come home drunk. It would be well to have something in the house when they came back.

The son had an affair on with a woman at the county seat, fifteen miles away. She was a rough enough woman, a tough one. Once, in the summer, the son had brought her to the house. Both she and the son had been drinking. Jake Grimes was away and the son and his woman ordered the old woman about like a servant. She didn't mind much; she was used to it. Whatever happened she never said anything. That was her way of getting along. She had managed that way when she was a young girl at the German's and ever since she had married Jake. That time her son brought his woman to the house they stayed all night, sleeping together just as though they were married. It hadn't shocked the old woman, not much. She had got past being shocked early in life.

With the pack on her back she went painfully along across an open field, wading in the deep snow, and got into the woods.

There was a path, but it was hard to follow. Just beyond the top of the hill, where the woods was thickest, there was a small clearing. Had some one once thought of building a house there? The clearing was as large as a building lot in town, large enough for a house and a garden. The path ran along the side of the clearing, and when she got there the old woman sat down to rest at the foot of a tree.

It was a foolish thing to do. When she got herself placed, the pack against the tree's trunk, it was nice, but what about getting up again? She worried about that for a moment and then quietly closed her eyes.

She must have slept for a time. When you are about so cold you can't get any colder. The afternoon grew a little warmer and the snow came thicker than ever. Then after a time the weather cleared. The moon even came out.

There were four Grimes dogs that had followed Mrs Grimes into town, all tall gaunt fellows. Such men as Jake Grimes and his son always keep just such dogs. They kick and abuse them, but they stay. The Grimes dogs, in order to keep from starving, had to do a lot of foraging for themselves, and they had been at it while the old woman slept with her back to the tree at the side of the clearing. They had been chasing rabbits in the woods and in adjoining fields and in their ranging had picked up three other farm dogs.

After a time all the dogs came back to the clearing. They were excited about something. Such nights, cold and clear and with a moon, do things to dogs. It may be that some old instinct, come down from the time when they were wolves and ranged the woods in packs on winter nights, comes back into them.

The dogs in the clearing, before the old woman, had caught two or three rabbits and their immediate hunger had been satisfied. They began to play, running in circles in the clearing. Round and round they ran, each dog's nose at the tail of the next dog. In the clearing, under the snow-laden trees and under the wintry moon they made a strange picture, running thus silently, in a circle their running had beaten in the soft snow. The dogs made no sound. They ran around and around in the circle.

It may have been that the old woman saw them doing that before she died. She may have awakened once or twice and looked at the strange sight with dim eyes.

She wouldn't be very cold now, just drowsy. Life hangs on a long time. Perhaps the old woman was out of her head. She may have dreamed of her girlhood, at the German's, and before that, when she was a child and before her mother lit out and left her.

Her dreams couldn't have been very pleasant. Not many pleasant things had happened to her. Now and then one of the Grimes dogs left the running circle and came to stand before her. The dog thrust his face close to her face. His red tongue was hanging out.

The running of the dogs may have been a kind of death ceremony. It may have been that the primitive instinct of the wolf, having been aroused in the dogs by the night and the running, made them somehow afraid.

'Now we are no longer wolves. We are dogs, the servants of

men. Keep alive, man! When man dies we becomes wolves again.'

When one of the dogs came to where the old woman sat with her back against the tree and thrust his nose close to her face he seemed satisfied and went back to run with the pack. All the Grimes dogs did it at some time during the evening, before she died. I knew all about it afterward, when I grew to be a man, because once in a woods in Illinois, on another winter night, I saw a pack of dogs act just like that. The dogs were waiting for me to die as they had waited for the old woman that night when I was a child, but when it happened to me I was a young man and had no intention whatever of dying.

The old woman died softly and quietly. When she was dead and when one of the Grimes dogs had come to her and had found her dead all the dogs stopped running.

They gathered about her.

Well, she was dead now. She had fed the Grimes dogs when she was alive, what about now?

There was the pack on her back, the grain bag containing the piece of salt pork, the liver the butcher had given her, the dog-meat, the soup bones. The butcher in town, having been suddenly overcome with a feeling of pity, had loaded her grain bag heavily. It had been a big haul for the old woman.

It was a big haul for the dogs now.

4

One of the Grimes dogs sprang suddenly out from among the others and began worrying the pack on the old woman's back. Had the dogs really been wolves that one would have been the leader of the pack. What he did, all the others did.

All of them sank their teeth into the grain bag the old woman had fastened with ropes to her back.

They dragged the old woman's body out into the open clearing. The worn-out dress was quickly torn from her shoulders. When she was found, a day or two later, the dress had been torn from her body clear to the hips, but the dogs had not touched her body. They had got the meat out of the grain bag, that was all. Her body was frozen stiff when it was found, and the shoulders were so narrow and the body so slight that in death it looked like the body of some charming young girl.

Such things happened in towns of the Middle West, on farms near town, when I was a boy. A hunter out after rabbits found the old woman's body and did not touch it. Something, the beaten round path in the little snow-covered clearing, the silence of the place, where the dogs had worried the body trying to pull the grain bag away or tear it open – something startled the man and he hurried off to town.

I was in Main street with one of my brothers who was town newsboy and who was taking the afternoon papers to the stores. It was almost night.

The hunter came into a grocery and told his story. Then he went to a hardware-shop and into a drugstore. Men began to gather on the sidewalks. Then they started out along the road to the place in the woods.

My brother should have gone on about his business of distributing papers but he didn't. Every one was going to the woods. The undertaker went and the town marshal. Several men got on a dray and rode out to where the path left the road and went into the woods, but the horses weren't very sharply shod and slid about on the slippery roads. They made no better time than those of us who walked.

The town marshal was a large man whose leg had been injured in the Civil War. He carried a heavy cane and limped rapidly along the road. My brother and I followed at his heels, and as we went other men and boys joined the crowd.

It had grown dark by the time we got to where the old woman had left the road, but the moon had come out. The marshal was thinking there might have been a murder. He kept asking the hunter questions. The hunter went along with his gun across his shoulders, a dog following at his heels. It isn't often a rabbit hunter has a chance to be so conspicuous. He was taking full advantage of it, leading the procession with the town marshal. 'I didn't see any wounds. She was a beautiful young girl. Her face was buried in the snow. No, I didn't know her.' As a matter of fact, the hunter had not looked closely at the body. He had been frightened. She might have been murdered and some one might spring out from behind a tree and murder him. In a woods, in the late afternoon, when the trees are all bare and there is white snow on the ground, when all is silent, something creepy steals over the mind and body. If something strange or uncanny has happened in the neighborhood all you think about is getting away from there as fast as you can.

The crowd of men and boys had got to where the old woman had crossed the field and went, following the marshal and the hunter, up the slight incline and into the woods.

My brother and I were silent. He had his bundle of papers in a bag slung across his shoulder. When he got back to town he would have to go on distributing his papers before he went home to supper, If I went along, as he had no doubt already determined I should, we would both be late. Either mother or our older sister would have to warm our supper.

Well, we would have something to tell. A boy did not get such a chance very often. It was lucky we just happened to go into the grocery when the hunter came in. The hunter was a country fellow. Neither of us had ever seen him before.

Now the crowd of men and boys had got to the clearing. Darkness comes quickly on such winter nights, but the full moon made everything clear. My brother and I stood near the tree, beneath which the old woman had died.

She did not look old, lying there in that light, frozen and still. One of the men turned her over in the snow and I saw everything. My body trembled with some strange mystical feeling and so did my brother's. It might have been the cold.

Neither of us had ever seen a woman's body before. It may have been the snow, clinging to the frozen flesh, that made it look so white and lovely, so like marble. No woman had come with the party from town; but one of the men, he was the town blacksmith, took off his overcoat and spread it over her. Then he gathered her into his arms and started off to town, all the others following silently. At that time no one knew who she was.

5

I had seen everything, had seen the oval in the snow, like a miniature race-track, where the dogs had run, had seen how the men were mystified, had seen the white bare young-looking shoulders, had heard the whispered comments of the men.

The men were simply mystified. They took the body to the undertaker's, and when the blacksmith, the hunter, the marshal and several others had got inside they closed the door. If father had been there perhaps he could have got in, but we boys couldn't.

I went with my brother to distribute the rest of his papers and when we got home it was my brother who told the story.

I kept silent and went to bed early. It may have been I was not satisfied with the way he told it.

Later, in the town, I must have heard other fragments of the old woman's story. She was recognized the next day and there was an investigation.

The husband and son were found somewhere and brought to town and there was an attempt to connect them with the woman's death, but it did not work. They had perfect enough alibis.

However, the town was against them. They had to get out. Where they went I never heard.

I remember only the picture there in the forest, the men standing about, the naked girlish-looking figure, face down in the snow, the tracks made by the running dogs and the clear cold winter sky above. White fragments of clouds were drifting across the sky. They went racing across the little open space among the trees.

The scene in the forest had become for me, without my knowing it, the foundation for the real story I am now trying to tell. The fragments, you see, had to be picked up slowly, long afterwards.

Things happened. When I was a young man I worked on the farm of a German. The hired-girl was afraid of her employer. The farmer's wife hated her.

I saw things at that place. Once later, I had a half-uncanny, mystical adventure with dogs in an Illinois forest on a clear, moon-lit winter night. When I was a schoolboy, and on a summer day, I went with a boy friend out along a creek some miles from town and came to the house where the old woman had lived. No one had lived in the house since her death. The doors were broken from the hinges; the window lights were all broken. As the boy and I stood in the road outside, two dogs, just roving farm dogs no doubt, came running around the corner of the house. The dogs were tall, gaunt fellows and came down to the fence and glared through at us, standing in the road.

The whole thing, the story of the old woman's death, was to me as I grew older like music heard from far off. The notes had to be picked up slowly one at a time. Something had to be understood.

The woman who died was one destined to feed animal life. Anyway, that is all she ever did. She was feeding animal life before she was born, as a child, as a young woman working on the farm of the German, after she married, when she grew old, and when she died. She fed animal life in cows, in chickens, in pigs, in horses, in dogs, in men. Her daughter had died in childhood and with her one son she had no articulate relations. On the night when she died she was hurrying homeward, bearing on her body food for animal life.

She died in the clearing in the woods and even after her death continued feeding animal life.

You see it is likely that, when my brother told the story, that night when we got home and my mother and sister sat listening, I did not think he got the point. He was too young and so was I. A thing so complete has its own beauty.

I shall not try to emphasize the point. I am only explaining why I was dissatisfied then and have been ever since. I speak of that only that you may understand why I have been impelled to try to tell the simple story over again.

Ring Lardner

WHO DEALT?

You know, this is the first time Tom and I have been with real friends since we were married. I suppose you'll think it's funny for me to call you *my* friends when we've never met before, but Tom has talked about you so much and how much he thought of you and how crazy he was to see you and everything – well, it's just as if I'd known you all my life, like he has.

We've got our little crowd out there, play bridge and dance with them; but of course we've only been there three months, at least I have, and people you've known that length of time, well, it isn't like knowing people all your life, like you and Tom. How often I've heard Tom say he'd give any amount of money to be with Arthur and Helen, and how bored he was out there with just poor little me and his new friends!

Arthur and Helen, Arthur and Helen – he talks about you so much that it's a wonder I'm not jealous; especially of you, Helen. You must have been his real pal when you were kids.

Nearly all of his kid books, they have your name in front – to Thomas Cannon from Helen Bird Strong. This is a wonderful treat for him to see you! And a treat for me, too. Just think, I've at last met the wonderful Helen and Arthur! You must forgive me calling you by your first names; that's how I always think of you and I simply can't say Mr and Mrs Gratz.

No, thank you, Arthur; no more. Two is my limit and I've already exceeded it, with two cocktails before dinner and now this. But it's a special occasion, meeting Tom's best friends. I bet Tom wishes he could celebrate too, don't you, dear? Of course he could if he wanted to, but when he once makes up his mind to a thing, there's nothing in the world can shake him. He's got the strongest will power of any person I ever saw.

I do think it's wonderful, him staying on the wagon this long, a man that used to – well, you know as well as I do;

probably a whole lot better, because you were with him so much in the old days, and all I know is just what he's told me. He told me about once in Pittsburgh – All right, Tommie; I won't say another word. But it's all over now, thank heavens! Not a drop since we've been married; three whole months! And he says it's forever, don't you dear? Though I don't mind a person drinking if they do it in moderation. But you know Tom! He goes the limit in everything he does. Like he used to in athletics –

All right, dear; I won't make you blush. I know how you hate the limelight. It's terrible, though, not to be able to boast about your own husband; everything he does or ever has done seems so wonderful. But is that only because we've been married such a short time? Do you feel the same way about Arthur, Helen? You do? And you married him four years ago, isn't that right? And you eloped, didn't you? You see I know all about you.

Oh, are you waiting for me? Do we cut for partners? Why can't we play families? I don't feel so bad if I do something dumb when it's Tom I'm playing with. He never scolds, though he does give me some terrible looks. But not very often lately; I don't make the silly mistakes I used to. I'm pretty good now, aren't I, Tom? You better say so, because if I'm not, it's your fault. You know Tom had to teach me the game. I never played at all till we were engaged. Imagine! And I guess I was pretty awful at first, but Tom was a dear, so patient! I know he thought I never would learn, but I fooled you, didn't I, Tommie?

No, indeed, I'd rather play than do almost anything. But you'll sing for us, won't you , Helen? I mean after a while. Tom has raved to me about your voice and I'm dying to hear it.

What are we playing for? Yes, a penny's perfectly all right. Out there we generally play for half a cent a piece, a penny a family. But a penny a piece is all right. I guess we can afford it now, can't we, dear? Tom hasn't told you about his raise. He was – All right, Tommie; I'll shut up. I know you hate to be talked about, but your wife can't help being just a teeny bit proud of you. And I think your best friends are interested in your affairs, aren't you, folks?

But Tom is the most secretive person I ever knew. I believe he even keeps things from me! Not very many, though. I can usually tell when he's hiding something and I keep after him till he confesses. He often says I should have been a lawyer or a detective, the way I can worm things out of people. Don't you, Tom?

For instance, I never would have known about his experience with those horrid football people at Yale if I hadn't just made him tell me. Didn't you know about that? No, Tom, I'm going to tell Arthur even if you hate me for it. I know you'd be interested, Arthur, not only because you're Tom's friend, but on account of you being such a famous athlete yourself. Let me see, how was it, Tom? You must help me out. Well, if I don't get it right, you correct me.

Well, Tom's friends at Yale had heard what a wonderful football player he was in high school so they made him try for a place on the Yale nine. Tom had always played half-back. You have to be a fast runner to be a half-back and Tom could run awfully fast. He can yet. When we were engaged we used to run races and the prize was – All right, Tommie, I won't give away our secrets. Anyway, he can beat me to pieces.

Well, he wanted to play half-back at Yale and he was getting along fine and the other men on the team said he would be a wonder and then one day they were having their practice and Tex Jones, no, Ted Jones – he's the main coach – he scolded Tom for having the signal wrong and Tom proved that Jones was wrong and he was right and Jones never forgave him. He made Tom quit playing half-back and put him tackle or end or some place like that where you can't do anything and being a fast runner doesn't count. So Tom saw that Jones had it in for him and he quit. Wasn't that it, Tom? Well, anyway, it was something.

Oh, are you waiting for me? I'm sorry. What did you bid, Helen? And you, Tom? You doubled her? And Arthur passed? Well, let's see. I wish I could remember what that means. I know that sometimes when he doubles he means one thing and sometimes another. But I always forget which is which. Let me see; it was two spades that he doubled, wasn't it? That means

I'm to leave him in, I'm pretty sure. Well, I'll pass. Oh, I'm sorry, Tommie! I knew I'd get it wrong. Please forgive me. But maybe we'll set them anyway. Whose lead?

I'll stop talking now and try and keep my mind on the game. You needn't look that way, Tommie. I *can* stop talking if I try. It's kind of hard to concentrate though, when you're, well, excited. It's not only meeting you people, but I always get excited traveling. I was just terrible on our honeymoon, but then I guess a honeymoon's enough to make anybody nervous. I'll never forget when we went into the hotel in Chicago – All right, Tommie, I won't. But I can tell about meeting the Bakers.

They're a couple about our age that I've known all my life. They were the last people in the world I wanted to see, but we ran into them on State Street and they insisted on us coming to their hotel for dinner and before dinner they took us up to their room and Ken – that's Mr Baker – Ken made some cocktails, though I didn't want any and Tom was on the wagon. He said a honeymoon was a fine time to be on the wagon! Ken said.

'Don't tempt him, Ken,' I said. 'Tom isn't a drinker like you and Gertie and the rest of us. When he starts, he can't stop.' Gertie is Mrs Baker.

So Ken said why should he stop and I said there was good reason why he should because he had promised me he would and he told me the day we were married that if I ever saw him take another drink I would know that –

What did you make? Two odd? Well, thank heavens that isn't a game! Oh, that does make a game, doesn't it? Because Tom doubled and I left him in. Isn't that wicked! Oh, dearie, please forgive me and I'll promise to pay attention from now on! What do I do with these? Oh, yes, I make them for Arthur.

I was telling you about the Bakers. Finally Ken saw he couldn't make Tom take a drink, so he gave up in disgust. But imagine meeting them on our honeymoon, when we didn't want to see anybody! I don't suppose anybody does unless they're already tired of each other, and we certainly weren't, were we, Tommie? And aren't yet, are we, dear? And never will be. But I guess I better speak for myself.

There! I'm talking again! But you see it's the first time we've been with anybody we really cared about; I mean, you're Tom's best friends and it's so nice to get a chance to talk to somebody who's known him a long time. Out there the people we run around with are almost strangers and they don't talk about anything but themselves and how much money their husbands make. You never can talk to them about things that are worth while, like books. I'm wild about books, but I honestly don't believe half the women we know out there can read. Or at least they don't. If you mention some really worth while novel like, say, *Black Oxen*, they think you're trying to put on the Ritz.

You said a no-trump, didn't you, Tom? And Arthur passed. Let me see; I wish I knew what to do. I haven't any five-card — it's terrible! Just a minute. I wish somebody could — I know I ought to take — but — well, I'll pass. Oh, Tom, this is the worst you ever saw, but I don't know what I could have done.

I do hold the most terrible cards! I certainly believe in the saying, 'Unlucky at cards, lucky in love'. Whoever made it up must have been thinking of me. I hate to lay them down, dear. I know you'll say I ought to have done something. Well, there they are! Let's see your hand, Helen. Oh, Tom, she's — but I mustn't tell, must I? Anyway, I'm dummy. That's one comfort. I can't make a mistake when I'm dummy. I believe Tom over-bids lots of times so I'll be dummy and can't do anything ridiculous. But at that I'm much better than I used to be, aren't I, dear?

Helen, do you mind telling me where you got that gown? Crandall and Nelsons's? I've heard of them, but I heard they were terribly expensive. Of course a person can't expect to get a gown like that without paying for it. I've got to get some things while I'm here and I suppose that's where I better go, if their things aren't too horribly dear. I haven't had a thing new since I was married and I've worn this so much I'm sick of it.

Tom's always after me to buy clothes, but I can't seem to get used to spending somebody else's money, though it was dad's money I spent before I did Tom's, but that's different, don't you think so? And of course at first we didn't have very much to spend, did we, dear? But now that we've had our raise – All right, Tommie, I won't say another word.

Oh, did you know they tried to get Tom to run for mayor? Tom is making faces at me to shut up, but I don't see any harm in telling it to his best friends. They know we're not the kind that brag, Tommie. I do think it was quite a tribute; he'd only lived there a little over a year. It came up one night when the Guthries were at our house, playing bridge. Mr Guthrie – that's A. L. Guthrie – he's one of the big lumbermen out there. He owns – just what does he own, Tom? Oh, I'm sorry. Anyway, he's got millions. Well, at least thousands.

He and his wife were at our house playing bridge. She's the queerest woman! If you just saw her, you'd think she was a janitor or something; she wears the most hideous clothes. Why, that night she had on a – honestly you'd have sworn it was a maternity gown, and for no reason. And the first time I met her – well, I just can't describe it. And she's a graduate of Bryn Mawr and one of the oldest families in Philadelphia. You'd never believe it!

She and her husband are terribly funny in a bridge game. He doesn't think there ought to be any conventions; he says a person might just as well tell each other what they've got. So he won't pay any attention to what-do-you-call-'em, informatory, doubles and so forth. And she plays all the conventions, so you can imagine how they get along. Fight! Not really fight, you know, but argue. That is, he does. It's horribly embarrassing to whoever is playing with them. Honestly, if Tom ever spoke to me like Mr Guthrie does to his wife, well – aren't they terrible, Tom? Oh, I'm sorry!

She was the first woman in Portland that called on me and I thought it was awfully nice of her, though when I saw her at the door I would have sworn she was a book agent or maybe a cook looking for work. She had on a – well, I can't describe it. But it was sweet of her to call, she being one of the real people there and me – well, that was before Tom was made a vice-president. What? Oh, I never dreamed he hadn't written you about that!

But Mrs Guthrie acted just like it was a great honor for her to meet me, and I like people to act that way even when I know it's all apple sauce. Isn't that a funny expression, 'apple sauce'? Some man said it in a vaudeville show in Portland the Monday night before we left. He was a comedian – Jack Brooks or Ned Frawley or something. It means – well, I don't know how to describe it. But we had a terrible time after the first few minutes. She is the silentest person I ever knew and I'm kind of bashful myself with strangers. What are you grinning about, Tommie? I am, too, bashful when I don't know people. Not exactly bashful, maybe, but, well, bashful.

It was one of the most embarrassing things I ever went through. Neither of us could say a word and I could hardly help from laughing at what she had on. But after you get to know her you don't mind her clothes, though it's a terrible temptation all the time not to tell how much nicer – And her hair! But she plays a dandy game of bridge, lots better than her husband. You know he won't play conventions. He says it's just like telling you what's in each other's hand. And they have awful arguments in a game. That is, he does. She's nice and quiet and it's a kind of mystery how they ever fell in love. Though there's a saying or a proverb or something, isn't there, about like not liking like? Or is it just the other way?

But I was going to tell you about them wanting Tom to be mayor. Oh, Tom, only two down? Why, I think you did splendidly! I gave you a miserable hand and Helen had – what didn't you have, Helen? You had the ace, king of clubs. No, Tom had the king. No, Tom had the queen. Or was it spades? And you had the ace of hearts. No, Tom had that. No, he didn't. What *did* you have, Tom? I don't exactly see what you bid on. Of course I was terrible, but – what's the difference anyway?

What was I saying? Oh, yes, about Mr and Mrs Guthrie. It's funny for a couple like that to get married when they are so different in every way. I never saw two people with such different tastes. For instance, Mr Guthrie is keen about motoring and Mrs Guthrie just hates it. She simply suffers all the time she's in a car. He likes a good time, dancing, golfing, fishing, shows, things like that. She isn't interested in anything but church work and bridge work.

'Bridge work.' I meant bridge, not bridge work. That's funny, isn't it? And yet they get along awfully well; that is when they're not playing cards or doing something else together. But it does seem queer that they picked each other out. Still, I guess hardly any husband and wife agree on anything.

You take Tom and me, though, and you'd think we were made for each other. It seems like we feel just the same about everything. That is, almost everything. The things we don't agree on are little things that don't matter. Like music. Tom is wild about jazz and blues and dance music. He adores Irving Berlin and Gershwin and Jack Kearns. He's always after those kind of things on the radio and I just want serious, classical things like 'Humoresque' and 'Indian Love Lyrics'. And then there's shows. Tom is crazy over Ed Wynn and I can't see anything in him. Just the way he laughs at his own jokes is enough to spoil him for me. If I'm going to spend time and money on a theater I want to see something worth while – *The Fool* or *Lightnin'*.

And things to eat. Tom insists, or that is he did insist, on a great big breakfast – fruit, cereal, eggs, toast, and coffee. All I want is a little fruit and dry toast and coffee. I think it's a great deal better for a person. So that's one habit I broke Tom of, was big breakfasts. And another thing he did when we were first married was to take off his shoes as soon as he got home from the office and put on bedroom slippers. I believe a person ought not to get sloppy just because they're married.

But the worst of all was pajamas! What's the difference, Tommie? Helen and Arthur don't mind. And I think it's kind of funny, you being so old-fashioned. I mean Tom had always worn a nightgown till I made him give it up. And it was a struggle, believe me! I had to threaten to leave him if he didn't buy pajamas. He certainly hated it. And now he's mad at me for telling, aren't you, Tommie? I just couldn't help it. I think it's so funny in this day and age. I hope Arthur doesn't wear them; nightgowns, I mean. You don't, do you, Arthur? I knew you didn't.

Oh, are you waiting for me? What did you say, Arthur? Two diamonds? Let's see what that means. When Tom makes an

original bid of two it means he hasn't got the tops. I wonder —
but of course you couldn't have the — heavens! What am I saying! I guess I better just keep still and pass.

But what was I going to tell you? Something about — oh, did
I tell you about Tom being an author? I had no idea he was
talented that way till after we were married and I was unpack-
ing his old papers and things and came across a poem he'd
written, the saddest, mushiest poem! Of course it was a long
time ago he wrote it; it was dated four years ago, long before
he met me, so it didn't make me very jealous, though it was
about some other girl. You didn't know I found it, did you,
Tommie?

But that wasn't what I refer to. He's written a story, too, and
he's sent it to four different magazines and they all sent it
back. I tell him though, that that doesn't mean anything. When
you see some of the things the magazines do print, why, it's an
honor to have them *not* like yours. The only thing is that Tom
worked so hard over it and sat up nights writing and rewriting,
it's a kind of a disappointment to have them turn it down.

It's a story about two men and a girl and they were all
brought up together and one of the men was awfully popular
and well off and good-looking and a great athlete — a man like
Arthur. There, Arthur! How is that for a T. L.? The other man
was just an ordinary man with not much money, but the girl
seemed to like him better and she promised to wait for him.
Then this man worked hard and got money enough to see him
through Yale.

The other man, the well-off one, went to Princeton and made
a big hit as an athlete and everything and he was through
college long before his friend because his friend had to earn the
money first. And the well-off man kept after the girl to marry
him. He didn't know she had promised the other one. Anyway
she got tired waiting for the man she was engaged to and
eloped with the other one. And the story ends up by the man
she threw down welcoming the couple when they came home
and pretending everything was all right, though his heart was
broken.

What are you blushing about, Tommie? It's nothing to be

ashamed of. I thought it was very well written and if the editors had any sense they'd have taken it.

Still, I don't believe the real editors see half the stories that are sent to them. In fact I know they don't. You've either got to have a name or a pull to get your things published. Or else pay the magazines to publish them. Of course if you are Robert Chambers or Irving R. Cobb, they will print whatever you write whether it's good or bad. But you haven't got a chance if you are an unknown like Tom. They just keep your story long enough so you will think they are considering it and then they send it back with a form letter saying it's not available for their magazine and they don't even tell why.

You remember, Tom, that Mr Hastings we met at the Hammonds'. He's a writer and knows all about it. He was telling me of an experience he had with one of the magazines; I forget which one, but it was one of the big ones. He wrote a story and sent it to them and they sent it back and said they couldn't use it.

Well, some time after that Mr Hastings was in a hotel in Chicago and a bell-boy went around the lobby paging Mr — I forget the name, but it was the name of the editor of this magazine that had sent back the story, Rungle, or Byers, or some such name. So the man, whatever his name was, he was really there and answered the page and afterwards Mr Hastings went up to him and introduced himself and told the man about sending a story to his magazine and the man said he didn't remember anything about it. And he was the editor! Of course he'd never seen it. No wonder Tom's story keeps coming back!

He says he is through sending it and just the other day he was going to tear it up, but I made him keep it because we may meet somebody some time who knows the inside ropes and can get a hearing with some big editor. I'm sure it's just a question of pull. Some of the things that get into the magazines sound like they had been written by the editor's friends or relatives or somebody whom they didn't want to hurt their feelings. And Tom really can write!

I wish I could remember that poem of his I found. I memorized it once, but — wait! I believe I can still say it! Hush, Tommie! What hurt will it do anybody? Let me see; it goes:

I thought the sweetness of her song
Would ever, ever more belong
To me; I thought (O thought divine!)
My bird was really mine!

But promises are made, it seems,
Just to be broken. All my dreams
Fade out and leave me crushed, alone.
My bird, alas, has flown!

Isn't that pretty. He wrote it four years ago. Why, Helen, you revoked! And, Tom, do you know that's Scotch you're drinking? You said — *Why, Tom!*

Katherine Anne Porter

FLOWERING JUDAS

BRAGGIONI sits heaped upon the edge of a straight-backed chair much too small for him, and sings to Laura in a furry, mournful voice. Laura has begun to find reasons for avoiding her own house until the latest possible moment, for Braggioni is there almost every night. No matter how late she is, he will be sitting there with a surly, waiting expression, pulling at his kinky yellow hair, thumbing the strings of his guitar, snarling a tune under his breath. Lupe the Indian maid meets Laura at the door, and says with a flicker of a glance towards the upper room, 'He waits.'

Laura wishes to lie down, she is tired of her hairpins and the feel of her long tight sleeves, but she says to him, 'Have you a new song for me this evening?' If he says yes, she asks him to sing it. If he says no, she remembers his favorite one, and asks him to sing it again. Lupe brings her a cup of chocolate and a plate of rice, and Laura eats at the small table under the lamp, first inviting Braggioni, whose answer is always the same: 'I have eaten, and besides, chocolate thickens the voice.'

Laura says, 'Sing, then,' and Braggioni heaves himself into song. He scratches the guitar familiarly as though it were a pet animal, and sings passionately off key, taking the high notes in a prolonged painful squeal. Laura, who haunts the markets listening to the ballad singers, and stops every day to hear the blind boy playing his reed-flute in Sixteenth of September Street, listens to Braggioni with pitiless courtesy, because she dares not smile at his miserable performance. Nobody dares to smile at him. Braggioni is cruel to everyone, with a kind of specialized insolence, but he is so vain of his talents, and so sensitive to slights, it would require a cruelty and vanity greater than his own to lay a finger on the vast cureless wound of his self-esteem. It would require courage, too, for it is dangerous to offend him, and nobody has this courage.

Braggioni loves himself with such tenderness and amplitude and eternal charity that his followers – for he is a leader of men, a skilled revolutionist, and his skin has been punctured in honorable warfare – warm themselves in the reflected glow, and say to each other: 'He has a real nobility, a love of humanity raised above mere personal affections.' The excess of this self-love has flowed out, inconveniently for her, over Laura, who, with so many others, owes her comfortable situation and her salary to him. When he is in a very good humour, he tells her, 'I am tempted to forgive you for being a *gringa. Gringita!*' and Laura, burning, imagines herself leaning forward suddenly, and with a sound back-handed slap wiping the suety smile from his face. If he notices her eyes at these moments he gives no sign.

She knows what Braggioni would offer her, and she must resist tenaciously without appearing to resist, and if she could avoid it she would not admit even to herself the slow drift of his intention. During these long evenings which have spoiled a long month for her, she sits in her deep chair with an open book on her knees, resting her eyes on the consoling rigidity of the printed page when the sight and sound of Braggioni singing threaten to identify themselves with all her remembered afflictions and to add their weight to her uneasy premonitions of the future. The gluttonous bulk of Braggioni has become a symbol of her many disillusions, for a revolutionist should be lean, animated by heroic faith, a vessel of abstract virtues. This is nonsense, she knows it now and is ashamed of it. Revolution must have leaders, and leadership is a career for energetic men. She is, her comrades tell her, full of romantic error, for what she defines as cynicism in them is merely 'a developed sense of reality'. She is almost too willing to say, 'I am wrong, I suppose I don't really understand the principles,' and afterward she makes a secret truce with herself, determined not to surrender her will to such expedient logic. But she cannot help feeling that she has been betrayed irreparably by the disunion between her way of living and her feeling of what life should be, and at times she is almost contented to rest in this sense of grievance as a private store of consolation. Sometimes she wishes to run away, but she stays. Now she longs to fly out of this room, down the narrow stairs, and into the street where the houses lean together like conspirators under a single mottled lamp, and leave Braggioni singing to himself.

Instead she looks at Braggioni, frankly and clearly, like a good child who understands the rules of behavior. Her knees cling together under sound blue serge, and her round white collar is not purposely nun-like. She wears the uniform of an idea, and has renounced vanities. She was born Roman Catholic, and in spite of her fear of being seen by someone who might make a scandal of it, she slips now and again into some crumbling little church, kneels on the chilly stone, and says a Hail Mary on the gold rosary she bought in Tehuantepec. It is no good and she ends by examining the altar with its tinsel flowers and ragged brocades, and feels tender about the battered doll-shape of some real saint whose white, lace-trimmed drawers hang limply around his ankles below the hieratic dignity of his velvet robe. She has encased herself in a set of principles derived from her early training, leaving no detail of gesture or of personal taste untouched, and for this reason she will not wear lace made on machines. This is her private heresy, for in her special group the machine is sacred, and will be the salvation of the workers. She loves fine lace, and there is a tiny edge of fluted cobweb on this collar, which is one of twenty precisely alike, folded in blue tissue paper in the upper drawer of her clothes chest.

Braggioni catches her glance solidly as if he had been waiting for it, leans forward, balancing his paunch between his spread knees, and sings with tremendous emphasis, weighing his words. He has, the song relates, no father and no mother, nor even a friend to console him; lonely as a wave of the sea he comes and goes, lonely as a wave. His mouth opens round and yearns sideways, his balloon cheeks grow oily with the labor of song. He bulges marvelously in his expensive garments. Over his lavender collar, crushed upon a purple necktie, held by a diamond hoop: over his ammunition belt of tooled leather worked in silver, buckled cruelly around his gasping middle: over the tops of his glossy yellow shoes Braggioni swells with ominous ripeness, his mauve silk hose stretched taut, his ankles bound with the stout leather thongs of his shoes.

When he stretches his eyelids at Laura she notes again that his eyes are the true tawny yellow cat's eyes. He is rich, not in money, he tells her, but in power, and this power brings with it the blameless ownership of things, and the right to indulge his love of small luxuries. 'I have a taste for the elegant refinements,' he said once, flourishing a yellow silk hankerchief before her nose. 'Smell that? It is Jockey Club, imported from New York.' Nonetheless he is wounded by life. He will say so presently. 'It is true everything turns to dust in the hand, to gall on the tongue.' He sighs and his leather belt creaks like a saddle girth. 'I am disappointed in everything as it comes. Everything.' He shakes his head. 'You, poor thing, you will be disappointed too. You are born for it. We are more alike than you realize in some things. Wait and see. Some day you will remember what I have told you, you will know that Braggioni was your friend.'

Laura feels a slow chill, a purely physical sense of danger, a warning in her blood that violence, mutilation, a shocking death, wait for her with lessening patience. She has translated this fear into something homely, immediate, and sometimes hesitates before crossing the street. 'My personal fate is nothing, except as the testimony of a mental attitude,' she reminds herself, quoting from some forgotten philosophic primer, and is sensible enough to add, 'Anyhow, I shall not be killed by an automobile if I can help it.'

'It may be true I am as corrupt, in another way, as Braggioni,' she thinks in spite of herself, 'as callous, as incomplete,' and if this is so, any kind of death seems preferable. Still she sits quietly, she does not run. Where could she go? Uninvited she has promised herself to this place; she can no longer imagine herself as living in another country, and there is no pleasure in remembering her life before she came here.

Precisely what is the nature of this devotion, its true motives, and what are its obligations? Laura cannot say. She spends part of her days in Xochimilco, near by, teaching Indian children to say in English, 'The cat is on the mat.' When she appears in the

classroom they crowd about her with smiles on their wise, innocent, clay-colored faces, crying, 'Good morning, my titcher!' in
immaculate voices, and they make of her desk a fresh garden
of flowers every day.

During her leisure she goes to union meetings and listens to
busy important voices quarrelling over tactics, methods, internal
politics. She visits the prisoners of her own political faith in their
cells, where they entertain themselves with counting cock-
roaches, repenting of their indiscretions, composing their
memoirs, writing out manifestoes and plans for their comrades
who are still walking about free, hands in pockets, sniffing fresh
air. Laura brings them food and cigarettes and a little money,
and she brings messages disguised in equivocal phrases from the
men outside who dare not set foot in the prison for fear of disappearing into the cells kept empty for them. If the prisoners
confuse night and day, and complain, 'Dear little Laura, time
doesn't pass in this infernal hole, and I won't know when it is
time to sleep unless I have a reminder,' she brings them their
favorite narcotics, and says in a tone that does not wound them
with pity, 'Tonight will really be night for you,' and though her
Spanish amuses them, they find her comforting, useful. If they
lose patience and all faith, and curse the slowness of their friends
in coming to their rescue with money and influence, they trust
her not to repeat everything, and if she inquires, 'Where do you
think we can find money, or influence?' they are certain to answer,
'Well, there is Braggioni, why doesn't he do something?'

She smuggles letters from headquarters to men hiding from
firing squads in back streets in mildewed houses, where they sit
in tumbled beds and talk bitterly as if all Mexico were at their
heels, when Laura knows positively they might appear at the
band concert in the Alameda on Sunday morning, and no one
would notice them. But Braggioni says, 'Let them sweat a little.
The next time they may be careful. It is very restful to have them
out of the way for a while.' She is not afraid to knock on any
door in any street after midnight, and enter in the darkness, and
say to one of these men who is really in danger: 'They will be
looking for you – seriously – tomorrow morning after six. Here
is some money from Vincente. Go to Vera Cruz and wait.'

She borrows money from the Roumanian agitator to give to his bitter enemy the Polish agitator. The favor of Braggioni is their disputed territory, and Braggioni holds the balance nicely, for he can use them both. The Polish agitator talks love to her over café tables, hoping to exploit what he believes is her secret sentimental preference for him, and he gives her misinformation which he begs her to repeat as the solemn truth to certain persons. The Roumanian is more adroit. He is generous with his money in all good causes, and lies to her with an air of ingenuous candor, as if he were her good friend and confidant. She never repeats anything they may say. Braggioni never asks questions. He has other ways to discover all that he wishes to know about them.

Nobody touches her, but all praise her gray eyes, and the soft, round under lip which promises gaiety, yet is always grave, nearly always firmly closed: and they cannot understand why she is in Mexico. She walks back and forth on her errands, with puzzled eyebrows, carrying her little folder of drawings and music and school papers. No dancer dances more beautifully than Laura walks, and she inspires some amusing, unexpected ardors, which cause little gossip, because nothing comes of them. A young captain who had been a soldier in Zapata's army attempted, during a horseback ride near Cuernavaca, to express his desire for her with the noble simplicity befitting a rude folk-hero: but gently, because he was gentle. This gentleness was his defeat, for when he alighted, and removed her foot from the stirrup, and essayed to draw her down into his arms, her horse, ordinarily a tame one, shied fiercely, reared and plunged away. The young hero's horse careered blindly after his stablemate, and the hero did not return to the hotel until rather late that evening. At breakfast he came to her table in full charro dress, gray buckskin jacket, and trousers with strings of silver buttons down the leg, and he was in a humorous, careless mood. 'May I sit with you?' and 'You are a wonderful rider. I was terrified that you might be thrown and dragged. I should never have forgiven myself. But I cannot admire you enough for your riding!'

'I learned to ride in Arizona,' said Laura.

'If you will ride with me again this morning, I promise you a horse that will not shy with you,' he said. But Laura remembered that she must return to Mexico City at noon.

Next morning the children made a celebration and spent their playtime writing on the blackboard, 'We lov ar titcher,' and with tinted chalks they drew wreaths of flowers around the words. The young hero wrote her a letter: 'I am a very foolish, wasteful, impulsive man. I should have first said I love you, and then you would not have run away. But you shall see me again.' Laura thought, 'I must send him a box of colored crayons,' but she was trying to forgive herself for having spurred her horse at the wrong moment.

A brown, shock-haired youth came and stood in her patio one night and sang like a lost soul for two hours, but Laura could think of nothing to do about it. The moonlight spread a wash of gauzy silver over the clear spaces of the garden, and the shadows were cobalt blue. The scarlet blossoms of the Judas tree were dull purple, and the names of the colors repeated themselves automatically in her mind, while she watched not the boy, but his shadow, fallen like a dark garment across the fountain rim, trailing in the water. Lupe came silently and whispered expert counsel in her ear: 'If you will throw him one little flower, he will sing another song or two and go away.' Laura threw the flower, and he sang a last song and went away with the flower tucked in the band of his hat. Lupe said, 'He is one of the organizers of the Typographers Union, and before that he sold corridos in the Merced market, and before that, he came from Guanajuato, where I was born. I would not trust any man, but I trust least those from Guanajuato.'

She did not tell Laura that he would be back again the next night, and the next, nor that he would follow her at a certain fixed distance around the Merced market, through the Zócolo, up Francisco I. Madero Avenue, and so along the Paseo de la Reforma to Chapultepec Park, and into the Philosopher's Footpath, still with that flower withering in his hat, and an indivisible attention in his eyes.

Now Laura is accustomed to him, it means nothing except that he is nineteen years old and is observing a convention with all propriety, as though it were founded on a law of nature, which in the end it might well prove to be. He is beginning to write poems which he prints on a wooden press, and he leaves them stuck like handbills in her door. She is pleasantly disturbed by the abstract, unhurried watchfulness of his black eyes which will in time turn easily towards another object. She tells herself that throwing the flower was a mistake, for she is twenty-two years old and knows better; but she refuses to regret it, and persuades herself that her negation of all external events as they occur is a sign that she is gradually perfecting herself in the stoicism she strives to cultivate against that disaster she fears, though she cannot name it.

She is not at home in the world. Every day she teaches children who remain strangers to her, though she loves their tender round hands and their charming opportunist savagery. She knocks at unfamiliar doors not knowing whether a friend or a stranger shall answer, and even if a known face emerges from the sour gloom of that unknown interior, still it is the face of a stranger. No matter what this stranger says to her, nor what her message to him, the very cells of her flesh reject knowledge and kinship in one monotonous word. No. No. No. She draws her strength from this one holy talismanic word which does not suffer her to be led into evil. Denying everything, she may walk anywhere in safety, she looks at everything without amazement.

No, repeats this firm unchanging voice of her blood; and she looks at Braggioni without amazement. He is a great man, he wishes to impress this simple girl who covers her great round breasts with thick dark cloth, and who hides long, invaluably beautiful legs under a heavy skirt. She is almost thin except for the incomprehensible fullness of her breasts, like a nursing mother's, and Braggioni, who considers himself a judge of women, speculates again on the puzzle of her notorious virginity, and takes the liberty of speech which she permits without a sign of modesty, indeed, without any sort of sign, which is disconcerting.

'You think you are so cold, *gringita*! Wait and see. You will surprise yourself some day! May I be there to advise you!' He stretches his eyelids at her, and his ill-humored cat's eyes waver in a separate glance for the two points of light marking the opposite ends of a smoothly drawn path between the swollen curve of her breasts. He is not put off by that blue serge, nor by her resolutely fixed gaze. There is all the time in the world. His cheeks are bellying with the wind of song. 'O girl with the dark eyes,' he sings, and reconsiders. 'But yours are not dark. I can change all that. O girl with the green eyes, you have stolen my heart away!' then his mind wanders to the song, and Laura feels the weight of his attention being shifted elsewhere. Singing thus, he seems harmless, he is quite harmless, there is nothing to do but sit patiently and say 'No', when the moment comes. She draws a full breath, and her mind wanders also, but not far. She dares not wander too far.

Not for nothing has Braggioni taken pains to be a good revolutionist and a professional lover of humanity. He will never die of it. He has the malice, the cleverness, the wickedness, the sharpness of wit, the hardness of heart, stipulated for loving the world profitably. *He will never die of it.* He will live to see himself kicked out from his feeding trough by other hungry world-saviours. Traditionally he must sing in spite of his life which drives him to bloodshed, he tells Laura, for his father was a Tuscany peasant who drifted to Yucatan and married a Maya woman: a woman of race, an aristocrat. They gave him the love and knowledge of music, thus: and under the rip of his thumbnail, the strings of the instrument complain like exposed nerves.

Once he was called Delgadito by all the girls and married women who ran after him; he was so scrawny all his bones showed under his thin cotton clothing, and he could squeeze his emptiness to the very backbone with his two hands. He was a poet and the revolution was only a dream then; too many women loved him and sapped away his youth, and he could never find enough to eat anywhere, anywhere! Now he is a leader of men, crafty men who whisper in his ear, hungry men who wait for hours outside his office for a word with him, emaciated men with wild faces who waylay him at the street gate with a timid, 'Comrade, let me tell you . . .' and they blow the foul breath from their empty stomachs in his face.

He is always sympathetic. He gives them handfuls of small

coins from his own pocket, he promises them work, there will be demonstrations, they must join the unions and attend the meetings, above all they must be on the watch for spies. They are closer to him than his own brothers, without them he can do nothing – until tomorrow, comrade!

Until tomorrow. 'They are stupid, they are lazy, they are treacherous, they would cut my throat for nothing,' he says to Laura. He has good food and abundant drink, he hires an automobile and drives in the Paseo on Sunday morning, and enjoys plenty of sleep in a soft bed beside a wife who dares not disturb him; and he sits pampering his bones in easy billows of fat, singing to Laura, who knows and thinks these things about him. When he was fifteen, he tried to drown himself because he loved a girl, his first love, and she laughed at him. 'A thousand women have paid for that,' and his tight little mouth turns down at the corners. Now he perfumes his hair with Jockey Club, and confides to Laura: 'One woman is really as good as another for me, in the dark. I prefer them all.'

His wife organizes unions among the girls in the cigarette factories, and walks in picket lines, and even speaks at meetings in the evening. But she cannot be brought to acknowledge the benefits of true liberty. 'I tell her I must have my freedom, net. She does not understand my point of view.' Laura has heard this many times. Braggioni scratches the guitar and meditates. 'She is an instinctively virtuous woman, pure gold, no doubt of that. If she were not, I should lock her up, and she knows it.'

His wife, who works so hard for the good of the factory girls, employs part of her leisure lying on the floor weeping because there are so many women in the world, and only one husband for her, and she never knows where nor when to look for him. He told her: 'Unless you can learn to cry when I am not here, I must go away for good.' That day he went away and took a room at the Hotel Madrid.

It is this month of separation for the sake of higher principles that has been spoiled not only for Mrs Braggioni, whose sense of reality is beyond criticism, but for Laura, who feels herself bogged in a nightmare. Tonight Laura envies Mrs Braggioni, who is alone, and free to weep as much as she pleases about a concrete wrong. Laura has just come from a visit to the prison, and she is waiting for tomorrow with a bitter anxiety as if tomorrow may not come, but time may be caught immovably in this hour, with herself transfixed, Braggioni singing on forever, and Eugenio's body not yet discovered by the guard.

Braggioni says: 'Are you going to sleep?' Almost before she can shake her head, he begins telling her about the May-day disturbances coming on in Morelia, for the Catholics hold a festival in honor of the Blessed Virgin, and the Socialists celebrate their martyrs on that day. 'There will be two independent processions starting from either end of town, and they will march until they meet, and the rest depends. ...' He asks her to oil and load his pistols. Standing up, he unbuckles his ammunition belt, and spreads it laden across her knees. Laura sits with the shells slipping through the cleaning cloth dipped in oil, and he says again he cannot understand why she works so hard for the revolutionary idea unless she loves some man who is in it. 'Are you not in love with someone?' 'No,' says Laura. 'And no one is in love with you?' 'No.' 'Then it is your own fault. No woman need go begging. Why, what is the matter with you? The legless beggar woman in the Alameda has a perfectly faithful lover. Did you know that?'

Laura peers down the pistol barrel and says nothing, but a long, slow faintness rises and subsides in her; Braggioni curves his swollen fingers around the throat of the guitar and softly smothers the music out of it, and when she hears him again he seems to have forgotten her, and is speaking in the hypnotic voice he uses when talking in small rooms to a listening, close-gathered crowd. Some day this world, now seemingly so composed and eternal, to the edges of every sea shall be merely a tangle of gaping trenches, of crashing walls and broken bodies. Everything must be torn from its accustomed place where it has rotted for centuries, hurled skyward and distributed, cast down again clean as rain, without separate identity. Nothing shall survive that the stiffened hands of poverty have created for the rich and no one shall be left alive except the elect spirits destined to procreate a new world cleansed of cruelty and injustice, ruled by benevolent anarchy: 'Pistols are good, I love them, cannon are even better, but in the end I pin my faith to good dynamite,' he concludes, and strokes the pistol lying in her hands. 'Once I dreamed of destroying this city, in case it offered resistance to General Ortíz, but it fell into his hands like an overripe pear.'

He is made restless by his own words, rises and stands waiting. Laura holds up the belt to him: 'Put that on, and go kill somebody in Morelia, and you will be happier,' she says softly. The presence of death in the room makes her bold. 'Today, I found Eugenio going into a stupor. He refused to allow me to call the prison doctor. He had taken all the tablets I brought him yesterday. He said he took them because he was bored.'

'He is a fool, and his death is his own business,' says Braggioni, fastening his belt carefully.

'I told him if he had waited only a little while longer, you would have got him set free,' says Laura. 'He said he did not want to wait.'

'He is a fool and we are well rid of him,' says Braggioni, reaching for his hat.

He goes away. Laura knows his mood has changed, she will not see him any more for a while. He will send word when he needs her to go on errands into strange streets, to speak to the strange faces that will appear, like clay masks with the power of human speech, to mutter their thanks to Braggioni for his help. Now she is free, and she thinks, I must run while there is time. But she does not go.

Braggioni enters his own house where for a month his wife has spent many hours every night weeping and tangling her hair upon her pillow. She is weeping now, and she weeps more at the sight of him, the cause of all her sorrows. He looks about the room. Nothing is changed, the smells are good and familiar, he is well acquainted with the woman who comes toward him with no reproach except grief on her face. He says to her tenderly: 'You are so good, please don't cry any more, you dear good creature.' She says, 'Are you tired, my angel? Sit here and I will wash your feet.' She brings a bowl of water, and kneeling, unlaces his shoes, and when from her knees she raises her sad eyes under her blackened lids, he is sorry for everything,

317

and bursts into tears. 'Ah, yes, I am hungry, I am tired, let us eat something together,' he says, between sobs. His wife leans her head on his arm and says, 'Forgive me!' and this time he is refreshed by the solemn, endless rain of her tears.

Laura takes off her serge dress and puts on a white linen nightgown and goes to bed. She turns her head a little to one side, and lying still, reminds herself that it is time to sleep. Numbers tick in her brain like little clocks, soundless doors close of themselves around her. If you would sleep, you must not remember anything, the children will say tomorrow, good morning, my teacher, the poor prisoners who come every day bringing flowers to their jailor. 1-2-3-4-5 – it is monstrous to confuse love with revolution, night with day, life with death – ah, Eugenio!

The tolling of the midnight bell is a signal, but what does it mean? Get up, Laura, and follow me: come out of your sleep, out of your bed, out of this strange house. What are you doing in this house? Without a word, without fear she rose and reached for Eugenio's hand, but he eluded her with a sharp, sly smile and drifted away. This is not all, you shall see – Murderer, he said, follow me, I will show you a new country, but it is far away and we must hurry. No, said Laura, not unless you take my hand, no; and she clung first to the stair rail, and then to the topmost branch of the Judas tree that bent down slowly and set her upon the earth, and then to the rocky ledge of a cliff, and then to the jagged wave of a sea that was not water but a desert of crumbling stone. Where are you taking me, she asked in wonder but without fear. To death, and it is a long way off, and we must hurry, said Eugenio. No, said Laura, not unless you take my hand. Then eat these flowers, poor prisoner, said Eugenio in a voice of pity, take and eat: and from the Judas tree he stripped the warm bleeding flowers, and held them to her lips. She saw that his hand was fleshless, a cluster of small white petrified branches, and his eye sockets were without light, but she ate the flowers greedily for they satisfied both hunger and thirst. Murderer! said Eugenio, and Cannibal! This is my body and my blood. Laura cried No! and at the sound of her own voice, she awoke trembling, and was afraid to sleep again.

F. Scott Fitzgerald

THE RICH BOY

I

BEGIN with an individual, and before you know it you find that you have created a type; begin with a type, and you find that you have created – nothing. That is because we are all queer fish, queerer behind our faces and voices than we want anyone to know or than we know ourselves. When I hear a man proclaiming himself an 'average, honest, open fellow', I feel pretty sure that he has some definite and perhaps terrible abnormality which he has agreed to conceal – and his protestations of being average and honest and open is his way of reminding himself of his misprision.

There are no types, no plurals. There is a rich boy, and this is his and not his brothers' story. All my life I have lived among his brothers but this one has been my friend. Besides, if I wrote about his brothers I should have to begin by attacking all the lies that the poor have told about the rich and the rich have told about themselves – such a wild structure they have erected that when we pick up a book about the rich, some instinct prepares us for unreality. Even the intelligent and impassioned reporters of life have made the country of the rich as unreal as fairy-land.

Let me tell you about the very rich. They are different from you and me. They possess and enjoy early, and it does something to them, makes them soft where we are hard, and cynical where we are trustful, in a way that, unless you were born rich, it is very difficult to understand. They think, deep in their hearts, that they are better than we are because we had to discover the compensations and refuges of life for ourselves. Even when they enter deep into our world or sink below us, they still think that they are better than we are. They are different. The only way I can describe young Anson Hunter is to approach him as if he

were a foreigner and cling stubbornly to my point of view. If I
accept his for a moment I am lost – I have nothing to show but
a preposterous movie.

2

Anson was the eldest of six children who would some day divide
a fortune of fifteen million dollars, and he reached the age of
reason – is it seven? – at the beginning of the century when
daring young women were already gliding along Fifth Avenue
in electric 'mobiles'. In those days he and his brother had an
English governess who spoke the language very clearly and
crisply and well, so that the two boys grew to speak as she did –
their words and sentences were all crisp and clear and not run
together as ours are. They didn't talk exactly like English children but acquired an accent that is peculiar to fashionable
people in the city of New York.

In the summer the six children were moved from the house
on 71st Street to a big estate in northern Connecticut. It was
not a fashionable locality – Anson's father wanted to delay as
long as possible his children's knowledge of that side of life. He
was a man somewhat superior to his class, which composed
New York society, and to his period, which was the snobbish
and formalized vulgarity of the Gilded Age, and he wanted his
sons to learn habits of concentration and have sound constitu-
tions and grow up into right-living and successful men. He and
his wife kept an eye on them as well as they were able until the
two older boys went away to school, but in huge establishments
this is difficult – it was much simpler in the series of small and
medium-sized houses in which my own youth was spent – I was
never far out of the reach of my mother's voice, of the sense of
her presence, her approval or disapproval.

Anson's first sense of his superiority came to him when he
realized the half-grudging American deference that was paid to
him in the Connecticut village. The parents of the boys he
played with always inquired after his father and mother, and
were vaguely excited when their own children were asked to the
Hunters' house. He accepted this as the natural state of things,
and a sort of impatience with all groups of which he was not the

center – in money, in position, in authority – remained with him for the rest of his life. He disdained to struggle with other boys for precedence – he expected it to be given him freely, and when it wasn't he withdrew into his family. His family was sufficient, for in the East money is still a somewhat feudal thing, a clan-forming thing. In the snobbish West, money separates families to form 'sets'.

At eighteen, when he went to New Haven, Anson was tall and thick-set, with a clear complexion and a healthy colour from the ordered life he had led in school. His hair was yellow and grew in a funny way on his head, his nose was beaked – these two things kept him from being handsome – but he had a confident charm and a certain brusque style, and the upper-class men who passed him on the street knew without being told that he was a rich boy and had gone to one of the best schools. Nevertheless, his very superiority kept him from being a success in college – the independence was mistaken for egotism, and the refusal to accept Yale standards with the proper awe seemed to belittle all those who had. So, long before he graduated, he began to shift the center of his life to New York.

He was at home in New York – there was his own house with 'the kind of servants you can't get any more' – and his own family, of which, because of his good humor and a certain ability to make things go, he was rapidly becoming the center, and the débutante parties, and the correct manly world of the men's clubs, and the occasional wild spree with the gallant girls whom New Haven only knew from the fifth row. His aspirations were conventional enough – they included even the irreproachable shadow he would some day marry, but they differed from the aspirations of the majority of young men in that there was no mist over them, none of that quality which is variously known as 'idealism' or 'illusion'. Anson accepted without reservation the world of high finance and high extravagance, of divorce and dissipation, of snobbery and of privilege. Most of our lives end as a compromise – it was as a compromise that his life began.

He and I first met in the late summer of 1917 when he was just out of Yale, and, like the rest of us, was swept up into the

systematized hysteria of the war. In the blue-green uniform of
the naval aviation he came down to Pensacola, where the hotel
orchestras played *I'm Sorry, Dear*, and we young officers danced
with the girls. Everyone liked him, and though he ran with the
drinkers and wasn't an especially good pilot, even the instructors
treated him with a certain respect. He was always having long
talks with them in his confident, logical voice – talks which
ended by his getting himself, or, more frequently, another
officer, out of some impending trouble. He was convivial, bawdy,
robustly avid for pleasure, and we were all surprised when he
fell in love with a conservative and rather proper girl.

Her name was Paula Legendre, a dark, serious beauty from
somewhere in California. Her family kept a winter residence
just outside of town, and in spite of her primness she was
enormously popular; there is a large class of men whose egotism
can't endure humor in a woman. But Anson wasn't that sort,
and I couldn't understand the attraction of her 'sincerity' – that
was the thing to say about her – for his keen and somewhat
sardonic mind.

Nevertheless, they fell in love – and on her terms. He no
longer joined the twilight gathering at the De Soto Bar, and
whenever they were seen together they were engaged in a long,
serious dialogue, which must have gone on several weeks. Long
afterward he told me that it was not about anything in particular but was composed on both sides of immature and even
meaningless statements – the emotional content that gradually
came to fill it grew up not out of the words but out of its enormous seriousness. It was a sort of hypnosis. Often it was interrupted, giving way to that emasculated humor we call fun;
when they were alone it was resumed again, solemn, low-keyed,
and pitched so as to give each other a sense of unity in feeling
and thought. They came to resent any interruptions of it, to be un-
responsive to facetiousness about life, even to the mild cynicism
of their contemporaries. They were only happy when the dialogue
was going on, and its seriousness bathed them like the amber
glow of an open fire. Toward the end there came an interruption
they did not resent – it began to be interrupted by passion.

Oddly enough, Anson was as engrossed in the dialogue as she

and as profoundly affected by it, yet at the same time aware that on his side much was insincere, and on hers much was merely simple. At first, too, he despised her emotional simplicity as well, but with his love her nature deepened and blossomed, and he could despise it no longer. He felt that if he could enter into Paula's warm safe life he would be happy. The long preparation of the dialogue removed any constraint – he taught her some of what he had learned from more adventurous women, and she responded with a rapt holy intensity. One evening after a dance they agreed to marry, and he wrote a long letter about her to his mother. The next day Paula told him that she was rich, that she had a personal fortune of nearly a million dollars.

3

It was exactly as if they could say 'Neither of us has anything: we shall be poor together' – just as delightful that they should be rich instead. It gave them the same communion of adventure. Yet when Anson got leave in April, and Paula and her mother accompanied him North, she was impressed with the standing of his family in New York and with the scale on which they lived. Alone with Anson for the first time in the rooms where he had played as a boy, she was filled with a comfortable emotion, as though she were pre-eminently safe and taken care of. The pictures of Anson in a skull-cap at his first school, of Anson on horseback with the sweetheart of a mysterious forgotten summer, of Anson in a gay group of ushers and bridesmaids at a wedding, made her jealous of his life apart from her in the past, and so completely did his authoritative person seem to sum up and typify these possessions of his that she was inspired with the idea of being married immediately and returning to Pensacola as his wife.

But an immediate marriage wasn't discussed – even the engagement was to be secret until after the war. When she realized that only two days of his leave remained, her dissatisfaction crystallized in the intention of making him as unwilling to wait as she was. They were driving to the country for dinner and she determined to force the issue that night.

Now a cousin of Paula's was staying with them at the Ritz, a severe, bitter girl who loved Paula but was somewhat jealous of her impressive engagement, and as Paula was late in dressing, the cousin, who wasn't going to the party, received Anson in the parlor of the suite.

Anson had met friends at five o'clock and drunk freely and indiscreetly with them for an hour. He left the Yale Club at a proper time, and his mother's chauffeur drove him to the Ritz, but his usual capacity was not in evidence, and the impact of the steam-heated sitting-room made him suddenly dizzy. He knew it, and he was both amused and sorry.

Paula's cousin was twenty-five, but she was exceptionally naïve, and at first failed to realize what was up. She had never met Anson before, and she was surprised when he mumbled strange information and nearly fell off his chair, but until Paula appeared it didn't occur to her that what she had taken for the odor of a dry-cleaned uniform was really whisky. But Paula understood as soon as she appeared; her only thought was to get Anson away before her mother saw him, and at the look in her eyes the cousin understood too.

When Paula and Anson descended to the limousine they found two men inside, both asleep; they were the men with whom he had been drinking at the Yale Club, and they were also going to the party. He had entirely forgotten their presence in the car. On the way to Hempstead they awoke and sang. Some of the songs were rough, and though Paula tried to reconcile herself to the fact that Anson had few verbal inhibitions, her lips tightened with shame and distaste.

Back at the hotel the cousin, confused and agitated, considered the incident, and then walked into Mrs Legendre's bedroom, saying: 'Isn't he funny?'

'Who is funny?'

'Why – Mr Hunter. He seemed so funny.'

Mrs Legendre looked at her sharply.

'How is he funny?'

'Why, he said he was French. I didn't know he was French.'

'That's absurd. You must have misunderstood.' She smiled: 'It was a joke.'

The cousin shook her head stubbornly.

'No. He said he was brought up in France. He said he couldn't speak any English, and that's why he couldn't talk to me. And he couldn't!'

Mrs Legendre looked away with impatience just as the cousin added thoughtfully, 'Perhaps it was because he was so drunk,' and walked out of the room.

This curious report was true. Anson, finding his voice thick and uncontrollable, had taken the unusual refuge of announcing that he spoke no English. Years afterwards he used to tell that part of the story, and he invariably communicated the uproarious laughter which the memory aroused in him.

Five times in the next hour Mrs Legendre tried to get Hempstead on the phone. When she succeeded, there was a ten-minute delay before she heard Paula's voice on the wire.

'Cousin Jo told me Anson was intoxicated.'

'Oh, no ...'

'Oh, yes. Cousin Jo says he was intoxicated. He told her he was French, and fell off his chair and behaved as if he was very intoxicated. I don't want you to come home with him.'

'Mother, he's all right! Please don't worry about –'

'But I do worry. I think it's dreadful. I want you to promise me not to come home with him.'

'I'll take care of it, Mother ...'

'I don't want you to come home with him.'

'All right, Mother. Good-bye.'

'Be sure now, Paula. Ask someone to bring you.'

Deliberately Paula took the receiver from her ear and hung it up. Her face was flushed with helpless annoyance. Anson was stretched out asleep in a bedroom upstairs, while the dinner-party below was proceeding lamely toward conclusion.

The hour's drive had sobered him somewhat – his arrival was merely hilarious – and Paula hoped that the evening was not spoiled, after all, but two imprudent cocktails before dinner completed the disaster. He talked boisterously and somewhat offensively to the party at large for fifteen minutes, and then slid silently under the table; like a man in an old print – but, unlike an old print, it was rather horrible without being at all quaint.

None of the young girls present remarked upon the incident – it seemed to merit only silence. His uncle and two other men carried him upstairs, and it was just after this that Paula was called to the phone.

An hour later Anson awoke in a fog of nervous agony, through which he perceived after a moment the figure of his Uncle Robert standing by the door.

'... I said are you better?'

'What?'

'Do you feel better, old man?'

'Terrible,' said Anson.

'I'm going to try you on another bromo-seltzer. If you can hold it down, it'll do you good to sleep.'

With an effort Anson slid his legs from the bed and stood up.

'I'm all right,' he said dully.

'Take it easy.'

'I thin' if you gave me a glassbrandy I could go downstairs.'

'Oh, no –'

'Yes, that's the only thin'. I'm all right now ... I suppose I'm in Dutch dow' there.'

'They know you're a little under the weather,' said his uncle deprecatingly. 'But don't worry about it. Schuyler didn't even get here. He passed away in the locker-room over at the Links.'

Indifferent to any opinion, except Paula's, Anson was nevertheless determined to save the débris of the evening, but when after a cold bath he made his appearance most of the party had already left. Paula got up immediately to go home.

In the limousine the old serious dialogue began. She had known that he drank, she admitted, but she had never expected anything like this – it seemed to her that perhaps they were not suited to each other, after all. Their ideas about life were too different, and so forth. When she finished speaking, Anson spoke in turn, very soberly. Then Paula said she'd have to think it over; she wouldn't decide tonight; she was not angry but she was terribly sorry. Nor would she let him come into the hotel with her, but just before she got out of the car she leaned and kissed him unhappily on the cheek.

The next afternoon Anson had a long talk with Mrs Legendre

while Paula sat listening in silence. It was agreed that Paula was to brood over the incident for a proper period and then, if mother and daughter thought it best, they would follow Anson to Pensacola. On his part he apologized with sincerity and dignity – that was all; with every card in her hand Mrs Legendre was unable to establish any advantage over him. He made no promises, showed no humility, only delivered a few serious comments on life which brought him off with rather a moral superiority at the end. When they came South three weeks later, neither Anson in his satisfaction nor Paula in her relief at the reunion realized that the psychological moment had passed forever.

4

He dominated and attracted her, and at the same time filled her with anxiety. Confused by his mixture of solidity and self-indulgence, of sentiment and cynicism – incongruities which her gentle mind was unable to resolve – Paula grew to think of him as two alternating personalities. When she saw him alone, or at a formal party, or with his casual inferiors, she felt a tremendous pride in his strong, attractive presence, the paternal, understanding stature of his mind. In other company she became uneasy when what had been a fine imperviousness to mere gentility showed its other face. The other face was gross, humorous, reckless of everything but pleasure. It startled her mind temporarily away from him, even led her into a short, covert experiment with an old beau, but it was no use – after four months of Anson's enveloping vitality there was an anaemic pallor in all other men.

In July he was ordered abroad, and their tenderness and desire reached a crescendo. Paula considered a last-minute marriage – decided against it only because there were always cocktails on his breath now, but the parting itself made her physically ill with grief. After his departure she wrote him long letters of regret for the days of love they had missed by waiting. In August Anson's plane slipped down into the North Sea. He was pulled on to a destroyer after a night in the water and sent to hospital with pneumonia; the armistice was signed before he was finally sent home.

Then, with every opportunity given back to them, with no material obstacle to overcome, the secret weavings of their temperaments came between them, drying up their kisses and their tears, making their voices less loud to one another, muffling the intimate chatter of their hearts until the old communication was only possible by letters, from far away. One afternoon a society reporter waited for two hours in the Hunters' house for a confirmation of their engagement. Anson denied it; nevertheless an early issue carried the report as a leading paragraph – they were 'constantly seen together at Southampton, Hot Springs, and Tuxedo Park'. But the serious dialogue had turned a corner into a long-sustained quarrel, and the affair was almost played out. Anson got drunk flagrantly and missed an engagement with her, whereupon Paula made certain behavioristic demands. His despair was helpless before his pride and his knowledge of himself: the engagement was definitely broken.

'Dearest,' said their letters now, 'Dearest, Dearest, when I wake up in the middle of the night and realize that after all it was not to be, I feel that I want to die. I can't go on living any more. Perhaps when we meet this summer we may talk things over and decide differently – we were so excited and sad that day, and I don't feel that I can live all my life without you. You speak of other people. Don't you know there are no other people for me, but only you ...'

But as Paula drifted here and there around the East she would sometimes mention her gaieties to make him wonder. Anson was too acute to wonder. When he saw a man's name in her letters he felt more sure of her and a little disdainful – he was always superior to such things. But he still hoped that they would some day marry.

Meanwhile he plunged vigorously into all the movement and glitter of post-bellum New York, entering a brokerage house, joining half a dozen clubs, dancing late, and moving in three worlds – his own world, the world of young Yale graduates, and that section of the half-world which rests one end on Broadway. But there was always a thorough and infractible eight hours devoted to his work in Wall Street, where the combination of his influential family connexion, his sharp intelligence, and his abundance of sheer physical energy brought him almost immediately forward. He had one of those invaluable minds with partitions in it; sometimes he appeared at his office refreshed by less than an hour's sleep, but such occurrences were rare. So early as 1920 his income in salary and commissions exceeded twelve thousand dollars.

As the Yale tradition slipped into the past he became more and more of a popular figure among his classmates in New York, more popular than he had ever been in college. He lived in a great house, and had the means of introducing young men into other great houses. Moreover, his life already seemed secure, while theirs, for the most part, had arrived again at precarious beginnings. They commenced to turn to him for amusement and escape, and Anson responded readily, taking pleasure in helping people and arranging their affairs.

There were no men in Paula's letters now, but a note of tenderness ran through them that had not been there before. From several sources he heard that she had 'a heavy beau', Lowell Thayer, a Bostonian of wealth and position, and though he was sure she still loved him, it made him uneasy to think that he might lose her, after all. Save for one unsatisfactory day she had not been in New York for almost five months, and as the rumors multiplied he became increasingly anxious to see her. In February he took his vacation and went down to Florida.

Palm Beach sprawled plump and opulent between the sparkling sapphire of Lake Worth, flawed here and there by houseboats at anchor, and the great turquoise bar of the Atlantic Ocean. The huge bulks of the Breakers and the Royal Poinciana rose as twin paunches from the bright level of the sand, and around them clustered the Dancing Glade, Bradley's House of Chance, and a dozen modistes and milliners with goods at triple prices from New York. Upon the trellised veranda of the Breakers two hundred women stepped right, stepped left, wheeled, and slid in that then celebrated calisthenic known as the double-shuffle, while in half-time to the music 2,000 bracelets clicked up and down on two hundred arms.

At the Everglades Club after dark Paula and Lowell Thayer and Anson and a casual fourth played bridge with hot cards. It seemed to Anson that her kind, serious face was wan and tired — she had been around now for four, five, years. He had known her for three.

'Two spades.'

'Cigarette? ... Oh, I beg your pardon. By me.'

'By.'

'I'll double three spades.'

There were a dozen tables of bridge in the room, which was filling up with smoke. Anson's eyes met Paula's, held them persistently even when Thayer's glance fell between them ...

'What was bid?' he asked abstractedly.

'Rose of Washington Square'

sang the young people in the corners:

> 'I'm withering there
> In basement air –'

The smoke banked like fog, and the opening of a door filled the room with blown swirls of ectoplasm. Little Bright Eyes streaked past the tables seeking Mr Conan Doyle among the Englishmen who were posing as Englishmen about the lobby.

'You could cut it with a knife.'

'... cut it with a knife.'

'... a knife.'

At the end of the rubber Paula suddenly got up and spoke to Anson in a tense, low voice. With scarcely a glance at Lowell Thayer, they walked out the door and descended a long flight of stone steps – in a moment they were walking hand in hand along the moonlit beach.

'Darling, darling ...' They embraced recklessly, passionately, in a shadow ... Then Paula drew back her face to let his lips say what she wanted to hear – she could feel the words forming as they kissed again ... Again she broke away, listening, but as he pulled her close once more she realized that he had said nothing – only *'Darling! Darling!'* in that deep, sad whisper that always made her cry. Humbly, obediently, her emotions yielded to him and the tears streamed down her face, but her heart kept on crying: 'Ask me – oh, Anson, ask me!'

'Paula ... *Paula!*'

The words wrung her heart like hands, and Anson, feeling her tremble, knew that emotion was enough. He need say no more, commit their destinies to no practical enigma. Why should he, when he might hold her so, biding his own time, for another year – forever? He was considering them both, her more than himself. For a moment, when she said suddenly that she must go back to her hotel, he hesitated, thinking first, 'This is the moment, after all,' and then: 'No, let it wait – she is mine ...'

He had forgotten that Paula too was worn away inside with the strain of three years. Her mood passed forever in the night.

He went back to New York next morning filled with a certain restless dissatisfaction. Late in April, without warning, he received a telegram from Bar Harbour in which Paula told him that she was engaged to Lowell Thayer, and that they would be married immediately in Boston. What he never really believed could happen had happened at last.

Anson filled himself with whisky that morning, and going to the office, carried on his work without a break – rather with a fear of what would happen if he stopped. In the evening he went out as usual, saying nothing of what had occurred; he was cordial, humorous, unabstracted. But one thing he could not help – for three days, in any place, in any company, he would suddenly bend his head into his hands and cry like a child.

5

In 1922 when Anson went abroad with the junior partner to investigate some London loans, the journey intimated that he was to be taken into the firm. He was twenty-seven now, a little heavy without being definitely stout, and with a manner older than his years. Old people and young people liked him and trusted him, and mothers felt safe when their daughters were in his charge, for he had a way, when he came into a room, of putting himself on a footing with the oldest and most conservative people there. 'You and I,' he seemed to say, 'we're solid. We understand.'

He had an instinctive and rather charitable knowledge of the weaknesses of men and women, and, like a priest, it made him the more concerned for the maintenance of outward forms. It was typical of him that every Sunday morning he taught in a fashionable Episcopal Sunday-school – even though a cold shower and a quick change into a cutaway coat were all that separated him from the wild night before.

After his father's death he was the practical head of his family, and, in effect guided the destinies of the younger children. Through a complication his authority did not extend to his father's estate, which was administered by his Uncle Robert, who was the horsey member of the family, a good-natured, hard-drinking member of that set which centers about Wheatley Hills.

Uncle Robert and his wife, Edna, had been great friends of Anson's youth, and the former was disappointed when his nephew's superiority failed to take a horsey form. He backed him for a city club which was the most difficult in America to enter – one could only join if one's family had 'helped to build up New York' (or, in other words, were rich before 1880) – and when Anson, after his election, neglected it for the Yale Club, Uncle Robert gave him a little talk on the subject. But when on top of that Anson declined to enter Robert Hunter's own conservative and somewhat neglected brokerage house, his manner grew cooler. Like a primary teacher who has taught all he knew, he slipped out of Anson's life.

There were so many friends in Anson's life – scarcely one for whom he had not done some unusual kindness and scarcely one whom he did not occasionally embarrass by his bursts of rough conversation or his habit of getting drunk whenever and however he liked. It annoyed him when anyone else blundered in that regard – about his own lapses he was always humorous. Odd things happened to him and he told them with infectious laughter.

I was working in New York that spring, and I used to lunch with him at the Yale Club, which my university was sharing until the completion of our own. I had read of Paula's marriage, and one afternoon, when I asked him about her, something moved him to tell me the story. After that he frequently invited me to family dinners at his house and behaved as though there was a special relation between us, as though with his confidence a little of that consuming memory had passed into me.

I found that despite the trusting mothers, his attitude toward girls was not indiscriminately protective. It was up to the girl – if she showed an inclination toward looseness, she must take care of herself, even with him.

'Life,' he would explain sometimes, 'has made a cynic of me.'

By life he meant Paula. Sometimes, especially when he was drinking, it became a little twisted in his mind, and he thought that she had callously thrown him over.

This 'cynicism', or rather his realization that naturally fast girls were not worth sparing, led to his affair with Dolly Karger. It wasn't his only affair in those years, but it came nearest to touching him deeply, and it had a profound effect upon his attitude toward life.

Dolly was the daughter of a notorious 'publicist' who had married into society. She herself grew up into the Junior League, came out at the Plaza, and went to the Assembly; and only a few old families like the Hunters could question whether or not she 'belonged', for her picture was often in the papers, and she had more enviable attention than many girls who undoubtedly did. She was dark-haired, with carmine lips and a high, lovely colour, which she concealed under pinkish-grey powder all through the first year out, because high colour was unfashionable – Victorian-pale was the thing to be. She wore black, severe suits and stood with her hands in her pockets leaning a little forward, with a humorous restraint on her face. She danced exquisitely – better than anything she liked to dance – better than anything except making love. Since she was ten she had always been in love, and, usually, with some boy who didn't respond to her. Those who did – and there were many – bored her after a brief encounter, but for her failures she reserved the warmest spot in her heart. When she met them she would always try once more – sometimes she succeeded, more often she failed.

It never occurred to this gypsy of the unattainable that there was a certain resemblance in those who refused to love her – they shared a hard intuition that saw through to her weakness, not a weakness of emotion but a weakness of rudder. Anson perceived this when he first met her, less than a month after Paula's marriage. He was drinking rather heavily, and he pretended for a week that he was falling in love with her. Then he dropped her abruptly and forgot – immediately he took up the commanding position in her heart.

Like so many girls of that day Dolly was slackly and indiscreetly wild. The unconventionality of a slightly older generation had been simply one facet of a post-war movement to discredit obsolete manners – Dolly's was both older and shabbier, and she saw in Anson the two extremes which the emotionally shiftless woman seeks, an abandon to indulgence alternating with a protective strength. In his character she felt both the sybarite and the solid rock, and these two satisfied every need of her nature.

She felt that it was going to be difficult, but she mistook the reason – she thought that Anson and his family expected a more spectacular marriage, but she guessed immediately that her advantage lay in his tendency to drink.

They met at the large débutante dances, but as her infatuation increased they managed to be more and more together. Like most mothers, Mrs Karger believed that Anson was exceptionally reliable, so she allowed Dolly to go with him to distant country clubs and suburban houses without inquiring closely into their activities or questioning her explanations when they came in late. At first these explanations might have been accurate, but Dolly's worldly ideas of capturing Anson were soon engulfed in the rising sweep of her emotion. Kisses in the back of taxis and motor-cars were no longer enough; they did a curious thing:

They dropped out of their world for a while and made another world just beneath it where Anson's tippling and Dolly's irregular hours would be less noticed and commented on. It was composed, this world, of varying elements – several of Anson's Yale friends and their wives, two or three young brokers and

334

bond salesmen, and a handful of unattached men, fresh from college, with money and a propensity to dissipation. What this world lacked in spaciousness and scale it made up for by allowing them a liberty that it scarcely permitted itself. Moreover, it centered around them and permitted Dolly the pleasure of a faint condescension – a pleasure which Anson, whose whole life was a condescension from the certitudes of his childhood, was unable to share.

He was not in love with her, and in the long feverish winter of their affair he frequently told her so. In the spring he was weary – he wanted to renew his life at some other source – moreover, he saw that either he must break with her now or accept the responsibility of a definite seduction. Her family's encouraging attitude precipitated his decision – one evening when Mr Karger knocked discreetly at the library door to announce that he had left a bottle of old brandy in the dining-room, Anson felt that life was hemming him in. That night he wrote her a short letter in which he told her that he was going on his vacation, and that in view of all the circumstances they had better meet no more.

It was June. His family had closed up the house and gone to the country, so he was living temporarily at the Yale Club. I had heard about his affair with Dolly as it developed – accounts salted with humor, for he despised unstable women, and granted them no place in the social edifice in which he believed – and when he told me that night that he was definitely breaking with her I was glad. I had seen Dolly here and there, and each time with a feeling of pity at the hopelessness of her struggle, and of shame at knowing so much about her that I had no right to know. She was what is known as 'a pretty little thing', but there was a certain recklessness which rather fascinated me. Her dedication to the goddess of waste would have been less obvious had she been less spirited – she would most certainly throw herself away, but I was glad when I heard that the sacrifice would not be consummated in my sight.

Anson was going to leave the letter of farewell at her house next morning. It was one of the few houses left open in the Fifth Avenue district, and he knew that the Kargers, acting upon erroneous information from Dolly, had foregone a trip abroad to give their daughter her chance. As he stepped out the door of the Yale Club into Madison Avenue the postman passed him, and he followed back inside. The first letter that caught his eye was in Dolly's hand.

He knew what it would be – a lonely and tragic monologue, full of the reproaches he knew, the invoked memories, and 'I wonder ifs' – all the immemorial intimacies that he had communicated to Paula Legendre in what seemed another age. Thumbing over some bills, he brought it on top again and opened it. To his surprise it was a short, somewhat formal note, which said that Dolly would be unable to go to the country with him for the week-end, because Perry Hull from Chicago had unexpectedly come to town. It added that Anson had brought this on himself: '– if I felt that you loved me as I love you I would go with you at any time, any place, but Perry is *so* nice, and he so much wants me to marry him –'

Anson smiled contemptuously – he had had experience with such decoy epistles. Moreover, he knew how Dolly had labored over this plan, probably sent for the faithful Perry and calculated the time of his arrival – even laboured over the note so that it would make him jealous without driving him away. Like most compromises, it had neither force nor vitality but only a timorous despair.

Suddenly he was angry. He sat down in the lobby and read it again. Then he went to the phone, called Dolly and told her in his clear, compelling voice that he had received her note and would call for her at five o'clock as they had previously planned. Scarcely waiting for the pretended uncertainty of her 'Perhaps I can see you for an hour', he hung up the receiver and went down to his office. On the way he tore his own letter into bits and dropped it in the street.

He was not jealous – she meant nothing to him – but at her pathetic ruse everything stubborn and self-indulgent in him came to the surface. It was a presumption from a mental inferior and it could not be overlooked. If she wanted to know to whom she belonged she would see.

He was on the door-step at quarter-past five. Dolly was

dressed for the street, and he listened in silence to the paragraph of 'I can only see you for an hour', which she had begun on the phone.

'Put on your hat, Dolly,' he said, 'we'll take a walk.'

They strolled up Madison Avenue and over to Fifth while Anson's shirt dampened upon his portly body in the deep heat. He talked little, scolding her, making no love to her, but before they had walked six blocks she was his again, apologizing for the note, offering not to see Perry at all as an atonement, offering anything. She thought that he had come because he was beginning to love her.

'I'm hot,' he said when they reached 71st Street. 'This is a winter suit. If I stop by the house and change, would you mind waiting for me downstairs? I'll only be a minute.'

She was happy; the intimacy of his being hot, of any physical fact about him, thrilled her. When they came to the iron-grated door and Anson took out his key she experienced a sort of delight.

Downstairs it was dark, and after he ascended in the lift Dolly raised a curtain and looked out through opaque lace at the houses over the way. She heard the lift machinery stop, and with the notion of teasing him pressed the button that brought it down. Then on what was more than an impulse she got into it and sent it up to what she guessed was his floor.

'Anson,' she called, laughing a little.

'Just a minute,' he answered from his bedroom ... then after a brief delay: 'Now you can come in.'

He had changed and was buttoning his vest.

'This is my room,' he said lightly. 'How do you like it?'

She caught sight of Paula's picture on the wall and stared at it in fascination, just as Paula had stared at the pictures of Anson's childish sweethearts five years before. She knew something about Paula – sometimes she tortured herself with fragments of the story.

Suddenly she came close to Anson, raising her arms. They embraced. Outside the area window a soft artificial twilight already hovered, though the sun was still bright on a back roof across the way. In half an hour the room would be quite dark.

The uncalculated opportunity overwhelmed them, made them both breathless, and they clung more closely. It was imminent, inevitable. Still holding one another, they raised their heads – their eyes fell together upon Paula's picture, staring down at them from the wall.

Suddenly Anson dropped his arms, and sitting down at his desk tried the drawer with a bunch of keys.

'Like a drink?' he asked in a gruff voice.

'No, Anson.'

He poured himself half a tumbler of whisky, swallowed it, and then opened the door into the hall.

'Come on,' he said.

Dolly hesitated.

'Anson – I'm going to the country with you tonight, after all. You understand that, don't you?'

'Of course,' he answered brusquely.

In Dolly's car they rode on to Long Island, closer in their emotions than they had ever been before. They knew what would happen – not with Paula's face to remind them that something was lacking, but when they were alone in the still, hot, Long Island night they did not care.

The estate in Port Washington where they were to spend the week-end belonged to a cousin of Anson's who had married a Montana copper operator. An interminable drive began at the lodge and twisted under imported poplar saplings toward a huge, pink Spanish house. Anson had often visited there before.

After dinner they danced at the Linx Club. About midnight Anson assured himself that his cousins would not leave before two – then he explained that Dolly was tired; he would take her home and return to the dance later. Trembling a little with excitement, they got into a borrowed car together and drove to Port Washington. As they reached the lodge he stopped and spoke to the night-watchman.

'When are you making a round, Carl?'

'Right away.'

'Then you'll be here till everybody's in?'

'Yes, sir.'

338

'All right. Listen: if any automobile, no matter whose it is, turns in at this gate, I want you to phone the house immediately.' He put a five-dollar bill into Carl's hand. 'Is that clear?'

'Yes, Mr Anson.' Being of the Old World, he neither winked nor smiled. Yet Dolly sat with her face turned slightly away.

Anson had a key. Once inside he poured a drink for both of them – Dolly left hers untouched – then he ascertained definitely the location of the phone, and found that it was within easy hearing distance of their rooms, both of which were on the first floor.

Five minutes later he knocked at the door of Dolly's room.

'Anson?' He went in, closing the door behind him. She was in bed, leaning up anxiously with elbows on the pillow; sitting beside her he took her in his arms.

'Anson, darling.'

He didn't answer.

'Anson ... Anson! I love you ... Say you love me. Say it now – can't you say it now? Even if you don't mean it?'

He did not listen. Over her head he perceived that the picture of Paula was hanging here upon this wall.

He got up and went close to it. The frame gleamed faintly with thrice-reflected moonlight – within was a blurred shadow of a face that he saw he did not know. Almost sobbing, he turned around and stared with abomination at the little figure on the bed.

'This is all foolishness,' he said thickly. 'I don't know what I was thinking about. I don't love you and you'd better wait for somebody that loves you. I don't love you a bit, can't you understand?'

His voice broke, and he went hurriedly out. Back in the saloon he was pouring himself a drink with uneasy fingers, when the front door opened suddenly, and his cousin came in.

'Why, Anson, I hear Dolly's sick,' she began solicitously. 'I hear she's sick ...'

'It was nothing,' he interrupted, raising his voice so that it would carry into Dolly's room. 'She was a little tired. She went to bed.'

For a long time afterward Anson believed that a protective

God sometimes interfered in human affairs. But Dolly Karger, lying awake and staring at the ceiling, never again believed in anything at all.

6

When Dolly married during the following autumn, Anson was in London on business. Like Paula's marriage, it was sudden, but it affected him in a different way. At first he felt that it was funny, and had an inclination to laugh when he thought of it. Later it depressed him – it made him feel old.

There was something repetitive about it – why, Paula and Dolly had belonged to different generations. He had a foretaste of the sensation of a man of forty who hears that the daughter of an old flame has married. He wired congratulations and, as was not the case with Paula, they were sincere – he had never really hoped that Paula would be happy.

When he returned to New York, he was made a partner in the firm, and, as his responsibilities increased, he had less time on his hands. The refusal of a life-insurance company to issue him a policy made such an impression on him that he stopped drinking for a year, and claimed that he felt better physically, though I think he missed the convivial recounting of those Celliniesque adventures which, in his early twenties, had played such a part in his life. But he never abandoned the Yale Club. He was a figure there, a personality, and the tendency of his class, who were now seven years out of college, to drift away to more sober haunts was checked by his presence.

His day was never too full nor his mind too weary to give any sort of aid to anyone who asked it. What had been done at first through pride and superiority had become a habit and passion. And there was always something – a younger brother in trouble at New Haven, a quarrel to be patched up between a friend and his wife, a position to be found for this man, an investment for that. But his specialty was the solving of problems for young married people. Young married people fascinated him and their apartments were almost sacred to him – he knew the story of their love-affair, advised them where to live and how, and re-

membered their babies' names. Toward young wives his attitude was circumspect: he never abused the trust which their
husbands – strangely enough in view of his unconcealed irregu-
larities – invariably reposed in him.

He came to take a vicarious pleasure in happy marriages,
and to be inspired to an almost equally pleasant melancholy by
those that went astray. Not a season passed that he did not witness the collapse of an affair that perhaps he himself had
fathered. When Paula was divorced and almost immediately re-
married to another Bostonian, he talked about her to me all one
afternoon. He would never love anyone as he had loved Paula,
but he insisted that he no longer cared.

'I'll never marry,' he came to say; 'I've seen too much of it,
and I know a happy marriage is a very rare thing. Besides, I'm
too old.'

But he did believe in marriage. Like all men who spring from
a happy and successful marriage, he believed in it passionately –
nothing he had seen would change his belief, his cynicism dissolved upon it like air. But he did really believe he was too old.
At twenty-eight he began to accept with equanimity the prospect of marrying without romantic love; he resolutely chose a
New York girl of his own class, pretty, intelligent, congenial,
above reproach – and set about falling in love with her. The
things he had said to Paula with sincerity, to other girls with
grace, he could no longer say at all without smiling, or with the
force necessary to convince.

'When I'm forty,' he told his friends, 'I'll be ripe. I'll fall for
some chorus girl like the rest.'

Nevertheless, he persisted in his attempt. His mother wanted
to see him married, and he could now well afford it – he had a
seat on the Stock Exchange, and his earned income came to
twenty-five thousand a year. The idea was agreeable: when his
friends – he spent most of his time with the set he and Dolly
had evolved – closed themselves in behind domestic doors at
night, he no longer rejoiced in his freedom. He even wondered
if he should have married Dolly. Not even Paula had loved him
more, and he was learning the rarity, in a single life, of en-
countering true emotion.

Just as this mood began to creep over him a disquieting story reached his ear. His Aunt Edna, a woman just this side of forty, was carrying on an open intrigue with a dissolute, hard-drinking young man named Cary Sloane. Everyone knew of it except Anson's Uncle Robert, who for fifteen years had talked long in clubs and taken his wife for granted.

Anson heard the story again and again with increasing annoyance. Something of his old feeling for his uncle came back to him, a feeling that was more than personal, a reversion towards that family solidarity on which he had based his pride. His intuition singled out the essential point of the affair, which was that his uncle shouldn't be hurt. It was his first experiment in unsolicited meddling, but with his knowledge of Edna's character he felt that he could handle the matter better than a district judge or his uncle.

His uncle was in Hot Springs. Anson traced down the sources of the scandal so that there should be no possibility of mistake and then he called Edna and asked her to lunch with him at the Plaza next day. Something in his tone must have frightened her, for she was reluctant, but he insisted, putting off the date until she had no excuse for refusing.

She met him at the appointed time in the Plaza lobby, a lovely, faded, grey-eyed blonde in a coat of Russian sable. Five great rings, cold with diamonds and emeralds, sparkled on her slender hands. It occurred to Anson that it was his father's intelligence and not his uncle's that had earned the fur and the stones, the rich brilliance that buoyed up her passing beauty.

Though Edna scented his hostility, she was unprepared for the directness of his approach.

'Edna, I'm astonished at the way you've been acting,' he said in a strong, frank voice. 'At first I couldn't believe it.'

'Believe what?' she demanded sharply.

'You needn't pretend with me, Edna. I'm talking about Cary Sloane. Aside from any other consideration, I didn't think you could treat Uncle Robert —'

'Now look here, Anson —' she began angrily, but his peremptory voice broke through hers:

'–and your children in such a way. You've been married eighteen years, and you're old enough to know better.'

'You can't talk to me like that! You –'

'Yes, I can. Uncle Robert has always been my best friend.' He was tremendously moved. He felt a real distress about his uncle, about his three young cousins.

Edna stood up, leaving her crab-flake cocktail untasted.

'This is the silliest thing –'

'Very well, if you won't listen to me I'll go to Uncle Robert and tell him the whole story – he's bound to hear it sooner or later. And afterward I'll go to old Moses Sloane.'

Edna faltered back into her chair.

'Don't talk so loud,' she begged him. Her eyes blurred with tears. 'You have no idea how your voice carries. You might have chosen a less public place to make all these crazy accusations.'

He didn't answer.

'Oh, you never liked me, I know,' she went on. 'You're just taking advantage of some silly gossip to try and break up the only interesting friendship I've ever had. What did I ever do to make you hate me so?'

Still Anson waited. There would be the appeal to his chivalry, then to his pity, finally to his superior sophistication – when he had shouldered his way through all these there would be admissions, and he could come to grips with her. By being silent, by being impervious, by returning constantly to his main weapon, which was his own true emotion, he bullied her into frantic despair as the luncheon hour slipped away. At two o'clock she took out a mirror and a handkerchief, shined away the marks of her tears and powdered the slight hollows where they had lain. She had agreed to meet him at her own house at five.

When he arrived she was stretched on a chaise-longue which was covered with cretonne for the summer, and the tears he had called up at luncheon seemed still to be standing in her eyes. Then he was aware of Cary Sloane's dark, anxious presence upon the cold hearth.

'What's this idea of yours?' broke out Sloane immediately. 'I understand you invited Edna to lunch and then threatened her on the basis of some cheap scandal.'

Anson sat down.

'I have no reason to think it's only scandal.'

'I hear you're going to take it to Robert Hunter, and to my father.'

Anson nodded.

'Either you break it off – or I will,' he said.

'What God damned business is it of yours, Hunter?'

'Don't lose your temper, Cary,' said Edna nervously. 'It's only a question of showing him how absurd –'

'For one thing, it's my name that's being handed around,' interrupted Anson. 'That's all that concerns you, Cary.'

'Edna isn't a member of your family.'

'She most certainly is!' His anger mounted. 'Why – she owes this house and the rings on her fingers to my father's brains. When Uncle Robert married her she didn't have a penny.'

They all looked at the rings as if they had a significant bearing on the situation. Edna made a gesture to take them from her hand.

'I guess they're not the only rings in the world,' said Sloane.

'Oh, this is absurd,' cried Edna. 'Anson, will you listen to me? I've found out how the silly story started. It was a maid I discharged who went right to the Chilicheffs – all these Russians pump things out of their servants and then put a false meaning on them.' She brought down her fist angrily on the table: 'And after Robert lent them the limousine for a whole month when we were South last winter –'

'Do you see?' demanded Sloane eagerly. 'This maid got hold of the wrong end of the thing. She knew that Edna and I were friends, and she carried it to the Chilicheffs. In Russia they assume that if a man and a woman –'

He enlarged the theme to a disquisition upon social relations in the Caucasus.

'If that's the case it better be explained to Uncle Robert,' said Anson dryly, 'so that when the rumors do reach him he'll know they're not true.'

Adopting the method he had followed with Edna at luncheon he let them explain it all away. He knew that they were guilty and that presently they would cross the line from explanation

344

into justification and convict themselves more definitely than he could ever do. By seven they had taken the desperate step of telling him the truth – Robert Hunter's neglect, Edna's empty life, the casual dalliance that had flamed up into passion – but like so many true stories it had the misfortune of being old, and its enfeebled body beat helplessly against the armor of Anson's will. The threat to go to Sloane's father sealed their helplessness, for the latter, a retired cotton broker out of Alabama, was a notorious fundamentalist who controlled his son by a rigid allowance and the promise that at his next vagary the allowance would stop forever.

They dined at a small French restaurant, and the discussion continued – at one time Sloane resorted to physical threats, a little later they were both imploring him to give them time. But Anson was obdurate. He saw that Edna was breaking up, and that her spirit must not be refreshed by any renewal of their passion.

At two o'clock in a small night-club on 53rd Street, Edna's nerves suddenly collapsed, and she cried to go home. Sloane had been drinking heavily all evening, and he was faintly maudlin, leaning on the table and weeping a little with his face in his hands. Quickly Anson gave them his terms. Sloane was to leave town for six months, and he must be gone within forty-eight hours. When he returned there was to be no resumption of the affair, but at the end of a year Edna might, if she wished, tell Robert Hunter that she wanted a divorce and go about it in the usual way.

He paused, gaining confidence from their faces for his final word.

'Or there's another thing you can do,' he said slowly, 'if Edna wants to leave her children, there's nothing I can do to prevent your running off together.'

'I want to go home!' cried Edna again. 'Oh, haven't you done enough to us for one day?'

Outside it was dark, save for a blurred glow from Sixth Avenue down the street. In that light those two who had been lovers looked for the last time into each other's tragic faces, realizing that between them there was not enough youth and

strength to avert their eternal parting. Sloane walked suddenly
off down the street and Anson tapped a dozing taxi-driver on the
arm.

It was almost four; there was a patient flow of cleaning water
along the ghostly pavement of Fifth Avenue, and the shadows
of two night women flitted over the dark façade of St Thomas's
church. Then the desolate shrubbery of Central Park where
Anson had often played as a child, and the mounting numbers,
significant as names, of the marching streets. This was his city,
he thought, where his name had flourished through five generations. No change could alter the permanence of its place here,
for change itself was the essential substratum by which he and
those of his name identified themselves with the spirit of New
York. Resourcefulness and a powerful will – for his threats in
weaker hands would have been less than nothing – had beaten
the gathering dust from his uncle's name, from the name of his
family, from even this shivering figure that sat beside him in
the car.

Cary Sloane's body was found next morning on the lower
shelf of a pillar of Queensboro Bridge. In the darkness and in
his excitement he had thought that it was the water flowing
black beneath him, but in less than a second it made no possible
difference – unless he had planned to think one last thought of
Edna, and call out her name as he struggled feebly in the water.

7

Anson never blamed himself for his part in this affair – the
situation which brought it about had not been of his making.
But the just suffer with the unjust, and he found that his oldest
and somehow his most precious friendship was over. He never
knew what distorted story Edna told, but he was welcome in his
uncle's house no longer.

Just before Christmas Mrs Hunter retired to a select Episcopal
heaven, and Anson became the responsible head of his family.
An unmarried aunt who had lived with them for years ran the
house, and attempted with helpless inefficiency to chaperone the
younger girls. All the children were less self-reliant than Anson,

more conventional both in their virtues and in their shortcomings. Mrs Hunter's death had postponed the début of one daughter and the wedding of another. Also it had taken something deeply material from all of them, for with her passing the quiet, expensive superiority of the Hunters came to an end.

For one thing, the estate, considerably diminished by two inheritance taxes and soon to be divided among six children, was not a notable fortune any more. Anson saw a tendency in his youngest sisters to speak rather respectfully of families that hadn't 'existed' twenty years ago. His own feeling of precedence was not echoed in them – sometimes they were conventionally snobbish, that was all. For another thing, this was the last summer they would spend on the Connecticut estate; the clamor against it was too loud: 'Who wants to waste the best months of the year shut up in that dead, old town?' Reluctantly he yielded – the house would go into the market in the fall, and next summer they would rent a smaller place in Westchester County. It was a step down from the expensive simplicity of his father's idea, and, while he sympathized with the revolt, it also annoyed him; during his mother's lifetime he had gone up there at least every other week-end – even in the gayest summers.

Yet he himself was part of this change, and his strong instinct for life had turned him in his twenties from the hollow obsequies of that abortive leisure class. He did not see this clearly – he still felt that there was a norm, a standard of society. But there was no norm, it was doubtful if there ever had been a true norm in New York. The few who still paid and fought to enter a particular set succeeded only to find that as a society it scarcely functioned – or, what was more alarming, that the Bohemia from which they fled sat above them at table.

At twenty-nine Anson's chief concern was his own growing loneliness. He was sure now that he would never marry. The number of weddings at which he had officiated as best man or usher was past all counting – there was a drawer at home that bulged with the official neckties of this or that wedding-party, neckties standing for romances that had not endured a year, for couples who had passed completely from his life. Scarf-pins, gold pencils, cuff-buttons, presents from a generation of grooms had passed through his jewel-box and been lost – and with every ceremony he was less and less able to imagine himself in the groom's place. Under his hearty good-will toward all those marriages there was despair about his own.

And as he neared thirty he became not a little depressed at the inroads that marriage, especially lately, had made upon his friendships. Groups of people had a disconcerting tendency to dissolve and disappear. The men from his own college – and it was upon them he had expended the most time and affection – were the most elusive of all. Most of them were drawn deep into domesticity, two were dead, one lived abroad, one was in Hollywood writing continuities for pictures that Anson went faithfully to see.

Most of them, however, were permanent commuters with an intricate family life centring around some suburban country club, and it was from these that he felt his estrangement most keenly.

In the early days of their married life they had all needed him; he gave them advice about their slim finances, he exorcized their doubts about the advisability of bringing a baby into two rooms and a bath, especially he stood for the great world outside. But now their financial troubles were in the past and the fearfully expected child had evolved into an absorbing family. They were always glad to see old Anson, but they dressed up for him and tried to impress him with their present importance, and kept their troubles to themselves. They needed him no longer.

A few weeks before his thirtieth birthday the last of his early and intimate friends was married. Anson acted in his usual role of best man, gave his usual silver tea-service, and went down to the usual *Homeric* to say good-bye. It was a hot Friday afternoon in May, and as he walked from the pier he realized that Saturday closing had begun and he was free until Monday morning.

'Go where?' he asked himself.

The Yale Club, of course; bridge until dinner, then four or five raw cocktails in somebody's room and a pleasant confused evening. He regretted that this afternoon's groom wouldn't be along – they had always been able to cram so much into such nights: they knew how to attach women and how to get rid of them, how much consideration any girl deserved from their intelligent hedonism. A party was an adjusted thing – you took certain girls to certain places and spent just so much on their amusement; you drank a little, not much, more than you ought to drink, and at a certain time in the morning you stood up and said you were going home. You avoided college boys, sponges, future engagements, fights, sentiment, and indiscretions. That was the way it was done. All the rest was dissipation.

In the morning you were never violently sorry – you made no resolutions, but if you had overdone it and your heart was slightly out of order, you went on the wagon for a few days without saying anything about it, and waited until an accumulation of nervous boredom projected you into another party.

The lobby of the Yale Club was unpopulated. In the bar three very young alumni looked up at him, momentarily and without curiosity.

'Hello, there, Oscar,' he said to the bartender. 'Mr Cahill been around this afternoon?'

'Mr Cahill's gone to New Haven.'

'Oh ... that so?'

'Gone to the ball game. Lot of men gone up.'

Anson looked once again into the lobby, considered for a moment, and then walked out and over to Fifth Avenue. From the broad window of one of his clubs – one that he had scarcely visited in five years – a grey man with watery eyes stared down at him. Anson looked quickly away – that figure sitting in vacant resignation, in supercilious solitude, depressed him. He stopped and, retracing his steps, started over 47th Street toward Teak Warden's apartment. Teak and his wife had once been his most familiar friends – it was a household where he and Dolly Karger had been used to go in the days of their affair. But Teak had taken to drink, and his wife had remarked publicly that Anson was a bad influence on him. The remark reached Anson in an exaggerated form – when it was finally cleared up, the delicate spell of intimacy was broken, never to be renewed.

'Is Mr Warden at home?' he inquired.

'They've gone to the country.'

The fact unexpectedly cut at him. They were gone to the

country and he hadn't known. Two years before he would have known the date, the hour, come up at the last moment for a final drink, and planned his first visit to them. Now they had gone without a word.

Anson looked at his watch and considered a week-end with his family, but the only train was a local that would jolt through the aggressive heat for three hours. And tomorrow in the country, and Sunday – he was in no mood for porch-bridge with polite undergraduates, and dancing after dinner at a rural roadhouse, a diminutive of gaiety which his father had estimated too well.

'Oh, no,' he said to himself ... 'No.'

He was a dignified, impressive young man, rather stout now, but otherwise unmarked by dissipation. He could have been cast for a pillar of something – at times you were sure it was not society, at others nothing else – for the law, for the church. He stood for a few minutes motionless on the sidewalk in front of a 47th Street apartment-house; for almost the first time in his life he had nothing whatever to do.

Then he began to walk briskly up Fifth Avenue, as if he had just been reminded of an important engagement there. The necessity of dissimulation is one of the few characteristics that we share with dogs, and I think of Anson on that day as some well-bred specimen who had been disappointed at a familiar back door. He was going to see Nick, once a fashionable bartender in demand at all private dances, and now employed in cooling non-alcoholic champagne among the labyrinthine cellars of the Plaza Hotel.

'Nick,' he said, 'what's happened to everything?'

'Dead,' Nick said.

'Make me a whisky sour.' Anson handed a pint bottle over the counter. 'Nick, the girls are different; I had a little girl in Brooklyn and she got married last week without letting me know.'

'That a fact? Ha-ha-ha,' responded Nick diplomatically. 'Slipped it over on you.'

'Absolutely,' said Anson. 'And I was out with her the night before.'

'Ha-ha-ha,' said Nick, 'ha-ha-ha!'

'Do you remember the wedding, Nick, in Hot Springs where I had the waiters and the musicians singing "God save the King"?'

'Now where was that, Mr Hunter?' Nick concentrated doubtfully. 'Seems to me that was –'

'Next time they were back for more, and I began to wonder how much I'd paid them,' continued Anson.

'– seems to me that was at Mr Trenholm's wedding.'

'Don't know him,' said Anson decisively. He was offended that a strange name should intrude upon his reminiscences; Nick perceived this.

'Na – aw –' he admitted, 'I ought to know that. It was one of *your* crowd – Brakins ... Baker –'

'Bicker Baker,' said Anson responsively. 'They put me in a hearse after it was over and covered me up with flowers and drove me away.'

'Ha-ha-ha,' said Nick. 'Ha-ha-ha.'

Nick's simulation of the old family servant paled presently and Anson went upstairs to the lobby. He looked around – his eyes met the glance of an unfamiliar clerk at the desk, then fell upon a flower from the morning's marriage hesitating in the mouth of a brass cuspidor. He went out and walked slowly toward the blood-red sun over Columbus Circle. Suddenly he turned around and, retracing his steps to the Plaza, immured himself in a telephone-booth.

Later he said that he tried to get me three times that afternoon, that he tried everyone who might be in New York – men and girls he had not seen for years, an artist's model of his college days whose faded number was still in his address book – Central told him that even the exchange existed no longer. At length his quest roved into the country, and he held brief disappointing conversations with emphatic butlers and maids. So-and-so was out, riding, swimming, playing golf, sailed to Europe last week. Who shall I say phoned?

It was intolerable that he should pass the evening alone – the private reckonings which one plans for a moment of leisure lose every charm when the solitude is enforced. There were always women of a sort, but the ones he knew had temporarily vanished, and to pass a New York evening in the hired company of a stranger never occurred to him – he would have considered that that was something shameful and secret, the diversion of a travelling salesman in a strange town.

Anson paid the telephone bill – the girl tried unsuccessfully to joke with him about its size – and for the second time that afternoon started to leave the Plaza and go he knew not where. Near the revolving door the figure of a woman, obviously with child, stood sideways to the light – a sheer beige cape fluttered at her shoulders when the door turned and, each time, she looked impatiently toward it as if she were weary of waiting. At the first sight of her a strong nervous thrill of familiarity went over him, but not until he was within five feet of her did he realize that it was Paula.

'Why, Anson Hunter !'

His heart turned over.

'Why, Paula –'

'Why, this is wonderful. I can't believe it, *Anson* !'

She took both his hands, and he saw in the freedom of the gesture that the memory of him had lost poignancy to her. But not to him – he felt that old mood that she evoked in him stealing over his brain, that gentleness with which he had always met her optimism as if afraid to mar its surface.

'We're at Rye for the summer. Pete had to come East on business – you know of course I'm Mrs Peter Hagerty now – so we brought the children and took a house. You've got to come out and see us.'

'Can I?' he asked directly. 'When?'

'When you like. Here's Pete.' The revolving door functioned, giving up a fine tall man of thirty with a tanned face and a trim moustache. His immaculate fitness made a sharp contrast with Anson's increasing bulk, which was obvious under the faintly tight cutaway coat.

'You oughtn't to be standing,' said Hagerty to his wife. 'Let's sit down here.' He indicated lobby chairs, but Paula hesitated.

'I've got to go right home,' she said. 'Anson, why don't you –

why don't you come out and have dinner with us tonight! We're just getting settled, but if you can stand that –'

Hagerty confirmed the invitation cordially.

'Come out for the night.'

Their car waited in front of the hotel, and Paula with a tired gesture sank back against silk cushions in the corner. 'There's so much I want to talk to you about,' she said, 'it seems hopeless.'

'I want to hear about you.'

'Well' – she smiled at Hagerty – 'that would take a long time too. I have three children – by my first marriage. The oldest is five, then four, then three.' She smiled again. 'I didn't waste much time having them, did I?'

'Boys?'

'A boy and two girls. Then – oh, a lot of things happened, and I got a divorce in Paris a year ago and married Pete. That's all – except that I'm awfully happy.'

In Rye they drove up to a large house near the Beach Club, from which there issued presently three dark, slim children who broke from an English governess and approached them with an esoteric cry. Abstractedly and with difficulty, Paula took each one into her arms, a caress which they accepted stiffly, as they had evidently been told not to bump into Mummy. Even against their fresh faces Paula's skin showed scarcely any weariness – for all her physical languor she seemed younger than when he had last seen her at Palm Beach seven years ago.

At dinner she was preoccupied, and afterward, during the homage to the radio, she lay with closed eyes on the sofa, until Anson wondered if his presence at this time were not an intrusion. But at nine o'clock, when Hagerty rose and said pleasantly that he was going to leave them by themselves for a while, she began to talk slowly about herself and the past.

'My first baby,' she said – 'the one we call Darling, the biggest little girl – I wanted to die when I knew I was going to have her, because Lowell was like a stranger to me. It didn't seem as though she could be my own. I wrote you a letter and tore it up. Oh, you were *so* bad to me, Anson.'

It was the dialogue again, rising and falling, Anson felt a sudden quickening of memory.

'Weren't you engaged once?' she asked – 'a girl named Dolly something?'

'I wasn't ever engaged. I tried to be engaged, but I never loved anybody but you, Paula.'

'Oh,' she said. Then after a moment: 'This baby is the first one I ever really wanted. You see, I'm in love now – at last.'

He didn't answer, shocked at the treachery of her remembrance. She must have seen that the 'at last' bruised him, for she continued:

'I was infatuated with you, Anson – you could make me do anything you liked. But we wouldn't have been happy. I'm not smart enough for you. I don't like things to be complicated like you do.' She paused. 'You'll never settle down,' she said.

The phrase struck at him from behind – it was an accusation that of all accusations he had never merited.

'I could settle down if women were different,' he said. 'If I didn't understand so much about them, if women didn't spoil you for other women, if they had only a little pride. If I could go to sleep for a while and wake up into a home that was really mine – why, that's what I'm made for, Paula, that's what women have seen in me and liked in me. It's only that I can't get through the preliminaries any more.'

Hagerty came in a little before eleven; after a whisky Paula stood up and announced that she was going to bed. She went over and stood by her husband.

'Where did you go, dearest?' she demanded.

'I had a drink with Ed Saunders.'

'I was worried. I thought maybe you'd run away.'

She rested her head against his coat.

'He's sweet, isn't he, Anson?' she demanded.

'Absolutely,' said Anson, laughing.

She raised her face to her husband.

'Well, I'm ready,' she said. She turned to Anson: 'Do you want to see our family gymnastic stunt?'

'Yes,' he said in an interested voice.

'All right. Here we go!'

Hagerty picked her up easily in his arms.

'This is called the family acrobatic stunt,' said Paula. 'He carries me upstairs. Isn't it sweet of him?'

'Yes,' said Anson.

Hagerty bent his head slightly until his face touched Paula's.

'And I love him,' she said. 'I've just been telling you haven't I, Anson?'

'Yes,' he said.

'He's the dearest thing that ever lived in this world; aren't you, darling? ... Well, good night. Here we go. Isn't he strong?'

'Yes,' Anson said.

'You'll find a pair of Pete's pyjamas laid out for you. Sweet dreams – see you at breakfast.'

'Yes,' Anson said.

8

The older members of the firm insisted that Anson should go abroad for the summer. He had scarcely had a vacation in seven years, they said. He was stale and needed a change. Anson resisted.

'If I go,' he declared, 'I won't come back any more.'

'That's absurd, old man. You'll be back in three months with all this depression gone. Fit as ever.'

'No.' He shook his head stubbornly. 'If I stop, I won't go back to work. If I stop, that means I've given up – I'm through.'

'We'll take a chance on that. Stay six months if you like – we're not afraid you'll leave us. Why, you'd be miserable if you didn't work.'

They arranged his passage for him. They liked Anson – everyone liked Anson – and the change that had been coming over him cast a sort of pall over the office. The enthusiasm that had invariably signalled up business, the consideration toward his equals and his inferiors, the lift of his vital presence – within the past four months his intense nervousness had melted down these qualities into the fussy pessimism of a man of forty. On every transaction in which he was involved he acted as a drag and a strain.

'If I go I'll never come back,' he said.

Three days before he sailed Paula Legendre Hagerty died in childbirth. I was with him a great deal then, for we were crossing together, but for the first time in our friendship he told me not a word of how he felt, nor did I see the slightest sign of emotion. His chief preoccupation was with the fact that he was thirty years old – he would turn the conversation to the point where he could remind you of it and then fall silent, as if he assumed that the statement would start a chain of thought sufficient to itself. Like his partners, I was amazed at the change in him, and I was glad when the *Paris* moved off into the wet space between the worlds, leaving his principality behind.

'How about a drink?' he suggested.

We walked into the bar with that defiant feeling that characterizes the day of departure and ordered four Martinis. After one cocktail a change came over him – he suddenly reached across and slapped my knee with the first joviality I had seen him exhibit for months.

'Did you see the girl in the red tam?' he demanded, 'the one with the high color who had the two police dogs down to bid her good-bye.'

'She's pretty,' I agreed.

'I looked her up in the purser's office and found out that she's alone. I'm going down to see the steward in a few minutes. We'll have dinner with her tonight.'

After a while he left me, and within an hour he was walking up and down the deck with her, talking to her in his strong, clear voice. Her red tam was a bright spot of color against the steel-grey sea, and from time to time she looked up with a flashing bob of her head, and smiled with amusement and interest, and anticipation. At dinner we had champagne, and were very joyous – afterward Anson ran the pool with infectious gusto, and several people who had seen me with him asked me his name. He and the girl were talking and laughing together on a lounge in the bar when I went to bed.

I saw less of him on the trip than I had hoped. He wanted to arrange a foursome, but there was no one available, so I saw him only at meals. Sometimes, though, he would have a cocktail in the bar, and he told me about the girl in the red tam, and his adventures with her, making them all bizarre and amusing, as he had a way of doing, and I was glad that he was himself again, or at least the self that I knew, and with which I felt at home. I don't think he was ever happy unless someone was in love with him, responding to him like filings to a magnet, helping him to explain himself, promising him something. What it was I do not know. Perhaps they promised that there would always be women in the world who would spend their brightest, freshest, rarest hours to nurse and protect that superiority he cherished in his heart.

William Faulkner

DELTA AUTUMN

SOON now they would enter the Delta. The sensation was
familiar to him. It had been renewed like this each last week in
November for more than fifty years – the last hill, at the foot of
which the rich unbroken alluvial flatness began as the sea began
at the base of its cliffs, dissolving away beneath the unhurried
November rain as the sea itself would dissolve away.

At first they had come in wagons: the guns, the bedding, the
dogs, the food, the whisky, the keen heart-lifting anticipation
of hunting; the young men who could drive all night and all
the following day in the cold rain and pitch a camp in the rain
and sleep in the wet blankets and rise at daylight the next morning and hunt. There had been bear then. A man shot a doe or a
fawn as quickly as he did a buck, and in the afternoons they
shot wild turkey with pistols to test their stalking skill and
marksmanship, feeding all but the breast to the dogs. But that
time was gone now. Now they went in cars, driving faster and
faster each year because the roads were better and they had
farther and farther to drive, the territory in which game still
existed drawing yearly inward as his life was drawing inward,
until now he was the last of those who had once made the
journey in wagons without feeling it and now those who accompanied him were the sons and even grandsons of the men who
had ridden for twenty-four hours in the rain or sleet behind the
steaming mules. They called him 'Uncle Ike' now, and he no
longer told anyone how near eighty he actually was because he
knew as well as they did that he no longer had any business
making such expeditions, even by car.

In fact, each time now, on that first night in camp, lying
aching and sleepless in the harsh blankets, his blood only faintly
warmed by the single thin whisky-and-water which he allowed
himself, he would tell himself that this would be his last. But

he would stand that trip – he still shot almost as well as he ever had, still killed almost as much of the game he saw as he ever killed; no longer even knew how many deer had fallen before his gun – and the fierce long heat of the next summer would renew him. Then November would come again, and again in the car with two of the sons of his old companions, whom he had taught not only how to distinguish between the prints left by a buck or a doe but between the sound they made in moving, he would look ahead past the jerking arc of the windshield wiper and see the land flatten suddenly and swoop, dissolving away beneath the rain as the sea itself would dissolve, and he would say, 'Well, boys, there it is again.'

This time though, he didn't have time to speak. The driver of the car stopped it, slamming it to a skidding halt on the greasy pavement without warning, actually flinging the two passengers forward until they caught themselves with their braced hands against the dash. 'What the hell, Roth!' the man in the middle said. 'Cant you whistle first when you do that? Hurt you, Uncle Ike?'

'No,' the old man said. 'What's the matter?' The driver didn't answer. Still leaning forward, the old man looked sharply past the face of the man between them, at the face of his kinsman. It was the youngest face of them all, aquiline, saturnine, a little ruthless, the face of his ancestor too, tempered a little, altered a little, staring sombrely through the streaming windshield across which the twin wipers flicked and flicked.

'I didn't intend to come back in here this time,' he said suddenly and harshly.

'You said that back in Jefferson last week,' the old man said. 'Then you changed your mind. Have you changed it again? This aint a very good time to –'

'Oh, Roth's coming,' the man in the middle said. His name was Legate. He seemed to be speaking to no one, as he was looking at neither of them. 'If it was just a buck he was coming all this distance for, now. But he's got a doe in here. Of course a old man like Uncle Ike can't be interested in no doe, not one that walks on two legs – when she's standing up, that is. Pretty light-coloured, too. The one he was after them nights last fall when he said he was coon-hunting, Uncle Ike. The one I figured maybe he was still running when he was gone all that month last January. But of course a old man like Uncle Ike aint got no interest in nothing like that.' He chortled, still looking at no one, not completely jeering.

'What?' the old man said. 'What's that?' But he had not even so much as glanced at Legate. He was still watching his kins-man's face. The eyes behind the spectacles were the blurred eyes of an old man, but they were quite sharp too; eyes which could still see a gun-barrel and what ran beyond it as well as any of them could. He was remembering himself now: how last year, during the final stage by motor-boat in to where they camped, a box of food had been lost overboard and how on the next day his kinsman had gone back to the nearest town for supplies and had been gone overnight. And when he did return, something had happened to him. He would go into the woods with his rifle each dawn when the others went, but the old man, watching him, knew that he was not hunting. 'All right,' he said. 'Take me and Will on to shelter where we can wait for the truck, and you can go on back.'

'I'm going in,' the other said harshly. 'Don't worry. Because this will be the last of it.'

'The last of deer hunting, or of doe hunting?' Legate said.

This time the old man paid no attention to him even by speech. He still watched the young man's savage and brooding face.

'Why?' he said.

'After Hitler gets through with it? Or Smith or Jones or Roosevelt or Wilkie or whatever he will call himself in this country?'

'We'll stop him in this country,' Legate said. 'Even if he calls himself George Washington.'

'How?' Edmonds said. 'By singing God bless America in bars at midnight and wearing dime-store flags in our lapels?'

'So that's what's worrying you,' the old man said. 'I aint noticed this country being short of defenders yet, when it needed them. You did some of it yourself twenty-odd years ago, before you were a grown man even. This country is a little mite stronger than any one man or group of men, outside of it or even inside of it either. I reckon, when the time comes and some of you have done got tired of hollering we are whipped if we dont go to war and some more are hollering we are whipped if we do, it will cope with one Austrian paper-hanger, no matter what he will be calling himself. My pappy and some other better men than any of them you named tried once to tear it in two with a war, and they failed.'

'And what have you got left?' the other said. 'Half the people without jobs and half the factories closed by strikes. Half the people on public dole that wont work and half that couldn't work even if they would. Too much cotton and corn and hogs, and not enough for people to eat and wear. The country full of people to tell a man how he cant raise his own cotton whether he will or wont, and Sally Rand with a sergeant's stripes and not even the fan couldn't fill the army rolls. Too much not-butter and not even the guns —'

'We got a deer camp — if we ever get to it,' Legate said. 'Not to mention does.'

'It's a good time to mention does,' the old man said. 'Does and fawns both. The only fighting anywhere that ever had any-thing of God's blessing on it has been when men fought to pro-tect does and fawns. If it's going to come to fighting, that's a good thing to mention and remember too.'

'Haven't you discovered in — how many years more than seventy is it? — that women and children are one thing there's never any scarcity of?' Edmonds said.

'Maybe that's why all I am worrying about right now is that ten miles of river we still have got to run before we can make camp,' the old man said. 'So let's go on.'

They went on. Soon they were going fast again, as Edmonds always drove, consulting neither of them about the speed just as he had given neither of them any warning when he slammed the car to stop. The old man relaxed again. He watched, as he did each recurrent November while more than sixty of them passed, the land which he had seen change. At first there had been only the old towns along the River and the old towns along the hills, from each of which the planters with their gangs of slaves and then of hired labourers had wrested from the impenetrable jungle of water-standing cane and cypress, gum and holly and oak and ash, cotton patches which as the years passed became fields and then plantations. The paths made by deer and bear became roads and then highways, with towns in turn springing up along them and along the rivers Tallahatchie and Sunflower which joined and became the Yazoo, the River of the Dead of the Choctaws – the thick, slow, black, unsunned streams almost without current, which once each year ceased to flow at all and then reversed, spreading, drowning the rich land and subsiding again, leaving it still richer.

Most of that was gone now. Now a man drove two hundred miles from Jefferson before he found wilderness to hunt in. Now the land lay open from the cradling hills on the East to the impenetrable jungle of water-standing cane and cypress, cotton for the world's looms – the rich black land, imponderable and vast, fecund up to the very doorsteps of the negroes who worked it and of the white men who owned it; which exhausted the hunting life of a dog in one year, the working life of a mule in five and of a man in twenty – the land in which neon flashed past them from the little countless towns and countless shining this-year's automobiles sped past them on the board plumb-ruled highways, yet in which the only permanent mark of man's occupation seemed to be the tremendous gins, constructed in sections of sheet iron and in a week's time though they were, since no man, millionaire though he be, would build more than a roof and walls to shelter the camping equipment he lived from when he knew that once each ten years or so his house would be flooded to the second storey and all within it ruined – the land across which there came now no scream of panther but instead the long hooting of locomotives: trains of incredible length and drawn by a single engine, since there was no gradient anywhere and no elevation save those raised by forgotten aboriginal hands as refuges from the yearly water and used by their Indian successors to sepulchre their fathers' bones, and all that remained of that old time were the Indian names on the little towns and usually pertaining to water – Aluschaskuna, Tillatoba, Homochitto, Yazoo.

By early afternoon, they were on water. At the last little Indian-named town at the end of pavement they waited until the other car and the two trucks – the one carrying the bedding and tents and food, the other the horses – overtook them. They left the concrete and, after another mile or so, the gravel too. In caravan they ground on through the ceaselessly dissolving afternoon, with skid-chains on the wheels now, lurching and splashing and sliding among the ruts, until presently it seemed to him that the retrograde of his remembering had gained an inverse velocity from their own slow progress, that the land had retreated not in minutes from the last spread of gravel but in years, decades, back toward what it had been when he first knew it: the road they now followed once more the ancient pathway of bear and deer, the diminishing fields they now passed once more scooped punily and terrifically by axe and saw and mule-drawn plough from the wilderness's flank, out of the brooding and immemorial tangle, in place of ruthless mile-wide parallelograms wrought by ditching the dyking machinery.

They reached the river landing and unloaded, the horses to go overland down stream to a point opposite the camp and swim the river, themselves and the bedding and food and dogs and guns in the motor-launch. It was himself, though no horseman, no farmer, not even a countryman save by his distant birth and boyhood, who coaxed and soothed the two horses, drawing them by his own single frail hand until, backing, filling, trembling a little, they surged, halted, then sprang scrambling down from the truck, possessing no affinity for them as creatures, beasts, but being merely insulated by his years and time from the corruption of steel and oiled moving parts which tainted the others.

Then, his old hammer double gun which was only twelve years younger than he standing between his knees, he watched even the last puny marks of man – cabin, clearing, the small and irregular fields which a year ago were jungle and in which the skeleton stalks of this year's cotton stood almost as tall and rank as the old cane had stood, as if man had to marry his planting to the wilderness in order to conquer it – fall away and vanish. The twin banks marched with wilderness as he remembered it – the tangle of brier and cane impenetrable even to sight twenty feet away, the tall tremendous soaring of oak and gum and ash and hickory which had rung to no axe save the hunter's had echoed to no machinery save the beat of old-time steamboats traversing it or to the snarling of launches like their own of people going into it to dwell for a week or two weeks because it was still wilderness. There was some of it left, although now it was two hundred miles from Jefferson when once it had been thirty. He had watched it, not being conquered, destroyed, so much as retreating since its purpose was served now and its time an outmoded time, retreating southward through this inverted-apex, this V-shaped section of earth between hills and River until what was left of it seemed now to be gathered and for the time arrested in one tremendous destiny of brooding and inscrutable impenetrability at the ultimate funnelling tip.

They reached the site of their last-year's camp with still two hours left of light. 'You go on over under that driest tree and set down,' Legate told him, '– if you can find it. Me and these other young boys will do this.' He did neither. He was not tired yet. That would come later. *Maybe it wont come at all this time*, he thought, as he had thought at this point each November for the last five or six of them. *Maybe I will go out on stand in the morning too*; knowing that he would not, not even if he took the advice and sat down under the driest shelter and did nothing until camp was made and supper cooked. Because it would not be the fatigue. It would be because he would not sleep tonight but would lie instead wakeful and peaceful on the cot amid the tent-filling snoring and the rain's whisper as he always did on the first night in camp; peaceful, without regret or fretting, telling himself that was all right too, who didn't have so many of them left as to waste one sleeping.

In his slicker he directed the unloading of the boat – the tents, the stove, the bedding, the food for themselves and the dogs until there should be meat in camp. He sent two of the Negroes to cut firewood; he had the cook-tent raised and the stove up and a fire going and supper cooking while the big tent was still being staked down. Then in the beginning of dusk he crossed in the boat to where the horses waited, backing and snorting at the water. He took the lead-ropes and with no more weight than that and his voice, he drew them down into the water and held them beside the boat with only their heads above the surface, as though they actually were suspended from his frail and strengthless old man's hands, while the boat recrossed and each horse in turn lay prone in the shallows, panting and trembling, its eyes rolling in the dusk, until the same weightless hand and unraised voice gathered it surging upward, splashing and thrashing up the bank.

Then the meal was ready. The last of light was gone now save the thin stain of it snared somewhere between the river's surface and the rain. He had the single glass of thin whisky-and-water, then, standing in the churned mud beneath the stretched tarpaulin, he said grace over the fried slabs of pork, the hot soft shapeless bread, the canned beans and molasses and coffee in iron plates and cups – the town food, brought along with them – then covered himself again, the others following. 'Eat,' he said. 'Eat it all up. I dont want a piece of town meat in camp after breakfast tomorrow. Then you boys will hunt. You'll have to. When I first started hunting in this bottom sixty years ago with old General Compson and Major de Spain and Roth's grandfather and Will Legate's too, Major de Spain wouldn't allow but two pieces of foreign grub in his camp. That was one side of pork and one ham of beef. And not to eat for the first supper and breakfast neither. It was to save until along toward the end of camp when everybody was so sick of bear meat and coon and venison that we couldn't even look at it.'

'I thought Uncle Ike was going to say the pork and beef was for the dogs,' Legate said, chewing. 'But that's right; I remember. You just shot the dogs a mess of wild turkey every evening when they got tired of deer guts.'

'Times are different now,' another said. 'There was game here then.'

'Yes,' the old man said quietly. 'There was game here then.'

'Besides, they shot does then too,' Legate said. 'As it is now, we aint got but one doe-hunter in –'

'And better men hunted it,' Edmonds said. He stood at the

end of the rough plank table, eating rapidly and steadily as the others ate. But again the old man looked sharply across at the sullen, handsome, brooding face which appeared now darker and more sullen still in the light of the smoky lantern. 'Go on. Say it.'

'I didn't say that,' the old man said. 'There are good men everywhere, at all times. Most men are. Some are just unlucky, because most men are a little better than their circumstances give them a chance to be. And I've known some that even the circumstances couldn't stop.'

'Well, I wouldn't say –' Legate said.

'So you've lived almost eighty years,' Edmonds said. 'And that's what you finally learned about the other animals you lived among. I suppose the question to ask you is, where have you been all the time you were dead?'

There was a silence; for the instant even Legate's jaw stopped chewing while he gaped at Edmonds. 'Well, by God, Roth –' the third speaker said. But it was the old man who spoke, his voice still peaceful and untroubled and merely grave:

'Maybe so,' he said. 'But if being what you call alive would have learned me any different, I reckon I'm satisfied, wherever it was I've been.'

'Well, I wouldn't say that Roth –' Legate said.

The third speaker was still leaning forward a little over the table, looking at Edmonds. 'Meaning that it's only because folks happen to be watching him that a man behaves at all,' he said. 'Is that it?'

'Yes,' Edmonds said. 'A man in a blue coat, with a badge on it watching him. Maybe just the badge.'

'I deny that,' the old man said. 'I don't –'

The other two paid no attention to him. Even Legate was listening to them for the moment, his mouth still full of food and still open a little, his knife with another lump of something balanced on the tip of the blade arrested halfway to his mouth. 'I'm glad I don't have your opinion of folks,' the third speaker said. 'I take it you include yourself.'

'I see,' Edmonds said. 'You prefer Uncle Ike's opinion of circumstances. All right. Who makes the circumstances?'

'Luck,' the third said. 'Chance. Happen so. I see what you are getting at. But that's just what Uncle Ike said: that now and then, maybe most of the time, man is a little better than the net result of his and his neighbors' doings, when he gets the chance to be.'

This time Legate swallowed first. He was not to be stopped this time. 'Well, I wouldn't say that Roth Edmonds can hunt one doe every day and night for two weeks and was a poor hunter or a unlucky one neither. A man that still have the same doe left to hunt on again next year –'

'Have some meat,' the man next to him said.

'– aint no unlucky. What?' Legate said.

'Have some meat.' The other offered the dish.

'I got some,' Legate said.

'Have some more,' the third speaker said. 'You and Roth Edmonds both. Have a heap of it. Clapping your jaws together that way with nothing to break the shock.' Someone chortled. Then they all laughed, with relief, the tension broken. But the old man was speaking, even into the laughter, in that peaceful and still untroubled voice:

'I still believe. I see proof everywhere. I grant that man made a heap of his circumstances, him and his living neighbours between them. He even inherited some of them already made, already almost ruined even. A while ago Henry Wyatt there said how there used to be more game here. There was. So much that we even killed does. I seem to remember Will Legate mentioning that too –' Someone laughed, a single guffaw, stillborn. It ceased and they all listened, gravely, looking down at their plates. Edmonds was drinking his coffee, sullen, brooding, inattentive.

'Some folks still kill does,' Wyatt said. 'There wont be just one buck hanging in this bottom tomorrow night without any head to fit it.'

'I didn't say all men,' the old man said. 'I said most men. And not just because there is a man with a badge to watch us. We probably wont even see him unless maybe he will stop here about noon tomorrow and eat dinner with us and check our licences –'

'We don't kill does because if we did kill does in a few years there wouldn't even be any bucks left to kill, Uncle Ike,' Wyatt said.

'According to Roth yonder, that's one thing we wont never have to worry about,' the old man said. 'He said on the way here this morning that does and fawns – I believe he said women and children – are two things this world aint ever lacked. But that aint all of it,' he said. 'That's just the mind's reason a man has to give himself because the heart dont always have time to bother with thinking up words that fit together. God created man and He created the world for him to live in and I reckon He created the kind of world He would have wanted to live in if He had been a man – the ground to walk on, the big woods, the trees and the water, and the game to live in it. And maybe He didn't put the desire to hunt and kill game in man but I reckon He knew it was going to be there, that man was going to teach it to himself, since he wasn't quite God himself yet –'

'When will he be?' Wyatt said.

'I think that every man and woman, at the instant when it dont even matter whether they marry or not, I think that whether they marry then or afterward or dont never, at that instant the two of them together were God.'

'Then there are some Gods in this world I wouldn't want to touch, and with a damn long stick,' Edmonds said. He set his coffee cup down and looked at Wyatt. 'And that includes myself, if that's what you want to know. I'm going to bed.' He was gone. There was a general movement among the others. But it ceased and they stood again about the table, not looking at the old man, apparently held there yet by his quiet and peaceful voice as the heads of the swimming horses had been held above the water by his weightless hand. The three Negroes – the cook and his helper and old Isham – were sitting quietly in the entrance of the kitchen tent, listening too, the three faces dark and motionless and musing.

'He put them both here: man, and the game he would follow and kill, foreknowing it. I believe He said, "So be it." I reckon He even foreknew the end. But He said, "I will give him his chance. I will give him warning and foreknowledge too, along

368

with the desire to follow and the power to slay. The woods and fields he ravages and the game he devastates will be the consequence and signature of his crime and guilt, and his punishment." – Bed time,' he said. His voice and inflexion did not change at all. 'Breakfast at four o'clock, Isham. We want meat on the ground by sun-up time.'

There was a good fire in the sheet-iron heater; the tent was warm and was beginning to dry out, except for the mud underfoot. Edmonds was already rolled into his blankets, motionless, his face to the wall. Isham had made up his bed too – the strong, battered iron cot, the stained mattress which was not quite soft enough, the worn, often-washed blankets which as the years passed were less and less warm enough. But the tent was warm; presently, when the kitchen was cleaned up and readied for breakfast, the young Negro would come in to lie down before the heater, where he could be roused to put fresh wood into it from time to time. And then, he knew now he would not sleep tonight anyway; he no longer needed to tell himself that perhaps he would. But it was all right now. The day was ended now and night faced him, but alarmless, empty of fret. *Maybe I came for this*, he thought: *Not to hunt, but for this. I would come anyway, even if only to go back home tomorrow*. Wearing only his bagging woollen underwear, his spectacles folded away in the worn case beneath the pillow where he could reach them readily and his lean body fitted easily into the old worn groove of mattress and blankets, he lay on his back, his hands crossed on his breast and his eyes closed while the others undressed and went to bed and the last of the sporadic talking died into snoring. Then he opened his eyes and lay peaceful and quiet as a child, looking up at the motionless belly of rain-murmured canvas upon which the glow of the heater was dying slowly away and would fade still further until the young Negro, lying on two planks before it, would sit up and stoke it and lie back down again.

They had a house once. That was sixty years ago, when the Big Bottom was only thirty miles from Jefferson and old Major de Spain, who had been his father's cavalry commander in '61 and '2 and '3 and '4, and his cousin (his older brother; his father

too) had taken him into the woods for the first time. Old Sam
Fathers was alive then, born in slavery, son of a Negro slave
and a Chickasaw chief, who had taught him how to shoot, not
only when to shoot but when not to; such a November dawn as
tomorrow would be and the old man led him straight to the
great cypress and he had known the buck would pass exactly
there because there was something running in Sam Father's
veins which ran in the veins of the buck too, and they stood
there against the tremendous trunk, the old man of seventy and
the boy of twelve, and there was nothing save the dawn until
suddenly the buck was there, smoke-colored out of nothing,
magnificent with speed: and Sam Fathers said, 'Now. Shoot
quick and shoot slow:' and the gun levelled rapidly without
haste and crashed and he walked to the buck lying still intact
and still in the shape of that magnificent speed and bled it with
Sam's knife and Sam dipped his hands into the hot blood and
marked his face for ever while he stood trying not to tremble,
humbly and with pride too though the boy of twelve had been
unable to phrase it then: *I slew you: my bearing must not
shame your quitting life. My conduct for ever onward must
become your death*: marking him for that and for more than
that: that day and himself and McCaslin juxtaposed not against
the wilderness but against the tamed land, the old wrong and
shame itself, in repudiation and denial at least of the land and
the wrong and shame even if he couldn't cure the wrong and
eradicate the shame, who at fourteen when he learned of it had
believed he could do both when he became competent and when
at twenty-one he became competent he knew that he could do
neither but at least he could repudiate the wrong and shame, at
least in principle, and at least the land itself in fact, for his son
at least: and did, thought he had: then (married then) in a
rented cubicle in a back-street stock-traders' boarding-house,
the first and last time he ever saw her naked body, himself and
his wife juxtaposed in their turn against that same land, that
same wrong and shame from whose regret and grief he would
at least save and free his son and, saving and freeing his son,
lost him. They had the house then. That roof, the two weeks of
each November which they spent under it, had become his

home. Although since that time they had lived during the two
fall weeks in tents and not always in the same place two years
in succession and now his companions were the sons and even
the grandsons of them with whom he had lived in the house and
for almost fifty years now the house itself had not even existed,
the conviction, the sense and feeling of home, had been merely
transferred into the canvas. He owned a house in Jefferson, a
good house though small, where he had had a wife and lived
with her and lost her, ay, lost her even though he had lost her in
the rented cubicle before he and his old clever dipsomaniac partner had finished the house for them to move into it: but lost her,
because she loved him. But women hope for so much. They
never live too long to still believe that anything within the scope
of their passionate wanting is likewise within the range of their
passionate hope: and it was still kept for him by his dead
wife's widowed niece and her children and he was comfortable
in it, his wants and needs and even the small trying harmless
crotchets of an old man looked after by blood at least related to
the blood which he had elected out of all the earth to cherish.
But he spent the time within those walls waiting for November,
because even this tent with its muddy floor, and the bed which
was not wide enough nor soft enough nor even warm enough,
was his home and these men, some of whom he only saw during
these two November weeks and not one of whom even bore any
name he used to know – De Spain and Compson and Ewell
and Hogganbeck – were more his kin than any. Because this
was his land –

The shadow of the youngest Negro loomed. It soared, blot-
ting the heater's dying glow from the ceiling, the wood billets
thumping into the iron maw until the glow, the flame, leaped
high and bright across the canvas. But the Negro's shadow still
remained, by its length and breadth, standing, since it covered
most of the ceiling, until after a moment he raised himself on
one elbow to look. It was not the Negro, it was his kinsman;
when he spoke the other turned sharp against the red firelight
the sullen and ruthless profile.

'Nothing,' Edmonds said. 'Go on back to sleep.'

'Since Will Legate mentioned it,' McCaslin said, 'I remember you had some trouble sleeping in here last fall too. Only you called it coon-hunting then. Or was it Will Legate called it that?' The other didn't answer. Then he turned and went back to his bed, McCaslin, still propped on his elbow, watched until the other's shadow sank down the wall and vanished, became one with the mass of sleeping shadows. 'That's right,' he said. 'Try to get some sleep. We must have meat in camp tomorrow. You can do all the setting up you want to after that.' He lay down again, his hands crossed again on his breast, watching the glow of the heater on the canvas ceiling. It was steady again now, the fresh wood accepted, being assimilated; soon it would begin to fade again, taking with it the last echo of that sudden upflare of a young man's passion and unrest. Let him lie awake for a little while, he thought; he will lie still some day for a long time without even dissatisfaction to disturb him. And lying awake here, in these surroundings, would sooth him if anything could, if anything could soothe a man just forty years old. Yes, he thought; forty years old or thirty, or even the trembling and sleepless ardor of a boy; already the tent, the rain-murmured canvas globe, was once more filled with it. He lay on his back, his eyes closed, his breathing quiet and peaceful as a child's, listening to it – that silence which was never silence but was myriad. He could almost see it, tremendous, primeval, looming, musing downward upon this puny evanescent clutter of human sojourn which after a single brief week would vanish and in another week would be completely healed, traceless in the unmarked solitude. Because it was his land, although he had never owned a foot of it. He had never wanted to, not even after he saw plain its ultimate doom, watching it retreat year by year before the onslaught of axe and saw the log-lines and then dynamite and tractor ploughs, because it belonged to no man. It belonged to all; they had only to use it well, humbly and with pride. Then suddenly he knew why he had never wanted to own any of it, arrest at least that much of what people called progress, measure his longevity at least against that much of its ultimate fate. It was because there was just exactly enough of it. He seemed to see the two of them – himself and the wilderness – as coevals, his own span as a hunter, a woodsman, not contemporary with his first breath but transmitted to him, assumed by him gladly, humbly, with joy and pride, from that old Major de Spain and that old Sam Fathers who had taught him to hunt, the two spans running out together, not toward oblivion, nothingness, but into a dimension free of both time and space where once more the untreed land warped and wrung to mathematical squares of rank cotton for the frantic old-world people to turn into shells to shoot at one another, would find ample room for both – the names, the faces of the old men he had known and loved and for a little while outlived, moving again among the shades of tall unaxed trees and sightless brakes where the wild strong immortal game ran for ever before the tireless belling immortal hounds, falling and rising phoenix-like to the soundless guns.

He had been asleep. The lantern was lighted now. Outside in the darkness the oldest Negro, Isham, was beating a spoon against the bottom of a tin pan and crying, 'Raise up and get yo foa clock coffy. Raise up and get yo foa clock coffy,' and the tent was full of low talk and of men dressing, and Legate's voice, repeating: 'Get out of here now and let Uncle Ike sleep. If you wake him up, he'll go out with us. And he aint got any business in the woods this morning.'

So he didn't move. He lay with his eyes closed, his breathing gentle and peaceful, and heard them one by one leave the tent. He listened to the breakfast sounds from the table beneath the tarpaulin and heard them depart – the horses, the dogs, the voice until it died away and there was only the sounds of the Negroes clearing breakfast away. After a while he might possibly even hear the first faint clear cry of the first hound ring through the wet woods from where the buck had bedded, then he would go back to sleep again – The tent-flap swung in and fell. Something jarred sharply against the end of the cot and a hand grasped his knee through the blanket before he could open his eyes. It was Edmonds, carrying a shotgun in place of his rifle. He spoke in a harsh, rapid voice:

'Sorry to wake you. There will be a –'

'I was awake,' McCaslin said. 'Are you going to shoot that shotgun today?'

'You just told me last night you want meat,' Edmonds said. 'There will be a –'

'Since when did you start having trouble getting meat with your rifle?'

'All right,' the other said, with that harsh, restrained, furious impatience. Then McCaslin saw in his hand a thick oblong: an envelope. 'There will be a message here some time this morning, looking for me. Maybe it wont come. If it does, give the messenger this and tell h— say I said No.'

'A what?' McCaslin said. 'Tell who?' He half rose on to his elbow as Edmonds jerked the envelope on to the blanket, already turning toward the entrance, the envelope striking solid and heavy and without noise and already sliding from the bed until McCaslin caught it, divining by feel through the paper as instantaneously and conclusively as if he had opened the envelope and looked, the thick sheaf of banknotes. 'Wait,' he said. 'Wait:' – more than the blood kinsman, more even than the senior in years, so that the other paused, the canvas lifted, looking back, and McCaslin saw that outside it was already day. 'Tell her No,' he said. 'Tell her.' They stared at one another – the old face, wan, sleep-raddled above the tumbled bed, the dark and sullen younger one at once furious and cold. 'Will Legate was right. This is what you called coon-hunting. And now this.' He didn't raise the envelope. He made no motion, no gesture to indicate it. 'What did you promise her that you haven't the courage to face her and retract?'

'Nothing!' the other said. 'Nothing! This is all of it. Tell her I said No.' He was gone. The tent flap lifted on an in-waft of faint light and the constant murmur of rain, and fell again, leaving the old man still-half-raised on to one elbow, the envelope clutched in the other shaking hand. Afterward it seemed to him that he had begun to hear the approaching boat almost immediately, before the other could have got out of sight even. It seemed to him that there had been no interval whatever: the tent flap falling on the same out-waft of faint and rain-filled light like the suspiration and expiration of the same breath and then in the next second lifted again – the mounting snarl of the outboard engine, increasing, nearer and nearer and louder and louder then cut short off, ceasing with the absolute instantaneity of a blown-out candle, into the lap and plop of water under the bows as the skiff slid in to the bank, the youngest Negro, the youth, raising the tent flap beyond which for that instant he saw the boat — a small skiff with a Negro man sitting in the stern beside the up-slanted motor — then the woman entering, in a man's hat and a man's slicker and rubber boots, carrying the blanket-swaddled bundle on one arm and holding the edge of the unbuttoned raincoat over it with the other hand: and bringing something else, something intangible, an effluvium which he knew he would recognize in a moment because Isham had already told him, warned him, by sending the young Negro to the tent to announce the visitor instead of coming himself, the flap falling at last on the young Negro and they were alone — the face indistinct and as yet only young and with dark eyes, queerly colorless but not ill and not of a country woman despite the garments she wore, looking down at him where he sat upright on the cot now, clutching the envelope, the soiled undergarment bagging about him and the twisted blankets huddled about his hips.

'Is that his?' he cried. 'Don't lie to me!'

'Yes,' she said. 'He's gone.'

'Yes. He's gone. You won't jump him here. Not this time. I don't reckon even you expected that. He left you this. Here.' He fumbled at the envelope. It was not to pick it up, because it was still in his hand; he had never put it down. It was as if he had to fumble somehow to co-ordinate physically his heretofore obedient hand with what his brain was commanding of it, as if he had never performed such an action before, extending the envelope at last, saying again, 'Here. Take it. Take it;' until he became aware of her eyes, or not the eyes so much as the look, the regard fixed now on his face with that immersed contemplation, that bottomless and intent color, of a child. If she had ever seen either the envelope or his movement to extend it, she did not show it.

'You're Uncle Isaac,' she said.

'Yes,' he said. 'But never mind that. Here. Take it. He said to tell you No.' She looked at the envelope, then she took it. It was sealed and bore no superscription. Nevertheless, even after she glanced at the front of it, he watched her hold it in the one free hand and tear the corner off with her teeth and manage to rip it open and tilt the neat sheaf of bound notes on to the blanket without even glancing at them and look into the empty envelope and take the edge between her teeth and tear it completely open before she crumpled and dropped it.

'That's just money,' she said.

'What did you expect? What else did you expect? You have known him long enough or at least often enough to have got that child, and you don't know him any better than that?'

'Not very often. Not very long. Just that week here last fall, and in January he sent for me and we went West, to New Mexico. We were there six weeks, where I could at least sleep in the same apartment where I cooked for him and looked after his clothes –'

'But not marriage,' he said. 'Not marriage. He didn't promise you that. Dont lie to me. He didn't have to.'

'No. He didn't have to. I didn't ask him to. I knew what I was doing. I knew that to begin with, long before honor I imagine he called it told him the time had come to tell me in so many words what his code I suppose he would call it would forbid him for ever to do. And agreed. Then we agreed again before he left New Mexico, to make sure. That that would be all of it. I believed him. No, I don't mean that; I mean I believed myself. I wasn't even listening to him any more by then because by that time it had been a long time since he had had anything else to tell me for me to have to hear. By then I wasn't even listening enough to ask him to please stop talking. I was listening to myself. And I believed it. I must have believed it. I dont see how I could have helped but believe it, because he was gone then as we had agreed and he didn't write as we had agreed, just the money came to the bank in Vicksburg in my name but coming from nobody as we had agreed. So I must have believed it. I even wrote him last month to make sure again and the letter came back unopened and I was sure. So I left the hospital and rented myself a room to live in until the deer season opened so I could make sure myself and I was waiting beside the road yesterday when your car passed and he saw me and so I was sure.'

'Then what do you want?' he said. 'What do you want? What do you expect?'

'Yes,' she said. And while he glared at her, his white hair awry from the pillow and his eyes, jacking the spectacles to focus them, blurred and irisless and apparently pupilless, he saw again that grave, intent, speculative and detached fixity like a child watching him. 'His great great – Wait a minute – great great *great* grandfather was your grandfather. McCaslin. Only it got to be Edmonds. Only it got to be more than that. Your cousin McCaslin was there that day when your father and Uncle Buddy won Tennie from Mr Beauchamp for the one that had no name but Terrel so you called him Tomey's Terrel to marry. But after that it got to be Edmonds.' She regarded him, almost peacefully, with that unwinking and heatless fixity – the dark wide bottomless eyes in the face's dead and toneless pallor which to the old man looked anything but dead, but young and incredibly and even ineradicably alive – as though she were not only not looking at anything, she was not even speaking to anyone but herself. 'I would have made a man of him. He's not a man yet. You spoiled him. You, and Uncle Lucas and Aunt Mollie. But mostly you.'

'Me?' he said. 'Me?'

'Yes. When you gave to his grandfather that land which didn't belong to him, not even half of it by will or even law.'

'And never mind that too,' he said. 'Never mind that too. You,' he said. 'You sound like you have been to college even. You sound almost like a Northerner even, not like the draggle-tailed women of these Delta peckerwoods. Yet you meet a man on the street one afternoon just because a box of groceries happened to fall out of a boat. And a month later you go off with him and live with him until he got a child on you: and then, by your own statement, you sat there while he took his hat and said good-bye and walked out. Even a Delta peckerwood would look after even a draggle-tail better than that. Haven't you got any folks at all?'

'Yes,' she said. 'I was living with one of them. My aunt, in Vicksburg. I came to live with her two years ago when my father died; we lived in Indianapolis then. But I got a job, teaching school here in Aluschaskuna, because my aunt was a widow, with a big family, taking in washing to sup —'

'Took in what?' he said. 'Took in washing?' He sprang, still seated even, flinging himself backward on to one arm, awry-haired, glaring. Now he understood what it was she had brought into the tent with her, what old Isham had already told him by sending the youth to bring her in to him — the pale lips, the skin pallid and dead-looking yet not ill, the dark and tragic and fore-knowing eyes. *Maybe in a thousand or two thousand years in America*, he thought. *But not now! Not now!* He cried, not loud, in a voice of amazement, pity, and outrage: 'You're a nigger !'

'Yes,' she said. 'James Beauchamp — you called him Tennie's Jim though he had a name — was my grandfather. I said you were Uncle Isaac.'

'And he knows?'

'No,' she said. 'What good would that have done?'

'But you did,' he cried. 'But you did. Then what do you expect here?'

'Nothing.'

'Then why did you come here? You said you were waiting in Aluschaskuna yesterday and he saw you. Why did you come this morning?'

'I'm going back North. Back home. My cousin brought me up the day before yesterday in his boat. He's going to take me on to Leland to get the train.'

'Then go,' he said. Then he cried again in that thin not loud and grieving voice: 'Get out of here ! I can do nothing for you ! Cant nobody do nothing for you !' She moved; she was not looking at him again, toward the entrance. 'Wait,' he said. She paused again, obediently still, turning. He took up the sheaf of banknotes and laid it on the blanket at the foot of the cot and drew his hand back beneath the blanket. 'There,' he said.

Now she looked at the money, for the first time, one brief blank glance, then away again. 'I don't need it. He gave me money last winter. Besides the money he sent to Vicksburg. Provided. Honor and code too. That was all arranged.'

'Take it,' he said. His voice began to rise again, but he stopped it. 'Take it out of my tent.' She came back to the cot and took up the money; whereupon once more he said, 'Wait:' although she had not turned, still stooping, and he put out his hand. But, sitting, he could not complete the reach until she moved her hand, the single hand which held the money, until he touched it. He didn't grasp it, he mere touched it – the gnarled, bloodless, bone-light bone-dry old man's fingers touching for a second the smooth young flesh where the strong old blood ran after its long-lost journey to home. 'Tennie's Jim,' he said. 'Tennie's Jim.' He drew the hand back beneath the blanket again: he said harshly now: 'It's a boy, I reckon. They usually are, except that one that was its own mother too.'

'Yes,' she said. 'It's a boy.' She stood for a moment longer, looking at him. Just for an instant her free hand moved as though she were about to lift the edge of the raincoat away from the child's face. But she did not. She turned again when once more he said Wait and moved beneath the blanket.

'Turn your back,' he said. 'I am going to get up. I aint got my pants on.' Then he could not get up. He sat in the huddled blanket, shaking, while again she turned and looked down at him in dark interrogation. 'There,' he said harshly, in the thin and shaking old man's voice. 'On the nail there. The tentpole.'

'What?' she said.

'The horn l' he said harshly. 'The horn.' She went and got it, thrust the money into the slicker's side pocket as if it were a rag, a soiled hankerchief, and lifted down the horn, the one which General Compson had left him in his will, covered with the unbroken skin from a buck's shank and bound with silver.

'What?' she said.

'It's his. Take it.'

'Oh,' she said. 'Yes. Thank you.'

'Yes,' he said, harshly, rapidly, but not so harsh now and soon not harsh at all but just rapid, urgent, until he knew that his voice was running away with him and he had neither intended it nor could stop it: 'That's right. Go back North.

Marry: a man in your own race. That's the only salvation for you – for a while yet, maybe a long while yet. We still have to wait. Marry a black man. You are young, handsome, almost white; you could find a black man who would see in you what it was you saw in him, who would ask nothing of you and expect less and get even still less than that, if it's revenge you want. Then you will forget all this, forget it ever happened, that he ever existed –' until he could stop it at last and did, sitting there in his huddle of blankets during the instant when, without moving at all, she blazed silently down at him. Then that was gone too. She stood in the gleaming and still dripping slicker, looking quietly down at him from under the sodden hat.

'Old man,' she said, 'you have lived so long and forgotten so much that you dont remember anything you ever knew or felt or even heard about love?'

Then she was gone too. The waft of light and the murmur of the constant rain flowed into the tent and then out again as the flap fell. Lying back once more, trembling, panting, the blanket huddled to his chin and his hands crossed on his breast, he listened to the pop and snarl, the mounting then fading whine of the motor until it died away and once again the tent held only silence and the sound of rain. And cold too: he lay shaking faintly and steadily in it, rigid save for the shaking. This Delta, he thought: This Delta. *This land which man has deswamped and denuded and derivered in two generations so that white men can own plantations and commute every night to Memphis and black men own plantations and ride in jim crow cars to Chicago to live in millionaires' mansions on Lakeshore Drive, where white men rent farms and live like niggers and niggers crop on shares and live like animals, where cotton is planted and grows man-tall in the very cracks of the sidewalks, and usury and mortgage and bankruptcy and measureless wealth, Chinese and African and Aryan and Jew, all breed and spawn together until no man has time to say which one is which nor cares.* . . . No wonder the ruined woods I used to know dont cry for retribution! he thought: The people who have destroyed it will accomplish its revenge.

The tent flap jerked rapidly in and fell. He did not move

save to turn his head and open his eyes. It was Legate. He went quickly to Edmonds's bed and stopped, rummaging hurriedly among the still-tumbled blankets.

'What is it?' he said.

'Looking for Roth's knife,' Legate said. 'I come back to get a horse. We got a deer on the ground.' He rose, the knife in his hand, and hurried toward the entrance.

'Who killed it?' McCaslin said. 'Was it Roth?'

'Yes,' Legate said, raising the flap.

'Wait,' McCaslin said. He moved, suddenly, on to his elbow. 'What was it?' Legate paused for an instant beneath the lifted flap. He did not look back.

'Just a deer, Uncle Ike,' he said impatiently. 'Nothing extra.' He was gone; again the flap fell behind him, wafting out of the tent again the faint light and the constant and grieving rain. McCaslin lay back down, the blanket once more drawn to his chin, his crossed hands once more weightless on his breast in the empty tent.

'It was a doe,' he said.

Ernest Hemingway

THE BATTLER

NICK stood up. He was all right. He looked up the track at the
lights of the caboose going out of sight around the curve. There
was water on both sides of the track, then tamarack swamp.

He felt of his knee. The pants were torn and the skin was
barked. His hands were scraped and there were sand and cinders
driven up under his nails. He went over to the edge of the track
down the little slope to the water and washed his hands. He
washed them carefully in the cold water, getting the dirt out
from the nails. He squatted down and bathed his knee.

That lousy crut of a brakeman. He would get him some day.
He would know him again. That was a fine way to act.

'Come here, kid,' he said. 'I got something for you.'

He had fallen for it. What a lousy kid thing to have done.

They would never suck him in that way again.

'Come here, kid, I got something for you.' Then *wham* and
he lit on his hands and knees beside the track.

Nick rubbed his eye. There was a big bump coming up. He
would have a black eye, all right. It ached already. That son of
a crutting brakeman.

He touched the bump over his eye with his fingers. Oh, well,
it was only a black eye. That was all he had gotten out of it.
Cheap at the price. He wished he could see it. Could not see it
looking into the water, though. It was dark and he was a long
way off from anywhere. He wiped his hands on his trousers and
stood up, then climbed the embankment to the rails.

He started up the track. It was well ballasted and made easy
walking, sand and gravel packed between the ties, solid walking.
The smooth roadbed like a causeway went on ahead through
the swamp. Nick walked along. He must get to somewhere.

Nick had swung on to the freight train when it slowed down
for the yards outside of Walton Junction. The train, with Nick

on it, had passed through Kalkaska as it started to get dark.

Now he must be nearly to Mancelona. Three or four miles of swamp. He stepped along the track, walking so he kept on the ballast between the ties, the swamp ghostly in the rising mist. His eye ached and he was hungry. He kept on hiking, putting the miles of track back of him. The swamp was all the same on both sides of the track.

Ahead there was a bridge. Nick crossed it, his boots ringing hollow on the iron. Down below the water showed black between the slits of ties. Nick kicked a loose spike and it dropped into the water. Beyond the bridge were hills. It was high and dark on both sides of the track. Up the track Nick saw a fire.

He came up the track toward the fire carefully. It was off to one side of the track, below the railway embankment. He had only seen the light from it. The track came out through a cut and where the fire was burning the country opened out and fell away into woods. Nick dropped carefully down the embankment and cut into the woods to come up to the fire through the trees. It was a beechwood forest and the fallen beechnut burrs were under his shoes as he walked between the trees. The fire was bright now, just at the edge of the trees. There was a man sitting by it. Nick waited behind the tree and watched. The man looked to be alone. He was sitting there with his head in his hands looking at the fire. Nick stepped out and walked into firelight.

The man sat there looking into the fire. When Nick stopped quite close to him he did not move.

'Hello!' Nick said.

The man looked up.

'Where did you get the shiner?' he said.

'A brakeman busted me.'

'Off the through freight?'

'Yes.'

'I saw the bastard,' the man said. 'He went through here 'bout an hour and a half ago. He was walking along the top of the cars slapping his arms and singing.'

'The bastard!'

'It must have made him feel good to bust you,' the man said seriously.

'I'll bust him.'

'Get him with a rock sometime when he's going through,' the man advised.

'I'll get him.'

'You're a tough one, aren't you?'

'No,' Nick answered.

'All you kids are tough.'

'You got to be tough,' Nick said.

'That's what I said.'

The man looked at Nick and smiled. In the firelight Nick saw that his face was misshapen. His nose was sunken, his eyes were slits, he had queer-shaped lips. Nick did not perceive all this at once, he only saw the man's face was queerly formed and mutilated. It was like putty in color. Dead looking in the firelight.

'Don't you like my pan?' the man asked.

Nick was embarrassed.

'Sure,' he said.

'Look here !' the man took off his cap.

He had only one ear. It was thickened and tight against the side of his head. Where the other should have been there was a stump.

'Ever seen one like that?'

'No,' said Nick. It made him a little sick.

'I could take it,' the man said. 'Don't you think I could take it, kid?'

'You bet !'

'They all bust their hands on me,' the little man said. 'They couldn't hurt me.'

He looked at Nick. 'Sit down,' he said. 'Want to eat?'

'Don't bother,' Nick said. 'I'm going on to the town.'

'Listen !' the man said. 'Call me Ad.'

'Sure !'

'Listen,' the little man said. 'I'm not quite right.'

'What's the matter?'

'I'm crazy.'

He put on his cap. Nick felt like laughing.

'You're all right,' he said.

'No, I'm not. I'm crazy. Listen, you ever been crazy?'

'No,' Nick said. 'How does it get you?'

'I don't know.' Ad said. 'When you got it you don't know about it. You know me, don't you?'

'No.'

'I'm Ad Francis.'

'Honest to God?'

'Don't you believe it?'

'Yes.'

Nick knew it must be true.

'You know how I beat them?'

'No,' Nick said.

'My heart's slow. It only beats forty a minute. Feel it.'

Nick hesitated.

'Come on,' the man took hold of his hand. 'Take hold of my wrist. Put your fingers there.'

The little man's wrist was thick and the muscles bulged above the bone. Nick felt the slow pumping under his fingers.

'Got a watch?'

'No.'

'Neither have I,' Ad said. 'It ain't any good if you haven't got a watch.'

Nick dropped his wrist.

'Listen,' Ad Francis said. 'Take ahold again. You count and I'll count up to sixty.'

Feeling the slow hard throb under his fingers, Nick started to count. He heard the little man counting slowly, one, two, three, four, five, and on – aloud.

'Sixty,' Ad finished. 'That's a minute. What did you make it?'

'Forty,' Nick said.

'That's right,' Ad said happily. 'She never speeds up.'

A man dropped down the railroad embankment and came across the clearing to the fire.

'Hello, Bugs!' Ad said.

'Hello!' Bugs answered. It was a Negro's voice. Nick knew from the way he walked that he was a Negro. He stood with his back to them, bending over the fire. He straightened up.

'This is my pal Bugs,' Ad said. 'He's crazy, too.'

'Glad to meet you,' Bugs said. 'Where you say you're from?'

'Chicago,' Nick said.

'That's a fine town,' the Negro said. 'I didn't catch your name.'

'Adams. Nick Adams.'

'He says he's never been crazy, Bugs,' Ad said.

'He's got a lot coming to him,' the Negro said. He was unwrapping a package by the fire.

'When are we going to eat, Bugs?' the prizefighter asked.

'Right away.'

'Are you hungry, Nick?'

'Hungry as hell.'

'Hear that, Bugs?'

'I hear most of what goes on.'

'That ain't what I asked you.'

'Yes. I heard what the gentleman said.'

Into a skillet he was laying slices of ham. As the skillet grew hot the grease sputtered and Bugs, crouching on long nigger legs over the fire, turned the ham and broke eggs into the skillet, tipping it from side to side to baste the eggs with the hot fat.

'Will you cut some bread out of that bag, Mister Adams?' Bugs turned from the fire.

'Sure.'

Nick reached in the bag and brought out a loaf of bread. He cut six slices. Ad watched him ad leaned forward.

'Let me take your knife, Nick,' he said.

'No, you don't,' the Negro said. 'Hang on to your knife, Mister Adams.'

The prizefighter sat back.

'Will you bring me the bread, Mister Adams?' Bugs asked. Nick brought it over.

'Do you like to dip your bread in the ham fat?' the Negro asked.

'You bet!'

'Perhaps we'd better wait until later. It's better at the finish of the meal. Here.'

The Negro picked up a slice of ham and laid it on one of the pieces of bread, then slid an egg on top of it.

'Just close the sandwich, will you, please, and give it to Mister Francis.'

Ad took the sandwich and started eating.

'Watch out how that egg runs,' the Negro warned. 'This is for you, Mister Adams. The remainder for myself.'

Nick bit into the sandwich. The Negro was sitting opposite him beside Ad. The hot fried ham and eggs tasted wonderful.

'Mister Adams is right hungry,' the Negro said. The little man whom Nick knew by name as a former champion fighter was silent. He had said nothing since the Negro had spoken about the knife.

'May I offer you a slice of bread dipped right in the hot ham fat?' Bugs said.

'Thanks a lot.'

The little white man looked at Nick.

'Will you have some, Mister Adolph Francis?' Bugs offered from the skillet.

Ad did not answer. He was looking at Nick.

'Mister Francis?' came the nigger's soft voice.

Ad did not answer. He was looking at Nick.

'I spoke to you, Mister Francis,' the nigger said softly.

Ad kept on looking at Nick. He had his cap down over his eyes. Nick felt nervous.

'How the hell do you get that way?' came out from under the cap sharply at Nick. 'Who the hell do you think you are? You're a snotty bastard. You come in here where nobody asks you and eat a man's food and when he asks to borrow a knife you get snotty.'

He glared at Nick, his face was white and his eyes almost out of sight under the cap.

'You're a hot sketch. Who the hell asked you to butt in here?'

'Nobody.'

'You're damn right nobody did. Nobody asked you to stay either. You come in here and act snotty about my face and smoke my cigars and drink my liquor and then talk snotty. Where the hell do you think you get off?'

Nick said nothing. Ad stood up.

'I'll tell you, you yellow-livered Chicago bastard. You're going to get your head knocked off. Do you get that?'

Nick stepped back. The little man came toward him slowly, stepping flat-footed forward, his left foot stepping forward, his right dragging up to it.

'Hit me,' he moved his head. 'Try and hit me.'

'I don't want to hit you.'

'You don't get out of it that way. You're going to take a beating, see? Come on and lead at me.'

'Cut it out,' Nick said.

'All right, then, you bastard.'

The little man looked down at Nick's feet. As he looked down the Negro, who had followed behind him as he moved away from the fire, set himself and tapped him across the base of the skull. He fell forward and Bugs dropped the cloth-wrapped blackjack on the grass. The little man lay there, his face in the grass. The Negro picked him up, his head hanging, and carried him to the fire. His face looked bad, the eyes open. Bugs laid him down gently.

'Will you bring me the water in the bucket, Mister Adams?' he said. 'I'm afraid I hit him just a little hard.'

The Negro splashed water with his hand on the man's face and pulled his ear gently. The eyes closed.

Bugs stood up.

'He's all right,' he said. 'There's nothing to worry about. I'm sorry, Mister Adams.'

'It's all right.' Nick was looking down at the little man. He saw the blackjack on the grass and picked it up. It had a flexible handle and was limber in his hand. It was made of worn black leather with a handkerchief wrapped around the heavy end.

'That's a whalebone handle,' the Negro smiled. 'They don't make them any more. I didn't know how well you could take care of yourself and, anyway, I didn't want you to hurt him or mark him up no more than he is.'

The Negro smiled again.

'You hurt him yourself.'

'I know how to do it. He won't remember nothing of it. I have to do it to change him when he gets that way.'

Nick was still looking down at the little man, lying, his eyes closed in the firelight. Bugs put some wood on the fire.

'Don't you worry about him none, Mister Adams. I seen him like this plenty of times before.'

'What made him crazy?' Nick asked.

'Oh, a lot of things,' the Negro answered from the fire. 'Would you like a cup of this coffee, Mister Adams?'

He handed Nick the cup and smoothed the coat he had placed under the unconscious man's head.

'He took too many beatings, for one thing,' the Negro sipped the coffee. 'But that just made him sort of simple. Then his sister was his manager and they was always being written up in the papers all about brothers and sisters and how she loved her brother and how he loved his sister, and then they got married in New York and that made a lot of unpleasantness.'

'I remember about it.'

'Sure. Of course they wasn't brother and sister no more than a rabbit, but there was a lot of people didn't like it either way and they commenced to have disagreements, and one day she just went off and never come back.'

He drank the coffee and wiped his lips with the pink palm of his hand.

'He just went crazy. Will you have some more coffee, Mister Adams?'

'Thanks.'

'I seen her a couple of times,' the Negro went on. 'She was an awful good-looking woman. Looked enough like him to be twins. He wouldn't be bad-looking without his face all busted.'

He stopped. The story seemed to be over.

'Where did you meet him?' asked Nick.

'I met him in jail,' the Negro said. 'He was busting people all the time after she went away and they put him in jail. I was in for cuttin' a man.'

He smiled, and went on soft-voiced:

'Right away I liked him and when I got out I looked him up. He likes to think I'm crazy and I don't mind. I like to be with

him and I like seeing the country and I don't have to commit
no larceny to do it. I like living like a gentleman.'

'What do you all do?' Nicked asked.

'Oh, nothing. Just move around. He's got money.'

'He must have made a lot of money.'

'Sure. He spent all his money, though. Or they took it away
from him. She sends him money.'

He poked up the fire.

'She's a mighty fine woman,' he said. 'She looks enough like
him to be his own twin.'

The Negro looked over at the little man, lying breathing
heavily. His blond hair was down over his forehead. His mutilated face looked childish in repose.

'I can wake him up any time now, Mister Adams. If you
don't mind I wish you'd sort of pull out. I don't like to not be
hospitable, but it might disturb him back again to see you. I
hate to have to thump him and it's the only thing to do when
he gets started. I have to sort of keep him away from people.
You don't mind, do you, Mister Adams? No, don't thank me,
Mister Adams. I'd have warned you about him but he seemed to
have taken such a liking to you and I thought things were going
to be all right. You'll hit a town about two miles up the track.
Mancelona they call it. Good-bye. I wish we could ask you to
stay the night but it's just out of the question. Would you like to
take some of that ham and some bread with you? No? You better
take a sandwich,' all this in a low, smooth, polite nigger voice.

'Good. Well, good-bye, Mister Adams. Good-bye and good
luck !'

Nick walked away from the fire across the clearing to the railway tracks. Out of range of the fire he listened. The low soft voice
of the Negro was talking. Nick could not hear the words. Then
he heard the little man say, 'I got an awful headache, Bugs.'

'You'll feel better, Mister Francis,' the Negro's voice soothed.
'Just you drink a cup of this hot coffee.'

Nick climbed the embankment and started up the track. He
found he had a ham sandwich in his hand and put it in his
pocket. Looking back from the mounting grade before the track
curved into the hills he could see the firelight in the clearing.

Bernard Malamud

THE JEWBIRD

THE window was open so the skinny bird flew in. Flappity-flap with its frazzled black wings. That's how it goes. It's open, you're in. Closed, you're out and that's your fate. The bird wearily flapped through the open window of Harry Cohen's top-floor apartment on First Avenue near the lower East River. On a rod on the wall hung an escaped canary cage, its door wide open, but this black-type long-beaked bird – its ruffled head and small eyes, crossed a little, making it look like a dissipated crow – landed if not smack on Cohen's thick lamb chop, at least on the table, close by. The frozen foods salesman was sitting at supper with his wife and young son on a hot August evening a year ago. Cohen, a heavy man with hairy chest and beefy shorts; Edie, in skinny yellow shorts and red halter; and their ten-year-old Morris (after her father) – Maurie, they called him, a nice kid though not overly bright – were all in the city after two weeks out, because Cohen's mother was dying. They had been enjoying Kingston, New York, but drove back when Mama got sick in her flat in the Bronx.

'Right on the table,' said Cohen, putting down his beer glass and swatting at the bird. 'Son of a bitch.'

'Harry, take care with your language,' Edie said, looking at Maurie, who watched every move.

The bird cawed hoarsely and with a flap of its bedraggled wings – feathers tufted this way and that – rose heavily to the top of the open kitchen door, where it perched staring down.

'Gevalt, a pogrom l'

'It's a talking bird,' said Edie in astonishment.

'In Jewish,' said Maurie.

'Wise guy,' muttered Cohen. He gnawed on his chop, then put down the bone. 'So if you can talk, say what's your business. What do you want here?'

391

'If you can't spare a lamb chop,' said the bird, 'I'll settle for a piece of herring with a crust of bread. You can't live on your nerve for ever.'

'This ain't a restaurant,' Cohen replied. 'All I'm asking is what brings you to this address?'

'The window was open,' the bird sighed; adding after a moment, 'I'm running. I'm flying but I'm also running.'

'From whom?' asked Edie with interest.

'Anti-Semeets.'

'Anti-Semites?' they all said.

'That's from whom.'

'What kind of anti-Semites bother a bird?' Edie asked.

'Any kind,' said the bird, 'also including eagles, vultures, and hawks. And once in a while some crows will take your eyes out.'

'But aren't you a crow?'

'Me? I'm a Jewbird.'

Cohen laughed heartily. 'What do you mean by that?'

The bird began dovening. He prayed without Book or tallith, but with passion. Edie bowed her head though not Cohen. And Maurie rocked back and forth with the prayer, looking up with one wide-open eye.

When the prayer was done Cohen remarked, 'No hat, no phylacteries?'

'I'm an old radical.'

'You're sure you're not some kind of ghost or dybbuk?'

'Not a dybbuk,' answered the bird, 'though one of my relatives had such an experience once. It's all over now, thanks God. They freed her from a former lover, a crazy jealous man. She's now the mother of two wonderful children.'

'Birds?' Cohen asked slyly.

'Why not?'

'What kind of birds?'

'Like me. Jewbirds.'

Cohen tipped back in his chair and guffawed. 'That's a big laugh. I've heard of a Jewfish but not a Jewbird.'

'We're once removed.' The bird rested on one skinny leg, then on the other. 'Please, could you spare maybe a piece of herring with a small crust of bread?'

Edie got up from the table.

'What are you doing?' Cohen asked her.

'I'll clear the dishes.'

Cohen turned to the bird. 'So what's your name, if you don't mind saying?'

'Call me Schwartz.'

'He might be an old Jew changed into a bird by somebody,' said Edie, removing a plate.

'Are you?' asked Harry, lighting a cigar.

'Who knows?' answered Schwartz. 'Does God tell us everything?'

Maurie got up on his chair. 'What kind of herring?' he asked the bird in excitement.

'Get down, Maurie, or you'll fall,' ordered Cohen.

'If you haven't got matjes, I'll take schmaltz,' said Schwartz.

'All we have is marinated, with slices of onion – in a jar,' said Edie.

'If you'll open for me the jar I'll eat marinated. Do you have also, if you don't mind, a piece of rye bread – the spitz?'

Edie thought she had.

'Feed him out on the balcony,' Cohen said. He spoke to the bird. 'After that take off.'

Schwartz closed both bird eyes. 'I'm tired and it's a long way.'

'Which direction are you headed, north or south?'.

Schwartz, barely lifting his wings, shrugged.

'You don't know where you're going?'

'Where there's charity I'll go.'

'Let him stay, papa,' said Maurie. 'He's only a bird.'

'So stay the night,' Cohen said, 'but no longer.'

In the morning Cohen ordered the bird out of the house but Maurie cried, so Schwartz stayed for a while. Maurie was still on vacation from school and his friends were away. He was lonely and Edie enjoyed the fun he had, playing with the bird.

'He's no trouble at all,' she told Cohen, 'and besides his appetite is very small.'

'What'll you do when he makes dirty?'

'He flies across the street in a tree when he makes dirty, and if nobody passes below, who notices?'

'So all right,' said Cohen, 'but I'm dead set against it. I warn you he ain't gonna stay here long.'

'What have you got against the poor bird?'

'Poor bird, my ass. He's a foxy bastard. He thinks he's a Jew.'

'What difference does it make what he thinks?'

'A Jewbird, what a chuzpah. One false move and he's out on his drumsticks.'

At Cohen's insistence Schwartz lived out on the balcony in a new wooden birdhouse Edie had bought him.

'With many thanks,' said Schwartz, 'though I would rather have a human roof over my head. You know how it is at my age. I like the warm, the windows, the smell of cooking. I would also be glad to see once in a while the *Jewish Morning Journal* and have now and then a schnapps because it helps my breathing, thanks God. But whatever you give me, you won't hear complaints.'

However, when Cohen brought home a bird feeder full of dried corn, Schwartz said, 'Impossible.'

Cohen was annoyed. 'What's the matter, crosseyes, is your life getting too good for you? Are you forgetting what it means to be migratory? I'll bet a helluva lot of crows you happen to be acquainted with, Jews or otherwise, would give their eyeteeth to eat this corn.'

Schwartz did not answer. What can you say to a grubber yung?

'Not for my digestion,' he later explained to Edie. 'Cramps. Herring is better even if it makes you thirsty. At least rainwater don't cost anything.' He laughed sadly in breathy caws.

And herring, thanks to Edie, who knew where to shop, was what Schwartz got, with an occasional piece of potato pancake, and even a bit of soupmeat when Cohen wasn't looking.

When school began in September, before Cohen would once again suggest giving the bird the boot, Edie prevailed on him to wait a little while until Maurie adjusted.

'To deprive him right now might hurt his school work, and you know what trouble we had last year.'

'So okay, but sooner or later the bird goes. That I promise you'.

Schwartz, though nobody had asked him, took on full responsibility for Maurie's performance in school. In return for favours granted, when he was let in for an hour or two at night, he spent most of his time overseeing the boy's lessons. He sat on top of the dresser near Maurie's desk as he laboriously wrote out his homework. Maurie was a restless type and Schwartz gently kept him to his studies. He also listened to him practise his screechy violin, taking a few minutes off now and then to rest his ears in the bathroom. And they afterwards played dominoes. The boy was an indifferent checkers player and it was impossible to teach him chess. When he was sick, Schwartz read him comic books though he personally disliked them. But Maurie's work improved in school and even his violin teacher admitted his playing was better. Edie gave Schwartz credit for these improvements though the bird pooh-poohed them.

Yet he was proud there was nothing lower than C minuses on Maurie's report card, and on Edie's insistence celebrated with a little schnapps.

'If he keeps up like this,' Cohen said, 'I'll get him in an Ivy League college for sure.'

'Oh I hope so,' sighed Edie.

But Schwartz shook his head. 'He's a good boy – you don't have to worry. He won't be a shicker or a wifebeater, God forbid, but a scholar he'll never be, if you know what I mean, although maybe a good mechanic. It's no disgrace in these times.'

'If I were you,' Cohen said, angered, 'I'd keep my big snoot out of other people's private business.'

'Harry, please,' said Edie.

'My goddamn patience is wearing out. That crosseyes butts into everything.'

Though he wasn't exactly a welcome guest in the house, Schwartz gained a few ounces although he did not improve in appearance. He looked bedraggled as ever, his feathers unkempt, as though he had just flown out of a snowstorm. He spent, he admitted, little time taking care of himself. Too much to think about. 'Also outside plumbing,' he told Edie. Still there was more glow to his eyes so that though Cohen went on calling him crosseyes he said it less emphatically.

Liking his situation, Schwartz tried tactfully to stay out of

Cohen's way, but one night when Edie was at the movies and Maurie was taking a hot shower, the frozen foods salesman began a quarrel with the bird.

'For Christ sake, why don't you wash yourself sometimes? Why must you always stink like a dead fish?'

'Mr Cohen, if you'll pardon me, if somebody eats garlic he will smell from garlic. I eat herring three times a day. Feed me flowers and I will smell like flowers.'

'Who's obligated to feed you anything at all? You're lucky to get herring.'

'Excuse me, I'm not complaining,' said the bird. 'You're complaining.'

'What's more,' said Cohen, 'even from out on the balcony I can hear you snoring away like a pig. It keeps me awake at night.'

'Snoring,' said Schwartz, 'isn't a crime, thanks God.'

'All in all you are a goddamn pest and free loader. Next thing you'll want to sleep in bed next to my wife.'

'Mr Cohen,' said Schwartz, 'on this, rest assured. A bird is a bird.'

'So you say, but how do I know you're a bird and not some kind of a goddamn devil?'

'If I was a devil you would know already. And I don't mean because your son's good marks.'

'Shut up, you bastard bird,' shouted Cohen.

'Grubber yung,' cawed Schwartz, rising to the tips of his talons, his long wings outstretched.

Cohen was about to lunge for the bird's scrawny neck but Maurie came out of the bathroom, and for the rest of the evening until Schwartz's bedtime on the balcony, there was pretended peace.

But the quarrel had deeply disturbed Schwartz and he slept badly. His snoring woke him, and awake, he was fearful of what would become of him. Wanting to stay out of Cohen's way, he kept to the birdhouse as much as possible. Cramped by it, he paced back and forth on the balcony ledge, or sat on the birdhouse roof, staring into space. In the evenings, while overseeing Maurie's lessons, he often fell asleep. Awakening, he nervously hopped around exploring the four corners of the room. He spent much time in Maurie's closet, and carefully examined his bureau drawers when they were left open. And once when he found a large paper bag on the floor, Schwartz poked his way into it to investigate what possibilities were. The boy was amused to see the bird in the paper bag.

'He wants to build a nest,' he said to his mother.

Edie, sensing Schwartz's unhappiness, spoke to him quietly.

'Maybe if you did some of the things my husband wants you, you would get along better with him.'

'Give me a for instance,' Schwartz said.

'Like take a bath, for instance.'

'I'm too old for baths,' said the bird. 'My feathers fall out without baths.'

'He says you have a bad smell.'

'Everybody smells. Some people smell because of their thoughts or because who they are. My bad smell comes from the food I eat. What does his comes from?'

'I better not ask him or it might make him mad,' said Edie.

In late November Schwartz froze on the balcony in the fog and cold, and especially on rainy days he woke with stiff joints and could barely move his wings. Already he felt twinges of rheumatism. He would have liked to spend more time in the warm house, particularly when Maurie was in school and Cohen at work. But though Edie was good-hearted and might have sneaked him in in the morning, just to thaw out, he was afraid to ask her. In the meantime Cohen, who had been reading articles about the migration of birds, came out on the balcony one night after work when Edie was in the kitchen preparing pot roast, and peeking into the birdhouse, warned Schwartz to be on his way soon if he knew what was good for him. 'Time to hit the flyways.'

'Mr Cohen, why do you hate me so much?' asked the bird. 'What did I do to you?'

'Because you're an A-number-one trouble maker, that's why. What's more, whoever heard of a Jewbird? Now scat or it's open war.'

But Schwartz stubbornly refused to depart so Cohen embarked on a campaign of harassing him, meanwhile hiding it from Edie and Maurie. Maurie hated violence and Cohen didn't want to leave a bad impression. He thought maybe if he played dirty tricks on the bird he would fly off without being physically kicked out. The vacation was over, let him make his easy living off the fat of somebody else's land. Cohen worried about the effect of the bird's departure on Maurie's schooling but decided to take the chance, first because the boy now seemed to have the knack of studying – give the black bird-bastard credit – and second, because Schwartz was driving him bats by being there always, even in his dreams.

The frozen foods salesman began his campaign against the bird by mixing watery cat food with the herring slices in Schwart's dish. He also blew up and popped numerous paper bags outside the birdhouse as the bird slept, and when he had got Schwartz good and nervous, though not enough to leave, he brought a full-grown cat into the house, supposedly a gift for little Maurie, who had always wanted a pussy. The cat never stopped springing up at Schwartz whenever he saw him, one day managing to claw out several of his tailfeathers. And even at lesson time, when the cat was usually excluded from Maurie's room, though somehow or other he quickly found his way in at the end of the lesson, Schwartz was desperately fearful of his life and flew from pinnacle to pinnacle – light fixture to clothes-tree to door-top – in order to elude the beast's wet jaws.

Once when the bird complained to Edie how hazardous his existence was, she said, 'Be patient, Mr Schwartz. When the cat gets to know you better he won't try to catch you any more.'

'When he stops trying we will both be in Paradise,' Schwartz answered. 'Do me a favour and get rid of him. He makes my whole life worry. I'm losing feathers like a tree loses leaves.'

'I'm awfully sorry but Maurie likes the pussy and sleeps with it.'

What could Schwartz do? He worried but came to no decision, being afraid to leave. So he ate the herring garnished with cat food, tried hard not to hear the paper bags bursting like fire crackers outside the birdhouse at night, and lived terror-stricken closer to the ceiling than the floor, as the cat, his tail flicking, endlessly watched him.

Weeks went by. Then on the day after Cohen's mother had died in her flat in the Bronx, when Maurie came home with a zero on an arithmetic test, Cohen, enraged, waited until Edie had taken the boy to his violin lesson, then openly attacked the bird. He chased him with a broom on the balcony and Schwartz frantically flew back and forth, finally escaping into his birdhouse. Cohen triumphantly reached in, and grabbing both skinny legs, dragged the bird out, cawing loudly, his wings wildly beating. He whirled the bird around and around his head. But Schwartz, as he moved in circles, managed to swoop down and catch Cohen's nose in his beak, and hung on for dear life. Cohen cried out in great pain, punched the bird with his fist, and tugging at its legs with all his might, pulled his nose free. Again he swung the yawking Schwartz around until the bird grew dizzy, then with a furious heave, flung him into the night. Schwartz sank like stone into the street. Cohen then tossed the birdhouse and feeder after him, listening at the ledge until they crashed on the sidewalk below. For a full hour, broom in hand, his heart palpitating and nose throbbing with pain, Cohen waited for Schwartz to return but the broken-hearted bird didn't.

That's the end of that dirty bastard, the salesman thought and went in. Edie and Maurie had come home.

'Look,' said Cohen, pointing to his bloody nose swollen three times its normal size, 'what that sonofabitchy bird did. It's a permanent scar.'

'Where is he now?' Edie asked, frightened.

'I threw him out and he flew away. Good riddance.'

Nobody said no, though Edie touched a handkerchief to her eyes and Maurie rapidly tried the nine-times table and found he knew approximately half.

In the spring when the winter's snow had melted, the boy, moved by a memory, wandered in the neighbourhood, looking for Schwartz. He found a dead black bird in a small lot near the river, his two wings broken, neck twisted, and both bird-eyes plucked clean.

'Who did it to you, Mr Schwartz?' Mauric wept.

'Anti-Semeets,' Edie said later.

Truman Capote

CHILDREN ON THEIR BIRTHDAYS

(This story is for Andrew Lyndon)

YESTERDAY afternoon the six-o'clock bus ran over Miss Bobbit. I'm not sure what there is to be said about it; after all, she was only ten years old, still I know no one of us in this town will forget her. For one thing, nothing she ever did was ordinary, not from the first time that we saw her, and that was a year ago. Miss Bobbit and her mother, they arrived on that same six-o'clock bus, the one that comes through from Mobile. It happened to be my cousin Billy Bob's birthday, and so most of the children in town were here at our house. We were sprawled off the front porch having tutti-frutti and devil cake when the bus stormed around Deadman's Curve. It was the summer that never rained; rusted dryness coated everything; sometimes when a car passed on the road, raised dust would hang in the still air an hour or more. Aunt El said if they didn't pave the highway soon she was going to move down to the sea-coast; but she'd said that for such a long time. Anyway, we were sitting on the porch, tutti-frutti melting on our plates, when suddenly, just as we were wishing that something would happen, something did; for out of the red road dust appeared Miss Bobbit. A wiry little girl in a starched, lemon-colored party dress, she sassed along with a grown-up mince, one hand on her hip, the other supporting a spinsterish umbrella. Her mother, lugging two cardboard valises and a wind-up victrola, trailed in the background. She was a gaunt shaggy woman with silent eyes and a hungry smile.

All the children on the porch had grown so still that when a cone of wasps started humming the girls did not set up their usual holler. Their attention was too fixed upon the approach of Miss Bobbit and her mother, who had by now reached the gate. 'Begging your pardon,' called Miss Bobbit in a voice that was at once silky and childlike, like a pretty piece of ribbon, and immaculately exact, like a movie-star or a schoolmarm, 'but might we speak with the grownup persons of the house?' This, of course, meant Aunt El; and, at least to some degree, myself. But Billy Bob and all the other boys, no one of whom was over fourteen, followed down to the gate after us. From their faces you would have thought they'd never seen a girl before. Certainly not like Miss Bobbit. As Aunt El said, whoever heard tell of a child wearing make-up? Tangee gave her lips an orange glow, her hair, rather like a costume wig, was a mass of rosy curls, and her eyes had a knowing pencilled tilt; even so, she had a skinny dignity, she was a lady, and, what is more, she looked you in the eye with manlike directness. 'I'm Miss Lily Jane Bobbit, Miss Bobbit from Memphis, Tennessee,' she said solemnly. The boys looked down at their toes, and, on the porch, Cora McCall, who Billy Bob was courting at the time, led the girls into a fanfare of giggles. 'Country children,' said Miss Bobbit with an understanding smile, and gave her parasol a saucy whirl. 'My mother,' and this homely woman allowed an abrupt nod to acknowledge herself, 'my mother and I have taken rooms here. Would you be so kind as to point out the house? It belongs to a Mrs Sawyer.' Why, sure, said Aunt El, that's Mrs Sawyer's, right there across the street. The only boarding house around here, it is an old tall dark place with about two dozen lightning rods scattered on the roof: Mrs Sawyer is scared to death in a thunderstorm.

Coloring like an apple, Billy Bob said, please, ma'am, it being such a hot day and all, wouldn't they rest a spell and have some tutti-frutti? and Aunt El said yes, by all means, but Miss Bobbit shook her head. 'Very fattening, tutti-frutti; but *merci* you very kindly,' and they started across the road, the mother half-dragging her parcels in the dust. Then, and with an earnest expression, Miss Bobbit turned back; the sunflower yellow of her eyes darkened, and she rolled them slightly sideways, as if trying to remember a poem. 'My mother has a disorder of the tongue, so it is necessary that I speak for her,' she announced rapidly and heaved a sigh. 'My mother is a very fine seamstress; she has made dresses for the society of many cities and towns, including Memphis and Tallahassee. No doubt you have noticed and admired the dress I am wearing. Every stitch of it was handsewn by my mother. My mother can copy any pattern, and just recently she won a twenty-five-dollar prize from the *Ladies' Home Journal*. My mother can also crochet, knit and embroider. If you want any kind of sewing done, please come to my mother. Please advise your friends and family. Thank you.' And then, with a rustle and a swish, she was gone.

Cora McCall and the girls pulled their hair-ribbons nervously, suspiciously, and looked very put out and prune-faced. I'm *Miss* Bobbit, said Cora, twisting her face into an evil imitation, and I'm Princess Elizabeth, that's who I am, ha, ha, ha. Furthermore, said Cora, that dress was just as tacky as could be; personally, Cora said, all my clothes come from Atlanta; plus a pair of shoes from New York, which is not even to mention my silver turquoise ring all the way from Mexico City, Mexico. Aunt El said they ought not to behave that way about a fellow child, a stranger in the town, but the girls went on like a huddle of witches, and certain boys, the sillier ones that liked to be with the girls, joined in and said things that made Aunt El go red and declare she was going to send them all home and tell their daddies, to boot. But before she could carry forward this threat Miss Bobbit herself intervened by traipsing across the Sawyer porch, costumed in a new and startling manner.

The older boys, like Billy Bob and Preacher Star, who had sat quietly while the girls razzed Miss Bobbit, and who had watched the house into which she'd disappeared with misty, ambitious faces, they now straightened up and ambled down to the gate. Cora McCall sniffed and poked out her lower lip, but the rest of us went and sat on the steps. Miss Bobbit paid us no mind whatever. The Sawyer yard is dark with mulberry trees and it is planted with grass and sweet shrub. Sometimes after a rain you can smell the sweet shrub all the way into our house; and in the centre of this yard there is a sundial which Mrs Sawyer installed in 1912 as a memorial to her Boston bull, Sunny, who died after having lapped up a bucket of paint. Miss Bobbit pranced into the yard toting the victrola, which she put on the sundial; she wound it up, and started a record playing, and it played the Count of Luxembourg. By now it was almost nightfall, a firefly hour, blue as milkglass; and birds like arrows swooped together and swept into the folds of trees. Before storms, leaves and flowers appear to burn with a private light, color, and Miss Bobbit, got up in a little white skirt like a powder-puff and with strips of gold-glittering tinsel ribboning her hair, seemed set against the darkening all around, to contain this illuminated quality. She held her arms arched over her head, her hands lily-limp, and stood straight up on the tips of her toes. She stood that way for a good long while, and Aunt El said it was right smart of her. Then she began to waltz around and around, and around and around she went until Aunt El said, why, she was plain dizzy from the sight. She stopped only when it was time to re-wind the victrola; and when the moon came rolling down the ridge, and the last supper bell had sounded, and all the children had gone home, and the night iris was beginning to bloom, Miss Bobbit was still there in the dark turning like a top.

We did not see her again for some time. Preacher Star came every morning to our house and stayed straight through to supper. Preacher is a rail-thin boy with a butchy shock of red hair; he has eleven brothers and sisters, and even they are afraid of him, for he has a terrible temper, and is famous in these parts for his green-eyed meanness: last fourth of July he whipped Ollie Overton so bad that Ollie's family had to send him to the hospital in Pensacola, and there was another time he bit off half a mule's ear, chewed it and spit it on the ground. Before Billy Bob got his growth, Preacher played the devil with him, too. He used to drop cockleburrs down his collar, and rub pepper in his eyes, and tear up his homework. But now they are the biggest friends in town: talk alike, walk alike; and occasionally they disappear together for whole days, Lord knows where to. But during these days when Miss Bobbit did not appear they stayed close to the house. They would stand around in the yard trying to slingshot sparrows off telephone poles, or sometimes Billy Bob would play his ukelele, and they would sing so loud Uncle Billy Bob, who is Judge for this county, claimed he could hear them all the way to the court-house: *send me a letter, send it by mail, send it in the care of the Birmingham jail.* Miss Bobbit did not hear them; at least she never poked her head out of the door. Then one day Mrs Sawyer, coming over to borrow a cup of sugar, rattled on a good deal about her new boarders. You know she said, squinting her chicken-bright eyes, the husband was a crook, uh huh, the child told me herself. Hasn't an ounce of shame, not a mite. Said her daddy was the dearest daddy and the sweetest singing man in the whole of Tennessee. ... And I said, honey, where is he? and just as offhand as you please she says, Oh, he's in the penitentiary and we don't hear from him no more. Say, now, does that make your blood run cold? Uh huh, and I been thinking, her mama, I been thinking she's some kinda foreigner: never says a word, and sometimes it looks like she don't understand what nobody says to her. And you know, they eat everything *raw. Raw eggs, raw turnips, carrots* – no meat whatsoever. For reasons of health, the child says, but ho! she's been straight out on the bed running a fever since last Tuesday.

That same afternoon Aunt El went out to water her roses, only to discover them gone. These were special roses, ones she'd planned to send to the flower show in Mobile, and so naturally she got a little hysterical. She rang up the Sheriff, and said, listen here, Sheriff, you come over here right fast. I mean somebody's got off with all my Lady Anne's that I've devoted myself to heart and soul since early spring. When the Sheriff's car pulled up outside our house, all the neighbors along the street came out on their porches, and Mrs Sawyer, layers of cold cream whitening her face, trotted across the road. Oh shoot, she said, very disappointed to find no one had been murdered, oh shoot, she said, nobody's stole them roses. Your Billy Bob brought them roses over and left them for little Bobbit. Aunt El did not say one word. She just marched over to the peach tree, and cut herself a switch. Ohhh, Billy Bob, she stalked along the street calling his name, and then she found him down at Speedy's garage where he and Preacher were watching Speedy take a motor apart. She simply lifted him by the hair and, switching blueblazes, towed him home. But she couldn't make him say he was sorry and she couldn't make him cry. And when she was finished with him he ran into the backyard and climbed high into the tower of a pecan tree and swore he wasn't ever going to come down. Then his daddy came home, and it was time to have supper. His daddy stood at the window and called to him: Son, we aren't mad with you, so come down and eat your supper. But Billy Bob wouldn't budge. Aunt El went and leaned against the tree. She spoke in a voice soft as the gathering light. I'm sorry, son, she said, I didn't mean whipping you so hard like that. I've fixed a nice supper, son, potato salad and boiled ham and devilled eggs. Go away, said Billy Bob, I don't want no supper, and I hate you like all-fire. His daddy said he ought not to talk like that to his mother, and she began to cry. She stood there under the tree and cried, raising the hem of her skirt to dab at her eyes. I don't hate you, son. ... If I don't love you I wouldn't whip you. The pecan leaves began to rattle; Billy Bob slid slowly to the ground, and Aunt El, brushing her fingers through his hair, pulled him against her. Aw, Ma, he said, Aw, Ma.

After supper Billy Bob came and flung himself on the foot of my bed. He smelled all sour and sweet, the way boys do, and I felt very sorry for him, especially because he looked so worried. His eyes were almost shut with worry. You're s'posed to send sick folks flowers, he said righteously. About this time we heard the victrola, a lilting faraway sound, and a night moth flew through the window, drifting in the air delicate as the music. But it was dark now, and we couldn't tell if Miss Bobbit was dancing. Billy Bob, as though he were in pain, doubled up on the bed like a jack-knife; but his face was suddenly clear, his grubby boy-eyes twitching like candles. She's so cute, he whispered, she's the cutest dickens I ever saw, gee, to hell with it, I don't care, I'd pick all the roses in China.

Preacher would have picked all the roses in China, too. He was as crazy about her as Billy Bob. But Miss Bobbit did not notice them. The sole communication we had with her was a note to Aunt El thanking her for the flowers. Day after day she sat on her porch, always dressed to beat the band, and doing a piece of embroidery, or combing curls in her hair, or reading a Webster's dictionary – formal, but friendly enough; if you said good day to her she said good day to you. Even so, the boys never could seem to get up the nerve to go over and talk with her, and most of the time she simply looked through them, even when they tomcatted up and down the street trying to get her eye. They wrestled, played Tarzan, did foolheaded bicycle tricks. It was a sorry business. A great many girls in town strolled by the Sawyer house two and three times within an hour just on the chance of getting a look. Some of the girls who did this were: Cora McCall, Mary Murphy Jones, Janice Ackerman. Miss Bobbit did not show any interest in them either. Cora would not speak to Billy Bob any more. The same was true with Janice and Preacher. As a matter of fact, Janice wrote Preacher a letter in red ink on lace-trimmed paper in which she told him he was vile beyond all human beings and words, that she considered their engagement broken, that he could have back the stuffed squirrel he'd given her. Preacher, saying he wanted to act nice, stopped her the next time she passed our house, and said, well, hell, she could keep that old squirrel if she wanted to. Afterwards, he couldn't understand why Janice ran away bawling the way she did.

Then one day the boys were being crazier than usual; Billy Bob was sagging around in his daddy's World War khakis, and Preacher, stripped to the waist, had a naked woman drawn on his chest with one of Aunt El's old lipsticks. They looked like perfect fools, but Miss Bobbit, reclining in a swing, merely yawned. It was noon, and there was no one passing in the street, except a colored girl, baby-fat and sugar-plum shaped, who hummed along carrying a pail of blackberries. But the boys, teasing at her like gnats, joined hands and wouldn't let her go by, not until she paid a tariff. I ain't studyin' no tariff, she said, what kinda tariff you talking about, mister? A party in the barn, said Preacher, between clenched teeth, mighty nice party in the barn. And she, with a sulky shrug, said, huh, she intended studyin' no barn parties. Whereupon Billy Bob capsized her berry pail, and when she, with despairing, piglike shrieks, bent down in futile gestures of rescue, Preacher, who can be mean as the devil, gave her behind a kick which sent her sprawling jellylike among the blackberries and the dust. Miss Bobbit came tearing across the road, her finger wagging like a metronome; like a schoolteacher she clapped her hands, stamped her foot, and said: 'It is a well-known fact that gentlemen are put on the face of the earth for the protection of ladies. Do you suppose boys behave this way in towns like Memphis, New York, London, Hollywood or Paris?' The boys hung back, and shoved their hands in their pockets. Miss Bobbit helped the colored girl to her feet; she dusted her off, dried her eyes, held out a handkerchief and told her to blow. 'A pretty pass,' she said, 'a fine situation when a lady can't walk safely in the public daylight.

Then the two of them went back and sat on Mrs Sawyer's porch; and for the next year they were never far apart, Miss Bobbit and this baby elephant, whose name was Rosalba Cat. At first, Mrs Sawyer raised a fuss about Rosalba being so much at her house. She told Aunt El that it went against the grain to have a nigger lolling smack there in plain sight on her front porch. But Miss Bobbit had a certain magic, whatever she did she did it with completeness, and so directly, so solemnly, that there was nothing to do but accept it. For instance, the tradespeople in town used to snicker when they called her *Miss* Bobbit; but by and by she was Miss Bobbit, and they gave her stiff little bows as she whirled by spinning her parasol. Miss Bobbit told everyone that Rosalba was her sister, which caused a good many jokes; but like most of her ideas, it gradually seemed natural, and when we would overhear them calling each other Sister Rosalba and Sister Bobbit none of us cracked a smile. But Sister Rosalba and Sister Bobbit did some queer things. There was the business about the dogs. Now there are a great many dogs in this town, rat-terriers, bird-dogs, bloodhounds; they trail along the forlorn noon-hot streets in sleepy herds of six to a dozen, all waiting only for dark and the moon, when straight through the lonesome hours you can hear them howling: someone is dying, someone is dead. Miss Bobbit complained to the Sheriff; she said that certain of the dogs always planted themselves under her window, and that she was a light sleeper to begin with; what is more, and as Sister Rosalba said, she did not believe they were dogs at all, but some kind of devil. Naturally the Sheriff did nothing; and so she took the matter into her own hands. One morning, after an especially loud night, she was seen stalking through the town with Rosalba at her side, Rosalba carrying a flower basket filled with rocks; whenever they saw a dog they paused while Miss Bobbit scrutinized him. Sometimes she would shake her head, but more often she said, 'Yes, that's one of them, Sister Rosalba,' and Sister Rosalba, with ferocious aim, would take a rock from her basket and crack the dog between the eyes.

Another thing that happened concerns Mr Henderson. Mr Henderson has a back room in the Sawyer house; a tough runt of a man who formerly was a wildcat oil prospector in Oklahoma, he is about seventy years old and, like a lot of old men, obsessed by functions of the body. Also, he is a terrible drunk. One time he had been drunk for two weeks; whenever he heard Miss Bobbit and Sister Rosalba moving around the house, he would charge to the top of the stairs and bellow down to Mrs Sawyer that there were midgets in the walls trying to get at his supply of toilet paper. They've already stolen fifteen cents' worth, he said. One evening, when the two girls were sitting under a tree in the yard, Mr Henderson, sporting nothing more than a nightshirt, stamped out after them. Steal all my toilet paper, will you? he hollered, I'll show you midgets. ... Somebody come help me, else these midget bitches are liable to make off with every sheet in town. It was Billy Bob and Preacher who caught Mr Henderson and held him until some grown men arrived and began to tie him up. Miss Bobbit, who had behaved with admirable calm, told the men they did not know how to tie a proper knot, and undertook to do so herself. She did such a good job that all the circulation stopped in Mr Henderson's hands and feet and it was a month before he could walk again.

It was shortly afterwards that Miss Bobbit paid us a call. She came on Sunday and I was there alone, the family having gone to church. 'The odors of a church are so offensive,' she said, leaning forward and with her hands folded primly before her. 'I don't want you to think I'm a heathen, Mr C.; I've had enough experience to know that there is a God and that there is a Devil. But the way to tame the Devil is not to go down there to church and listen to what a sinful mean fool he is. No, love the Devil like you do Jesus: because he is a powerful man, and will do you a good turn if he knows you trust him. He has frequently done me good turns, like at dancing school in Memphis. ... I always called in the Devil to help me get the biggest part in our annual show. That is common sense; you see, I knew Jesus wouldn't have any truck with dancing. Now, as a matter of fact, I have called in the Devil just recently. He is the only one who can help me get out of this town. Not that I live here, not exactly. I think always about somewhere else, somewhere else where everything is dancing, like people dancing in the streets, and everything is pretty, like children on their birthdays. My precious papa said I live in the sky, but if he'd lived more in the sky he'd be rich like he wanted to be. The trouble with my papa was he did not love the Devil, he let the Devil love him. But I am very smart in that respect, I know the next best thing is very often the best. It was the next best thing for us to move to this town; and since I can't pursue my career here, the next best thing for me is to start a little business on the side. Which is what I have done. I am sole subscription agent in this county for an impressive list of magazines, including *Reader's Digest, Popular Mechanics, Dime Detective* and *Child's Life*. To be sure, Mr C., I'm not here to sell you anything. But I have a thought in mind. I was thinking those two boys that are always hanging around here, it occurred to me that they are men, after all. Do you suppose they would make a pair of likely assistants?'

Billy Bob and Preacher worked hard for Miss Bobbit, and for Sister Rosalba, too. Sister Rosalba carried a line of cosmetics called Dewdrop, and it was part of the boys' job to deliver purchases to her customers. Billy Bob used to be so tired in the evening he could hardly chew his supper. Aunt El said it was a shame and a pity, and finally one day when Billy Bob came down with a touch of sunstroke she said, all right, that settled it, Billy Bob would just have to quit Miss Bobbit. But Billy Bob cursed her out until his daddy had to lock him in his room; whereupon he said he was going to kill himself. Some cook we'd had told him once that if you ate a mess of collards all slopped over with molasses it would kill you sure as shooting; and so that is what he did. I'm dying, he said, rolling back and forth on his bed, I'm dying and nobody cares.

Miss Bobbit came over and told him to hush up. 'There's nothing wrong with you, boy,' she said. 'All you've got is a stomach ache.' Then she did something that shocked Aunt El very much: she stripped the covers off Billy Bob and rubbed him down with alcohol from head to toe. When Aunt El told her she did not think that was a nice thing for a little girl to do, Miss Bobbit replied: 'I don't know whether it's nice or not, but it's certainly very refreshing.' After which Aunt El did all she could to keep Billy Bob from going back to work for her, but his daddy said to leave him alone, they would have to let the boy lead his own life.

Miss Bobbit was very honest about money. She paid Billy Bob and Preacher their exact commission and she never let them treat her, as they often tried to do, at the drugstore or to the picture-show. 'You'd better save your money,' she told them. 'That is, if you want to go to college. Because neither one of you has got the brains to win a scholarship, not even a football scholarship.' But it was over money that Billy Bob and Preacher had a big falling out; that was not the real reason, of course: the real reason was that they had grown cross-eyed jealous over Miss Bobbit. So one day, and he had the gall to do this right in front of Billy Bob, Preacher said to Miss Bobbit that she'd better check her accounts carefully because he had more than a suspicion that Billy Bob wasn't turning over to her all the money he collected. That's a damned lie, said Billy Bob, and with a clean left hook he knocked Preacher off the Sawyer porch and jumped after him into a bed of nasturtiums. But once Preacher got a hold on him, Billy Bob didn't stand a chance. Preacher even rubbed dirt in his eyes. During all this, Mrs Sawyer, leaning out an upper-storey window, screamed like an eagle, and Sister Rosalba, fatly cheerful, ambiguously shouted, Kill him! Kill him! Kill him! Only Miss Bobbit seemed to know what she was doing. She plugged in the lawn hose, and gave the boys a close-up, blinding bath. Gasping, Preacher staggered to his feet. Oh, honey, he said, shaking himself like a wet dog, honey, you've got to decide. 'Decide *what*?' said Miss Bobbit, right away in a huff. Oh, honey, wheezed Preacher, you don't want us boys killing each other. You got to decide who is your real true sweetheart. 'Sweetheart, my eye,' said Miss Bobbit. 'I should've known better than to get myself involved with a lot of country children. What sort of businessman are you going to make? Now, you listen here, Preacher Star : I don't want a sweetheart, and if I did, it wouldn't be you. As a matter of fact, you don't even get up when a lady enters the room.'

Preacher spit on the ground and swaggered over to Billy Bob. Come on, he said, just as though nothing had happened, she's a hard one, she is, she don't want nothing but to make trouble between two good friends. For a moment it looked as if Billy Bob was going to join him in a peaceful togetherness; but suddenly, coming to his senses, he drew back and made a gesture. The boys regarded each other a full minute, all the closeness between them turning an ugly colour : you can't hate so much unless you love, too. And Preacher's face showed all of this. But there was nothing for him to do except go away. Oh, yes, Preacher, you looked so lost that day that for the first time I really liked you, so skinny and mean and lost going down the road all by yourself.

They did not make it up, Preacher and Billy Bob; and it was not because they didn't want to, it was only that there did not seem to be any straight way for their friendship to happen again. But they couldn't get rid of this friendship: each was always aware of what the other was up to; and when Preacher found himself a new buddy, Billy Bob moped around for days, picking things up, dropping them again, or doing sudden wild things, like purposely poking his finger in the electric fan. Some times in the evenings Preacher would pause by the gate and talk with Aunt El. It was only to torment Billy Bob, I suppose, but he stayed friendly with all of us, and at Christmas time he gave us a huge box of shelled peanuts. He left a present for Billy Bob, too. It turned out to be a book of Sherlock Holmes; and on the flyleaf there was scribbled, 'Friends Like Ivy On The Wall Must Fall'. That's the corniest thing I ever saw, Billy Bob said. Jesus, what a dope he is! But then, and though it was a cold winter day, he went in the backyard and climbed up into the pecan tree, crouching there all afternoon in the blue December branches.

But most of the time he was happy, because Miss Bobbit was there, and she was always sweet to him now. She and Sister Rosalba treated him like a man; that is to say, they allowed him to do everything for them. On the other hand, they let him win at three-handed bridge, they never questioned his lies, nor discouraged his ambitions. It was a happy while. However, trouble started again when school began. Miss Bobbit refused to go. 'It's ridiculous,' she said, when one day the principal, Mr Copland, came around to investigate, 'really ridiculous; I can read and write and there are *some* people in this town who have every reason to know that I can count money. No, Mr Copland, consider for a moment and you will see neither of us has the time nor energy. After all, it would only be a matter of whose spirit broke first, yours or mine. And besides, what is there for you to teach me? Now, if you knew anything about dancing, that would be another matter; but under the circumstances, yes, Mr Copland, under the circumstances, I suggest we forget the whole thing.' Mr Copland was perfectly willing to. But the rest of the town thought she ought to be whipped. Horace Deasley wrote a piece in the paper which was titled 'A Tragic Situation'. It was, in his opinion, a tragic situation when a small girl could defy what he, for some reason, termed the Constitution of the United States. The article ended with a question: *Can she get away with it?* She did; and so did Sister Rosalba. Only she was colored, so no one cared. Billy Bob was not so lucky. It was school for him, all right; but he might as well have stayed home for all the good it did him. On his first report card he got three Fs, a record of some sort. But he is a smart boy. I guess he just couldn't live through those hours without Miss Bobbit; away from her he always seemed half-asleep. He was always in a fight, too; either his eye was black, or his lip was split, or his walk had a limp. He never talked about these fights, but Miss Bobbit was shrewd enough to guess the reason why. 'You are a dear, I know. And I appreciate you, Billy Bob. Only don't fight with people because of me. Of course they say mean things about me. But do you know why that is, Billy Bob? It's a compliment, kind of. Because deep down they think I'm absolutely wonderful.'

And she was right: if you are not admired no one will take the trouble to disapprove. But actually we had no idea of how wonderful she was until there appeared the man known as Manny Fox. This happened late in February. The first news we had of Manny Fox was a series of jovial placards posted up in the stores around town: Manny Fox Presents the Fan Dancer Without the Fan; then, in smaller print: Also, Sensational Amateur Programme Featuring Your Own Neighbors – First Prize, A Genuine Hollywood Screen Test. All this was to take place the following Thursday. The tickets were priced at one dollar each, which around here is a lot of money; but it is not often that we get any kind of flesh entertainment, so everybody shelled out their money and made a great to-do over the whole thing. The drugstore cowboys talked dirty all week, mostly about the fan dancer without the fan, who turned out to be Mrs Manny Fox. They stayed down the highway at the Chuckle-wood Tourist Camp; but they were in town all day, driving around in an old Packard which had Manny Fox's full name stencilled on all four doors. His wife was a deadpan pimento-tongued redhead with wet lips and moist eyelids; she was quite large actually, but compared to Manny Fox she seemed rather frail, for he was a fat cigar of a man.

They made the pool hall their headquarters, and every afternoon you could find them there, drinking beer and joking with the town loafs. As it developed, Manny Fox's business affairs were not restricted to theatrics. He also ran a kind of employment bureau: slowly he let it be known that for a fee of $150 he could get for any adventurous boys in the county high-class jobs working on fruit ships sailing from New Orleans to South America. The chance of a lifetime, he called it. There are not two boys around here who readily lay their hands on so much as five dollars; nevertheless, a good dozen managed to raise the money. Ada Willingham took all she'd saved to buy an angel tombstone for her husband and gave it to her son, and Acey Trump's papa sold an option on his cotton crop.

But the night of the show! That was a night when all was forgotten: mortgages, and the dishes in the kitchen sink. Aunt El said you'd think we were going to the opera, everybody so dressed up, so pink and sweet-smelling. The Odeon had not been so full since the night they gave away the matched set of sterling silver. Practically everybody had a relative in the show, so there was a lot of nervousness to contend with. Miss Bobbit was the only contestant we knew real well. Billy Bob couldn't sit still; he kept telling us over and over that we mustn't applaud for anybody but Miss Bobbit; Aunt El said that would be very rude, which sent Billy Bob off into a state again; and when his father bought us all bags of popcorn he wouldn't touch his because it would make his hands greasy, and please, another thing, we mustn't be noisy and eat ours while Miss Bobbit was performing. That she was to be a contestant had come as a last-minute surprise. It was logical enough, and there were signs that should've told us; the fact, for instance, that she had not set foot outside the Sawyer house in how many days? And the victrola going half the night, her shadow whirling on the window-shade, and the secret, stuffed look on Sister Rosalba's face whenever asked after Sister Bobbit's health. So there was her name on the programme, listed second, in fact, though she did not appear for a long while. First came Manny Fox, greased and leering, who told a lot of peculiar jokes, clapping his hands, ha, ha. Aunt El said if he told another joke like that she was going to walk straight out: he did, and she didn't. Before Miss Bobbit came on there were eleven contestants, including Eustacia Bern-stein, who imitated movie stars so that they all sounded like Eustacia, and there was an extraordinary Mr Buster Riley, a jug-eared old wool-hat from way in the back country who played 'Waltzing Matilda' on a saw. Up to that point, he was the hit of the show; not that there was any marked difference in the various receptions, for everybody applauded generously, every-body, that is, except Preacher Star. He was sitting two rows ahead of us, greeting each act with a donkey-loud boo. Aunt El said she was never going to speak to him again. The only person he ever applauded was Miss Bobbit. No doubt the Devil was on her side, but she deserved it. Out she came, tossing her hips, her curls, rolling her eyes. You could tell right away it wasn't going to be one of her classical numbers. She tapped across the stage, daintily holding up the sides of a cloud-blue skirt. That's the

cutest thing I ever saw, said Billy Bob, smacking his thigh, and
Aunt El had to agree that Miss Bobbit looked real sweet. When
she started to twirl the whole audience broke into spontaneous
applause; so she did it all over again, hissing, 'Faster, faster,' at
poor Miss Adelaide, who was at the piano doing her Sunday-
school best. 'I was born in China, and raised in Jay-pan ...' We
had never heard her sing before, and she had a rowdy sand-
paper voice. '... if you don't like my peaches, stay away from
my can, o-ho o-ho!' Aunt El gasped; she gasped again when
Miss Bobbit, with a bump, up-ended her skirt to display blue-
lace underwear, thereby collecting most of the whistles the
boys had been saving for the fan dancer without the fan, which
was just as well, as it later turned out, for that lady, to the tune
of 'An apple for the Teacher' and cries of gyp gyp, did her
routine attired in a bathing suit. But showing off her bottom was
not Miss Bobbit's final triumph. Miss Adelaide commenced an
ominous thundering in the darker keys, at which point Sister
Rosalba, carrying a lighted Roman candle, rushed on-stage and
handed it to Miss Bobbit, who was in the midst of a full split;
she made it, too, and just as she did the Roman candle burst into
fiery balls of red, white and blue, and we all had to stand up because she was singing 'The Star Spangled Banner' at the top of
her lungs. Aunt El said afterwards that it was one of the most
gorgeous things she'd ever seen on the American stage.

Well, she surely did deserve a Hollywood screen test and,
inasmuch as she won the contest, it looked as though she were
going to get it. Manny Fox said she was: honey, he said, you're
real star stuff. Only he skipped town the next day, leaving nothing but hearty promises. Watch the mails, my friends, you'll all
be hearing from me. That is what he said to the boys whose
money he'd taken, and that is what he said to Miss Bobbit.
There are three deliveries daily, and this sizable group gathered
at the post office for all of them, a jolly crowd growing gradually joyless. How their hands trembled when a letter slid into
their mailbox. A terrible hush came over them as the days
passed. They all knew what the other was thinking, but no one
could bring himself to say it, not even Miss Bobbit. Postmistress
Patterson said it plainly, however: the man's a crook, she said,

I knew he was a crook to begin with, and if I have to look at your faces one more day I'll shoot myself.

Finally, at the end of two weeks, it was Miss Bobbit who broke the spell. Her eyes had grown more vacant than anyone had ever supposed they might, but one day, after the last mail was up, all her old sizzle came back. 'O.K., boys, it's lynch law now,' she said, and proceeded to herd the whole troupe home with her. This was the first meeting of the Manny Fox Hangman's Club, an organization which, in a more social form, endures to this day, though Manny Fox has long since been caught and, so to say, hung. Credit for this went quite properly to Miss Bobbit. Within a week she'd written over three hundred descriptions of Manny Fox and dispatched them to sheriffs throughout the South; she also wrote letters to papers in the larger cities, and these attracted wide attention. As a result, four of the robbed boys were offered good-paying jobs by the United Fruit Company, and late this spring, when Manny Fox was arrested in Uphigh, Arkansas, where he was pulling the same old dodge, Miss Bobbit was presented with a Good Deed Merit award from the Sunbeam Girls of America. For some reason, she made a point of letting the world know that this did not exactly thrill her. 'I do not approve of the organization,' she said. 'All that rowdy bugle blowing. It's neither good-hearted nor truly feminine. And anyway, what is a good deed? Don't let anybody fool you, a good deed is something you do because you want something in return.' It would be reassuring to report she was wrong, and that her just reward, when at last it came, was given out of kindness and love. However, this is not the case. About a week ago the boys involved in the swindle all received from Manny Fox cheques covering their losses, and Miss Bobbit, with clodhopping determination, stalked into a meeting of the Hangman's Club, which is now an excuse for drinking beer and playing poker every Thursday night. 'Look, boys,' she said, laying it on the line, 'none of you ever thought to see that money again, but now that you have, you ought to invest it in something practical – like me.' The proposition was that they should pool their money and finance her trip to Hollywood; in return, they would get ten per cent of her life's earnings which, after she was a star, and that would not be very long, would make them all rich men. 'At least,' as she said, 'in this part of the country.' Not one of the boys wanted to do it: but when Miss Bobbit looked at you, what was there to say?

Since Monday, it has been raining buoyant summer rain shot through with sun, but dark at night and full of sound, full of dripping leaves, watery chimneys, sleepless scuttlings. Billy Bob is wide-awake, dry-eyed, though everything he does is a little frozen and his tongue is as stiff as a bell tongue. It has not been easy for him, Miss Bobbit's going. Because she'd meant more than that. Than what? Than being thirteen years old and crazy in love. She was the queer things in him, like the pecan tree and liking books and caring enough about people to let them hurt him. She was the things he was afraid to show anyone else. And in the dark the music trickled through the rain: won't there be nights when we will hear it just as though it were really there? And afternoons when the shadows will be all at once confused, and she will pass before us, unfurling across the lawn like a pretty piece of ribbon? She laughed to Billy Bob; she held his hand, she even kissed him. 'I'm not going to die,' she said. 'You'll come out there, and we'll climb a mountain, and we'll all live there together, you and me and Sister Rosalba.' But Billy Bob knew it would never happen that way, and so when the music came through the dark he would stuff the pillow over his head.

Only there was a strange smile about yesterday, and that was the day she was leaving. Around noon the sun came out, bringing with it into the air all the sweetness of wisteria. Aunt El's yellow Lady Anne's were blooming again, and she did something wonderful, she told Billy Bob he could pick them and give them to Miss Bobbit for good-bye. All afternoon Miss Bobbit sat on the porch surrounded by people who stopped by to wish her well. She looked as though she were going to Communion, dressed in white and with a white parasol. Sister Rosalba had given her a handkerchief, but she had to borrow it back because she couldn't stop blubbering. Another little girl brought a baked chicken, presumably to be eaten on the bus; the only trouble was she'd forgotten to take out the insides before cooking it. Miss

Bobbit's mother said that was all right by her, chicken was chicken, which is memorable because it is the single opinion she ever voiced. There was only one sour note. For hours Preacher Star had been hanging around down at the corner, sometimes standing at the kerb tossing a coin, and sometimes hiding behind a tree, as if he didn't want anyone to see him. It made everybody nervous. About twenty minutes before bus time he sauntered up and leaned against our gate. Billy Bob was still in the garden picking roses; by now he had enough for a bonfire, and their smell was as heavy as wind. Preacher stared at him until he lifted his head. As they looked at each other the rain began again, falling fine as sea spray and coloured by a rainbow. Without a word, Preacher went over and started helping Billy Bob separate the roses into two giant bouquets: together they carried them to the kerb. Across the street there were bumblebees of talk, but when Miss Bobbit saw them, two boys whose flower-masked faces were like yellow moons, she rushed down the steps, her arms outstretched. You could see what was going to happen; and we called out, out voices like lightning in the rain, but Miss Bobbit, running toward those moons of roses, did not seem to hear. That is when the six o'clock bus ran over her.

John Updike

WIFE-WOOING

OH my love. Yes. Here we sit, on warm broad floorboards,
before a fire, the children between us, in a crescent, eating. The
girl and I share one half-pint of French-fried potatoes; you and
the boy share another; and in the centre, sharing nothing, making simple reflections within himself like a jewel, the baby,
mounted in an Easybaby, sucks at his bottle with frowning
mastery, his selfish, contemplative eyes stealing glitter from
the center of the flames. And you. You. You allow your skirt,
the same black skirt in which this morning you with woman's
soft bravery mounted a bicycle and sallied forth to play hymns
in difficult keys on the Sunday school's old piano – you allow
this black skirt to slide off your raised knees down your thighs,
slide *up* your thighs in your body's absolute geography, so the
parallel whiteness of their undersides is exposed to the fire's
warmth and to my sight. Oh. There is a line of Joyce. I try to
recover it from the legendary, imperfectly explored grottoes of
Ulysses: a garter snapped, to please Blazes Boylan, in a deep
Dublin den. What? Smackwarm. That was the crucial word.
Smacked smackwarm on her smackable warm woman's thigh.
Something like that. A splendid man, to feel that. Smackwarm
woman's. Splendid also to feel the curious and potent, inexplicable and irrefutably magical life language leads within itself.
What soul took thought and knew that adding 'wo' to man
would make a woman? The difference exactly. The wide w, the
receptive o. Womb. In our crescent the children for all their
size seem to come out of you towards me, wet fingers and eyes,
tinted bronze. Three children, five persons, seven years. Seven
years since I wed wide warm woman, white-thighed. Wooed
and wed. Wife. A knife of a word that for all its final bite did
not end the wooing. To my wonderment.

We eat meat, meat I wrested warm from the raw hands of

419

the hamburger girl in the diner a mile away, a ferocious place, slick with savagery, wild with chrome; young predators snarling dirty jokes menaced me, old men reached for me with coffee-warmed paws; I wielded my wallet and won my way back. The fat brown bag of buns was warm beside me in the cold car; the smaller bag holding the two tiny cartons of French-fries emitted an even more urgent heat. Back through the black winter air to the fire, the intimate cave, where halloos and hurrahs greeted me, the deer, mouth agape and its cotton throat gushing, stretched dead across my shoulders. And now you, beside the white O of the plate upon which the children discarded with squeals of disgust the rings of translucent onion that came squeezed in the hamburgers – you push your toes an inch closer to the blaze, and the ashy white of the inside of your deep thigh is lazily laid bare, and the eternally elastic garter snaps smackwarm against my hidden heart.

Who would have thought, wide wife, back there in the white tremble of the ceremony (in the corner of my eye I held, despite the distracting hail of ominous vows, the vibration of the cluster of stephanotis clutched against your wrist), that seven years would bring us no distance, through all those warm beds, to the same trembling point, of beginning? The cells change every seven years, and down in the atom, apparently, there is a strange discontinuity; as if God wills the universe anew every instant. (Ah God, dear God, tall friend of my childhood, I will never forget you, though they say dreadful things. They say rose windows in cathedrals are vaginal symbols.) Your legs, exposed as fully as by a bathing suit, yearn deeper into the amber wash of heat. Well: begin. A green jet of flame spits out sideways from a pocket of resin in a log, crying, and the orange shadows on the ceiling sway with fresh life. Begin.

'Remember, on our honeymoon, how the top of the kerosene heater made a great big rose window on the ceiling?'

'Vnn.' Your chin goes to your knees, your shins draw in, all is retracted. Not much to remember, perhaps, for you; blood badly spilled, clumsiness of all sorts. 'It was cold for June.'

'Mommy, what was cold? What did you say?' the girl asks,

enunciating angrily, determined not to let language slip on her tongue and tumble her so that we laugh.

'A house where Daddy and I stayed one time.'

'I don't like dat,' the boy says, and throws a half bun painted with chartreuse mustard on to the floor.

You pick it up with beautiful sombre musing ask, 'Isn't that funny? Did any of the others have mustard on them?'

'I *hate* dat,' the boy insists; he is two. Language is to him thick vague handles swirling by; he grabs what he can.

'Here. He can have mine. Give me his.' I pass my hamburger over, you take it, he takes it from you, there is nowhere a ripple of gratitude. There is no more praise of my heroism in fetching Sunday supper, saving your labour. Cunning, you sense, and sense that I sense your knowledge, that I had hoped to hoard your energy towards a more ecstatic spending. We sense everything between us, every ripple, existent and non-existent; it is tiring. Courting a wife takes tenfold the strength of winning an ignorant girl. The fire shifts, shattering fragments of newspaper that carry in lighter grey the ghost of the ink of their message. You huddle your legs and bring the skirt back over them. With a sizzling noise like the sighs of the exhausted logs, the baby sucks the last from his bottle, drops it to the floor with its distasteful hoax of vacant suds, and begins to cry. His egotist's mouth opens; the delicate membrane of his satisfaction tears. You pick him up and stand. You love the baby more than me.

Who would have thought, blood once spilled, that no barrier would be broken, that you would be each time healed into a virgin again? Tall, fair, obscure, remote, and courteous.

We put the children to bed, one by one, in reverse order of birth. I am limitlessly patient, paternal, good. Yet you know. We watch the paper bags and cartons ignite on the breathing pillow of embers; read, watch television, eat crackers, it does not matter. Eleven comes. For a tingling moment you stand on the bedroom rug in your underpants, untangling your nightie; oh, fat white sweet fat fatness. In bed you read. About Richard Nixon. He fascinates you; you hate him. You know how he defeated Jerry Voorhis, martyred Mrs Douglas, how he played poker in the Navy despite being a Quaker, every fiendish trick, every low adaptation. Oh my Lord. Let's let the poor man go to bed. We're none of us perfect. 'Hey let's turn out the light.'

'Wait. He's just about to get Hiss convicted. It's very strange. It says he acted honorably.'

'I'm sure he did.' I reach for the switch.

'No. Wait. Just till I finish this chapter. I'm sure there'll be something at the end.'

'Honey, Hiss was guilty. We're all guilty. Conceived in concupiscence, we die unrepentant.' Once my ornate words wooed you.

I lie against your filmy convex back. You read sideways, a sleepy trick. I see the page through the fringe of your hair, sharp and white as a wedge of crystal. Suddenly it slips. The book has slipped from your hand. You are asleep. Oh cunning trick, cunning. In the darkness I consider. Cunning. The headlights of cars accidentally slide fanning slits of light around our walls and ceiling. The great rose window was projected upward through the petal-shaped perforations in the top of the black kerosene stove, which we stood in the center of the floor. As the flame on the circular wick flickered, the wide soft star of interlocked penumbra moved and waved as if it were printed on a silk cloth being gently tugged or slowly blown. Its color soft blurred blood. We pay dear in blood for our peaceful homes.

In the morning, to my relief, you are ugly. Monday's wan breakfast light bleaches you blotchily, drains the goodness from your thickness, makes the bathrobe a limp stained tube flapping disconsolately, exposing sallow décolletage. The skin between your breasts a sad yellow. I feast with the coffee on your drabness. Every wrinkle and sickly tint a relief and a revenge. The children yammer. The toaster sticks. Seven years have worn this woman.

The man, he arrows off to work, jousting for right-of-way, veering on the thin hard edge of the legal speed limit. Out of domestic muddle, softness, pallor, flaccidity: into the city. Stone is his province. The winning coin. The manoeuvring of abstractions. Making heartless things run. Oh the inanimate, adamant joys of job!

I return with my head enmeshed in a machine. A technicality it would take weeks to explain to you snags my brain; I fiddle with phrases and numbers all the blind evening. You serve me supper as a waitress – as less than a waitress, for I have known you. The children touch me timidly, as they would a steep girder bolted into a framework whose height they don't understand. They drift into sleep securely. We survive their passing in calm parallelity. My thoughts rework in chronic right angles the same snagging circuits on the same professional grid. You rustle the book about Nixon; vanish upstairs into the plumbing; the bathtub pipes cry. In my head I seem to have found the stuck switch at last: I push at it; it jams; I push; it is jammed. I grow dizzy, churning with cigarettes, I circle the room aimlessly.

So I am taken by surprise at a turning when at the meaningful hour of ten you come with a kiss of toothpaste to me moist and girlish and quick; the momentous moral of this story being, An expected gift is not worth giving.

READ MORE IN PENGUIN

In every corner of the world, on every subject under the sun, Penguin represents quality and variety – the very best in publishing today.

For complete information about books available from Penguin – including Puffins, Penguin Classics and Arkana – and how to order them, write to us at the appropriate address below. Please note that for copyright reasons the selection of books varies from country to country.

In the United Kingdom: Please write to *Dept. JC, Penguin Books Ltd, FREEPOST, West Drayton, Middlesex UB7 0BR*

If you have any difficulty in obtaining a title, please send your order with the correct money, plus ten per cent for postage and packaging, to *PO Box No. 11, West Drayton, Middlesex UB7 0BR*

In the United States: Please write to *Penguin USA Inc., 375 Hudson Street, New York, NY 10014*

In Canada: Please write to *Penguin Books Canada Ltd, 10 Alcorn Avenue, Suite 300, Toronto, Ontario M4V 3B2*

In Australia: Please write to *Penguin Books Australia Ltd, 487 Maroondah Highway, Ringwood, Victoria 3134*

In New Zealand: Please write to *Penguin Books (NZ) Ltd,182–190 Wairau Road, Private Bag, Takapuna, Auckland 9*

In India: Please write to *Penguin Books India Pvt Ltd, 706 Eros Apartments, 56 Nehru Place, New Delhi 110 019*

In the Netherlands: Please write to *Penguin Books Netherlands B.V., Keizersgracht 231 NL–1016 DV Amsterdam*

In Germany: Please write to *Penguin Books Deutschland GmbH, Friedrichstrasse 10–12, W–6000 Frankfurt/Main 1*

In Spain: Please write to *Penguin Books S. A., C. San Bernardo 117–6° E–28015 Madrid*

In Italy: Please write to *Penguin Italia s.r.l., Via Felice Casati 20, I–20124 Milano*

In France: Please write to *Penguin France S. A., 17 rue Lejeune, F–31000 Toulouse*

In Japan: Please write to *Penguin Books Japan, Ishikiribashi Building, 2–5–4, Suido, Tokyo 112*

In Greece: Please write to *Penguin Hellas Ltd, Dimocritou 3, GR–106 71 Athens*

In South Africa: Please write to *Longman Penguin Southern Africa (Pty) Ltd, Private Bag X08, Bertsham 2013*

READ MORE IN PENGUIN

A SELECTION OF OMNIBUSES

Italian Folktales Italo Calvino

Greeted with overwhelming enthusiasm and praise, Calvino's anthology is already a classic. These tales have been gathered from every region of Italy and retold in Calvino's own inspired and sensuous language. 'A magic book' – *Time*

The Penguin Book of Ghost Stories Edited by J. A. Cuddon

An anthology to set the spine tingling, from the frightening and bloodcurdling to the witty and subtle, to those that leave a strange and sinister feeling of unease and fear, including stories by Zola, Kleist, Sir Walter Scott, M. R. James, and A. S. Byatt.

The Collected Dorothy Parker

Dorothy Parker, more than any of her contemporaries, captured in her writing the spirit of the Jazz Age. Here, in a single volume, is the definitive Dorothy Parker: poetry, prose, articles and reviews. 'A good, fat book ... greatly to be welcomed' – Richard Ingrams

Graham Greene: Collected Short Stories

The thirty-seven stories in this immensely entertaining volume reveal Graham Greene in a range of moods: sometimes cynical, flippant and witty, sometimes searching and philosophical. Each one confirms V. S. Pritchett's statement that Greene is 'a master of storytelling'.

The Stories of William Trevor

'Trevor's short stories are a joy' – *Spectator*. 'Trevor packs into each separate five or six thousand words more richness, more laughter, more ache, more multifarious human-ness than many good writers manage to get into a whole novel' – *Punch*

READ MORE IN PENGUIN

A SELECTION OF OMNIBUSES

The Cornish Trilogy   Robertson Davies

'He has created a rich oeuvre of densely plotted, highly symbolic novels
that not only function as superbly funny entertainments but also give the
reader, in his character's words, a deeper kind of pleasure – delight, awe,
religious intimations, "a fine sense of the past, and of the boundless depth
and variety of life"' – *The New York Times*

For Good or Evil: Collected Stories   Clive Sinclair

'An ever-changing kaleidoscope of character and scenery and time, some
bewilderingly surreal, others starkly cold ... powerfully written, extremely
clever and very unpleasant' – *The Times*

The Pop Larkin Chronicles   H. E. Bates

'Tastes ambrosially of childhood. Never were skies so cornflower blue or
beds so swansbottom ... Life not as it is or was, but as it should be'
– *Guardian*. 'Pop is as sexy, genial, generous and boozy as ever, Ma is a
worthy match for him in these qualities' – *The Times*

The Penguin Book of British Comic Stories
Compiled by Patricia Craig

A rich blend of comic styles ranging from the sunny humour of
Wodehouse and the droll comedy of Graham Greene to the grim irony of
Fay Weldon and the inventive wit of Muriel Spark.

Lucia Victrix   E. F. Benson

Mapp and Lucia, Lucia's Progress, Trouble for Lucia – now together in
one volume, these three chronicles of English country life will delight a
new generation of readers with their wry observation and delicious satire.

READ MORE IN PENGUIN

A SELECTION OF OMNIBUSES

The Penguin Book of Modern Women's Short Stories
Edited by Susan Hill

'They move the reader to give a cry of recognition and understanding time and time again' – Susan Hill in the Introduction. 'These stories are excellent. They are moving, wise, and finely conceived ... a selection of stories that anyone should be pleased to own' – *Glasgow Herald*

Great Law-and-Order Stories
Edited and Introduced by John Mortimer

Each of these stories conjures suspense with consummate artistry. Together they demonstrate how the greatest mystery stories enthrall not as mere puzzles but as gripping insights into the human condition.

The Duffy Omnibus Dan Kavanagh

Nick Duffy – bisexual ex-cop turned private detective – is on the loose, for four rackety adventures in the grimiest streets of old London town... 'Exciting, funny and refreshingly nasty' – *Sunday Times*

The Best of Roald Dahl Roald Dahl

Twenty tales to curdle your blood and scorch your soul, chosen from his bestsellers *Over to You*, *Someone Like You*, *Kiss Kiss* and *Switch Bitch*. *The Best of Roald Dahl* is, quite simply, Roald Dahl at his sinister best!

The Rabbit Novels John Updike

'One of the finest literary achievements to have come out of the US since the war ... It is in their particularity, in the way they capture the minutiae of the world ... that [the Rabbit] books are most lovable' – John Banville in the *Irish Times*

READ MORE IN PENGUIN

INTERNATIONAL WRITERS – A SELECTION

The Butcher's Wife   Li Ang

Inspired by a murder case, Li Ang's novel has won international acclaim and made a profound impact on contemporary Chinese literature. With compelling power and daring it unravels the motive, the raw pain and the desperation that drove a woman to murder her husband. 'Fascinating … the story never loses the reader's sympathy' – *Guardian*

Marbles: A Play in Three Acts   Joseph Brodsky

Imprisoned in a mighty steel tower, where yesterday is the same as today and tomorrow, Publius and Tullius consider freedom, the nature of reality and illusion and the permanence of literature versus the transience of politics. In a Platonic dialogue set 'two centuries after our era' in ancient Rome, Nobel prizewinner Joseph Brodsky takes us beyond the farthest reaches of the theatre of the absurd.

Scandal   Shusaku Endo

'Spine-chilling, erotic, cruel … it's very powerful' – *Sunday Telegraph*. '*Scandal* addresses the great questions of our age. How can we straddle the gulf between faith and modernity? How can humankind be so tender, and yet so cruel? Endo's superb novel offers only an unforgettable bafflement for an answer' – *Observer*

Love and Garbage   Ivan Klíma

The narrator of Ivan Klíma's novel has temporarily abandoned his work-in-progress – an essay on Kafka – and exchanged his writer's pen for the orange vest of a Prague road-sweeper. As he works, he meditates on Czechoslovakia, on Kafka, on life, on art and, obsessively, on his passionate and adulterous love affair with the sculptress Daria.

A Scrap of Time   Ida Fink

'A powerful, terrifying story, an almost unbearable witness to unspeakable anguish,' wrote the *New Yorker* of the title story in Ida Fink's award-winning collection. Herself a survivor, she portrays Poland during the Holocaust, the lives of ordinary people in hiding as they resist, submit, hope, betray, remember.